Dear Reader,

Welcome to the world of *The Keepers: L.A.* I hope you enjoy this new four-book foray into the world of the guardians of the supernatural known as the Keepers. Writing these books—joined for this go-round by Harley Jane Kozak and Alexandra Sokoloff, two very good friends—has been a true labor of love.

When Harley and Alex and I began to think about this second go-round, our first concern was...where else? The answer came to all of us at the same time: Los Angeles, City of Angels, City of Dreams.

And a city where at any given time you might see any kind of performance, any kind of costume, any kind of *anything* happening right there in broad daylight—or the dark.

I'm actually in L.A. as I write this. Contestants for *The Voice* are scurrying around my hotel, all of them filled with hopes and dreams. And naturally, to sustain all the dreamers in the city, you have the exclusive clubs, the new "it" places and all the people who own and run them. And then there are those with the true power: the producers, the agents and the directors, who are thrilled—and sometimes challenged—by the choices the producers make.

What better place for a few new Keepers—a bit disconcerted by their sudden call to duty—to govern those denizens wearing masks beneath their masks?

I hope you'll have as much fun reading about these new Keepers as we had writing about them.

Thank you, and enjoy!

Heather Graham

HEATHER GRAHAM

New York Times bestselling author Heather Graham has written more than a hundred novels, many of which have been featured by the Doubleday Book Club and the Literary Guild. An avid scuba diver, ballroom dancer and a mother of five, she still enjoys her south Florida home, but loves to travel as well, from locations such as Cairo, Egypt, to her own backyard, the Florida Keys. Reading, however, is the pastime she still loves best, and she is a member of many writing groups. She's currently vice president of the Horror Writers' Association, and she's also an active member of International Thriller Writers. She is very proud to be a Killerette in the Killer Thriller Band, along with many fellow novelists she greatly admires. For more information, check out her website, theoriginalheathergraham.com.

KEEPER OF THE NIGHT & THE KEEPERS

New York Times and *USA TODAY* Bestselling Author

HEATHER GRAHAM

HARLEQUIN®

entertain, enrich, inspire™

Recycling programs for this product may not exist in your area.

ISBN-13: 978-0-373-83786-1

KEEPER OF THE NIGHT

Copyright © 2013 by Harlequin Books S.A.

The publisher acknowledges the copyright holder of the individual works as follows:

KEEPER OF THE NIGHT
Copyright © 2013 by Slush Pile Productions, LLC

THE KEEPERS
Copyright © 2010 by Heather Graham Pozzessere

This edition published by arrangement with Harlequin Books S.A.

For questions and comments about the quality of this book, please contact us at CustomerService@Harlequin.com.

® and TM are trademarks of the publisher. Trademarks indicated with ® are registered in the United States Patent and Trademark Office, the Canadian Trade Marks Office and in other countries.

www.Harlequin.com

Printed in U.S.A.

CONTENTS

Sometimes in life we get to meet people and in a few minutes we feel we've known them all our lives. I've known both Harley and Alex now for years, but from the time I met them I felt that I'd known them since childhood. To my prized and beloved cohorts on this Keepers journey, Alexandra Sokoloff and Harley Jane Kozak. I cannot remember a time when we weren't friends, and I certainly can't imagine not having you in my life.

KEEPER OF THE NIGHT

Prologue

Perception, to paraphrase the old saying, is nine-tenths of the law.

And so the world happily—well, mostly happily—accepts the truth of that. And, perception, of course, is the main duty of those born to be Keepers and maintain order among the paranormal races.

As centuries slipped by, man became a "show me" species and lost his belief in what he couldn't see plainly with his own eyes, and that was good for all the decent and law-abiding creatures. As the twenty-first century progressed, populations exploded. Human beings covered the earth, with birth rates at an all-time high.

And other *beings* flourished, too, learning how to coexist in a world where the magic of the earth and skies was no longer recognized, and human credence was more and more limited to one particular sense: sight. Many people began to lose faith not just in the

unexplainable or unknown, but even in their own om-
nipresent God.

While those of an…unusual bent had once headed
strictly to places like New Orleans, where even many
among the human population believed themselves to be
vampires or other denizens of the night, many places in
the world became the destinations of choice for the *truly*
different. The well-known among the races—vampires,
werewolves and shapeshifters—were ready to expand
their territory, as were Others who had once chosen to
remain in their native lands, the Elven, gnomes, leprechauns, fairies and more.

With that expansion came the need for an international council, the first of its kind, to keep order, and
Keepers from across the world were selected to meet
at a secret rendezvous in order to construct a code that
would be universally accepted. They would serve as
the last word when it came to events that could disturb
the status quo, because even the Otherworld races considered the most vile and beastly in human mythology
were trying to blend in and survive.

With so many of the most experienced Keepers serving on the council, some of the most promising young
Keepers were thrown into difficult situations with little warning.

And since so many of the paranormal races still liked
to settle where the abnormal was the norm, where the-
atrics abounded, even the most absurd people and situations frequently went unnoticed, it was no wonder
that the population of the Otherworld exploded off the
charts in one particular place: La-La Land, also known
as Hollywood, California.

City of dreams to many, and city of lost dreams for

too many others. A place where waiters and waitresses spent their tips on head shots, and the men and women behind the scenes—the producers—reigned as the real kings.

So many of the paranormal races—the vampires, the shifters, the Elven and more—traveled there, and many stayed, because where better to blend in than a place where even the human beings hardly registered as normal half the time? With so much going on, no one set of Keepers could control the vast scope of the Greater Los Angeles Otherworld, and so it was that the three Gryffald cousins, daughters of the three renowned Gryffald brothers, were called to take their place as peacekeepers a bit earlier than had been expected.

And right when L.A. was on the verge of exploding with Otherworld activity.

Hollywood, they were about to discover, could truly be murder.

Chapter 1

There was blood. So much blood.

From her position on the stage, Rhiannon Gryffald could see the man standing just outside the club door. He was tall and well built, his almost formal attire a contrast to the usual California casual and strangely at odds with his youth, with a Hollywood tan that added to the classic strength of his features and set off his light eyes and golden hair.

And he was bleeding from the throat.

Bleeding profusely.

There was blood everywhere. It was running down the side of his throat and staining his tailored white shirt and gold-patterned vest.

"Help! I've been bitten!" he cried. He was staggering, hands clutching his throat.

No! she thought. *Not yet!*

She had barely arrived in Los Angeles. This was too

soon, far too soon, to be called upon to take action. She was just beginning to find her way around the city, just learning how to maneuver through the insane traffic—not to mention that she was trying to maintain something that at least resembled steady employment.

"I've been bitten!" he screamed again. "By a vampire!"

There were two women standing near him, staring, and he seemed to be trying to warn them, but they didn't seem frightened, although they were focused on the blood pouring from his wound.

They started to move toward him, their eyes fixed on the scarlet ruin of his neck.

They weren't concerned, Rhiannon realized. They weren't going to help.

They were hungry.

She tossed her guitar aside and leaped off the stage. She was halfway to the group milling just outside the doors of the Mystic Café when she nearly plowed into her boss. Hugh Hammond, owner and manager, was staring at the spectacle.

"Hugh," she said, trying to sound authoritative and confident. "Let me by."

Hugh, a very tall man, turned and looked down at her, weary amusement in his eyes. He wasn't a bad sort, even though he could be annoyingly patronizing at times. She supposed that was natural, given that he had been friends with her father and her two uncles. Once upon a time he'd been a B-list leading man, and he was aging very slowly and with great dignity.

He was also the Keeper of the Laurel Canyon werewolves.

"Hugh!" she snapped.

"By all means, Miss Gryffald, handle the situation," he told her.

She frowned and started to step past him, refraining from simply pushing him out of the way. This was serious. Incredibly serious. If a vampire was ripping out throats in broad daylight, in front of witnesses...

"Stop!" someone called out.

Another man, dark where the victim was blond, not quite as tall, his face lean and menacing, broke through the crowd and addressed the bleeding man. "Give in to me! Give in to me and embrace the night. Savor the darkness. Give your soul to me and find eternal life and enjoy eternal lust. Drink from the human soul, the fountain of delight, and enjoy carnal delights with no fear of reprisal."

She was ready to shove through the crowd to reach the victim's side and defend him against the newcomer, but Hugh had his hand on her arm. "Wait," he whispered. "Rhiannon, take a look at what they're wearing and how they're acting, and *think about it*."

She was dying to move, but she stood still, blinked and heeded Hugh's words.

The two young women reached for the victim's arms, holding him up as the dark man spoke. One licked her lips in a provocative and sensual manner.

"Lord, forgive me," the bleeding man pleaded. "God, help me, for Drago comes and would have his terrible way until none but monsters walk the earth."

Drago walked forward threateningly, then stopped suddenly and turned to the crowd. He grinned pleasantly, and menace became humor as he said, "If you want to see any more, you need to listen up."

Where there had been silence, as if people were frozen with fear, there was a sudden eruption of laughter and applause.

"Thank you! Thank you!" the "victim" announced, lifting his hands to silence the crowd. "I'm Mac Brodie, actor at large. The diabolical Drago is portrayed by the illustrious Jack Hunter, and…" He turned to the sensual vixens at his side. "Erika is being performed by the beautiful Audrey Fleur and Jeneka by Kate Delaney. Please, everyone, take a bow."

They did. Drago was darkly handsome, and both young women—Audrey, a brunette, and Kate, a blonde—were extremely pretty. They, like the two men, were in Victorian attire, but in their case it was Victorian night attire. Beautiful white gossamer dresses, with gorgeous bone corsets beneath, and silky pantalets.

Mac continued to speak. "Please, join us at the Little Theater on the Hill this evening or anytime throughout the next three months, where we're presenting *Vampire Rampage,* which will soon begin production as a major motion picture, as well. We ask that you come and tell us what you think. Shows start at eight o'clock every night except Sunday and Monday, but to make up for that, we do have matinees on Wednesdays. Thank you!"

He bowed low, lifted his head and waved to the appreciative crowd.

Hugh stepped up close behind Rhiannon. "Actors," he said, sounding tired, as if he knew the profession and its attendant promo stunts far too well—which of course he did. "This is Hollywood, Miss Gryffald. Everyone's a bloody actor. Get used to it. You've got a lot to learn about life out here." He smiled down at her in that patronizing way that made her crazy, and shook his head. "Looks like your tip jar just disappeared."

Rhiannon turned quickly toward the stage. It was true. The lovely little tip jar her great-aunt Olga had made for her was gone. Along with her tips. And they hadn't been half bad today; a lot of people had thrown in bills instead of nickels.

She wanted to scream. Worse, she wanted to run back to Savannah, where so many people—and…Others—survived on the tourist trade alone that they behaved with old-fashioned courtesy and something that resembled normal human decency.

But Hugh was right. This was Hollywood, where everyone was an actor. Or a producer, or a writer, or an agent, or a would-be whatever. And everyone was cutthroat.

It's Hollywood, she told herself. *Get used to it.*

Go figure that the Otherworld's denizens would be starstruck, too.

"I'm calling it quits for the day, Hugh. I'm heading home."

He lifted her chin and stared into her eyes. "Calling it quits? That's what they sent us? A quitter? It's up to you, but I'd get up there and play if I were you. You can't quit every time there's a snafu. Lord above! We need Teddy Roosevelt, and they send us a sniveling child."

"I'm not a sniveling child, Hugh. I just don't see the sense of going on working today. Since there's certainly no imminent or inherent danger—"

He interrupted her, laughing. "Imminent or *inherent* danger? The world is *filled* with inherent danger—that's why you exist, Rhiannon. And imminent? How often do we really know when danger is imminent? Did you think being a Keeper was going to be like living in a *Superman* comic? You see someone in distress, throw on a red cape, save the day, then slip back down to earth and put your glasses on? How can you be your grandfather's descendant?"

Rhiannon felt an instant explosion of emotions. One was indignation.

One was shame.

And thankfully, others were wounded pride and determination.

"Hugh, I know my duty," she said quietly. "But my cousins and I were not supposed to take over as Keepers for years to come. No one knew that our fathers would be called to council, that the population explosion of Otherworlders in L.A. would skyrocket the way it has and we would need to start our duties now. It's only been a week. I'm not quitting, I'm adjusting. And it's not easy."

Hugh grinned, released her chin and smoothed back her hair. "Life ain't easy for anyone, kid. Now get up there and knock 'em dead."

She looked around the place and wondered drily if it was possible to "knock anyone dead" here. It was basically a glorified coffee shop, but she did need to make something of herself and her career here in L.A.

She'd left Savannah just when Dark As Night, her last band, had gotten an offer to open for a tour. Her bandmates had been incredulous when she'd said that she was moving, and distressed. Not distressed enough to lose the gig, though. They had found another lead guitarist slash backup singer before she'd even packed a suitcase.

Wearily, she made her way back to the stage. Screw the tip jar. She didn't have another, and she wasn't going to put out an empty coffee cup like a beggar.

She could not only play the guitar; she was good.

Unfortunately, given the recent twists in her life, it seemed she was never going to have the chance to prove it.

She stepped slowly back up on the stage. Earlier the crowd had been watching her, chatting a bit, too, and enjoying her slow mix of folk, rock and chart toppers.

Now they were all talking about the latest Hollywood promo stunt.

Rhiannon began to play and sing, making up the lyrics as she went along, giving in to her real feelings despite her determination not to be bitter that she was suddenly here—and with little chance for a life.

> *I hate Hollywood, I hate Hollywood, oh, oh,*
> *I hate Hollywood, I hate Hollywood, oh, oh, oh,*
> *oh.*
> *Everyone's an actor, it's a stark and frightening*
> *factor,*
> *I hate Hollywood....*
> *And I hate actors, too,*
> *Oh, yeah, and I hate actors, too.*

Okay, her cousin Sailor was an actress, and she didn't hate Sailor, although she wasn't certain that Sailor was actually living in the real world, either. She was too much the wide-eyed innocent despite the fact that she'd grown up in L.A. County—and had also spent a few years pounding the pavement trying to crack Broadway and the New York television scene. Maybe the wide-eyed innocence in Sailor was an act, too. No, no, Sailor really wanted the world to be all sunshine and roses. And, actually, Rhiannon loved her cousin; Sailor always meant well. And now, according to the powers that be, she and Sailor and another of their cousins, Barrie, a journalist with a good head on her shoulders, were to take their place as Keepers of three of the Otherworld races right here in L.A.

Oh, yeah, yeah, yeah, yeaaaah, I hate Hollywood,
And I hate actors, too.

If anyone disagreed with her lyrics, they didn't say so. No one was really listening, anyway. And maybe that was the point. Easy music in the background while the coffee, tea, latte, mocha and chai drinkers enjoyed their conversations.

Polite applause followed the song. Rhiannon looked down, not wanting the audience to see her roll her eyes.

At ten o'clock Hugh asked her to announce that the café was closed for the night. She was shutting her guitar case when one of the coffee drinkers came up to her, offering her a twenty. Surprised by the amount of the tip, she looked at him more closely and realized that he was Mac Brodie, the actor who had been covered in fake blood earlier.

She looked at the twenty but didn't touch it, then looked back into his eyes.

Elven, she realized.

Six foot five, she thought, judging that he stood a good seven inches over her own respectable five feet ten inches. And he had the telltale signs: golden hair streaked with platinum, eyes of a curious blue-green that was almost lime. And, of course, the lean, sleekly muscled physique.

She lowered her head again, shaking it. *"Elven,"* she

murmured. "It's all right. You *did* ruin my night, but that's okay." She made a point of not looking directly at him. Elven could read minds, but most of them had to have locked eye contact, so looking away made it possible to block the intrusion. And, luckily, the process was hard on them, so they didn't indulge in it frivolously.

"Keeper," he said, drawing out the word. "And new to the job, of course. Sorry. I saw that look of panic on your face. I'm assuming you're here for the blood-suckers?"

She stiffened. In Savannah she'd been a fledgling vampire Keeper, apprenticing with an old family friend who'd kept the city peacefully coexisting for years, but she'd always known that one day she would take her father's place in L.A.

As she'd told Hugh, this had all been so sudden. There hadn't been a warning, no "Tie up your affairs, you're needed in six months" —or even three months, or one. The World Council had been chosen, and in two weeks a core group of some of the country's wisest Keepers was gone and their replacements moved into their new positions. And there was no such thing as calling the Hague for help. No Keeper business could ever be discussed by cell phone, since in the day and age they lived in, anything could be recorded or traced.

So the new Keepers were simply yanked and resettled, and the hell with their past lives.

"Yes, of course, Keeper for the bloodsuckers," Mac said, his tone low.

"Some of my best friends are bloodsuckers," she said sweetly, looking quickly around. She'd been about to chastise him for speaking so openly, but the clientele was gone and the workers were cleaning the kitchen, well out of earshot. Of course, he might know exactly what she was thinking even without her saying it aloud. Some Elven were capable of telepathy even without eye contact, so she braced her mind against him. In fact, she knew she was playing a brutal game. It cost an Elven dearly to mind-read, especially without locking gazes, but it cost the target a great deal of strength to block the mind probe, as well.

There were a lot of Others in L.A. County. One thing they all did was keep the secret that they were…unusual. It was the key to survival—for all of them. History had taught them that when people feared any group, that group was in trouble.

"Same here," he told her. "I'm fond of a lot of vampires."

She stared at him for a moment. He was undeniably gorgeous. Like a sun god or some such thing. And he undoubtedly knew that Elven usually got their way, because they were born with grace and charm—not to mention the ability to teleport, or, as they defined it, move at the speed of light.

She was annoyed. She had no desire to be hit on by an Elven actor, of all things, but she didn't want to fight, either. All she wanted was to make her point. "I don't want money from a struggling actor," she said. "You don't need to feel guilty. I'm fine. I work because, Keeper or not, I still have to pay the bills. But Hugh gives me a salary, so go do some more promo stunts. I'm fine."

"You're more than fine," he said quietly. "And I'm truly sorry that we ruined the evening for you." He offered her his hand. "I'm Mac. Mac Brodie."

She hesitated and then accepted his hand. "Rhiannon. Rhiannon Gryffald.

"It's a pleasure, Miss Gryffald. And am I right?" he asked her.

"About?"

"The vampires?"

"Are you asking me so that you could avoid me if I were Keeper of the Elven?"

"Hey, we Elven have spent centuries keeping the peace because we're strong, sure of ourselves, some might say arrogant—" he smiled "—and we can talk almost anyone into almost anything. I'm asking you out of pure curiosity," he told her. "And because I'm trying to make casual conversation—and amends. I really am sorry."

Rhiannon waved a hand in the air. "I told you, it's all right. However, it has been a long day, and I would like to go home now."

"No nightcap with me, eh?" he asked.

He was smiling at her again. And like all his kind, he had charm to spare.

That's why the Elven fared so well in Hollywood. They were almost universally good looking. Tall, and perfectly built. They were made for the world of acting.

She realized, looking at him, that he was exceptionally godlike. She was surprised, actually, that he bothered with small theater at all. He would have been great in a Greek classic, a Viking movie or a sword and sorcery fantasy. He was lean, but she knew that he was strong—and would look amazing without a shirt.

Then again, he'd announced that the play was going to turn into a major movie. Maybe he was sticking with it for the stardom it might bring.

"No nightcap," she said. "I'm simply ready to go home."

"Perhaps you'll consider letting me buy you that apology another time?"

"Doubtful," she assured him.

He pulled a card from his pocket and handed it to her. "Well, be that as it may, you really should come see the show."

"Thank you, but I really don't enjoy a mockery being made of my—my charges," she told him.

He leaned closer to her, and the teasing, flirty smile left his face. He almost appeared to be a different person: older, more confident and deadly serious.

"No, you really *should* come see the show," he said. "My number is on the card, Miss Gryffald. And I'm sure you know L.A. well enough to find the theater."

He turned and walked out the door, nearly brushing the frame with the top of golden head.

Puzzled, she watched him go.

Hugh appeared just then. "Still here? I'm impressed," he said.

"I'm leaving, I'm leaving," she told him.

"I'll see you tomorrow. And be on time."

The man could be extremely aggravating. Werewolf Keepers were often like that, she had discovered. But then, the more experienced a Keeper was, the more he or she often took on the characteristics of a charge to a greater or lesser degree. She suspected that Hugh could become a wolf at the drop of a hat.

With her precious Fender in hand, she left the café. She heard Hugh locking the door behind her.

She headed to the ten-year-old Volvo that her uncle had left for her use, set her guitar in the trunk and started off down the street. Her song really hadn't been half bad. "Hollywood, oh, I hate Hollywood," she sang as she drove.

Brodie nodded to the attendant on duty and proceeded down the hallway of the morgue, past rooms where dozens of bodies in various stages of investigation were stored.

That was one thing about L.A. that wasn't so good. The city was huge, and the number of people who died on the streets, many of them nameless and unknown, was high. Possibly even sadder were the ones whose names were known—but whose deaths went by unnoticed and unmourned.

Of course, the morgue also housed the remains of people who were known and loved—but who had died under circumstances that ranged from suspicious to outright violent.

That night, however, he passed by the autopsy rooms, remembering all too clearly the one he'd entered when he was sixteen, a room filled with corpse after corpse wrapped in plastic shrouds—so many dead. His father had arranged it after discovering that Mac had left a party after drinking. Luckily he had only creamed the garage door. But it might have been a person, and his father had made sure he knew what the consequences could have been.

He reached a door marked Dr. Anthony Brandt, Senior Pathologist.

Tony undoubtedly knew that he was coming. Tony knew a lot. He had an amazing sense of smell that had served him well as a medical examiner. He could smell most poisons a mile away.

Before Brodie could tap on the door, Tony had answered it. "I was expecting you tonight," he said.

"Oh?"

"We've gotten another body that I think belongs to your killer."

"Where did he leave his mark this time?" Brodie asked.

Tony just looked at him, ignoring the question. "You still doing the show?" he asked.

"Yep."

"I saw that the cast included a Mac Brodie. That's you, I'm assuming. Not much of an alias," Tony said.

"None of the other actors actually know me. Being Mac Brodie instead of Brodie McKay works all right—if anyone looks me up, the captain has made sure that they'll find my online résumé and all the right information. Makes it easier if someone who does know me calls me either Mac or Brodie."

Tony mused on that for a minute. "You're not the only one going by a stage name, are you? I noticed a Jack Hunter in the credits."

Brodie shrugged. "You're right—that's Hunter Jackson. Obviously the cast and crew know who he really is—they're just sworn to secrecy."

"So he *is* the well-known director?"

"Yes. The play is his baby, really. He found the script and decided to produce it, then sell the film rights. The play was written by a friend of his, our stage manager. Name's Joe Carrie. Nice guy, about forty—and definitely human."

"So you don't think he's our murderer?" Tony asked.

Brodie shook his head. "No, and there's no proof the killer's even involved with the play itself. He could just be a theater buff. But the play does seem a solid place to start, at least. So, anyway, what makes you think our killer is responsible for this corpse?"

"Exsanguination, for one thing."

Tony was an interesting guy; he looked like what you would expect a werewolf to look like in human form. He was big and muscular, with broad shoulders and an equally broad chest. He had a head full of thick, curly light brown hair, and when he was on vacation, he grew a beard that would do Santa proud.

"And?"

"There's never anything obvious about the marks he leaves behind, but this time it looks like they're on the thigh. This is one clever vampire. He makes sure that he disposes of the bodies in a way that will lead to the most decay and deterioration in the shortest time."

"Want to show me the body?" Brodie asked.

"I thought you'd never ask."

Tony led the way down the hall to one of the autopsy rooms.

It was a large room, big enough for several autopsies to take place at one time. Now, however, the room was quiet and dim, and only a single body lay on a gurney on the far side of the room.

Strange, Brodie thought. He was Elven, although the Elven were pretty damned close to human in a lot of ways, maybe more human than they wanted to be. And he was a detective, often working undercover in some of the grittiest neighborhoods of a tough town where bluebloods crossed paths with derelict drug dealers. But despite both those things, he'd never gotten over the strange sensations that nearly overwhelmed him at an autopsy. Life—flesh and blood—reduced to sterile equipment and the smell of chemicals on the air. The organs that sustained life ripped from the body to be held and weighed and studied. It was just somehow... wrong, despite the fact that the work done here was some of the most important that could be done for the dead and the living both.

Tony pulled down the sheet that covered the victim, and Brodie stared first at the face, his jaw hardening.

"You've seen him before?"

Brodie nodded. "It's hard to tell, really, the body is so decomposed. But I think I recognize him. I think he was at the first performance of the show."

"Any idea who he is?" Tony asked.

"No, he was just a face in the crowd. Second row center. Have you gotten a hit off dental records? What about fingerprints?"

"Look at the hands," Tony told him, pulling the sheet down farther.

Brodie did, and he felt his stomach lurch sharply, even though he'd expected the scene that met his eyes.

The killer had chopped off the fingers.

Tony nodded toward the body. "Just like the other two. And here's what I found—you'll need that magnifier there." He pointed.

Brodie picked up the small magnifying glass that Tony had indicated, then walked down to join Tony by the foot of the gurney. Tony slipped on gloves and moved the thigh. The skin was mottled and bruised looking.

"No lividity?" Brodie asked.

"The discoloration and bloating you see are because he was dumped in a pond out by one of those housing projects they never finished off Laurel Canyon—suspiciously near your theater," Tony said. "But use the magnifying glass and check out his thigh. There are marks. They're tiny, and they're practically buried in swollen flesh, but they're there. And, of course, the body was pretty much drained of blood. There *is* a slash at the throat, but despite the damage and decay, I believe it was postmortem."

Despite his feelings about autopsy and corpses, Brodie donned gloves, shifted the dead man's leg and peered through the microscope, searching for the telltale marks, then looked up at Tony.

"Third body in two weeks with the same marks and same method of disposal," Tony said.

"And I *know* I've seen this one at the theater," Brodie said wearily.

"And the killer dumped them all close to that theater," Tony told him. "Your captain seems to have been on the mark."

Brodie nodded. "Yeah, without his insight the victims might have fallen onto the big pile of cold cases, with no leads to go on. The captain is…a smart guy."

"Guess that means you stay undercover," Tony said. "Too bad L.A.'s three best Keepers have been called to council. This is one hell of a mess."

Brodie thought about the stunning young auburn-haired woman with the big green eyes he had seen at the café. She'd rushed to what she thought was a crime scene like a bat out of hell. She'd been ready, he thought. But she wasn't ready *enough*. She loved her music too much. In a way, he understood. It was difficult to realize that you could—*had to*—lead a normal life, then let it all go to hell when necessary.

He wished to hell that Piers Gryffald, Rhiannon's father and the previous Keeper of the Canyon vampires, was still there.

But he wasn't.

And the body count was rising.

Driving in L.A. was not like driving in Savannah. People in Savannah moved at a far more *human* pace. Everyone in L.A. was in a hurry, which seemed strange, because often they were hurrying just to go sit in a coffee shop and while away their time, hoping to make the right connection. Some hopefuls still believed that they could be "discovered" in an ice cream parlor, and God knew, in Hollywood, anything could happen, even if the statistics weren't in their favor.

At least coming home—to the house that had been her old summer home and was now her permanent base—was appealing. She had to admit, she loved the exquisite old property where she lived with Sailor and Barrie. Each of them had her own house on the estate— the compound, really—that had been left to their grandfather, Rhys Gryffald, by the great Merlin, magician extraordinaire, real name Ivan Schwartz.

Somehow during his younger years, Merlin had learned about the Keepers. He'd longed to be one, but only those born in the bloodline, born with the telltale birthmark indicating what they were destined to become—werewolf Keeper, vampire Keeper, shapeshifter Keeper and so on—could inherit the role. Since he couldn't *be* a Keeper, Ivan did the next best thing: he befriended one. In fact, he had become such good friends with Rhiannon's grandfather that he had first built him a house on the property, opposite the guesthouse that already existed, and then, on his death, Merlin had willed the entire compound to him.

Good old Ivan. He had loved them all so much that he had never actually left.

The House of the Rising Sun, the main house, loomed above her as she drove along the canyon road, and she had to admit, it was magnificent. It wasn't as if she hadn't known the house all her life. Her grandparents had three sons—her father and her two uncles—and her dad had been mentored by a Keeper in Savannah, which had turned out to be a very good thing, since he'd fallen in love with her mother, a musical director for a Savannah theater. But then he'd returned to L.A. and assumed responsibility for the Canyon vampires—and she shouldn't have had to take over for another zillion years, give or take. She had grown up in Savannah, where her mother had kept her job, and her father had traveled back and forth on a regular basis. Despite the distance, her parents enjoyed one of the best marriages she had ever seen. And she'd grown close with her L.A. family, because she'd spent summers and most holidays there at the House of the Rising Sun. Sailor had always lived in the House of the Rising Sun itself, except for her acting stint in New York.

Barrie was now in Gwydion's Cave, the house Merlin had built for their grandfather, and she herself had the original 1920s guesthouse, called Pandora's Box.

Pandora's Box. A fitting name for all of L.A. in her opinion.

The main house really was beautiful! Regal, haunting and majestic, high up on a cliff. The style was Mediterranean Gothic, and it seemed to hold a thousand secrets as it stood proud against the night sky.

As a matter of fact, it *did* hold a thousand secrets. All right, maybe not *a thousand,* but a lot of them. Like the tunnels that connected all three houses. And the little red buttons that looked like light switches and were set randomly around the three houses. Little red buttons that set off alarms in all three residences, in case someone in any one of them needed help.

The property could only be reached via a winding driveway that scaled the cliff face, and the entire property was protected by a tall stone wall. She had to open the massive electric gate with a remote she kept in her car or else buzz in and hope someone was home to answer.

Grudgingly, she had to admit that she loved the House of the Rising Sun and living on the estate wasn't any kind of punishment. It was still breathtaking to watch the gate swing wide to allow entry to the compound, and then awe inspiring to see the beautiful stone facades of the houses appear.

Sometimes she wondered why Merlin had bothered with the wall. The Others that the Keepers were assigned to watch weren't the type to be stopped by walls or gates. But then again, Merlin had lived in the real world with its real dangers, too, as did they—although calling the surreal world of Hollywood "real" seemed like a contradiction in terms.

She clicked the gate shut behind her and drove forward slowly, noting that Barrie's car was parked on the left side of the property, while Sailor's, unsurprisingly, was not. Since there was no garage—all the available land had been used for the houses—she assumed that if Sailor's car wasn't there, neither was Sailor herself. Barrie was determined to save the world, not only by overseeing the shapeshifters but also by practicing the kind of hard-hitting journalism that could bring about change in L.A., if not the world, so, she tended to keep reasonable hours. Sailor, Keeper of the Elven, was determined to rule the world from the silver screen, which meant she was likely to be out and networking at all hours.

Still thinking about the way the Elven had handed her his card and told her that she *should* see the play, Rhiannon pulled into her usual parking place and exited the car, bringing her guitar with her as she headed for Pandora's Box. Slipping her key into the lock, she shoved a shoulder wearily against the door, stepped in and flicked on the lights.

She was tired. And she worked in a café, for God's sake. She should have brought home a gourmet tea to sip while she unwound, but after only a few minutes with Mac Brodie she had been too disconcerted to think of it.

She set her guitar case in its stand and headed into the kitchen. There she quickly brewed a cup of tea and added a touch of milk, then headed back out to the living room to sink into the comfortable old sofa and lean back. She closed her eyes.

"No, you really should *come see the show...."*

There was a tap at her door. She listened for a minute without rising. She was tired. And frustrated. And, she had to admit, unnerved.

An Elven had come to her and told her that she needed to see a vampire play.

Why?

It was just a play, a pretense. No vampires were out there killing people. Or other vampires, or anyone else. If they were, she would have heard about it on the news, wouldn't she?

The tapping became more persistent. Rhiannon forced herself to rise. It could only be one of a very few people at this time of night. Maybe Sailor had come home early and might listen to the story of Rhiannon's night and give her some advice.

It wasn't Sailor or even Barrie who stood at her door. Merlin had come by to visit. "I hope I'm not disturbing you?" he asked anxiously.

Yes, you are, she almost said, but she refrained. Merlin was a ghost. If he wanted to, he could be anywhere—perched on the end of the grand piano in the living room, day and night, if he felt like it. But he was a polite ghost, one who had learned to manifest corporeally. He had mastered the art of knocking on doors to announce his presence and behaved at all times as if he was not only living but a gentleman. He had maintained his old room in the main house, and he was careful to be the best possible "tenant." They all loved him, but Sailor, in particular, was accustomed to living with him—both before and after his death.

They had all sobbed at his funeral—until they realized that he was standing right there with them, comforting them in his new and unearthly form.

"Come in, Merlin, please," she said. "Have a seat. My home is your home, you know. Literally," she added with a warm smile.

Merlin had always been so good to her family, and it had been a two-way street. Her grandfather had saved him from jail when a shapeshifter had impersonated him and perpetrated several lewd crimes while posing as the noted magician. Her grandfather had been the shapeshifter Keeper and had worked with a friend on the police force—a werewolf—to prove that someone had been impersonating Merlin, and ensure that the proper person was caught and punished.

She stepped back from the door, sweeping a hand wide to indicate that he should join her.

Merlin stepped inside, looked around and sighed with happiness. "I'm so glad that you girls are living here," he told her.

He walked to the sofa and sank onto it, looking like a dignified and slightly weary old man. Which was exactly what he had been when he'd died. He'd lived a good, long life that had left him with a charmingly lined face, bright blue eyes and a cap of snow-white hair. Having him around really was like having a grandfather on the property.

"And we're glad to be here," Rhiannon said.

What a liar she was, she thought. She'd been about to get her big break when she'd been called home and been told that she was an adult and the good times were over. Her responsibilities had crashed down upon her with no time for her to think about it, to say yes or no. Suddenly all three Gryffald brothers were being sent overseas and their daughters were taking their places, and that was that.

Of course her father and her uncles hadn't been given a chance to say yes or no any more than she and Sailor and Barrie had.

The brothers had been summoned to serve on the new high council of Keepers at the Hague, a council that would act as a worldwide governing body for the Otherworld and the Others.

"Are you fitting in okay?" Merlin asked her, sincere concern in his voice.

"Of course." She forced a smile. None of this was

Merlin's fault. Or her father's. He'd tried to be so fierce when he'd talked to her. *You are the Keeper for the vampires, Rhiannon. They are powerful and deadly, and yours is a grave responsibility.*

At the time, of course, all she'd seen was that her band was finally getting a real break—and she wasn't going to be there to experience it.

Merlin nodded thoughtfully. "I was just wondering… I mean, this *is* L.A. It's not as if there isn't plenty of murder, mayhem and scandal on a purely human level."

"Merlin, what are you talking about?" she asked wearily.

"You might want to talk to Barrie. There have been a few mysterious deaths lately."

Something hard seemed to fall to the pit of her stomach. This couldn't involve her. Not already.

"Mysterious deaths?" she asked.

Merlin nodded. "They haven't gotten a lot of coverage, because none of them have been on one of those trashy reality shows or even made Hollywood's D list. These poor people have gone from this world unnoticed and unknown."

"Like you said—this *is* L.A.," Rhiannon said, frowning.

"Well, speak to your cousin, because she's got contacts who have told her a few things. There have been three similar deaths, and all three corpses were discovered in a similarly advanced state of decay."

"And?" She whispered the word, as if that could keep her fears from becoming real.

"The cops have been trying to keep the details out of the papers, but someone leaked one important fact," Merlin told her grimly.

"And that fact is…?" she asked.

He winced. "I'm sorry, Rhiannon. The corpses were almost bone dry, sucked dry of…"

"Of?" she asked, even though in her heart she knew the answer.

"Blood," Merlin said gravely. "Sucked dry of blood."

Chapter 2

To a lot of people in L.A., it wasn't all that late.

But to Rhiannon, after her wretched shift at the café, nothing sounded more welcome than her bed and a pillow.

Still, she knew she wouldn't sleep if she didn't try to talk to Barrie, though with any luck Barrie would already be in bed and wouldn't answer the knock at her door.

To Rhiannon's dismay, Barrie was up.

A single light was on in Barrie's living room, where she had been sitting on her sofa and working. Her laptop was sitting on a pile of newspapers and magazines.

Barrie definitely tended to be a workaholic.

She had a good job in her chosen field, but she still wasn't where she wanted to be in her career. At the moment she mostly got stories that ran under headlines—often handed to her whether she liked them or not—like "West Hollywood Woman Reveals Secret Behind Amazing Weight Loss."

Barrie was a crusader; she had strong opinions on right and wrong. She wanted to be where the action was. She wanted to get off the crime beat and into issue-based investigative journalism, but her Keeper duties would always have to take precedence, and that was a problem.

Rhiannon sympathized with her. She knew how difficult it was, trying to have a real career and deal with this sudden shift in purpose.

"Hey, I didn't expect to see you tonight." Barrie grinned and rolled her eyes. "Merlin, maybe—sometimes he forgets the time. Thought you'd come home exhausted and ready to crash."

"Am I interrupting?" Rhiannon asked her.

"No. Yes—but it's all right, honestly." She sighed. "I'm trying to come up with a story and an angle no one's thought of yet, so I can take it to my boss and maybe—finally—get a green light."

"Good luck," Rhiannon offered.

"So, how did things go at the café tonight?"

"They sucked. Totally sucked. Some actors staged a vampire attack right out front to publicize their play and nearly gave me heart failure—and in all the fuss my tip jar was stolen."

"You're right. That sucks. Want a cup of tea?"

"I just had one, but sure," Rhiannon said.

Barrie led the way into the kitchen.

All three of their houses might have been curio museums, filled as they were with Merlin's collections from a lifetime of loving magic—and the bizarre. The main house held the bulk of it, because it was so large, with five bedrooms upstairs, a grand living room and a family room that led out to the pool. Tiffany lamps were everywhere, along with Edwardian furniture, and busts and statues, and paintings that covered the walls. Pandora's Box had a Victorian feel, with rich, almost stuffy furniture, and a collection of sculpted birds, with the largest being a magnificent gesso rendition of Poe's raven. It also boasted a few of Merlin's old coin-drop fortune-teller machines.

Gwydion's Cave, Barrie's house, was decorated with old peacock fans, marble sideboards and rich wood pieces from the decadent days of the speakeasy. The service she used for tea was Royal Doulton. As she entered the kitchen, Rhiannon caught sight of herself in one of the antique hall mirrors, and though she knew it was distorted by the old glass, her own image troubled her.

She had the shocked look of someone who had stuck a finger in a live socket.

Barrie hummed as she boiled water and then looked at Rhiannon. "Something more happened than what you're telling me, didn't it? I always think of you as the go-getter among us. Nothing fazes you. But tonight you look…fazed."

"What if that attack had been real? Would I actually have been able to do anything to stop it? I guess we didn't think we'd be handling this kind of thing so quickly," Rhiannon said.

"None of us did. But it's not like we had a choice."

"I know. I just want to play my music, you know? It's all I've ever wanted. I missed my shot with the band, but at least I get to play at the café, you know? And that's what I was doing when those idiots interrupted."

"Listen to you, being so whiny."

"Whiny?" Rhiannon protested indignantly.

"Yes, whiny. 'Everybody but me gets to play in the band, while I'm stuck in a coffee shop playing for tips.' Buck up, buttercup."

"All right, all right, I have been whining. A little bit. But, honestly, I just wish…I wish we'd been a little better prepared. I mean, my dad is in great health. I never thought…"

"You never thought you'd have to be a Keeper until you were old and gray. I know. Neither did I. But here we are. So, what else is bothering you? Because I know there's something."

"All right, I came here to tell you, so…one of the actors was an Elven. I saw him when I was closing up my guitar case for the night. He came up to me and chatted, and I—I wasn't exactly rude, but I felt like he was comparing me to my dad and it bugged me. You know that Keepers all over the state put us down all the time. 'The Gryffald girls. What a shame their fathers were *all* put on the council. There used to be *good* Keepers in the Canyon.' So I guess I was a little rude. But really, I don't want to get all warm and cozy with the Elven— I'm going to have my hands full with the vampires."

"I understand all that," Barrie said calmly. "So, why are you so upset?"

"Well, he invited me to see his show. Like I want to see some ridiculous play about a bunch of vampire attacks. I brushed him off. But he knew who I was, and he said, 'No, no, you really *should* see the show,' or something weird like that, and when I got home…" She paused for breath.

"When you got home?" Barrie prompted.

"Merlin dropped in on me. And he told me that I

should speak to you—that there have been three recent murders in L.A.—"

"Only three?" Barrie interjected drily.

"Three in which the bodies have been found drained of blood and decayed and…I don't know. Merlin just said to talk to you."

"Oh," Barrie said.

"Oh?" Rhiannon repeated. "Come on, Barrie. You must know something. You work at a newspaper, for God's sake."

"You know all they give me is fluff," Barrie reminded her.

"Yes, but you're there and you must hear things."

"I don't remember anything that sensational, but maybe the police are keeping the details quiet. I do remember hearing about a John Doe found in a lake near some half-built apartment complex. That might have been one of your victims. I'll see what I can find out," she promised. "So—when are you going to see the show?"

"Now that Merlin's talked to me? Tomorrow night," Rhiannon told her, then sighed. "Hugh told me not to be late tomorrow night. He's going to give me a buttload of grief, not to mention dock my pay."

"Tell him you can't be there—that you have Keeper duties and that's it. I've seen you in action. You're great fighting other people's wars—fight this one for yourself. For all three of us," Barrie added. "We have to prove ourselves. You might as well start tomorrow night with Hugh."

As Barrie poured hot water into the teapot, they heard the sound of a car door slamming. "Sailor's home," she commented.

"So she is."

"I'll get another cup."

Rhiannon walked to the door and opened it just as Sailor was about to knock.

"Hi," her cousin said.

Sailor spoke with a cheerful voice and had a perfect smile to go with it. Rhiannon thought that while they were all decent looking, Sailor was their true beauty. It made sense that she was so passionate about being an actress. She had both the talent and the looks.

Maybe it had to do with the fact that Sailor had been destined to be Keeper of the Canyon Elven. Elven were beautiful, Rhiannon reminded herself drily, thinking of Mac Brodie.

Guilt bit into her. Several times she'd caught herself feeling impatient with Sailor for not taking their calling seriously, but hadn't she wanted to deny it herself? And now she was facing her first real challenge—because even if the murders proved to have nothing to do with the Canyon vampire community, standing up to Hugh was going to be no picnic—and all she wanted was to run away.

"I saw the light, so I thought I'd stop by," Sailor said.

"Come on in," Rhiannon said.

Sailor swept past her and headed straight for the kitchen. "I had a great night—I mean a *great* night. I went to this fantastic party at the club—Declan Wainwright's club, the Snake Pit."

Declan Wainwright was the shapeshifter Keeper for the Malibu area. They'd known him forever, though Rhiannon wasn't sure she would actually call him a friend.

"Declan told me he was going to ask you to play there a few nights a week. Well, he didn't tell *me*. He's kind of an ass to me. I'm not A-list enough for him, so mostly he ignores me. But I was with Darius Simonides, and he told Darius that he was going to talk to you. Pretty great, huh?"

"It's nice that you spent some time with Darius," Rhiannon said, filing away the potential offer of employment to consider later. Darius Simonides was Sailor's godfather and a big-deal Hollywood agent, but as far as Rhiannon could tell, he hadn't done much for her. At least not professionally. There was also something… slimy about him, she thought. Maybe it was because he was so…Hollywood. In his line of business, double-talk was really the only talk. Maybe that was at the heart of her reaction to him, but she still didn't trust him.

"Not only that, we hung with Hunter Jackson, too— do you know who he is?"

"Hunter Jackson," Rhiannon repeated, trying to remember why he sounded so familiar. "I've heard the name," she said.

"He's a director," Barrie said.

"He's *the* director these days, and he says that he has a role for me in a big-budget vampire thriller he's going to start filming in January. He and Darius actually invited me to the Snake Pit tonight to talk to me about it." Sailor beamed. "And it turns out there's a reason why Darius has kept his hands off me."

"That's good to hear," Barrie muttered sarcastically.

"I mean as far as my career goes," Sailor said. "Darius is a sweetie—people just think he's tough because he's so powerful. The thing is, he wanted me to make my own way, to prove I could succeed on my own before he stepped in. But tonight—it was wonderful!" Sailor looked rapturous. She drew a breath, and Rhiannon was sure she was going to go on some more about her amazing night, but instead she said, "Barrie, you have artificial sweetener, don't you? I don't want to gain an ounce right now."

Rhiannon decided that she would once again have to rethink Sailor's role in ensuring the safety of the world.

"I have everything I can think of for anyone's choice in tea," Barrie said. "Dig into the cabinet and help yourself."

"So, tell me more," Rhiannon said, genuinely happy for her cousin and momentarily putting aside her fears for the fate of the world.

Sailor turned to her, beaming. "The two leads will be major A-list actors. I don't know who yet. But what I'll make for just a few days' work will pay my bills for months."

Rhiannon lowered her head. At least one of them would be making a decent income, though if what Sailor had said about the offer to play the Snake Pit was true, she would be earning some real money, too, even if Hugh got mad enough to fire her. She looked up quickly, frowning. "Hunter Jackson... I remember reading something about him." She looked at Sailor. "He's a vampire, right? But he's the responsibility of the West Hollywood Keeper, Geoff Banner."

"Yes," Barrie said. "And he's the perfect person to direct a vampire thriller. The movies always have it wrong. Like all that crap about how vampires can't go out during the day."

"Seriously," Rhiannon agreed. "But no one wants to hear that the only problem is their eyes are exceptionally sensitive to light, so they always wear sunglasses—something that seems to be expected in Hollywood, anyway." She met Sailor's eyes. "You did know that he's a vampire, right?"

Sailor stared at her, indignant. "Of course I did. I'm the one who really grew up here, remember? I know the lowdown on almost everyone. Am I supposed to suddenly be suspicious of him because he's a vampire? And of all people who might be down on vampires, it shouldn't be you!"

"I'm not down on vampires," Rhiannon said quickly.

"Then what's your problem?" Sailor asked.

"I just wanted to make sure you knew what you were dealing with, that's all," Rhiannon said.

Sailor looked at her as if she knew Rhiannon doubted her abilities—and her competence in the face of a crisis. "Yes, I am well aware, thank you. And if you come across any Elven, I hope you'll try to be a little less judgmental."

Failed that one, Rhiannon thought. But she kept silent.

"Hey!" Barrie said, lifting a hand. "I get that we're all a little jittery right now, with our new responsibilities and all, but it's important that we get along. The world respected our fathers, but we're going to have to prove ourselves. And that will be a lot easier if we respect each other."

"Yes, you're right," Rhiannon said softly.

"There's nothing to prove, at least not right now," Sailor said. "Thanks to our dads, everything in the Canyon is running smoothly." She turned to Rhiannon. "Can't you just be happy for me?" she asked.

"I'm sorry. I *am* happy for you," Rhiannon said. She

hugged Sailor, who resisted for a moment then eased up and hugged Rhiannon in return. "I'm sorry. It was a bad night for me," Rhiannon said.

"Her tip jar was stolen," Barrie explained. "Among other things."

"Those bastards stole your tip jar!" Sailor said, straightening, her protest loyal and fierce.

"It's all right," Rhiannon said. "I'll live." She put an arm around Sailor's shoulders. "We need to go home. Barrie has an early morning, as usual." She turned to her other cousin. "Night, Barrie, thanks for listening."

"Hey, wait," Barrie said, following Rhiannon and Sailor to the door. "Rhiannon, I'll see what I can dig up tomorrow. And also, I was thinking that Sailor and I should go see that play with you."

"You don't have to," Rhiannon said.

"Play?" Sailor said, perking up. "What play?"

"Vampire Rampage," Rhiannon said.

To Rhiannon's surprise, Sailor's jaw dropped. "You're kidding, right?"

"No, not at all. They pulled a promo stunt in front of the coffee shop tonight."

Sailor's eyes were wide. "The movie—the one I've been asked to be in—is called *Vampire Rampage,* and it's based on the play. Yes, let's all go. It will really help me to see the original."

"And to think, I was just hoping it might keep someone alive," Rhiannon said.

Sailor turned slowly and stared at her. "What's going on?" she asked.

"An Elven actor stopped by the café tonight, and he told me that I really need to see the play. And then Merlin told me tonight that three murder victims have been found drained of blood. So now I'm kind of worried that a vampire, well, you know...."

Sailor stared at Rhiannon for a long moment, and then reached out and pulled her into a hug. "Oh, I am so sorry! You know...maybe someone has been itching to break the rules and waited until our fathers were gone, figuring that—"

"We'd be ineffectual," Rhiannon said wearily.

Barrie and Sailor were silent.

"Well, I don't intend to be ineffectual," Rhiannon said. "So tomorrow night, the three of us, the theater..."

"We'll be ready," Sailor assured her. "It will be great."

"All I can think about is three bodies drained of blood—and I've barely been here a week," Rhiannon said.

"We'll get through this. We'll help you get the answers," Barrie said. "Right, Sailor?"

"Right," Sailor agreed.

Rhiannon left Gwydion's Cave and headed back to her own house. The moon was out, shining down and creating a crystal trail across the surface of the pool.

Three bodies drained of blood.

Tomorrow she would get out her dad's list of helpful contacts in the city. She had to get into the morgue and see what she could find out, and then, tomorrow night, the play.

"Vampire Rampage," she murmured.

She reached into her pocket and fingered the business card the Elven had given her, then pulled it out and looked at it. *Mac Brodie, Actor.* And then it offered a cell phone number. It was curious that an actor's card didn't have his website and résumé listed.

She thought about calling him, then decided to wait until she'd seen the show. She might be a novice Keeper, but she was going to have to be strong and prove that she could be as effective as her father.

Because she was very afraid that there was already a vampire on the rampage in L.A.

Brodie sat, reading over the files on his desk.

The first body had been discovered three weeks ago at the bottom of the molding pool at an abandoned house off Hollywood and Vine—the owner had gone into foreclosure and no enterprising real estate mogul had as yet snapped up the place. The victim, who was in his twenties, remained unidentified, despite the fact that they'd combed through missing person reports from across the country. Of course, he'd been missing his fingers and though the morgue had taken dental impressions, they were worthless when there were no records with which to compare them.

The dead man must have had friends or family somewhere, but apparently none of them had reported him missing. Then again, young people often took off to "find themselves," so their nearest and dearest didn't always know they were missing.

Because of the fetid water where the body had been dumped, the soft tissue had been in an advanced state of decomposition. Despite the mess he'd had to work with, Tony Brandt's report stated that he'd tentatively identified the puncture marks at the throat that had led to exsanguination, which he listed as cause of death. Because the body had been in the water and then in the morgue for several weeks—and because it was a John

Doe the case had ended up at the bottom of a pile of open cases that had gone cold.

There was one interesting fact, though. A water-logged playbill had been discovered in his pocket.

Ten days ago, with the discovery of the second body, two files had landed on Brodie's desk. His captain was concerned. The second file contained another John Doe. This one had been found in a small man-made lake in Los Feliz—near a rehearsal hall that had been rented to a local theatrical group, the same group now performing *Vampire Rampage*. Once again dental impressions had been taken, and they were still hoping to make a match. Also once again, no fingerprint identification was possible because there were no fingers.

That body had also been decaying for some time. It was in fact so decayed that Tony Brandt could only find the suggestion of puncture marks in the jugular vein. But the similarities had been enough for Brodie's captain to decide that the two murders might be the work of a serial killer, and that it was time to get to the truth.

Captain Edwin Riley knew something about the Others and the Otherworld. He was one of the few individuals trusted by the city's Other community, being the son of a practicing Wiccan and high priestess who'd been targeted for death. Brodie didn't really know the whole story, and the captain didn't like talking about it, so he didn't pry. But it had something to do with a religious cult that had decided his parents were devil worshippers, and that they needed to have an accident—one that would remove them from the earth.

They'd survived the accident, thanks to Brodie's father, then a young Elven, who had seen what was happening and jumped from his own car in time to rescue the Rileys' car before their car went over a cliff.

Most human beings had no idea about the existence of the Others, but the captain knew about Brodie, which made him the logical choice to find out what was happening.

The next thing he knew, he was auditioning. There had been an opening in the cast because an actor had suddenly and, from the cops' point of view conveniently, left, sending Jackson Hunter an email stating that he had to get back to Connecticut and stop the love of his life from marrying another man.

It had seemed a weak link—joining the play—but it was better than nothing, and the theater was the only connection, however vague, between the murders. He'd been suspicious that the missing actor might be one of the John Does in the morgue cooler, but Adam Lansky, in the police tech assistance unit, had tracked him down, and he was indeed back in Connecticut. Whether he'd stopped the love of his life from marrying another man or not, Brodie didn't know.

Tonight, after seeing the third corpse on Tony Brandt's autopsy table, he was more convinced than ever that the killer was somehow involved with the play. Not only had the corpse been found in the lake that was just past the parking lot and a stretch of overgrown brush behind the theater, but there was the fact that he'd actually seen the man in the audience.

Three John Does, all of them connected in one way or another to the theater and *Vampire Rampage*. And, he was very much afraid, to a real vampire, too.

All right after the three strongest peacekeepers in the area had left.

And in their place…

Three untested…girls.

Brodie stood and walked to the rear of his bungalow apartment in central Hollywood. He could see the crescent moon rising boldly in the clear heavens. He tried to tell himself that the fact that the bodies had been drained did not definitely mean that the killer was a vampire. The victims might have been drained so that their deaths *appeared* to be the work of a vampire. And God knew, there were plenty of crazy humans who *thought* they were vampires. And there were dozens of reasons for draining a body of blood, starting with…

Hunger.

Like it or not, he had the feeling that a vampire was guilty.

All he had to do was find him—and kill him.

Obviously he couldn't count on any help from the new Keeper, Ms. Rhiannon Gryffald, and yet the case definitely fell under her jurisdiction. He'd given her his card, damn it, and she hadn't even bothered to call him. Okay, so she didn't know he was a cop. But still, she should have realized that something important was up—something she, as a Keeper, needed to investigate.

He gritted his teeth, wondering just how many corpses they would find before the killer was unmasked.

Chapter 3

Rhiannon wasn't as close to Darius Simonides as Sailor was, but their families had always been involved, so she was confident enough to head for his office late the next morning, despite the fact that she had no real idea of what she was about to say. She hadn't seen him since she'd come to town to take over her father's duties, so she could just chat, of course, and hope something useful came out of it.

Darius was a powerhouse; his offices were chrome and glass, impeccably modern. Head shots of his A-list clients covered the walls, along with movie posters. Artistic little Greek columns held statues of movie scenes. The offices were elegant, as they should be. Darius had earned his reputation.

She made her way past the guard on the first floor and up the broad marble staircase to the second floor, aware that security cameras followed her all the way.

When she reached Darius's office she was stopped by his secretary. She smiled when she saw the woman; she had known Mary Bickly from the time she'd been a child. Mary was no-nonsense. She had iron-gray hair and a manner to match. No one saw Darius unless she chose to let them in.

"Well, hello there, Rhiannon," Mary said, rising and coming around her large desk, her arms outstretched for a hug. Rhiannon quickly accepted. "Welcome. I understand that you and your cousin Barrie have moved to Los Angeles. It was quite bizarre, the way your families all moved to Europe. Did they go back to Wales?"

"No, no, my father and his brothers were always close, and I guess they just decided that they'd tour Europe together. My dad has always been fascinated by the Hague, so that's where they're spending most of their time." Not only was Mary human, but she had no idea that Darius was a vampire. It was amazing, really, that the Others were so heavily represented in L.A., and yet most of them managed to remain completely below the radar.

"Well, I know that Darius misses your father and his brothers, but I'm sure he'll be delighted to see you. He's in a meeting right now, if you can wait a few minutes? Would you like some coffee, dear?"

"I don't mind waiting, and you needn't bother—" Rhiannon began.

"No bother. The little pod maker thing is right there, on the shelf. Go help yourself."

"Thanks."

Rhiannon walked over and selected something that promised to be "bold and eye-opening, the best breakfast blend." As she played with the coffeemaker, the inner door to Darius's sanctum opened. She turned quickly, and to her surprise she saw not just Darius and Declan Wainwright, but one of the men who had destroyed her evening at the Magic Café. Jack Hunter, she remembered. Aka "Drago." And right behind them, another man. Mac Brodie.

Darius saw her just as Declan did, and both men offered her broad, welcoming smiles.

Jack Hunter stared at her curiously, as if he felt he should know her but didn't.

Nice to be remembered, she thought, then caught Mac's eyes. From his expression it was obvious that he, at least, definitely remembered her.

And the way he looked at her…

She was surprised to feel heat burning inside her. He unsettled her. Well, he was Elven, of course. But she should have been immune, and it annoyed her that she wasn't. Despite that annoyance, she felt her pulse thudding, the blood rising in her throat.

"Rhiannon! Sailor was saying that you and Barrie had moved to L.A.," Darius said, striding toward her, arms open wide. He was a little over six feet, a striking man with sharp hazel eyes, dark, slightly graying hair and an air of power that was unconsciously seductive. She had no idea how old he was; he definitely retained a dignified sexual appeal, but his face bore the character of centuries.

"Yes, Darius, we're both living on the estate. I was hoping that I might see you, just quickly, because I know you're incredibly busy." She turned to Declan and said, "I got your email this morning, and I'd love to play the club on weekends."

Darius introduced Mac next.

"No need for introductions, Darius. Ms. Gryffald and I met last night. In fact, we had a brief but very... interesting conversation." He met her eyes. "I do hope you'll think about what I said."

"Certainly. I'm weighing its importance," she said pleasantly.

"I think—for you—the importance could be high," he said.

He spoke lightly, but she felt his eyes on hers in a way that made her uncomfortable. Afraid that if he looked for too long he would read far too much, she quickly lowered her gaze.

He turned away to address the other men.

"I hate to meet and run, but if you'll excuse me, I have to be somewhere." He nodded curtly at Rhiannon then. "I meant what I said last night, as well as just now. Think about it."

And then, with a wave, he was gone. Rhiannon stared at his retreating back, feeling a bit as if she'd just been run over by a very attractive truck, then realized the men looked as stunned as she felt by his abrupt departure.

Darius shook his head as if recalling himself to the present and turned to Jack Hunter.

"Hunter Jackson, meet a very dear friend of mine, Rhiannon Gryffald," he said. "Jack is adapting a fantastic vampire play for the screen. Rhiannon, Hunter Jackson."

Hunter took her hand and smiled at her, his eyes bright with amusement. "It took me a moment to recognize you, but we almost met last night. I must say, Ms. Gryffald, you're a courageous young woman. Everyone else was screeching and screaming, and you rushed out like Joan of Arc on a mission."

The others laughed. Rhiannon forced a smile, not feeling the least bit amused.

"I believe you were introduced last night as Jack Hunter," she said, frowning, not the least bit impressed that she was meeting the illustrious director Hunter Jackson. Sailor was going to be thrilled, though.

"You've unmasked me, Darius," Jackson said, then turned back to Rhiannon. "Like a lot of directors, I started off with an acting career, and I decided to direct and star in the stage version of the show myself. A little bit of ego going on there, I'm afraid."

"You should be careful with your promo stunts, Mr. Jackson," she said. "I'm just a musician. What if there had been a cop there last night and he'd pulled a gun on you?"

"It's not likely, Ms. Gryffald," Hunter said, and shrugged. "This is Hollywood. The cops usually know a show from the real thing." He looked at Darius and laughed. "So I take it that *this* charming Miss Gryffald is *not* looking for a career on the big screen?"

Darius shook his head. "Musician, as she said."

Hunter turned back to Rhiannon, grinning. "Good for you. Because—my ego speaking again, I'm afraid— aspiring actresses always feel the need to suck up to me, and it can get pretty tiresome."

She forced a pleasant smile. "I'm sure that when you choose a star for one of your productions, you base your choice on talent and not just because she sucked up to you."

"Such a diplomat," Hunter said, but he was laughing.

Rhiannon realized that she ought to be nice to the

man; she wanted to know why one of his actors had insisted that she come to the show. She managed to keep her smile in place. "My cousins and I are going to see the show tonight," she told him.

"That's great. Is one of the cousins you're referring to Sailor Gryffald?" Hunter asked.

She nodded.

"I'm glad. She'll get a good feel for the material by seeing the play. It's not just a horror story. It's about the many different kinds of hunger that can drive us, even ruin our lives, and about what we're willing to do for love. Of course," he said thoughtfully, "it's about redemption, as well."

"It sounds interesting," Rhiannon said.

"It's a musical," Darius said. "You're going to love it, Rhiannon."

Declan smiled. "They're going to film some scenes at the Snake Pit," he said.

She nodded, trying very hard to keep a pleasant smile glued to her lips. She might have accepted a job offer from the man, but she didn't trust shapeshifters. They were pranksters. And when they went bad, their ability to shift into any guise meant major trouble. Their Keepers could be just as...shifty, and Declan definitely was.

"Sounds just great," she finally said, knowing how lame she sounded.

"Gotta go," Declan said. "I'll see you Friday night?"

"Yes, thank you."

He shook hands with the other men and started toward the stairs. As he was leaving, Hunter said, "Well, I'd best be on my way, too, Darius. Ms. Gryffald...a pleasure. And please, come see me backstage tonight. I'd love your opinion on the show."

"I'm not really a theater expert, but I'd be delighted to see you after the show," she said.

"Any audience member is an excellent theatrical judge," he said. "I'll see you later." He gave them both a wave and left.

Darius looked at Rhiannon assessingly, and she could see that he was well aware that she hadn't just dropped in on him for a casual chat.

"Shall we enter the inner sanctum, my dear?" he asked.

She nodded. "Thanks."

Mary had returned to her desk while the others talked, but she spoke up then. "Darius, shall I hold your calls?"

"Yes, please, Mary," Darius said. "Thank you."

Rhiannon grabbed her coffee and followed Darius into his office. It was huge, with massive windows that looked out over the city. In addition to the requisite de-signer chairs in front of a chrome and glass desk, the room boasted a comfortable sofa against a wall, a full stereo and wide-screen system and a wet bar. There was also a bathroom—all chrome and glass and mar-ble. Darius easily could have lived there and sometimes did, despite the fact that he had a fabulous mansion in the Hollywood Hills.

"Drink?" he asked her.

"I've got coffee. I'm fine," she told him.

"I'll help myself, then," he said.

He reached into his refrigerator, which was filled with his "specials." Mary didn't fill his refrigerator; his assistant, Rob Cantor, took care of that chore. His spe-cials looked like Bloody Marys, but they would have gagged a vegetarian. His blood came from a meatpacking plant he owned in west Texas.

"Sit," he told her, taking his own chair behind the desk, easing back and planting his feet on the shiny surface. "You doing okay?" he asked her once she'd taken a seat.

"I'm all right, yes, thanks," she told him.

"You can't be all right if you're here to see me so soon. What's the problem?" He took a sip from his glass, sighed and seemed to sink back farther in sensual delight.

"I saw a piece of the play last night, Darius. Your friends staged it right in front of the Mystic Café."

"How is that old dog Hugh Hammond?" Darius asked, laughing at his own joke.

"As growly as ever," Rhiannon assured him.

Darius enjoyed that. He didn't reply, but his easy smile deepened. He took another sip of blood and then looked at her. "And…?"

"Your play—or movie," she said.

He frowned. "What about it?"

"Darius, it's about a vampire on a killing spree," she said.

"Oh, please!" Darius said. He was clearly irritated. He swung his feet down and stared at her hard across the desk. "What? I'm going to stop the world from making vampire movies?"

Rhiannon drew a deep breath. "It's come to my attention, Darius, that three bodies have turned up in the area, drained of blood."

He arched a brow. "Really?"

"Really."

"Then you're not doing a very good job, are you?" he asked her.

She froze but refused to let him see her reaction in her expression. Instead, she leaned closer, staring at him. "The first body appeared before I ever arrived, Darius, and the second when I had just gotten here. But now there's a third."

"Then I suggest you bring it up at the local council meeting," he told her. "I haven't heard anything about this."

She didn't know that much herself yet, but she decided to fake it. "It sounds like a serial killer—a vampire serial killer—is at work."

"How dramatic, Rhiannon. Maybe you *should* have gone into acting," he said. "Bodies drained of blood. If you're accusing me of covering up for someone—which you had best not be—remember that I've been making my way by playing the human game for a very long time now. I love my life, and I'm not about to jeopardize it. If I did know of any suspicious vampires, I'd let you know. But I don't. Period."

"I didn't accuse you of anything," she said.

He continued to eye her suspiciously. "Did you come to me for help?"

"Yes, I suppose I did."

That, at least, mollified him.

"You still need to bring it up at the council meeting," he told her. "But I think it's pretty unlikely that a vampire's really behind this. I'm not the only one out here who is extremely happy. We make movies. We have a great supply of blood—I bring a lot of it in from my home state, where people are always lined up to donate—booze and women. We live in peace out here.

All of us, not just the vampires. I know a dozen gorgeous Elven who are big successes in this business—I get them roles, they make me money. Werewolves, shifters and all the rest…things work for them here in L.A. This is a city where we get along."

"It's also a city where lots of people don't make it," she reminded him. "Waitresses remain waitresses. Valets remain valets."

He lifted a hand. "I still don't see it, Rhiannon. I really don't." He leaned toward her. "What makes you think the murders have some connection to the play?"

"I never said they did," Rhiannon said. That was true; she hadn't said any such thing. She had suggested that both the play and movie might be in bad taste—for a vampire, at least—but that was all.

Suddenly she didn't want to tell him about Mac Brodie's insistence that she see the show. She wasn't sure why. Maybe because it seemed that Darius, like everyone else, didn't have any faith in her. Maybe it was because the two men knew each other, and until she knew how well, she didn't want to take chances.

And on top of that, she was a *Keeper*.

Which meant, for the time, as she felt her way forward and dealt with situations as they were thrust upon her, she was going to learn to *keep* things to herself.

She rose, determined not to make an enemy. "Darius, thank you. I'm glad I can look to you for help. I *will* bring this up at the council meeting."

"It's going to be your first," he told her. "I'll be happy to introduce you."

"Thanks."

"Thursday at midnight, the old church off Bertram," he told her.

"I'll be early," she promised.

He escorted her out of his office, giving her a hug. Moments later she found herself out on the street, wondering what to do next.

The answer was obvious. It was time to pay a visit to a werewolf.

Dr. Anthony Brandt arrived in the reception area of the morgue in his clean white coat.

He smiled when he saw Rhiannon, as if he were actually happy to see her. "Well, look who's come to see me," he said, then gave her a hug she was sure was intended for the benefit of the receptionist. She knew Tony—she'd known him since she was a child. He thought she was spoiled and had felt free to tell her parents so on occasion.

"It's so nice to finally see you, Tony," she said, her tone filled with artificial warmth. "You could have called me, you know."

"Well, I was thinking that you'd just arrived, that you were busy," he said.

As in, too busy to do what you should have been doing—being a good Keeper!

"I'm here now," she said.

"Well, then, come on back to my office," he told her. "Sign in first, though. You'll need a visitor's pass."

She got her pass and then followed him down the hallway.

His office was neat—sparse, actually. His desk held his computer and a stack of files, bookshelves lined two walls, while a single window looked out on the city. L.A. and life were all around him, but Tony lived in the realm of the dead.

"Have a seat," he told her.

He'd closed the door as they entered. She took a chair in front of the desk and leaned forward. "Don't go giving me that superior-than-thou look. I just got to town. If there was a problem and you knew about it, it was your responsibility to tell me. I shouldn't have had to rely on the grapevine to tell me about these murders—and the condition of the bodies." She stared challengingly at him. "You would have called my father."

He was quiet for a minute. "Yeah, I would have," he said quietly.

"Tony, I know you're a werewolf and you don't officially owe me anything, but can't you help me—the way you always helped my father?"

He looked a little abashed. "All right, Rhiannon, I'm sorry."

"Thank you. I'm learning, Tony. I can use all the help I can get."

He lifted the files on his desk and riffled through them, then produced three and handed them to her. "John Does, all of them. We can't get IDs on any of them."

"Did you find anything on the bodies? Any DNA from the killer? What about the bites? Any saliva?" Rhiannon asked.

"You know as well as I do that if they were bitten by a vampire, there would be no DNA. Vampire DNA disintegrates almost instantly. But, beyond that, all the bodies were found submerged in water and massively decomposed."

"No fibers, tickets, wallets, anything?"

"Totally empty pockets. All I know for sure is that they were bitten and exsanguinated."

"Is that what you put on the death certificates?" Rhiannon asked him.

He shook his head, indicating the reports. "The bodies *were* drained of blood, but due to the condition in which they were found, I couldn't determine an absolute cause of death. In fact, the really strange thing is that there was water in the lungs, so it's a crapshoot as to whether they drowned or died from blood loss, but whatever happened probably happened in the water. Or maybe they were just this side of dead when the killer tossed them in the water. No way to know, really."

"You're sure you found puncture marks?" Rhiannon asked, flipping through the files. There was information the police had given the medical examiners, and there were outlines of the male bodies, with notations and drawings. She looked back up at him. "It looks like they were tiny…you'd think that they'd be obvious. Vampire marks aren't usually as tiny as pinpricks."

"The fact that the flesh was so swollen around would have compressed them and made them harder to see. Still, there's nothing usual about these cases."

"I'm assuming you have a contact in the department?" she said.

"I have a lot of police contacts, but I don't think they'd appreciate my sharing their names. For now, you've got what you need to go on, so don't go barging into the station, telling one and all that you're the new vampire Keeper—especially since most of the bodies look like vampire victims."

Rhiannon had never actually ever been in a morgue in her life; even coming into the reception area had seemed difficult. Now…

You're at the morgue, she told herself. *This is what you're supposed to be doing, seeing the dead.*

She rose and followed Tony, who led her to a chilly room holding what appeared to be massive file cabinets, except that she knew they weren't. Each drawer contained one of the county's dead—those who still needed an autopsy, and those who were waiting....

To be claimed? Or because they were unclaimed?

Either way, it was sad.

She slipped into the white gown, mask and gloves Tony handed her, despite the fact that she had no intention of touching the bodies. She tried to appear professional.

But, no matter what her resolve, she wasn't ready for what she saw when he opened the first drawer.

The body was recognizable as human, but just barely.

"John Doe number one," Tony said. "He's our oldest, dead about a month. As you can see, the decomp is very bad. And, as you can also see, his fingers are missing."

Rhiannon willed herself not to gag. Despite the mask and the chemical smells in the air, the scent of decomposition was overwhelming. The flesh appeared absolutely putrid. His eyeballs were missing, and the flesh of his face was so puffed up that she couldn't have recognized anyone in such a state—even her own mother.

"The fingers...were they eaten by some creature? Or maybe they...rotted off?" she asked.

He shook his head. "There are telltale signs that a blade was used to remove them."

"So no one could make an ID?" she asked.

"It certainly makes it impossible to search the fingerprint database," he said.

She swallowed hard. "This seems like the work of a madman."

Tony looked around, but they were alone. "Or a hungry vampire, breaking the rules, attacking humans and trying to remain anonymous by making sure we can't ID the victims and connect them to him."

She stared into his eyes. "Yes, the killer *could* be a vampire. But it's far from certain. Do you have anything else to show me?"

Tony reached out and turned the head. "Here, right here. As the report said, they're tiny and surrounded by swelling, but the puncture marks are here. Now let's move on to John Doe number two."

He shut the drawer and didn't even glance her way as he led her to the next. The second body was in no better shape. Again he showed her what he had determined to be puncture marks and pointed out the missing fingers. The third body was the worst. He swept the sheet all the way down to show her the thighs, and at that point she thought she was going to black out or at least vomit.

Somehow she managed not to do either.

"Alcohol? Drugs? Had they been doing anything prior to their deaths? Stomach contents? Can their last meals be traced?" she asked.

Tony looked at her for a moment, then nodded. "All three men had been drinking. They were just above the legal limit, for whatever that's worth. I'm afraid that their last meals had been well digested, suggesting that they'd been drinking rather than eating during their final excursions into the wilds of the L.A. nightlife. Or day life. I don't have a time of death—I can't even guarantee a *day* of death. Water is vicious on human remains. And it's summer, so…" His voice trailed off.

Rhiannon silently willed him to close the last drawer. He did so, and then walked her back out to the hallway, where she dropped her lab coat, mask and gloves into the appropriate disposal bins.

She hadn't needed the gloves. She'd known she wouldn't.

She could still smell the terrible stench of death. She steeled herself against it. Had the hall smelled so strongly when she had arrived, or was the scent engrained in her forever?

"No poisons in the tox screens, right? You would have told me," she said.

"Nothing our screens have detected so far."

"Thank you, Tony," she said stiffly.

He nodded. "I'll let you know if…anything happens. And you'll return the favor?"

"Of course," she told him.

"Where are you going from here?" he asked her.

"To prepare for a night at the theater. I'm going to see a new vampire play. One of the actors told me I should see it." She tried not to think about how much she was actually looking forward to seeing Mac Brodie again— no matter how hard she tried to convince herself she didn't care. "And then I found out about the bodies."

"Yes, Rhiannon," he said after a moment, "I believe you *should* go to the theater. I think it will be a very enlightening evening for you."

Chapter 4

Brodie stood by the lake that lay about a hundred and fifty yards behind the theater. He knew that if he turned and faced the theater he would see a service station to the left, beyond the parking lot. To the right there was a warehouse. The lake itself was man-made. It had been dredged to build the housing project on the other side; however, the contractors had apparently run out of funds. The entire shore was overgrown, the lake itself green with alga, and, as twilight fell, the scene was forlorn.

He had already walked the area, carefully surveying the ground, but any clues that might have been left behind were long gone.

But he hadn't come to see if the crime-scene unit had missed anything; he had come to figure out why the perpetrator had chosen this location.

The killer had a method. He drained his victims of

blood, then discarded the bodies in water, which washed away any biological evidence, making it impossible for the M.E. to tell if the punctures had been inflicted by the fangs of a vampire or a sharp, probably metal, object of some kind.

All three locations where the bodies had been found were lonely, derelict—perfect for leaving a body without being seen, and with a reasonable expectation that it wouldn't be found for days or weeks, if ever.

It chafed Brodie no end to realize that he'd been working at the theater when the last victim had been dumped.

Frustrated, he hunkered down and skipped a stone across the lake. He had no leads. The bodies were giving them nothing—not even identities. The crime scenes had been cleansed by nature long before any first-on-scene officer could examine them.

The only possible connection between the victims and their killer was the play. He thanked whatever stroke of luck had led to the role being open just when he needed it. His natural Elven abilities had seen to it that he'd landed it without any trouble.

In his mind, his abilities made him a good cop. Unlike so many of his kind, he'd never yearned for the stage; he'd longed to keep order. He hated realizing that he and so many Others would be loathed and feared if their true natures were known by the general populace. He believed in equality, and that meant he believed in the law, as well, not to mention simple decency. Everyone deserved respect, the right to live, to seek happiness and to enjoy the freedom to follow their dreams.

He turned away from the lake. He wasn't particularly fond of water. Elven were creatures of the earth.

They didn't melt or anything, but they hadn't populated the new world until the airplane had been invented—they couldn't be away from solid ground for the time it took an ocean liner to make it across the Atlantic. They lost strength and eventually died if they didn't feel the power of the earth beneath their feet.

He glanced at his watch. It was almost his call time, and he prided himself on never being late. He made a point of talking with his cast mates every night, though so far his investigation hadn't netted him anything. He hadn't been sure about the connection to the play at first, but now he was. Instinct, perhaps. Which meant he had to be close to someone who at least knew what was going on—even if they didn't know they knew.

As he reached the cast entrance, he noticed that an old Volvo had pulled into the parking lot. Three women emerged.

The Gryffald cousins had arrived.

He was pleasantly surprised. Rhiannon hadn't called him, but at least she was coming to see the play.

He watched Rhiannon Gryffald as she stood by the driver's door, surveying the area. Her eyes were on the lake. She didn't see him as she studied the water.

She'd found out, he thought. She knew bodies had been found drained of blood. And she knew *where* they had been found; he could tell from the way she was looking at the water.

Yes, she definitely knew. Which meant she *definitely* hadn't come to see *him*. Damn it.

Intrigued, he stood by the rear door for a moment. He recognized Sailor Gryffald, of course. She'd grown up in L.A. and had often accompanied her father when he'd met with the Elven elders. She was an actress.

He hoped that she wouldn't recognize him, though of course she would know that he was Elven. Her interest in being a Keeper had been minimal when he had last seen her, so hopefully she hadn't paid any attention to him.

He smiled, taking a moment's pride in his people. She was the Elven Keeper, so by definition she possessed a bit of Elven charm. She didn't seem to have a passion for her hereditary responsibilities, but maybe that didn't matter so much. The Elven tended to be peaceful. They brooked no interference and could fight when drawn into battle, but they tended to live according to a philosophy of "Do as you will but harm no others." It was unlikely that she was going to have to solve a massive Elven crime spree.

Barrie Gryffald was now the Keeper of the shape-shifters. They were mischief-makers, and if any race was prone to misbehavior, it was them. But from what he knew, Barrie was a serious young woman, dedicated to becoming an investigative reporter.

For a moment he swept his concerns about the situation and the Gryffald cousins from his mind. They were all standing together, looking out at the stagnant lake. They were close to one another in height, and they all had varying shades of the same sleek hair. They looked like three Muses as they stood there, young, still naive and hopeful, and beautiful.

And, he feared, ineffectual.

He opened the stage door and came face-to-face with Bobby Conche, the tall, leanly muscled shapeshifter who'd been hired to take care of security. Bobby was from the Malibu area and fell under the jurisdiction of Declan Wainwright. He loved the theater, but as a fan, not a participant. He loved to guard the stage door, because it meant he got to see new productions in rehearsal. He knew, of course, that Brodie was Elven.

He didn't know he was cop.

"Hey, Bobby, thanks. I think I have some friends coming tonight. Three young women, the Gryffald—"

"Yeah, yeah, the Gryffald girls, the new Keepers," Bobby said, and grinned at Brodie. "Glad I'm with the Malibu pack—takes new Keepers a while to learn the ropes, you know?" Bobby nodded. "I'll make sure they find their way to you."

"Thanks," Brodie told him, then left to start getting ready for that night's performance.

Mac Brodie was a good actor. Damn him.

Not that Rhiannon had really expected anything else. Elven were known for their ability to charm—and to make others see them as they chose to be seen.

Vampire Rampage took place in modern London, but it was a riff on Bram Stoker's *Dracula*. It opened in a sea of mist, and then a car appeared. Mac Brodie, as Vince Anderson, stepped out, along with Lena Ashbury, who was playing a character named Lucy. They were lost in Transylvania, seeking her old family home, while on an extended honeymoon, and poor Lucy—who had dreamed of finding her distant cousins—was now terrified. Their rental car had died; the sound of wolves howling filled the air with a plaintive and spooky symphony. The writing was good, the dialogue occasionally funny as Lucy dreamed of the Transylvanian Automobile Association coming to the rescue. And then the fog thinned, revealing lights in the darkness, and they headed off to the house they saw in the distance.

The house was, of course, Drago's ancestral castle, where they were greeted there by Nickolai Drago and his household, which included an eerie butler and several sinfully sexual maids, all the action accompanied by a winning combination of dialogue and duets. Drago was charming, assuring Lucy that he would help her find her relatives in the morning, then having the newlyweds shown to a room. Later that night, however, Lucy rose and wandered downstairs to Drago's lair, where he proceeded to turn on his supernatural charm. Meanwhile, two of the sexy maids—Rhiannon recognized the actresses she'd seen outside the Mystic Café—broke in on Vince and attempted to seduce him. Rhiannon found her attention riveted on him with an intensity she couldn't fight as he escaped his would-be seducers and broke in on Drago and his wife. The audience was left to wonder if the vampire's teeth had or hadn't sunk into Lucy's lily-white throat.

In the morning Vince tried to convince his wife, who had no memory of the night's events, that they had to get away, because there was something evil afoot in the castle. Lucy, however, was clearly under Drago's spell, and refused to leave. That night Vince lay awake and waited, and when he heard the howling of the wolves in the forest, he saw Lucy awaken as if in response to their call. He followed her downstairs and managed to get her out of the castle without running into Drago, who was waiting with fangs bared. Vince dragged her through the forest, until they finally came upon an inn, where they were welcomed and warned that those who go to the castle were usually never seen again. Lucy met her long-lost cousins, who warned her that she had to be vigilant and avoid Drago and his castle at all costs.

Rhiannon tried to think why Mac had been so insistent that she see the show, because while she'd certainly enjoyed it—and him—she hadn't found anything so far that seemed relevant to the murders. Of course, maybe the problem was that she had been paying too much attention to Mac and not enough to the play.

There was a fifteen-minute intermission. As Rhiannon rose, she noticed that Sailor was still staring at the stage.

Her cousin looked up at her, rapt. "Isn't he magnificent?" She lowered her voice. "Imagine, Hunter Jackson playing Jack Hunter playing Drago. I can't believe the press hasn't pointed that out yet. I mean, someone besides me must have recognized him."

"I'm sure he'll be recognized once the show finishes previews and the reviewers descend. It's probably all part of his plan to start a major buzz about the whole project. He wants huge box office numbers when the movie opens. Clever, really," Rhiannon admitted.

"I am beyond excited. I'm going to be playing Erika, the upstairs maid."

"I wonder how the current upstairs maid feels," Barrie said drily.

"They're not using any of this cast for the movie," Sailor explained. "The show is going to keep running while the movie is being made. They're expecting to open on Broadway and hoping for a long run. After that, touring companies, if all goes well. It's not as if any of this cast will be out of a job."

"Still," Rhiannon said, "I wonder how they feel about not even getting the chance to be in the movie."

Sailor sniffed. "Well, certainly not angry enough to go around killing innocent strangers as if they were real vampires," she said. "They're working. In Hollywood, if you're not waiting on tables, you're a success."

A few minutes later, out in the lobby after Sailor decided she wanted a glass of wine, Rhiannon idly scanned the crowd. She was startled to see that Declan Wainwright was there. He must have known that he was going to be there that night when he'd seen her at Darius's office, but he hadn't said a word.

Not that he looked as if he really wanted to be found. He, too, seemed to be watching the audience members as they milled around, but unlike her, he was leaning against a support wall, mostly hidden from view.

Declan was a shifter Keeper, and he'd worked hard to take on the abilities of his charges. With enough concentration, he was capable of shifting. If he really hadn't wanted to be seen, he could have come to the show as anyone.

He could even have come as the proverbial fly on the wall.

Of course, shifting was taxing and exhausting. Maybe he was just here because he had an interest in the show. But why hadn't he mentioned that he was coming?

He hadn't seen her, so she walked up behind him and cleared her throat.

He whirled around in surprise. For a moment he looked disconcerted. Then he smiled. "Ah, there you are. I was looking for you and your cousins. How are you enjoying the play?"

"I love it. The songs are excellent," she said. "I didn't know that you were coming tonight."

He grinned at her. "I didn't know if I'd make it or not. The Snake Pit doesn't get busy 'til late, but I lost a manager a few weeks ago, and if I don't have someone I can trust going in to open, I don't like to be away. But I found someone to handle it, so I'm here to get a feel for how they're going to be using the club when they film there." He shrugged. "I'm hoping the film's a big hit. We do extremely well, but it's a fickle world. One day the lines are out the door. The next day you've been dropped for the newest thing down on Sunset or Vine."

Rhiannon smiled. "Declan, the Snake Pit has a built-in clientele."

It did, of course. Otherworld denizens flocked there by the dozens—especially vampires, who really liked the nightlife.

Declan shrugged. "I know. But I have to say, it would be pretty cool to be as well known as the Viper Room."

"Maybe not, given the deaths associated with it."

He waved a hand dismissively. "Death happens everywhere, Rhiannon. You must be aware of that. Deaths don't happen because of clubs, they happen because people—and Others—can get out of control." The lights began to flicker, indicating that intermission was over. "It's always good to see you, Rhiannon," he said, inclining his head slightly.

There was something old world about him, she realized. And she was lucky, getting a chance to perform at the Snake Pit. Not only was it a well-known venue, but it had after-hours and then it had *after-hours*. The club was a success in the world at large—and in the Otherworld, as well.

He turned and walked back into the theater. Rhiannon walked back toward the snack bar, but her cousins were gone. She quickly returned to her seat, just in time for the lights to go down once again.

Act II brought Vince and Lucy back to L.A., where they returned to their jobs in Hollywood, Lucy in animation and Vince in casting. Vince believed they'd gotten away clean, but shortly after their return he was visited at work by one of Drago's maids, and then another maid turned up as a barista in his favorite coffee shop. He realized that Drago was not far behind.

In the next scene the vampire arrived at Lucy's studio looking for work as a sketch artist. Vince found out when he showed up to take her home and saw sketches of characters that looked like Drago—and Lucy. Afraid, he called on an old friend—Dr. Van Helsing—who told him about vampires and explained that there was only one way to save Lucy from Drago.

The customary climax brought a twist. Vince had allowed himself to be infected by the vampire barista in order to fight Drago. Van Helsing met them in a Hollywood wax museum's chamber of horrors with a priest in tow, and Drago was put down. The scene ended with Vince and Lucy happy and still together—although they both had to adjust to a new lifestyle, since they'd both become vampires. Hand in hand, they headed off to a blood bank, starving after their exertions.

The finale had Drago rising again after the couple had departed, and he had a fantastic solo number—before dining on one of the policemen left to guard the "crime" scene.

Rhiannon didn't think it was the best show she'd ever seen—and she still wasn't sure what deeper meaning she'd been meant to discover—but it had certainly been entertaining.

The audience rose to give the cast a standing ovation, and she politely rose, as well. She noticed that Sailor was still staring at the stage as if hypnotized. "Hey," she said, and nudged her cousin. "It's over."

"Oh, my God, I'm in love with it," Sailor breathed.

"It did have a few twists," Barrie commented.

"There was a lot that was the usual," Rhiannon said. *And,* she thought, *a lot that could only have been written by an Other, someone aware of what was and wasn't real. Vampires didn't need to wait for night to come out, and while they—like everyone in California—enjoyed sunglasses, they weren't blinded by the sun. They could sleep pretty much wherever they wanted—after all, you couldn't get dirt from a mausoleum.*

Perhaps those were the points Mac had wanted her to notice? But why?

"I can't believe I'm going to be in the movie!" Sailor said, still wide-eyed with awe.

"Let's head backstage," Rhiannon said.

"Can we?" Barrie asked.

"I don't see why not," Rhiannon said. "After all, I was practically ordered to be here."

They walked out the front door and around to the stage entrance. Rhiannon felt someone walk up and slip an arm through hers. Startled, she turned to see that Declan Wainwright had joined them.

He gave her a grin and a shrug. "Safety in numbers," he told her.

She arched a brow at him but couldn't resist the blatant attempt to make her smile. "Sure, safety in numbers."

Declan turned to greet Sailor and Barrie, but his tone was merely polite, as if he had no real interest in them. Barrie nodded and said hello in return, but Sailor actually gritted her teeth and turned away.

At the stage door, Declan spoke to the guard, greeting him familiarly. "Hey, Bobby."

"Hey, Mr. Wainwright," the guard said. He was tall, fairly young and muscular. He smiled—clearly he knew Declan well—and Rhiannon realized he was a shapeshifter.

"Bobby Conche is with the Coastal shifters," Declan said softly, introducing them. Given that she was now a shifter Keeper, it made sense that Bobby stared at Barrie longest. He grinned. "Welcome, ladies," he said. "Just walk on in."

They walked along a hallway that ran parallel to the stage and stood to one side to wait, their eyes on the dressing room doors.

A moment later Mac Brodie came around a corner. His face was scrubbed clean of stage makeup, and his golden hair was still slightly damp. He walked toward her. "Miss Gryffald, I'm delighted to see that you took me up on my invitation. And these lovely ladies must be your cousins, Sailor and Barrie."

"Yes, Sailor, Barrie, please meet Mac Brodie. And of course you know Declan."

"Of course," Mac said, smiling and shaking Declan's hand. Their eyes met and seemed to convey an unspoken message, which disturbed Rhiannon.

They knew something she didn't. Exasperating! How could she work when everyone kept secrets from her?

"Nice to see you here. And, Barrie, Sailor—a pleasure," Mac said. "So, what did you think?"

"I thought everyone was wonderful," Sailor said. "Especially Drago." She frowned slightly. "Do I know you?" she asked him.

"I hope you feel that you do—that's the ultimate compliment for an actor," Mac said.

"Really?" she asked.

"So I hear," he said, and shrugged.

"One thing amazes me," Sailor said, then lowered her voice to a whisper. "I had no idea that Mr. Jackson was playing the role himself."

"He's a multitalented man," Mac said. "Come on, I'm sure you want to tell him yourself how much you enjoyed the show. And he'll be delighted to hear it. We're having a bit of a celebration tonight, because things are coming together so well. You can meet everyone."

He led them down the hall to a door marked Jack Hunter/Mac Brodie. Mac opened the door, and they entered.

The entire cast was there, everyone in civilian clothes. Hunter Jackson was seated in front of his dressing table, and the others were gathered around him. Champagne was flowing, and hors d'oeuvre trays covered every available surface. Hunter was laughing up at Audrey Fleur, the brunette playing Erika. Kate Delaney, the blonde who played Jeneka, was chatting with the actor who had portrayed the innkeeper. "Lucy," real name Lena Ashbury, was chatting with the actress who had played the innkeeper's wife. The buzz in the room didn't stop when they entered; apparently this group was ready to party with any and all comers.

"I've got to talk to Hunter," Sailor said, and walked over to the director.

Kate, bearing three glasses of champagne, walked over and welcomed them, then handed glasses to Rhiannon and Barrie, and then Declan. "Mac, you can grab your own champagne. And you must all be friends of

Mac. Oh, wait! I know who you are," she gushed to Dec-lan. "I've seen your face in the paper. You're Declan Wainwright, and you own the Snake Pit."

"Guilty," he said.

"Now I wish I was going to be in the movie," Kate said, smiling.

She made a good vamp, Rhiannon thought. Vamp, in the old-school sense, not vampire. The woman was definitely human.

Declan introduced the women, and Kate continued playing hostess.

"So nice to meet you, Barrie, Rhiannon," she said, and smiled, lifting her champagne glass, a slight knot of confusion tightening her brow as she asked Rhian-non, "Are you, um, with Mac?"

Mac, who had gone to get some champagne, slipped close to Rhiannon's side. "Yes," he said, before she could protest.

Rhiannon got the impression that Kate wasn't pleased by his answer. She wondered if Mac had ever given the woman any reason to feel proprietary, then reminded herself that Elven had a talent for engaging people on a sensual level even without intending to. And when they *did* intend to... Well, they were extremely sexual beings, and the numbers of them that now popu-lated L.A. bore witness to that fact.

"I've seen *you* before, too," Kate said. "Somewhere."

"Rhiannon sings at the Mystic Café," Mac explained.

"I've never actually been in there," Kate said. Then, having decided that Mac was interested in Rhiannon, so there was no point making a play for him, she turned to Declan. "Of course, I *have* been to the Snake Pit," she enthused.

"I'm going to introduce Rhiannon to the rest of the cast," Mac said to Declan as Barrie wandered off to check out the canapés. Once again Rhiannon had the uncomfortable feeling that the two men were sharing information she wasn't privy to.

"What the hell is going on here?" Rhiannon demanded as they walked away, standing on tiptoe and whispering in his ear. She steadied herself with a hand on his shoulder and was annoyed by the jolt of lightning that seemed to sweep through her as she touched him. *Elven!* She hated knowing he had that kind of power over her. She wanted to snatch her hand away, but he caught it, and Elven were strong. She couldn't have pulled free without creating a scene.

He leaned down and whispered back, his lips close to her ear, "Not the time to ask." His tone carried a warning.

"I want answers," she said.

He told her softly, "Smile. Kiss my cheek. I'm trying to buy you entry around here as the woman I'm seeing. Go with it."

She kissed his cheek. Her lips felt as if they were on fire.

Worse.

She felt *hungry*.

"Ah, the lovely Rhiannon," Hunter said as they approached. "So—I said I wanted your opinion. What did you think?"

"I particularly loved the musical numbers," she told him honestly.

"I thought you might," he said. "And?"

"I like the twist at the end, too. I think you're going to be a success on stage *and* on screen," she told him.

That was honest, too. A show didn't have to be brilliant to make it big; it just needed the right ingredients. Hunter Jackson would see that this one did.

Rhiannon felt someone close behind her.

Vampire.

She turned. Audrey Fleur was standing there. She smiled at Rhiannon, then dipped her head in acknowledgment that Rhiannon was a Keeper.

"Hi," Audrey said cheerfully.

"Hi, I'm Rhiannon—"

"Gryffald. I know. I just met your cousins. It's great that you came to the show. Mac brought you, of course."

"Yes, good old Mac," Rhiannon said, and shot him a look to be sure he didn't miss her meaning. "I didn't know that you would be having a celebration."

"I'm sure that's why he brought you and your cousins tonight," Audrey said. She clinked her champagne glass against Rhiannon's. "This is our last night of previews. It's a big deal for us. We're crowing with delight—except for Mac. He acts like it's just another day's work for him."

Mac shrugged. "I just know the game, Audrey. One day you're hot, one day you're not." He smiled to take any sting out of the words. "Now, if you'll excuse us, I want to show Rhiannon around the theater."

She smiled, far too aware of him slipping his arm through hers as he led her out of the dressing room and toward the back of the theater.

"Where are you taking me?" she asked him.

"First, to meet Joe Carrie. The playwright. He's out onstage."

"Shouldn't he be at the party?"

"He should, but Joe's a funny guy. Kind of quiet, not a big party animal."

He took her hand and led her along a narrow passageway and out onto the stage. "Joe?" he called.

There was a man onstage, pad in hand, talking to several others about where to reset props for the next performance.

He was tall, dark and probably about forty-five.

When he turned to look at Rhiannon, she knew.

Vampire.

"Joe, meet Rhiannon Gryffald. Rhiannon, our playwright and stage manager, Joe Carrie."

Joe Carrie immediately stopped what he was doing, a broad smile on his face. He came forward and shook Rhiannon's hand enthusiastically. He looked around and lowered his voice. "Piers Gryffald's daughter? Great to meet you. You're the new Keeper for the Canyon vampires, aren't you?"

"Yes, and it's great to meet you, as well," she said.

"What did you think?" he asked anxiously. "Factually speaking, I mean. Bram Stoker didn't have it so wrong, really. Most of all, did you have a good time tonight?"

"Yes, of course, I especially love the musical numbers," she said.

He beamed. "Thank you!"

"Rhiannon's a singer, so I thought you two should meet," Mac said. "I'm going to show her around a bit more now, Joe."

"Enjoy," Joe said, still smiling.

"Where to now?" Rhiannon asked as Mac led her away.

"Outside," he said.

She didn't know why she felt such a sudden surge of dread.

Yes, she did. She knew she was going to hear more about the murders.

She wanted desperately to get away from him. Maybe it was because he had way too much of the legendary Elven charm, and she was afraid that when he told her bad news she was going to curl up against him in the hope that he could somehow make all the bad stuff go away.

"You coming back?" Bobby asked when they reached the door.

"We'll be back before the party breaks up, I promise," Mac assured him.

"Where are we going?" she asked again as he practically dragged her toward the rear of the parking lot—and the lake beyond. She was going to be strong, she decided. Strong as befit the Keeper he didn't think she had the capability of being. And *he* needed to know that she was strong, as well. "You do realize that I have the ability to wrench someone's head off if I need to, right?"

He paused at that. She didn't think he'd meant to be rough—Elven were just over endowed with strength as well as charm. She found herself being spun around to face him and read incredulity in his eyes.

"You think I intended to *hurt* you?" he demanded. "Why, you…brat! I'm trying to *help* you, you little idiot. This is your jurisdiction—you should have stopped this!"

"This? You mean the murders? Yes, this is my jurisdiction—and has been for a whole week, which means the killer started working before I even got here, not to mention that he chose victims who wouldn't be missed and was careful to hide his crimes. And you know what else? If you knew what was going on, you could have called me. You know, picked up a phone, introduced yourself and explained that there was a matter that required my attention. And what's it to *you,* anyway? You're an Elven. Do you know who one of the victims is or something? Have you lost a friend, a fellow actor… what? Don't you dare get mad and put me down when you have me running around in circles for simple information!"

"First off, Miss Gryffald, I don't have any information on who the dead might be. And I didn't call you because we'd never met, and it was more important that you see the play, because I think the play and the murders are related, and that's why I'm even in the damned thing."

"What do you mean that's why you're in the damned thing?" Rhiannon demanded.

"I'm not an actor, Rhiannon. I'm a cop. My name is Brodie McKay, not Mac Brodie. I'm working undercover, and before my captain gets impatient with the fact that I haven't discovered a damned thing yet and brings in more cops who aren't part of the Other community, I could really use some help—from the vampire Keeper."

Rhiannon stared back at him, feeling like a fool.

He was a cop.

Working undercover.

He could have told her that earlier. Or that hairy bastard of a medical examiner might have mentioned it. They were withholding information as if she didn't matter—and then getting mad when she didn't perform up to their standards.

She straightened her shoulders and smoothed down her wounded pride, dredging up her strength and determination. "Thank you for the information," she said, then stared at him for a long moment, shaking her head. "You're Elven, so why don't you just read minds until you find the connection?"

"Whoever is doing this knows how to be careful. It's almost impossible to get into the subconscious, and so far all I'm getting is people running lines and bitching because so-and-so has a bigger part. Most or maybe all of it is legit. If the killer *is* here, I'm being blocked," he told her. "I need the killer to slip up—and having the vampire Keeper actually involved just might provoke that."

"Well, the vampire Keeper might have been involved already if the cop had seen fit to tell her what was going on," she retorted.

Then she turned and started heading back to the theater, moving with as much dignity as she could manage.

"Hey!"

She didn't want to halt her perfect exit, but she did. Turning around sharply, she asked, "What?"

"I didn't bring you out here for a tryst. I thought you might like to see where the last victim was discovered," he told her, sounding weary.

"Is that going to help us at all?" she asked.

"I don't know. I'm not the vampire Keeper," he replied.

She walked back to him. At that moment she hated the crystalline hypnotic power of his eyes, eyes that so often seemed to mock her.

"No. It won't help me—certainly not at this point. If there was something to be discovered there, either the crime-scene investigation unit or *you* would have found it by now. On the other hand, hearing the truth from everyone rather than being taunted will help a hell of a lot. If you don't have anything solid for me, excuse me. I'm going to go home and sort out the lies and omissions from the truth. Somehow I don't feel that I'm going to get any assistance with that from the people who should be helping me. Good night, Mac— or whoever the hell you really are."

This time she completed her exit, relieved to see that Sailor and Barrie were already at the car. She unlocked it and slammed her way in.

Barrie might have questioned her mood, but Sailor was still going on and on about the play.

Rhiannon turned up the radio, but Sailor didn't notice. With the cacophony rising in her ears, Rhiannon drove as quickly as she safely could, fighting the urge to scream the whole way home.

Once she was home, Rhiannon headed up to bed, thoughts about the night swirling through her head. Brodie McKay was absolutely the most annoying man she had ever met.

He could have just told her right away that he was a cop. No—she had to meet him while he was pulling a ridiculous stunt in front of her place of work.

Her pillow took the brunt of her anger as she curled into bed, but her mind continued to race. Aggravated, she tossed and turned for hours. Then, somehow, she drifted into sleep.

Somewhere in her mind, darkness turned to a soft swirling silver mist, and in that mist, he was walking toward her.

He was shirtless. She groaned, longing to touch the sleek and shimmering contours of his well-muscled chest. He walked fluidly, a small smile curving his lips as he approached her. He was coming to taunt her, of course, to make a comment about her lack of prowess as a Keeper, to tell her…

But he didn't speak. When he stopped directly in front of her, she could feel the heat that emanated from him, could feel his breath.

He was Elven.

Perfect face, beautiful and yet masculine, with strong cheekbones and a stronger jaw, a full mouth, and those eyes of his…eyes that read her mind, delved into her soul.

Still without speaking, he lifted a hand and cupped her face, and she knew that when he looked into her eyes, he could tell that she was waiting, longing, for him to do more.

And then his lips touched hers. She could feel the sense of power and passion that lay beneath his gentle touch. Her arms lifted without conscious thought on her part and wound around his neck. The kiss deepened; it was simmering and liquid, and ignited a fire inside her.

And then he touched her, truly touched her.

His hands slid over her flesh, and their clothing was magically gone. She ran her fingers down the hard length of his back and over his buttocks as she felt him crushing her to him. The silver mist formed a bed, and they fell back on it together. He broke the kiss and straddled her, and his eyes continued to hold hers as he lowered himself again, capturing her mouth. His hands were amazing…Elven hands. They caressed her midriff, teased her breasts.

She arched toward him, trying to deepen the kiss, but he pulled away. Then his lips moved to her collarbone and her breasts, then lower still. She could barely breathe as he teased her in every imaginable and intimate way, until she was whispering his name, then crying it aloud as she threaded her fingers into his golden Elven hair and drew him back to her. At last they were making love, and she was twisting and writhing in awe and wonder, the world nothing but the heat and fire of the man in the silver mist....

She cried out.

And woke herself from her dream.

She realized she was lying alone in her bed and groaned out loud, humiliated—and desperately glad that she lived alone and that Merlin was far too polite to have glanced into her bedroom. Her cheeks burned with embarrassment—even though she was by herself.

She threw her pillow across the room.

"I hate Elven!" she announced to the empty air. "Hate them, hate them, hate them!"

She shuddered and glanced at the clock on her bedside table. 5:00 a.m.

What the hell. She rose, strode into the bathroom and took a very cold shower.

Chapter 5

Back at the station house, Brodie handed a copy of the full audition list for *Vampire Rampage* to Adam Lansky, one of the department's research techs.

The younger man looked at the size of it and then looked up at him. "And you want me to…?"

"I want you to track down the people on that list and make sure they're alive and well," Brodie told him.

Adam was the best at searching through the internet for clues, and he had figured out how to access almost every database imaginable. If there was a code, Adam could crack it. Brodie had long ago decided it was best if he didn't always know how Adam got his information.

"I don't even know who our victims are," Brodie told him. "Maybe this will help."

Adam frowned. "You think the dead men are actors who didn't make the cut? Maybe I haven't lived in

L.A. long enough, but wouldn't a rejected actor want to kill an actor who *did* get into the play, not vice-versa?"

"I think," Brodie told him, "that the killer is involved with the play somehow. I think that he might have gotten to know some of the people on that list to find out who might not be missed for a long time. If we can go through the list and find out who's missing, I might be able to find out who the victims are, and if I can find out who they are I might have a chance of finding out who's killing them and stopping the violence before it escalates."

Adam nodded. "Any order? Alphabetical?"

"Start with the top page—the group that made the callbacks. The people who made the final cut had a greater chance of getting to know each other."

Adam nodded again. "I'm on it."

As Brodie headed back to his desk in Homicide he noticed that Bryce Edwards, an old werewolf working in vice now, was leading in a guest. A guest—not a detainee, since she was walking without benefit of handcuffs.

It was Rhiannon Gryffald. Visiting Edwards. Well, he should have suspected that she would find a way to circumvent him. Then again, maybe he hadn't gone about things in the right way or the right order. Maybe he felt more bitterness than he'd realized that all this was happening just when Piers Gryffald had gone off to join the World Council.

He watched as she went into Edwards's office. The old wolf was a lieutenant now. She sat in front of his desk in a tailored dress suit and appropriate heels, looking to all the world like some kind of a completely competent businesswoman.

Pain-in-the-ass Keeper!

As he watched, one of Edwards's men rushed in, staring at her with puppy-dog eyes. Brodie gathered that the man was asking if he could bring her something to drink, and Rhiannon, with one of her alluring smiles, was assuring him that she was just fine.

Should he walk on over? he asked himself. Or let her ask a vice detective what he knew about a string of murders?

Without giving himself time to question his decision, he walked into the office to join them. "Good morning."

"Hey, Brodie!" Edwards said, greeting him. "Come on in. You two should meet, if you haven't already. This is Rhiannon Gryffald, Piers Gryffald's daughter. Rhiannon, this is Brodie McKay, Homicide."

Rhiannon stared at him. "Good to see you, Detective," she said.

"Good to see *you,* Miss Gryffald." He turned to Edwards. "We've met," he explained.

"This is the man you need to talk to," Edwards said. "Come on in, Brodie, come on in—and close the door." He kept speaking as Brodie complied. "We've had a long history of working together, you know," he began. "The police—and the Keepers. We need to maintain that tradition."

"I know," Brodie said. "And I think that Rhiannon and I are ready to continue that tradition now. At least, I hope so."

Rhiannon looked at him and nodded. "Thank you. I'd just come by to see Uncle Bryce, but I'm glad you're here."

Uncle Bryce? Yes, Brodie supposed, that was…kind of right. Bryce had been instrumental years ago in helping out an old magician, the same magician who had built the House of the Rising Sun and befriended Rhiannon's grandparents.

"Perhaps we should discuss where we are with the case at the moment?" Brodie said.

"I'd like that," Rhiannon told him.

Brodie stood and opened the door for her, and they both looked back at Bryce Edwards, who had a fatherly grin on his weathered face.

"Thanks," Brodie and Rhiannon said at the same time.

He ushered her out. "Let me grab my coat," he said. "We should go somewhere where we can really talk. The office is too hectic—and even though there are a fair number of Others on the force, it's just easier to talk out of the office."

"I know where we can go," she told him. "My place." She smiled and winked. "I'll drive."

"Let me get my files," he said.

Five minutes later they were out on the road, heading to her home in the Canyon. He'd known the old Keepers, but he'd never been out to the estate. He was curious; there were fantastic rumors about the place, which was supposedly still filled with all kinds of magical paraphernalia. It was well guarded—against human interference, at least. Despite the famous internal alarm system and the wall that surrounded the property, it was easily accessible to most Others. Despite that, as far as he knew, no one had ever tried to breach the walls.

But that, he thought now, *was because of the extraordinary strength of the Keepers who had once lived there.*

Rhiannon—who maneuvered the tricky California

freeways like a native—broke into his thoughts as they reached the compound and she pushed the button that opened the gate. "You look worried," she said.

"I was just thinking," he said.

"Thinking that...?"

"That this should be a very safe place to live."

"That it should be—but isn't?" she asked. "And of course you're also thinking that the Canyon is due to erupt into violence—because my cousins and I are just girls, and weak."

He shook his head. "No, I'm thinking that evil exists no matter what, and that there is an evil element out there that will put you to the test just because you're new."

She smiled as they drove onto the property. "That one is mine," she said, pointing. "Pandora's Box."

"Very nice."

"It's the original guesthouse. Gwydion's Cave, where Barrie lives, is across the pool, and of course the main house is impossible to miss. Sailor lives there. She has since she was a child."

Rhiannon parked, and they exited the car. She walked to her house and he was glad to see that she had locked the door, even though this was a gated compound. She opened it, and he entered her inner sanctum.

The old magician's legacy was immediately obvious in the three fortune-teller machines in the living room. The first was an old Gypsy, the second a magician and the third an ethereal ghost dressed all in white.

Statuettes and curios filled the shelves that lined the walls, along with countless books. He glanced at the spines and saw that most were on pagan religions, Druids, witchcraft and the occult. Others were magicians' manuals, and the collection was rounded out by an eclectic mix of world history, modern mysteries and fantasy.

He noted a number of guitar stands, each one holding one of her precious instruments. There was also a beautiful old grand piano in the center of the room. His gut told him that the piano had been there long before she took over the house, and that the guitars were her own property, brought with her when she made the permanent move to L.A.

"So...stuffy? Creepy?" she asked him, aware that he was assessing the place.

"Cool. Very cool," he told her.

"I like it very much. I've put up a few pictures, but honestly, I haven't been here long enough to really put my stamp on the place. But it really is nice. The three of us might have struggled just to afford a lousy apartment in a so-so part of town, but instead we have beautiful homes of our own," she said. "So sit. The sofa is comfortable, and there's the big coffee table there for the files."

"Sure. Thanks." He sat down and spread out the folders he had brought.

She sat down next to him, and he started to talk.

"Victim one, victim two, victim three. I didn't know anything about the first murders—it went to a good cop, a guy on night shift. But when the second body was discovered, my captain brought both cases to me. He saw the link to the theater, so I took the part in the play to see if I could find out anything. And then the last victim was found just behind the theater, which pretty much clinched it—especially when I realized I'd seen him in the audience one night."

The crime-scene photos were horrible, but she didn't flinch. And after what she had said last night, he was certain she'd been to the morgue.

"The killer is taking the fingers," she said.

He nodded. "Usually you take fingertips because you're trying to hide the victim's ID, and it's certainly feasible that this killer took the fingers for that reason. But he didn't destroy the teeth, not that that's helped us any. So far there's been no way to get a viable sample of the killer's DNA, because the bodies have been too degraded by the time they were discovered." And I gather you've seen Anthony Brandt down at the morgue, so you probably already know that the victims were drowned while they were being sucked dry of blood, or maybe right after they'd pretty much been drained."

She nodded, staring down at the files. "So they're all still unidentified."

"Like I said, I saw number three at the theater, watching the show."

"And he was killed in the lake behind the theater," she said.

He nodded, watching her face. She looked so serious, biting her lower lip as she carefully studied the crime-scene photos. The Gryffalds really did have beautiful eyes. They were like prisms, catching the light in all kinds of fantastic patterns. At first he'd found her annoying...irritating....

And now... Now he couldn't stop thinking about her. The Elven were blessed with charm and the ability to use it to get what they wanted. But with it came a heightened sexuality. They loved the carnal pleasures, and he suddenly felt as if her allure was almost overwhelming.

It was easy for Elven to satisfy their sexual urges,

thanks to their charm, but at least they accomplished it with respect for morality. It was an unwritten Elven rule that only those who wished to be seduced were charmed into relationships, whether for a night or for a longer time.

But Rhiannon was a Keeper, and Keepers were all but taboo. They weren't to be treated lightly.

People were being murdered, he reminded himself harshly. He needed to keep his mind on the case.

And still the subtle scent of her perfume was seducing him almost to the point where resistance would be futile.

He stood and walked over to one of the fortune-telling machines. She barely seemed to realize that he had walked away, which was more than a little disappointing.

"I had a talk with Darius Simonides yesterday, after you left," she said. "You know, of course, that he's a vampire."

"A vampire who lives by the rules. He wants to be a Hollywood success story far more than he wants to be a vampire," Brodie said.

"I wasn't accusing Darius of anything," she said. "I just felt that he might know something, that he might have heard something. And what about Hunter Jackson? And Declan Wainwright?"

"What about them? A human and a Keeper, a shape-shifter Keeper," he said. "Both well-known and respected."

"And both involved in the play," she reminded him. "So, what's happening with your investigation? Where have you gone with it?"

"Right now I have someone working on the audition

sheets, tracking down everyone who tried out for the show and didn't make it."

"You think a disgruntled actor is doing this?" Rhiannon asked, and laughed suddenly.

Her smile, he realized, was radiant. His eyes had wandered down to her curves, and he forced them back to hers.

"I'd like to think it's an actor," she told him, still laughing. "They suddenly seem to be the bane of my existence."

"I'm sorry we ruined your night at the café," he told her.

She shrugged. "This is far more important. Of course, when I told Hugh Hammond that I wasn't coming in last night… Honestly! One minute he thinks I'm a total disaster as a Keeper, but the next, when I'm trying to do what a Keeper should do, he gives me a lecture about my obligation to my job and how I need it to survive in the real world."

"He's old guard. He'll come around. Maybe he's disappointed that he wasn't asked to be on the council while all three of the Gryffald men were," Brodie suggested.

Rhiannon shrugged. "Maybe. But I still have to make a living, and that means I still have to work with him," she said. "So—tell me about the victims. Do they have anything in common?"

He nodded. "All three of them were around thirty years old, the prime age to audition for the show. If I'm right that they were all among those who auditioned, then we know for a fact that the killer is somehow involved with the play."

"What about the cast?" she asked him.

He nodded, taking a seat again, this time a few feet away from her.

Not far enough. The soft, subtly sexual scent of her perfume still reached him.

"Here's what I think," he told her. "Joe Carrie's a vampire and thrilled to have his show being produced. Hunter Jackson's human, and I admit it, I think he's willing to do a hell of a lot to make *Vampire Rampage* a part of horror history, but I can't see a human as being physically capable of these murders. Lena Ashbury's another human, and as far as I've been able to ascertain, she's just a struggling actress who's delighted to have gotten the part. Then we have the two maids. Kate Delaney is human, and I can't find anything suspicious about her. Audrey Fleur is a vampire, and, she knows I'm Elven, of course, but again, there's nothing to cast suspicion on her."

He stopped and took a breath, then went on. "I've dismissed the old couple at the inn, the cousins and the backup dancers and singers. They're all human, so it's doubtful that they're involved. There are techs and seamstresses, stage managers...but I haven't discovered a single thing that would lead me to believe that any of them is the killer, either."

Rhiannon nodded. "What about Hunter Jackson? I know you don't think a human could have done it, but if he's willing to do anything to make this show the biggest thing since The Beatles, would he resort to murder just to show that vampires might be out there?"

"I *have* thought of that. I've searched his dressing room, and I've followed him, and I haven't seen him do a single thing that would suggest he's capable of murder," Brodie told her. "If we could pinpoint the time of the murders, I'd be able to trace people's movements and know if they had alibis. But with the bodies left in the water to accelerate decomp, it's impossible for Tony to determine time of death, so it's also impossible to eliminate anyone."

Rhiannon sighed. "And it could just be…a vampire on the rampage. Taking advantage of the fact that my father is gone, and that…and that the Canyon vampires may now have free rein."

The idea had occurred to Brodie a number of times, but now he wanted to deny the possibility.

Now he wanted to defend her.

"I don't think so. I really don't. Whatever's behind this, it has something to do with the play. I'm certain of it."

"All right, so we need to follow everyone—except the humans—who has anything to do with *Vampire Rampage*," Rhiannon said. "That's not going to be easy."

"Maybe you can find us some help," he told her.

"How?"

"Make the announcement to the vampire community that the police are actively seeking a killer who's draining his victims of blood. Your constituents—most of them, anyway—will be outraged and more than happy to keep an eye out." He was quiet for a moment, shaking his head. "I know that in a lot of cities the Others all have meetings together. In L.A., maybe because of the sheer sizes of the different populations and the physical size of the city, every race has its own council meetings. Obviously, Barrie and I can ask for help from the Elven community, and Hugh Hammond and Anthony Brandt can speak with the werewolves. And your cousin Sailor can help out with the shapeshifters."

"Maybe Barrie can get the press involved, too," Rhiannon suggested.

Brodie was thoughtful for a minute. "Let's hold off on that a bit."

"But one of the problems recognizing that a serial killer was at work was the fact that no one seemed to care about the victims," Rhiannon said. "If there's a big splash—"

"Let's just see what we can find out about our victims right now and follow the leads as we get them," Brodie suggested.

Rhiannon nodded grudgingly. "I'm going to have to go to work soon," she said, and grimaced. "I only work Monday through Thursday at the café. If I don't show up at all—"

"The Mystic Café is a good place for you to be," he told her. "You don't know what you might hear there. It's a favorite hangout for Others as well as human beings, so do your best to get to know the customers. And Hugh may be a pain in the ass to work for, but he's been a Keeper for a very long time, so he knows damn near everything. You can learn a lot from him."

She nodded again. "Should I meet you after the show tonight, so we can compare notes?"

"I'll pick you up from the café after the play. A lot of the cast and crew head to the Snake Pit after a performance. We can head over and show the world that we're an item, and you can also take a good look at where you'll be working on Friday."

"All right," she said. "And Declan is involved, too, in a way. They're going to film some scenes at the club, and he was at the play last night, too. What's weird is that he didn't tell me he was going to be there, even though I said *I* would be." She frowned. "Brodie, if any of the powerhouse guys—like Declan or Darius—*is* involved, you could be in real danger. They know what you are, right? That you're a cop, I mean."

"Yes, they do. But that's the point. I *am* a cop, Rhiannon."

"Yes, and you're Elven. But you're not…well, werewolves can rip a person to shreds, and shapeshifters—"

"Shapeshifters aren't really a threat. They can become anything, but they use up their strength to be it, though I admit Declan will bear watching. But please, don't go underestimating the Elven," he said.

He walked over to her, hunkering down so that he was almost kneeling in front of her. He took her hand, ignoring the electric jolt that ripped through him as he touched her. "Thank you for worrying, but I'm going to be fine. But we'll watch each other's backs, all right? Because, you know, I'm pretty worried about you, too."

She flushed. "I'm a Keeper."

"That's not going to protect you—not against a vampire who's truly on a rampage," he told her. "Keepers have been killed in the past, Rhiannon. Some of them by their charges, because they weren't prepared."

He stood quickly, unable to go on touching her or even be so close to her. A burning sensation was filling him, heating his blood to boiling.

He was a cop, he reminded himself. And she was a Keeper. This was a serious situation. Three men were dead already, with more to come if he couldn't stop the cycle of violence….

He stepped back. "You've got to get to work, and I

have to check in at the station and then get out to the theater. I'll see you later, and you can tell me everything you overheard at the café."

She nodded and stood, as well. She seemed a little shaky, and when he reached out to take her shoulders, for a moment their eyes met.

Hers were deep, beautiful pools of green. He felt as if he was sinking, as if he were lost in the depths of an ocean.

She forced a laugh, stepping by him. "Sorry about that. Clearly I need more sleep," she said.

As he walked toward the door, Brodie found himself stopping by one of the fortune-teller machines. It was the Magician, an older man with bright blue eyes and a mischievous smile, dressed in a magician's traditional tux.

Brodie didn't touch the machine.

Suddenly the magician started moving, picking up a card in one white-gloved hand as eerie music played. The card dropped into the receptacle, as if daring Brodie to pick it up.

He glanced over at Rhiannon, slowly arching a brow in question and smiling.

"Faulty wiring. Mr. Magic goes off now and then by himself," she said.

He picked up the card.

"What does it say?" she asked him.

"'Remember to keep your enemies close, and as you do, beware of those you would call friend,'" he read aloud.

"Merlin, are you here?" Rhiannon called out.

Brodie was surprised; even when his opinion of her had been at its lowest, he had considered her sane.

There was no answer, and she didn't attempt to explain herself. She simply picked up one of her guitars and joined him, carrying the instrument as if she were carrying gold from Fort Knox.

He followed her out, and as she turned to lock the door she at last caught the way he was looking at her. "He's still here, you know."

"Pardon?"

"Ivan Schwartz. Merlin. He's still here."

"The old man who used to own the place? The magician? Are you telling me that he's still here...as a ghost?" he asked skeptically.

She laughed suddenly. "You're Elven. I'm the Keeper responsible for the Canyon vampires. We deal with werewolves and shifters on a daily basis. And you're going to doubt the existence of a *ghost?* Speak to me. Tell me what you're thinking. I don't want any more cover-ups and half-truths between us, please."

Brodie had to laugh, too. "Okay, for a moment I was thinking you were crazy. I didn't know who you were talking to."

"And now?"

"Now I'm curious to meet him."

She let out a soft sigh and smiled slowly. "I'll try to see that you get that opportunity," she said.

They were close again. Too close.

This time she was the one who stepped away quickly.

"Work," she said firmly as if to remind herself. And then she led the way toward her car.

Brodie greeted the cast and crew as he went into his dressing room to change for the night's performance.

He shared the room with Hunter Jackson, but the other man hadn't come in yet.

He was just finishing getting dressed when he heard the door open and turned, assuming that Jackson had arrived, but it wasn't Hunter Jackson who stepped into the room.

It was Audrey.

"Audrey? Do you need something?" he asked.

"No, I'm just ready and getting bored waiting," she told him.

She had perched on the chair in front of his dressing table. She was dressed for her first scene, and her costume was provocative, to say the least. Victorian finery in shreds, with plenty of heaving bosom. She was attractive and flirtatious, but so far she'd been professional, as well, even if her conversation was always full of innuendo.

Brodie buttoned his shirt and walked closer, ready to start on his makeup, but she didn't move from his chair.

"So you're seeing the vampire Keeper," she said. "My Keeper. But you know that, of course."

"Of course."

"Is that allowed?" she asked.

"She's the vampire Keeper. I'm Elven."

Audrey laughed, a sound that originated low in her throat and was meant to seduce. "Oh, yes, you certainly *are* Elven. I've been rather surprised that you haven't been acting like one."

"We're in a play together, Audrey. And, as you just commented, I'm in a relationship."

"Would that really stop an Elven?"

"Audrey…"

"I wouldn't mind a threesome. And I'll bet you wouldn't, either."

"Audrey, I don't know what you *think* you know about Elven, but we pretty much function the same way human males do," he told her.

That elicited another delighted laugh. "Then you're willing to bed pretty much anyone, under the right circumstances."

She stood and walked over to him, and before he knew what she was doing, she had slipped a hand down and grabbed his crotch. His reaction was purely physical.

"Oh, no, you are much better than other men," she assured him.

Was she really bent on seducing him? Or was something else really on her mind?

It was worth temporarily sacrificing some of his strength to practice telepathy, he decided.

But what he could read was purely carnal.

Nice dick. He'd be scrumptious if I could get him into bed. I'll bet he knows what he's doing, too. That would so relieve some of the boredom....

At this moment, at least, her thoughts weren't worth reading.

He caught her hand, glad of the strength of his race, which was greater than hers in such a battle. He pulled her hand away and spoke to her gently. "Audrey, you're beautiful, you're sexy and I'm in a relationship."

Angry, she flushed and stepped away. "Are you *really* in a relationship? Or are you two really just snooping around to see what *I'm* doing?"

"What?"

"You heard me," Audrey snapped at him. "Yes, I can

be a little wild at times. I do like three-ways, and yes, dammit, I really do like sex! And yes, I'm bisexual. That's not a bad thing—it just means I love everyone. So what if I organized an orgy at the Theater on the Square last month? Half the people in this city are having sex with anyone who'll look at them. If your little prude thinks she's going to come after me for my behavior, she'll have to clean out the whole city—not to mention the rest of the country!"

Brodie stared at her, ready to break out laughing. He fought the urge.

"Audrey, I swear to you that Rhiannon is not planning to chastise you for your sexual behavior. I sincerely doubt she knows about it, and if she did, I'm sure she'd say that so long as you're having your fun with consenting adults, more power to you."

She looked back at him, her anger fading, though she was still frowning slightly.

"You really don't want to get it on with me?"

Brodie pondered that question. Since he'd been here, he'd been focused on catching a murderer. He'd barely noticed Audrey's playful sexual innuendos on anything other than an intellectual level. And yet he'd seen Rhiannon and immediately responded with every fiber of his being.

Audrey was extremely attractive and sexual, but she just wasn't his type. Rhiannon, on the other hand…

"It's a real relationship, Audrey," he said quietly, and he knew it was true, even though they hadn't so much as kissed yet.

"Hmm," Audrey mused thoughtfully, studying him. "She's only been here a week."

"It only took a few days," he told her.

She lowered her head for a moment and then looked back at him. "Then congratulations. What you have is rare. Anywhere, but especially here in La-La Land. And I promise, I'll behave, and I'll even be nice to her. For you."

"That's great of you, Audrey," Brodie assured her.

As Audrey was going out, Hunter Jackson was coming in. He brushed past her in the doorway.

"Good evening, Hunter," Audrey said. There it was again: that sultry, sexual purr in her voice.

Hunter watched her as she walked away. "Damn, she's sexy," he said. Then he turned back to Brodie and said, "Hey, full house last night. And it was nice to meet your lady, Mac."

"Yeah, thanks. I heard it's another full house tonight," Brodie said. "Here's hoping for good reviews."

Hunter nodded, pleased. "This could be it, Mac. This could be the project that takes me from being successful to being legendary." He raised an imaginary glass. "Here's to another great night."

"To another great night," Brodie agreed.

A few minutes later Joe Carrie, in his role as stage manager, stuck his head into the room. "Curtain, gentlemen, ten minutes."

"Thanks, Joe," Brodie said.

Another night, another show.

And he still needed answers.

It seemed that her song "I Hate Hollywood" had earned her some fans the other night; she received a request to play it not long after she took to the stage.

The night was, in all, a great deal better than that night had been, at least musically speaking.

Yet as for making any progress toward learning the identity of the murderer, she didn't come up with any information at all. The clientele was virtually all human; the only Other she saw was Anthony Brandt, who stopped in after his shift at the morgue. She took a break while he was there and sat down beside him, cradling a cup of blended black tea that was delicious.

"Anything?" she asked him softly.

He shook his head wearily. "Tonight? Nothing to do with the murders. A woman in her nineties who had to have an autopsy because she died in her son's custody. The son is seventy and on oxygen himself, but by law…"

"And she died of…?"

"Pulmonary arrest," he said. "The son isn't going to be far behind her. Heavy smoker—likely to blow himself up. He goes from his oxygen to a cigarette."

"Well, at least no one was murdered," she said.

"Yeah, at least no one was murdered. Today."

"I'm really angry with you, by the way," Rhiannon informed him. "Thanks a lot for telling me the truth about your buddy."

He flushed, looking down at his tea. "So," he said softly, "you've figured out that your Elven actor is a cop?"

"Yes, thank you, I've figured it out," she said.

"So?"

"We're working it," she said.

"Good," he told her.

"You could have just told me the truth, you know. Much easier on both of us."

"Maybe. Maybe not. Maybe you two had to learn to respect each other."

"Do you know anything else you haven't told me yet?" she asked him.

"No, do you?"

She nodded. "If it should come up in conversation anywhere, I'm with Brodie. Or Mac. The actor Mac Brodie. As in we're seeing each other," Rhiannon said.

"Good ruse," Brandt said. "I like it. You've filled Hugh in?"

"Yes, I had to. And he still gave me grief about taking last night off so I could see the play," she said indignantly.

It was almost as if she had given Hugh a cue. He walked up to where they were sitting and stared at her. "You're slacking off again."

Rhiannon looked at her watch. "I actually have sixty seconds of break left, Hugh. I'm not slacking off at all."

"Hey, Hugh, let's give the kid a chance here, huh?" Brandt asked.

"She's getting her chance," Hugh said. "She's working for me, isn't she? I'm showing her the ropes." He turned to Rhiannon. "This is Hollywood, kid. You fly or you die. Brutal, but that's the way it is. I'm doing you a favor toughening you up," he assured her.

"Thank you. Thank you ever so much," she said, then turned away and smiled at Brandt. "Brodie is coming by after the play. We're going to the Snake Pit, if you want to join us."

"Hey, don't mind if I do," Hugh said as if she had spoken to him. "Don't mind if I do at all," he repeated as he headed back behind the counter.

Rhiannon decided that she really wanted to write a song about how much she hated werewolf Keepers, but she decided that she wouldn't, discretion being the better part of valor and all. Instead, she sang songs she knew by rote, watching as Hugh came back and sat down with Anthony Brandt, then wound up deep in a heated discussion with him.

She couldn't help it. She wondered what they were talking about and whether it was something she should know, too.

Chapter 6

Brodie was grateful for one special Elven attribute that night: his ability to move like the speed of light. Since the theater, the Magic Café and his apartment were just different stops right off the 101, he left quickly after the show and stopped at his apartment for a shower. For some reason—maybe it had been his few moments of something like intimacy with Audrey Fleur and the realization they'd forced him to reach about his feelings for Rhiannon Gryffald—he'd felt the heat of the lights and the grease of his makeup a little too much that night.

He arrived at the Mystic Café to find that Rhiannon was ready to go.

"We should have met at the Snake Pit," she told him apologetically. "I have my car here, and also, I'd really love a quick shower. I feel like twenty varieties of Hugh's best Colombian beans tonight, for some reason."

"That's fine. I'll follow you to your place and wait

for you. We don't need two cars at the Snake Pit. Parking off Sunset is a bitch."

"All right," she told him. "Thanks."

"Hugh will be at the Snake Pit tonight, too," she told him as they walked out to their cars.

"Oh?"

"Anthony Brandt stopped by, and I suggested he come. Hugh assumed that I was inviting him, too."

Brodie shrugged. "Maybe Hugh wants to keep an eye on you," he suggested. "Keep his newest employee safe."

"Hugh doesn't want to keep me safe from the wolves, he wants to throw me to them—or rather, to the werewolves," she said. "He gave me a speech about life being brutal—sink or fly, that kind of thing."

"In a pinch, I think he'd help," Brodie said. And then he found himself wondering if that was true. Maybe Hugh was bitter about not being asked to be on the council and wanted to exact his petty revenge on Rhiannon, since she was handy. He decided to keep that thought to himself.

At his side, Rhiannon shrugged.

He followed her to the estate and up the drive to her house. "You all keep late hours," he commented when he saw that her cousins' cars were absent.

"Sailor is always schmoozing—and Barrie is always on the hunt for a good story she can use to make her name," she explained as she led him inside. She set her guitar case carefully in its place as they entered and indicated the living room and kitchen. "Make yourself at home. I promise, I'll be back down in ten minutes."

She raced up the stairs and he was left to wander the house. The fortune-telling machines fascinated him. He walked over to the Mr. Magician machine. "Any more fortunes for me?" he asked it aloud.

But it didn't answer, and no card dropped into the receptacle.

He could faintly hear the shower start to run above him. With his supernaturally acute hearing, he could hear it clearly. And with the sound of water splashing against tile came the visual. He could imagine her standing there, water cascading down on the naked beauty of her flesh, red hair streaming behind her. He could imagine being a bar of soap, sliding over that sleek naked flesh....

He gritted his teeth sharply. He might be Elven and still acutely aware of where and how Audrey had grabbed him earlier, and yet...

Audrey's blatant approach hadn't done a thing for him. All it had done was make him think of the red-headed Gryffald beauty who was up in the shower at this very minute. All he could think about was mounting the stairs and wrenching back the shower curtain. She would turn to him in surprise, of course, but he had a feeling she wouldn't really be surprised. She would be waiting for him, and he would see in the green depth of her eyes the look she had given him earlier....

"Good evening."

He was startled from his imagination-run-amok by an elderly man.

"I'm sorry. You *do* see me, right?"

Brodie blinked. Of course he saw the man, clear as day. He frowned sharply. "Who are you, and what the hell are you doing here?" he demanded, his hand dropping to the Smith & Wesson tucked into its holster at his waist.

"I'm so sorry. I usually knock. I'm Merlin, master magician. And who are you, please?"

Brodie paused, stunned into silence. He'd met all kinds of creatures in his life, but he'd never had a ghost come up and introduce himself.

"Sir, I can see that you are Elven, but even the Elven are far more attractive with their mouths shut," Merlin said.

Brodie came quickly back to life, instinctively offering his hand, then realizing that the ghost couldn't shake it. "Detective Brodie McKay, Mr. Merlin. I'm Rhiannon's guest."

"Finally! Thank the Lord above us, the two of you have connected," Merlin said.

Brodie decided not to broach the subject of just *how* he had imagined being connected to Rhiannon just moments before.

"Have you found out what's happening yet?" Merlin asked him. "With those murders?"

"No, sir, we haven't."

"What are you waiting for?" Merlin demanded indignantly. "You need to solve this case quickly. Men are dying—and you're doing Rhiannon a huge disservice. The girl just got out here, and you're behaving as if she should have done all your work for you by now."

"Merlin!" Brodie was startled by Rhiannon's sharp tone as he turned to look up the stairs. She'd been true to her word. Less than ten minutes had gone by, and she was transformed. Her hair looked like pure floating fire, and she had donned a short, sleek blue dress and matching high heels with lacy ribbons that tied around her ankles and drew attention to her long legs. The effect was truly wicked in the sexiest possible way.

"Hello, my dear. I was just introducing myself to your young gentleman here," he told her.

"He knows I'm a cop," Brodie said.

"And an Elven," Merlin added, looking at Rhiannon. His tone indicated that as far as he was concerned, *Elven* meant *beware*.

Rhiannon's attitude had shifted to one of amusement. She walked over to the ghost, and Brodie almost laughed at the way she seemed to take the older man by his nonexistent shoulders and bend to give him a kiss on the cheek. In her heels she was over six feet, and Merlin...wasn't.

"Thanks for worrying about me, Merlin. We're heading out to the Snake Pit to see if we can pick up any information—and so I can see where I'll be working," Rhiannon said.

"Just be careful," Merlin said. He turned and studied Brodie again. "Vampires . . . they're cagey, and they're powerful. If your killer really is a vampire..."

Brodie smiled. "Elven aren't weaklings, you know."

Merlin nodded. "All right, then. My dear," he said to Rhiannon, "my apologies, but I feel it's my duty to your dear parents to look out for your welfare."

Rhiannon smiled. "You're a sweetheart, Merlin. But you don't need to worry when you see Brodie in the future, okay?"

Merlin nodded, though he still looked doubtful. "I'll be returning to the main house," he told her. "But remember, I'm very close, if you ever need me."

"Thank you, Merlin," she said with a smile.

Brodie kept an eye on the ghost as he led Rhiannon to his car. When Merlin rounded the pool, he seemed to vanish into thin air.

"You did say you wanted to meet him," Rhiannon reminded him.

"Yes, my first ghost," he told her as he opened the passenger door for her. Once he was in the driver's seat, he added, "Actually, it's good that you have a watchdog."

"I suppose. Though, come to think of it, I've always wanted a real dog. Something huge, like a Saint Bernard."

"Scottish deerhound," Brodie suggested. "Or a good old German shepherd would be good, too. They make great guard dogs. They aren't vicious, but they're loyal, and they know who belongs and who doesn't. And—"

"And like all dogs, they have extra senses that we don't have," Rhiannon said.

No, he thought, *because neither of us is a werewolf.* Then again…compared to the human population, he *did* have extra powers. And once Rhiannon had enough experience that she could take on some of the abilities of her charges, *she* would have extra senses, too.

He realized that he was afraid she wouldn't know in time when she needed to use all her innate abilities. He didn't have the right to dictate to her, he thought. And yet…

This situation had given him the *feeling,* even if he didn't have the right.

"Now that I know I'm going to be living here, I think I *will* look for a dog," she said.

He nodded. "I don't have a pet. I keep lousy hours. It wouldn't be fair."

She smiled. "When I get my pup, you can borrow him. How's that?"

"Sounds like a plan," he said, trying to speak lightly.

He felt a catch in his throat. This was getting ridiculous. It was one thing to feel a strong sexual attraction. He was what he was—and she was a stunning woman. It was even all right to feel a little protective, whether she felt it was an insult or not. It was quite another to feel things that went beyond that.

A few minutes later he pulled off the freeway and was pleased to pull right up to the valet.

The attendant was one of the extremely tall leprechauns living in the L.A. area. The doorman was a shapeshifter. It was only natural that Declan Wainwright would employ so many of the city's Others.

As the valet took the car, Brodie stepped onto the sidewalk, where Rhiannon was waiting. He thought again that she looked absolutely breathtaking, and he wondered how the hell he had gone so quickly from finding her an annoying interruption in the functioning of his beloved city to seeing her as an exotic and nearly irresistible beauty.

She smiled; he took her arm. He felt magic in the air—unbelievable for an Elven who spent his days—and nights—dealing with the seamiest sides of the world, human and Other.

And then the moment was completely blown as a flash went off.

He turned to see Jake Reynolds, one of the paparazzi—and a gnome—snapping pictures from behind one of the ivied trellises that protected the front of the Snake Pit and added to its air of exclusivity.

Damn it! *Jake knew exactly who and what he was.*

He swore softly beneath his breath, ready to rip into Jake. Rhiannon set a calming hand on his arm.

"Let me," she told him softly.

He watched as she hurried over to the photographer. By then a small crowd was watching with interest. But, to her credit, Rhiannon seemed to be completely in control, smiling and laughing with Jake. But when she returned, she didn't have the photographer's memory card or camera.

"That damn gnome is going to blow my cover," Brodie told her.

She shook her head. "Smile over at the gnome. He's going to use your stage name. He wants a picture, so let him have one. He'll list Mac Brodie and Rhiannon Gryffald under the shot and sell it on the web. Everything's fine, and it will be great PR for the show."

"I don't trust gnomes," he said.

"We don't have a choice—unless you want to cause the kind of scene that will definitely create the wrong kind of publicity, not to mention give you away," she said.

"I still think he's going to out me as a cop," Brodie said, and he knew that his voice sounded like a growl.

"What if he does? All you have to do is say that you've always wanted to be an actor but didn't want to resign from the department." She touched his cheek as she spoke, and her fingers felt like silk against his skin.

Control yourself, he thought. He needed to get over her. Maybe he should sleep with the oversexed Ms. Audrey Fleur and get this out of his system.

"I'm all right," he said. He bared his teeth in a semblance of a grin. "I'm smiling at the gnome. See?"

"Good." She gave the gnome a beautiful smile of her own, waved and then they went on into the club.

Declan himself met them at the door.

"Welcome," he said, taking Rhiannon's hands and

kissing her cheek. "I saw what happened," he said, and looked at Brodie. "Do you want me to do something about him?"

"No! I already told Brodie not to strong-arm him. That would only cause a bigger problem," Rhiannon said.

Declan grinned. "I wasn't going to strong-arm anyone. I was going to shift into cop form and demand he hand over his memory card."

"No need," she said. "I asked him to post it using Brodie's stage name, so it will only help with what he's trying is to do."

Declan nodded and looked at Brodie. "Some of the other cast members are already here. Do you want to join them?"

"Maybe later. I think we should make a point of being alone," Brodie said. "As if we're out for a romantic evening."

"Gotcha," Declan said, grinning, as they entered the club. "By the way, Rhiannon, you're going to be appearing in the Midnight Room. Shall I show you as soon as you're inside?"

"Yes, thank you," she said.

"Brodie," Declan told him, "your friends are in the Velvet Lounge. Tell Humphrey I said to give you a VIP table in the back."

"Thanks," Brodie said. He kept Rhiannon's arm through his as they made their entry into the club. As soon as they had been noticed, he made a point of caressing her cheek, feeling her eyes burn across his skin as he touched her. Then, looking for all the world like reluctant lovers, they parted.

He watched for a moment as Declan escorted Rhiannon up the stairs to show her the Midnight Room, which was only open on the weekends. He imagined he was going to be spending a lot of time at the Snake Pit now—so long as Rhiannon kept playing there.

She might be a Keeper, with the potential to take on the abilities of her vampire charges. But she was still human—with all the weaknesses that went with that.

Brodie approached the Velvet Lounge and found Humphrey, one of Declan's werewolf maître d's, at the door. He was a big guy, the kind that brooked no trouble. He greeted Brodie with a smile, listened as Brodie repeated Declan's words and then led him to a table in the back.

Everything was velvet and silk at the Snake Pit. The back tables were like intimate tents, surrounded by velvet curtains that could be drawn back for a view of the entertainment or pulled closed for privacy.

Brodie sat. Several tables away, toward a magician who was performing the usual hat tricks, he could see Hunter Jackson sipping champagne and enjoying the company of Audrey Fleur and Kate Delaney. Both women were beautifully dressed and didn't seem to mind sharing his attention. Bobby Conche was with them, sitting back and enjoying a drink, clearly enjoying the reflected glory that came with sharing a table with the cast. Strange, Brodie thought. In essence, shapeshifters were actors, capable of taking on any role. But this shapeshifter didn't want to be anyone else—he just wanted to be around those who did.

At another table he saw Darius Simonides, accompanied by Sailor Gryffald. She seemed to be in seventh heaven. Of course, she wanted to act, and Darius was a major player.

A moment later Rhiannon returned and slid onto the chair next to him. She noticed her cousin, and she didn't seem happy. "I can't believe Sailor's here with him again. I know he's her godfather, but…"

"He *is* giving her a part in a major movie," Brodie offered.

"And I still don't trust him," she said.

"He's one of yours," he said, then leaned forward and spoke softly. "Let's keep an open mind and look at tonight as a fact-finding mission. We could be going in the wrong direction entirely, thinking everything's connected to the play. Maybe you'll know more after the council meeting tomorrow night."

She nodded but looked unhappy. Before he could say more, a waitress came by. Elven. She was tall, striking and sensual.

"May I take your order?" she asked sweetly.

"Rhiannon?" he asked.

"Do you carry Harp?" she asked.

"Absolutely. What about you, sir?" the waitress asked Brodie.

"The same, thanks."

As soon as their waitress left, Rhiannon rose.

"Where are you going?" he asked her.

"I can't just pretend that I don't see them," she said. "That would be rude."

"Rhiannon, we're observing—" he began.

But she was already gone. He rose quickly to follow her. She headed first to the table where Hunter Jackson was holding court, sweeping over as if she were just saying hello, and she played the scene perfectly, stopping to speak for just a moment, then moving on. Then she moved on to the table where her cousin was sitting. Brodie noted the way Jackson's eyes followed her.

And he saw that Audrey noticed, too.

Darius rose when Rhiannon reached the table, and they traded air kisses. Sailor rose, too, and gave her a hug, but she didn't look happy to see Rhiannon.

He decided to join them. Sailor stared at him in surprise, and then looked from him to her cousin. "So you two really are a couple."

"Would you like to sit down?" Darius asked.

Brodie suddenly regretted joining them. He had only met the man that one time at his office, when he'd invited himself along with Jackson and Declan, supposedly to talk about the filming but really because he wanted to meet everyone who had any connection to the show. He'd been Mac Brodie, actor, then. He hoped Sailor knew only his cover story, or that, if she knew the truth, she would remember that he was undercover. She should. She was the Elven Keeper, so she must have some sense.

"For a moment, sure, thanks," Brodie said, sliding in by Sailor.

"Out with your godfather—how nice," Rhiannon told Sailor.

"We were having a lovely discussion about my future," Sailor said. "It was all about me," she said with a rueful laugh.

Rhiannon grinned at that. "I came to see where I was going to be working."

"You know, Rhiannon, there might be a place for you when we record the soundtrack," Darius said.

"That would be great—especially if it pays well," Rhiannon said.

Darius laughed. "Honesty. I like that in women. How about you…Mr. Brodie? How do you feel about not being asked to be in the film?"

Sailor turned to him. "Seriously, Mr. Brodie, how *do* you feel about knowing someone else will play your role on the big screen?" She sounded genuinely curious. Maybe she'd forgotten what he did for a living, or maybe she really didn't know.

"I'm just happy to be working," he told her. "I don't have any problem with not being in the movie. Hunter Jackson won't be in it, either, and the whole project is his baby. Even the writer is stepping aside. He has consultation on the script, but that's it."

Sailor lowered her voice. "I feel a little awkward. I'm going to be playing Audrey Fleur's role in the movie, and I'm not sure she feels the way you do. We stopped by to say hello, and she was outright rude to me."

"This is Hollywood. People should be happy for whatever they get," Brodie said.

"But most of us aspire to be stars," Sailor said. "And I'm sure she was hoping this would be her big break."

"Sailor, are you worried about her?" Rhiannon asked.

"You may not believe this, but I honestly hate to hurt anyone," Sailor said.

"You're perfect for this role, Sailor," Darius said. "Stage and screen are different, and you shine on film. Besides, it was Hunter's plan from the start to do it this way. Lord, if I had to take a bullet for every unhappy actor in Hollywood, I'd be so riddled with holes there would be nothing left."

"And now, a volunteer from our audience, please," the magician called out, drawing their attention away from their conversation.

Hands went up all through the room. Audrey was waving wildly, but the magician ignored her and walked into the audience saying, "Sometimes the best volunteers are those who must be coerced onstage."

He was coming straight for them, announcing, "Tonight my good friend Declan Wainwright has given me permission to invite you all to visit the House of Illusion, where my fellow illusionists and I practice *real* magic. If you come on Sunday night, I promise you'll see the show of a lifetime."

When he stopped at their table, Brodie knew immediately that the tall, white-haired man was Elven. "I do hope you'll join us on Sunday night," he said directly to Brodie, who realized he'd seen the man at council meetings, though he didn't even know his name.

"My dear, you would make a wonderful assistant," the magician said.

He stretched out a hand, and Brodie thought he was reaching for Sailor, seeing as she was the new Elven Keeper.

But he wasn't offering his hand to Sailor. He was offering it to Rhiannon, who looked as if she wanted to crawl beneath the table.

"My dear?" the magician said. She stood reluctantly, accepting his hand, and they walked to the stage. "Now all I need you to do is lie down in this box…and then I'll cut you in half," he said.

Brodie had to stop himself from jumping to his feet and rushing to her side.

Sailor was clearly unhappy, too. "What's he doing?" she whispered. "I don't see why—"

"Just kidding!" the magician said. "If you would just

enter this glass dome…and then, when you hear a question, I swear you'll know the answer."

He opened the door to the glass dome, and Rhiannon entered.

"Beautiful, beautiful!" the magician said, then started soliciting questions from the audience and deferring to Rhiannon to provide the answers.

At the beginning, all the answers were amusing. One girl asked if she would find her true love, and the answer was, "Many times." That question segued into one from a pretty girl who asked if she would marry her boyfriend, and once again the answer was, "Many times." Then a young man asked if the pilot he had just shot would make it as a series. The response was, "Not this one, but it will lead to a movie role."

The next few questions all concerned Hollywood and the movies. And then a young guy asked, "Will I find my friend Jordan?"

The answer was, "He has already been found."

The man's gasp was frightening. He started walking toward the stage, his hand at his throat and his expression so intense that Humphrey the werewolf started toward him.

"Where? Where is he?" the man asked desperately. "I have to find him, I told him not to beat his head against the wall, but he loved that show, so he kept on trying…"

He didn't get any further, because Humphrey caught up to him. The magician seemed to realize that his session had veered from entertaining to all-too-real, and he helped Rhiannon from the answer box and asked that the audience give her a big hand.

As soon as he saw that Rhiannon was safely off the

stage, Brodie hurried after the young man—then being escorted out by Humphrey.

He caught the two of them just outside the room. "Humphrey, may I?" he asked.

The werewolf shrugged. Brodie took the young man's arm and led him toward the door. "Who are you looking for? How long has he been missing?"

Miserably, the man looked at Brodie. "Jordan Bellow. We've been together since high school. He's an actor. A *good* actor. We're from San Francisco, and he came down here to audition for some vampire play. He left me a message about some kind of a tour, but he didn't say anything specific, and now he's not answering emails and his cell goes straight to voice mail. I don't know where to look or what to do."

"And you are…?" Brodie asked.

"Nick. Nick Cassidy," the young man said. "This was just a silly game, right? He hasn't really been found, has he?"

"I don't know," Brodie said, and hesitated. If he did have the answer to Jordan Bellow's disappearance, his longtime lover wasn't going to like it. "Stay here. I'll be right back, and I'll see if I can help you."

He started back into the Snake Pit, but Rhiannon was already walking out in search of him. He practically collided with her at the door.

"Can you get a ride home with Sailor?" he asked her. "I'm going to take this man to the morgue and…find out if Jordan really has been found."

She nodded. "Of course."

"Before I go… How were you getting the answers?"

"They appeared in the glass, which isn't just normal clear glass. You were seeing a picture of the lower half of my body, while I had a computer monitor beside me," she explained. "I have no idea how the magician got the answers to show up there, though."

"Go talk to that magician. Find out who he is—and what he knows," Brodie told her. "But don't go talk to him alone—don't go *anywhere* alone. Sailor is going to have to give you a ride anyway, so make her stay with you. She's the Elven Keeper, so that might give you some clout."

"I'll be fine—go," Rhiannon told him.

Brodie rejoined Nick Cassidy.

"Where are we going?" Cassidy asked him.

"The morgue," Brodie said.

The magician had seemed a nice enough guy, and since she was going to be working at the Snake Pit herself, Rhiannon didn't think it would to be difficult to get a chance to speak with him. It was a little more difficult to disentangle Sailor from Darius Simonides, but Rhiannon feigned a total fascination with magic and finally drew her cousin away.

Sailor made her unhappiness known, though. "Rhiannon, I know this means nothing to you, but I want a life beyond this Keeper thing, and Darius can help me with that."

"Yes, and your future looks just peachy. But you *are* a Keeper. That's the way it is. The Elven Keeper. I don't even want to live in L.A., Sailor, but here I am." Rhiannon stared into her cousin's eyes. "And right now I need you."

Instantly Sailor looked contrite. "I'm sorry. Let's go see your magician."

Backstage, the magician—who billed himself as the

Count de Soir—was happy to greet them. He thanked
Rhiannon for participating in the show, and he held
Sailor's hands and kissed her cheeks, telling her that
the Elven were extremely lucky that their new Keeper
was so young and beautiful.

Rhiannon let them flatter each other for a few minutes and then stepped in. "Count, can you tell me,
please, where the answers were coming from? I didn't
see a ringer out in the audience who could have been
sending them to me."

"Ah, the answers," the count said, drumming his fingers on his dressing table. Then he looked at her and
said, "You live with my old mentor."

Rhiannon frowned, and then arched her brows. "You
mean…Merlin?"

He nodded. "I saw him in a dream, and he said that
I was to help you."

"You saw him in a dream?" Rhiannon repeated. That
sly old dog. He was haunting the magician, and the man
didn't even know it.

"He told me to use my magic for good. I don't have
all the answers, of course, but I read the newspapers.
Not online, either. The real thing, front to back, and
I've been waiting for someone to ask about a friend or
family member who's gone missing here in L.A. There
is no such thing as a John Doe. Not really. Everyone
is someone. I listen and I learn. I knew that you'd be
working here." He lowered his voice, looking around
his small dressing room. "I know that the man you
were sitting with is Brodie McKay, a cop, not an actor
named Mac Brodie."

"But how did you know that someone looking for

a dead man would come to the Snake Pit and ask you about him?" Rhiannon asked.

"That's easy," the count told her. "Everyone who wants to see or be seen comes to the Snake Pit."

Rhiannon thanked him and said goodbye. Before they left, the count kissed Sailor's hand and told her that he would see her the next night at the council meeting.

When they left, Rhiannon took Sailor's keys from her. "I'm driving," she said.

"I'm perfectly sober," Sailor told her.

"I'm sure you are, but I'm more sober, since I never even got my beer," Rhiannon said.

Traffic was comparatively light, and the drive home was quick.

When Rhiannon parked, Sailor looked over at her. "I know you think my whole life is all about me—me, me, me—but I really am here to help you. And I'll be a good Keeper, you know. Luckily I have the Elven, mostly law-abiding citizens who prefer mind games and getting along in life to fighting. You and Barrie are cut from tougher cloth, so it makes sense you inherited the vampires and the shifters. But whatever you think, I *am* here for you."

Rhiannon immediately felt guilty. She gave Sailor a hug. "Good night—and I'll count on that."

Sailor nodded. "By the way, watch out."

"Of course."

"No, I mean, watch out for your heart—and your sanity. With Brodie."

"I'll be fine," Rhiannon said. "He's a cop and I'm the vampire Keeper. We're working together, that's all."

"No, you're playing the part of lovers. And you're going to want it to be real," Sailor warned her.

"Don't worry, I know what I'm doing," Rhiannon assured her, then watched Sailor go into the main house before letting herself into Pandora's Box. She was exhausted, and she quickly prepared for bed, dully wondering if anything she'd learned tonight would help them in their investigation. Brodie, she knew, was just as frustrated.

Brodie.

Watch out!

Lying in bed, she found that she was thinking about the Elven detective, and that she was thinking about him in the very way Sailor had just warned her that she shouldn't. She was a sucker for tall men to begin with, probably because of her own height. And there was no way out of the fact that Elven males were...

Beautiful. Gorgeous. Men probably didn't want to be thought of as beautiful and gorgeous, she told herself drily. Too bad.

Elven males were also athletic, well-muscled, agile....

But it wasn't Brodie's physique that drew her, she thought. Or not only that. It was his eyes; it was his intensity. It was the way he looked at her, and the way she felt when he touched her.

She tossed, pounding her pillow, a blush rising to her cheeks. That afternoon, when she'd been in the shower, she'd had the most absurd fantasy of stepping out of the shower, grabbing a towel and walking downstairs. His flesh was almost as golden as his hair, and she longed to touch it. She'd imagined stepping up to him and letting the towel drop, telling him that too much work would leave them exhausted and incapable of logical thought, and that surrendering to the desires of the flesh could leave them ready to tackle the world again.

Pride was a great savior, though, and she'd done no such thing.

And yet...

She was imagining him again now, tall and imposing, seductive in his chinos and tailored shirt and black leather jacket.

A sound broke into her fantasy, something high-pitched and continuous. The sound of...

The alarm. One of her cousins had hit the little red button.

The House of the Rising Sun was under attack.

Chapter 7

The worst part about his job wasn't the dead, Brodie thought. It was the living.

He watched Nick Cassidy as he waited anxiously in the family "viewing" room at the morgue. Tony Brandt had no intention of walking the young man into the back and right up to the corpse of his partner. He was showing the face—cleaned up and as human as it was going to be without the talents of an expert mortician— on a monitor.

There was no doubt that Nick Cassidy had loved the man he saw on the screen. Brodie saw what he had expected and dreaded. First the look of denial, followed by the dawning of realization—and then the horror that what he saw couldn't be denied.

And last of all the tears.

Nick Cassidy convulsed and sank to the floor, shoulders shaking, hands to his face, tears streaming through his fingers.

Brodie let him cry, because there were no words to say. It wasn't going to "be all right," and nothing would make this moment better.

"Do you have family in the area?" he asked at last.

Nick shook his head. "Our families disowned us. We haven't seen or talked to any of them in…a decade. Not that I really had any family. My dad took off when I was two…my mother remarried some macho jock and I…I left at sixteen. Never looked back." He shook his head. "I'm not going back to my family now."

"Family doesn't always have to do with an accident of birth," Brodie told Nick. "Do you know anyone at all in the L.A. area?"

"Acquaintances, that's all," Nick said as he stood up slowly. He was suddenly angry. "Who did this? Why Jordan? He was the nicest guy in the world, never hurt anyone, loved the world, even when the world kicked him in the teeth."

"I don't know," Brodie said. "But I intend to find out. And you can help me with that. I need any emails you got from Jordan, and I need you to try to remember every conversation you had with him after he came down here." He paused, shaking his head. "Why didn't you file a missing person report?"

"Because last time I talked to Jordan he was all excited. He'd auditioned for the road show, and if he could travel, he was basically guaranteed the part. I just thought he was traveling at first, and when I started getting worried, I guess I was too upset to think of anything but coming down here to look for him myself."

"Nick, does the title *Vampire Rampage* mean anything to you?"

Nick stared back at him blankly. "It was a vampire play. I don't know if he ever said the name."

Tony showed up in the viewing room just then. He looked at Brodie, and Brodie nodded.

"I'm going to need you to help me," he said gently to Nick. "Can you help me fill out some papers so the detectives can find out who did this to your friend? He really needs you to be strong right now."

"I—I…yes. Jordan…oh, Jordan!" Nick started to sob again.

Tony got him seated and looked at Brodie. "I've got this," he said. "You look like hell. Can't burn the candle at both ends forever, you know. Get out of here. Go home and get some sleep."

"I drove Mr. Cassidy here," Brodie said.

"I only came in to meet you," Tony said. "When he and I are finished, I'll see that he gets back to his car or his hotel."

"I'm going to need to interview him tomorrow," Brodie said.

"Of course. I'll make sure to get an address where you can reach him."

Brodie still stood there. He would never get used to having to tell people that their loved ones were dead.

"I've got this," Tony assured him.

"Thanks," Brodie said gruffly.

He was on the freeway when his phone started ringing.

He answered it quickly. "Brodie."

It was Rhiannon. "I need you. Can you get over here? Now? *Please!*"

* * *

Never in a thousand years had Rhiannon expected that the compound alarm would ever actually go off.

She was out of bed in two seconds and racing downstairs. A cabinet in the living room held an array of weapons. She opened it and hastily decided on a small crossbow that shot silver-tipped arrows—an effective choice against both werewolves and vampires.

She started to race for the door and then realized she wasn't even sure where she was going, because only the signal system at the tunnel entry would tell her whether it was coming from the main house or Gwydion's Cave. She grabbed her phone off the desk and stilled her shaking fingers long enough to dial Brodie's number, and then she dropped the phone, racing toward the kitchen. As she ran to the basement and reached the tunnel, she saw that the alarm had come from Sailor.

Rhiannon knew that it was her fault if Sailor had been targeted—she had involved her cousin in everything that was going on.

The tunnels were equipped with emergency lightning, so she had no problem finding her way. She took the turn to the left, toward the main house, and nearly collided with Barrie, who was racing from Gwydion's Cave.

"What's happening?" Barrie asked anxiously.

"I don't know!"

They burst into the basement of the main house and ran for the stairs that led up to the kitchen. They found Merlin waiting for them at the top.

"What is it?" Rhiannon demanded.

"Shadows, dark shadows, swirling around Sailor.

And there was a raven—a *real* raven—sitting on her bedpost. And I can't wake her up!" Merlin said.

With Rhiannon a step ahead of Barrie, they raced through the house and upstairs, then into Sailor's room.

Merlin had told the truth. A massive raven was now sitting on Sailor's chest.

Right on her chest!

Rhiannon couldn't use her weapon without skewering her cousin, so she tossed it down and made a dive for the bird. It flapped its giant wings and rose from Sailor's chest, then flew at Rhiannon with talons extended toward her. But Rhiannon felt the adrenaline pumping through her and ducked back down for the weapon. She didn't have time to discharge it, but she swiped with all her strength at the raging black creature throwing itself at her.

Barrie made a dive for Sailor, shaking her. "Sailor, wake up!"

Rhiannon managed to slam the crossbow right into the raven. It let out a terrible screech of wrath and began to flap wildly toward the ceiling; then it wheeled and headed for the stairs, flying down toward the first floor.

Rhiannon heard a furious oath explode from the stairway, and she realized that Brodie was there, running up the stairs as the *thing* raced down them. He slammed a fist into the massive bird and it fell to the floor, but when he reached down to grab it, it surged to life again and flew toward the living room.

"Catch it! I think it got her—I think it did something to Sailor!" Barrie shouted.

Rhiannon joined Brodie in the living room, where the raven was flying in frantic circles, searching for a way out. But as fast as it moved, Brodie moved faster.

He caught it with his fist again, and again it fell to the floor.

Rhiannon took aim and caught it with a silver-tipped arrow.

What happened next seemed like a scene in a movie built on digital special effects. The raven disintegrated into a cloud of black ash that first seemed to take the form of a man and then a skeleton, before raining down in a haze of black particles.

At the end something bounced down to the floor.

A skull, quickly followed by fragments of bone.

Rhiannon stared at Brodie, shell-shocked and speechless.

He looked back at her and walked over to the pile of ash. He bent low, taking a pen from his pocket to poke at the skull so he could study it. The lower jaw was missing—it had landed across the room.

He looked at Rhiannon. "Old vampire," he said. "Very old. They only crumble to dust like this when they're old. The new ones can be…messy."

Barrie came rushing down the stairs, accompanied by Sailor, who looked as if she didn't quite know where she was, much less what had happened.

"What's going on?" Sailor asked.

Rhiannon spun around to look at her cousin. "You don't know?"

"I was dreaming. A nice dream," Sailor said.

"A *sexual* dream?" Brodie asked her.

Sailor flushed scarlet. "Yes…and then I felt Barrie shaking me…and then I woke up. I—what happened? Why are you all in my house—and why is there a giant pile of dirt on my floor?"

Brodie strode over to Sailor and inspected her throat.

"Clean, thank God…." He looked thoughtful as he said, "It's a good thing that we got him. Whoever the hell he was. Whatever poison he put into Sailor died with him."

"Poison?" Sailor gasped.

"It's all right—it's gone," Brodie said wearily. He looked at Rhiannon. She thought that she saw the slightest sparkle of respect in his eyes.

"A vampire dared to enter the home of a Keeper?" Sailor asked incredulously.

"And it went after Sailor, not Rhiannon," Barrie pointed out.

"Rhiannon can access the power of her charges," Brodie said. "And vampires can sicken and die from attacking other vampires. What I want to figure out right now is how the hell the damned thing got in," Brodie mused aloud.

"The window," Sailor said. "I was…warm, so I got up and opened the window, then fell asleep again."

"I guess it was that kind of a dream," Barrie said.

"Let's make sure all the windows are closed, because eventually we're going to have to get some sleep," Rhiannon said.

Rhiannon had forgotten Merlin, who had appeared at some point and was now standing near the sofa, looking thoughtful.

"Whoever it was, one of us had to know him," Merlin said.

"What?" Sailor asked.

Merlin looked at them in exasperation. "Whoever he was—"

"Or she," Brodie interjected.

"Or she," Merlin agreed. "One of us had to know them. A vampire can't come in without being invited.

There are a lot of silly rumors about vampires, invented by everyone from Stoker to Hollywood, but that one thing is quite true. Whoever you just killed was someone who'd been invited into the House of the Rising Sun. Might have been yesterday, might have been decades ago—but somewhere along the way, it happened."

"And they were old, very old," Rhiannon murmured.

"We'll find out who it was—and why," Brodie said. "For now, though, let's search the house and close it up tight."

"It had to be *her!*" Sailor said suddenly.

"Her?" Rhiannon asked.

Sailor looked at Brodie. "You know. Audrey Fleur. She's angry at me because she wants to be in the movie and I got the part instead of her."

"Sailor, I just can't see any vampire taking a chance on entering the home of a *Keeper* over a role in a movie," Rhiannon said.

"We'll worry about who it was later," Brodie said. "For now, Barrie, go upstairs with Sailor and keep an eye on her. Rhiannon and Merlin and I will check out the house. And when we're done, well, we're all staying here tonight. That's a nice big couch over there, and it will do me just fine."

"All right," Barrie said. "Sailor, let's go. I have to be at the paper early tomorrow, so I need to get some sleep."

"Are you nuts? I couldn't possibly sleep right now," Sailor said.

"Well, then, you can watch me sleep," Barrie said. "Let's go."

They went up the stairs, and Merlin followed them, saying, "I'll holler if I find another open window."

"Thanks, Merlin," Rhiannon called to him.

She was suddenly acutely aware of the fact that she was alone with Brodie and wearing nothing but an oversize T-shirt and a pair of lacy panties.

Luckily he seemed focused on the possibility of renewed danger at that moment. And he could have no clue whatsoever that she'd been fantasizing about him when the alarm had gone off.

"How many rooms?" he asked her.

"Living room, dining room, kitchen and a family room out back on this floor. And a few closets," she added quickly.

"Start from the back, and I'll start from the front, and we'll meet in the middle," he told her.

Rhiannon was thorough; she even looked into cabinets when she hit the kitchen. Brodie met her there. "Merlin says Sailor closed her bedroom window and there's nothing else open upstairs."

"Thanks," she said. "Brodie, how did you get onto the property?"

"I'm Elven," he reminded her. "I parked at the top of the drive and cleared the wall in a single bound, just like Superman," he said lightly.

She laughed and realized that whatever might come of it, she was suddenly glad that he was in her life.

"Thank you," she said. "Thank you for getting here so quickly."

He nodded. "It's my job. It's what I do," he said. There was a husky tone to his voice, and he added quickly, "We might want to sweep up our uninvited guest."

"Good idea," she said, going for a broom.

"Are there two of those?" he asked her.

"You don't have to—"

"Yeah, I do," he said as she handed him a second broom.

He went back to the living room with her, and they began sweeping up the piles of ash. "The place is definitely going to need a good dusting tomorrow," she said.

Brodie hunkered down by the skull, then retrieved the jaw. "I'm going to take these to Tony Brandt. It's a long shot, given his age, but maybe we can trace our vampire through his dental work."

"Can you tell from the skull what sex our visitor was?" she asked him.

Brodie shook his head. "I can't. Maybe Tony can. You have some kind of a tote here? Something I can carry this in?"

"Sure." She went into the kitchen and delved into the broom closet. She found a reusable fabric grocery bag and took it to him.

"Perfect," he told her as he put the skull and disarticulated jawbone into the bag.

They stood there awkwardly for a moment. Then Rhiannon swung into hostess mode. "There are four extra rooms upstairs—you're welcome to a real bed."

"I think I'll just stay down here," he said. "Maybe not awake and aware, but ready to be up, awake and aware if I need to."

"Okay. You know, you don't have to stay. I can…I can keep watch 'til morning."

"I'd be happier staying the night."

"Okay. But at least let me get you a pillow and a blanket."

"That would be great."

She ran upstairs to the linen closet, then hurried back

bearing a pillow and bedding. "The couch opens up into a bed," she told him.

"I'll be just fine the way it is," he assured her.

"Okay. Well, then, I'll leave you," she told him. "If you're the first one up, there's coffee in the pot already—a tradition in the main house—and there are tea bags and hot chocolate and cereal… Help yourself."

"I'll do that."

"Good night, then."

"Good night."

He smiled and nodded but didn't turn away. For a moment she envisioned a strange fantasy in which he stepped forward and took her into his arms. She pictured herself touching his face, fascinated by the lines and strength of it. Then his lips touched hers, and she was infused with the fire his gaze ignited when she least expected it.

She blinked quickly, offered him a brief nod of acknowledgment and turned away.

Rhiannon hurried up the stairs and looked into Sailor's room. Despite Sailor's earlier protest that she was wide awake, she was sound asleep, just as Barrie seemed to be at her side. Rhiannon smiled, surprised to realize that she felt like a mother hen looking in on them. She *was* the oldest; she had Barrie by a year, and Sailor a year and a half.

And now, here in the Canyon, it was down to the three of them to keep order.

They'd done all right tonight, she thought. Yes, Brodie had helped, but most people in the world got by with a little help, and she realized that to be the best she could be, she had to be open to help when it was available.

She walked down to the guest room where she had

always slept when she came out to California to visit. There were still posters of her favorite rock bands on the walls. No one had ever taken them down. The room had been hers, and if things hadn't worked out the way they had she wouldn't even be in L.A. No, the main house was Sailor's, and she didn't begrudge her cousin in the least.

She walked over to the dresser. The years of her youth seemed combined there. Ticket stubs from plays, concerts and movies had gone into a cup. She opened the little jewelry box. A tiny statue of Judy Garland popped up, and "Over the Rainbow" began to play.

She needed to clean out the room, she thought drily. It was wonderful, but it was hers no more. The old Keepers were not coming back.

But for tonight...

She turned off the overhead light and lay down, but unlike her cousins, she really was wide awake. Her heart was still pounding too quickly.

Sleep, she needed sleep.

It would be nice to slip back into that fantasy she'd been having when she was so abruptly awakened by the alarm.

No, not a good idea, not when the object of her fantasy was lying on a couch just below. Flesh and blood. So close she felt she could still feel the leather of his jacket, the touch of his hand, and hear his voice.

No, no, no, no.

Dear God, he was Elven! She had to stop thinking about his eyes, his face, his body and his touch! He would read her mind if she didn't keep her guard up, and then she would die of humiliation. She barely knew him, and she was having hot, sweaty, imaginative dreams about what she'd seen of him and wondering about the parts she hadn't.

To distract herself she started thinking about tomorrow night and the council meeting. Her first...

They probably assumed that she would just listen.

If so, they were assuming wrong.

It wasn't mandatory that every Other attend every council meeting, much less the informal multi-race get-togethers afterward, but most liked to enjoy an evening where there was no need for pretense. It was wonderful to live in a mixed world, but there was a real relief in escaping pretense for a place where everyone was different and the various races could mingle. Sure, throughout the years and across the globe prejudice had reared its ugly head, even between the Other races. Shapeshifters who hated werewolves. Werewolves who thought they were better than the vampires. Vampires who looked down on the Elven. Most of the time that prejudice came from the same sources as in the human world: fear or poverty or envy. But with the Others' supernatural abilities, the consequences could be much worse, and that was why the Keepers existed. They were the hand of tolerance and balance in a world where, even taken all together, the Others were still just a fraction of the population, always in danger of discovery and extinction. Dissension and malicious behavior could endanger them all.

She rolled over in misery.

And the vampires were at it right now—when she had barely arrived.

She felt her anger begin to burn again. There was no doubt that a vampire had invaded Sailor's home tonight, no doubt that somewhere out there, at least one vampire was pursuing evil.

She would never fall asleep if she stayed this angry.

She forced herself to go over song lyrics, and eventually she dozed off. When she opened her eyes again, the sun was sending delicate patterns of gold through the curtains.

Brodie woke at seven, and he could smell coffee brewing. When he opened his eyes, he saw that one of the Gryffald cousins was standing by the couch, holding a cup of coffee and staring down at him. It was Barrie. Disappointment filled him.

"Good morning, Detective, and thank you for staying the night. Coffee?"

"Sure. Thank you."

Barrie handed him the cup. As he sat up, she perched next to him, staring at him. "Are the police going to give any kind of a press conference about the murders? I've been doing my best to get information out of my sources on the street, but no one seems to know anything about a vampire on a killing spree. I was thinking that some press coverage might make someone remember something, maybe lead to ID'ing the victims."

"And it could make a killer hungrier," Brodie said.

"Hungrier?" That was Rhiannon. Freshly showered and dressed for the day, she was coming down the stairs. "A vampire broke into this house last night. Sailor could have died. I think we might as well go for broke and give Barrie a chance at a big story."

Rhiannon was angry, he thought. He didn't need to read her mind to know that.

She was taking last night's attack personally, which,

he supposed, was natural. She was the vampire Keeper, and her cousin might have been killed by one of her out-of-control charges.

"All right, slow down and let's think about this," he said. "The attack last night might have been intended purely to enrage you, Rhiannon, and make you react rashly. It was meant personally, yes, but you can't let yourself take it that way. You're a Keeper. You have to remain in control at all times." He turned to her cousin. "Barrie, I'll talk to my captain about your idea for a press conference. I have an identity now on one of the victims, and I have a tech working on trying to figure out who the others were, but you're right that getting the public involved might help. I'll see that a police spokesman calls you about any press conference, all right?" He looked back at Rhiannon, who nodded curtly and walked into the kitchen, presumably in search of coffee.

"Thanks," Barrie said, rising. "I have to get to work." She paused, though, and asked, "Do you think that attack was specifically directed at Sailor? Or are we all in danger now?"

Brodie looked at Barrie. "I don't know. I think you all need to be careful until we figure this out. Maybe I should drop you at work."

"I'm game," she told him.

"Rhiannon? How about you?" he asked as she came back into the living room.

"I don't have to be anywhere until this evening, so I think I'll stay here with Sailor, who's still asleep. I'm still a little worried, though. Will you give me a call and let me know whatever you find out?"

He nodded, finished his coffee and carried the cup to the kitchen.

Rhiannon followed him and leaned against the sink, looking serious. "Should we…meet tonight? After the council meetings?"

He wished she hadn't followed him into the kitchen. They were too close.

"Absolutely. Go to the Snake Pit. Barrie will already be there, because that's where the shifters meet. I'll bring Sailor, since we'll be at the same meeting, and meet you there."

Yes, being this close to her was definitely a mistake. He was dying to reach out and touch her. He could smell the shower-fresh dampness of her skin, and he could almost feel the touch of her hair against him.

This wasn't going to work. He had to get out of here. "I need to get home for a quick shower, and then to the station and the morgue," he told her. "I'll drop Barrie, make sure she's safely at the paper. Can you take Sailor to the café with you this afternoon, then drop her at the old church for her council meeting before you head to your own?" His voice sounded like a growl. Hell, at that moment, he might as well have been a werewolf. He offered her a forced smile before he collected the tote bag and headed back to the living room to collect Barrie.

It was an easy ride to the newspaper office, and from there he went back to his own place to shower and change, before making his way to the station.

Adam was grinning when Brodie approached his desk. "You should kiss me!" Adam told him. "I mean, don't, but you should."

"You've found something?"

Adam nodded. "Five names. One was Jordan Bellow—but I understand that he was identified last night.

There are four more—two are women, though, so they aren't your corpses. The two remaining men are Oscar Garcia and Deacon Steitz. Oscar grew up in foster homes, but he'd been at a halfway house in Oregon before going to Hollywood—to audition for a play. The guy running the halfway house said that he'd been a good guy, but he kept slipping in and out of AA. Kept having relapses. When he never came back to the halfway house, the guy just figured he'd gotten the part. Deacon Steitz was a loner. Both parents died in a car crash when he was twenty-two. He spent time in Chicago working the comedy clubs, then told a friend he was heading to California to try for the big time. The two women—Lila Mill and Rose Gillespie—were two more acting wannabes. Lila was a Southern California girl, twenty-three, tried three different colleges, always shopping around for scholarships, and then told a friend that she was going to audition for the 'perfect' play and not to expect to hear from her until she'd made it big. Similar story for the other woman. She was excited, heading out to audition for a play that was going to be her big break. She was being very secretive about it, though, so no one actually knew where she'd gone. Still don't, since we don't have two dead women."

Brodie felt as if a rock had slipped down his throat to his stomach. "We don't have them yet," he said wearily. "All five of them auditioned for *Vampire Rampage?*"

"Yep—I went off the lists you gave me. Four of them made the callbacks. I found the fifth when I checked the initial audition lists."

"Good work. Thanks, Adam," Brodie said, but the words felt dry in his mouth. "Pull up a map of the

Canyon area for me, will you? Find me something that shows me all lakes and waterways."

Adam groaned. "You'll have to give me a few minutes."

"You've got it."

"So, why are you still standing there?" Adam asked him.

"I can stand for a few minutes."

Adam turned back to his computer.

Brodie waited.

There were two more bodies out there. Two women. He had to find them.

While Adam worked at the computer, Brodie drew out his cell and gave Tony the names he had just gotten from Adam; he was certain that they could officially ID their John Does now that he had the names.

Five people had disappeared, unnoticed because of the lives they had led, until finally one's lover had come looking for him.

"You're sure?" Tony asked.

"Nothing is sure until you do the forensic testing."

"I'll get right on it."

"I'm ninety-nine percent sure there are two dead women out there, too. I'm going to find them."

Tony sighed. "I'll be waiting," he said.

Adam was still on his computer when Brodie hung up. "By the way, have you seen the paper today?" the younger man asked.

Brodie tensed, remembering that picture Jake Reynolds had snapped last night.

"No. Why?"

Adam glanced up for a minute. "You look good. Hot

Hollywood star all the way. And your date—she's even hotter. Up and coming singer, huh?"

"Adam, where's the paper?" Brodie asked, trying to keep his temper in check.

"Right there, other side of my desk. I know I can get the news on the computer, but I still get a paper every day. I like turning the pages, doing the crossword puzzle."

Brodie wasn't listening as Adam droned on, telling him the advantages of real paper over a computer screen. He picked up the newspaper and began riffling through it—the picture was on the nightlife page.

It was a good picture, actually. He and Rhiannon were looking into each other's eyes. He had to admit that if he'd seen that picture of two others, he would be convinced they were a real couple.

He hurriedly read the caption underneath the photo, which didn't say much. *Actor Mac Brodie from the play Vampire Rampage, out with the Mystic Café's trending new singer, Rhiannon Gryffald. Could she be the girl of his dreams?*

And that was it.

Brodie let out a sigh. He decided that gnomes weren't really such nasty little beasts.

"I've got your maps," Adam said. "You've got a lot of water to cover."

"Then I'd better get started," Brodie said, taking the maps from Adam with a terrible sense of foreboding. The minute he looked at the first map, he knew exactly where he was going to find the next body.

Chapter 8

Rhiannon took Sailor with her to work at the Mystic Café, where she had an evening set scheduled, since the council meetings didn't start 'til late, when most of L.A. was safely tucked into bed.

She was surprised to see that the café was full when she arrived, and that most of the clientele seemed to have coffee and pastries already, and were actually waiting—for her.

"Hey, it's a crowd!" Sailor told her happily.

"I wonder why."

"I don't," Sailor said, pointing to a little table next to the small stage. "Look."

Sailor looked. The newspaper was lying on the table, folded open to the nightlife page. And there she was, staring into Brodie's eyes. Jake Reynolds had done everything she had asked him.

"Oh, my God, I am so jealous," Sailor said. "And look at all the people in here. Hugh is going to be thrilled."

"Yes…but…"

"Oh, come on, Rhiannon. You were irritated about coming to California, sure your career was over. Now you have a real audience," Sailor said.

"Yes, but…"

Yes, she had an audience. But what did that mean next to the fact that people were dead? And most likely at the hands—or fangs—of a vampire, maybe even one of *her* vampires. She realized now that she wanted to be a good Keeper—a respected Keeper, like her father before her.

Hugh made an appearance just then, a huge smile on his face. He actually paused to hug them both. "I've made a fortune already tonight, so don't mess up. None of that 'I Hate Hollywood' crap tonight, Rhiannon. No more 'I hate actors.'"

Sailor looked at her. "You hate actors?" she asked.

"Of course not. I was just angry about the interruption from—oh, never mind." She turned away to get her guitar out of the case. She should have known that impromptu song was going to come back to haunt her.

The night went well, so well that at one point the place was standing room only.

"I can't believe it's council meeting night. I wouldn't close! I'd stay open 'til dawn," Hugh said to her during a break. "Here's hoping tomorrow will be just as good."

"I don't work here tomorrow," she reminded him. "I'm at the Snake Pit tomorrow, remember?"

"Tell that slimy shapeshifter you can't make it," he said.

"I can't do that and you know it. But we've still got an hour 'til closing, so let's make some money, okay?"

Hugh was unhappy, but when 10:00 p.m. rolled around he made the announcement that they were closing and people began filing out. When the last customers were gone, and Rhiannon had her guitar and equipment ready to go, Sailor let out a soft whistle.

"Rhiannon!"

"What?"

"You made money—a lot of money. You have a few hundred bucks here."

"Good. The way things are going, I'm going to need it," Rhiannon said. "Come on, we have to get moving. I have to drop you at the church and get to the House of Illusion before eleven."

"Hey, aren't you going to take the paper?" Sailor asked her.

"No, why?"

"Because that picture is hot, that's why. Do you two have a real thing going on?"

"We just met."

Sailor laughed. "That doesn't mean anything. You either have chemistry or you don't. And you two seem to sizzle."

"There's a serious situation going on," Rhiannon said primly.

"You *are* attracted to him. Natural, I suppose. He *is* Elven, after all."

"I've known dozens of Elven," Rhiannon said, "and I assure you, I didn't want to jump in bed with them."

"Just Brodie."

"Sailor!"

"Hey, you know what they say? Once you go Elven, you know you've been to heaven."

"It's taboo," Rhiannon murmured. "We're not supposed to…mix."

"Why?" Sailor said.

"I don't know. That's just what they say," Rhiannon told her.

"I've heard of a vampire Keeper down in New Orleans who fell in love with a vampire cop," Sailor said.

"I think there could be repercussions."

Sailor laughed. "Then just give in and sleep with him."

"Sailor…"

"Hey, I wish *I* could stumble on to a Mr. Right."

"Come on, we're wasting time," Rhiannon said.

The freeway was moving smoothly enough, but Rhiannon swore at every driver who slowed her down for two seconds. Sailor just rolled her eyes and told her, "Calm down."

"It's our first time attending council meetings as Keepers," Rhiannon reminded her.

"That's right, and they'll wait for us if we're late," Sailor said, grinning.

Rhiannon looked at her and smiled slowly in return. There was something in her cousin's tone—a touch of steel—that said she was going to do just fine.

She dropped Sailor at the deconsecrated 1890s church on Vine—by day it was a very trendy boutique carrying very trendy clothing. She saw the magician from the night before—the Count de Soir—and several other Elven at the entry. Sailor would be in good hands, but still Rhiannon was afraid to leave her. Then she saw that Brodie was there. He saw her, too, and came walking over to the car. He looked grim.

"What's wrong?" she asked him.

He waved a hand in the air. "We'll talk later. Come on, Sailor, I'll walk you in."

"Wish me luck," Sailor whispered to her.

Rhiannon nodded, but she was looking at Brodie. "Keep her safe. Please."

"Count on it. We'll see you at the Snake Pit after this," Brodie promised her.

Then he and Sailor turned away, and Rhiannon quickly drove on to her own destination.

Because the House of Illusion was owned by a vampire magician, Jerry Oglethorpe, the vampire council was held there. Jerry knew all the traditional magician's moves, but he also liked to do a little cheating that left his audience—and his peers—awed. As a vampire, he could perform illusions that the others couldn't begin to match. Some young magicians were counting on the hope that when he died, his secrets would be revealed. Rhiannon often felt sorry for them; they had no idea that Jerry would probably outlive them, and his secrets would never be known.

Rhiannon hadn't been to the House of Illusion often. The majestic castle hidden away in the Canyon was really a social club for magicians, but on Friday and Saturday nights it functioned as a magicians' showcase. They sold tickets, but you had to be invited to buy one. That kept the House of Illusion a fantasy—and made attendance there a must-manage-to-do for many of the tourists who came to Hollywood. And it made the count's invitation to the audience at the Snake Pit a real coup.

But once every two months, on the second Thursday night, the vampire council was held. There was an elected president who presided over the meeting, but the Keeper was the real power.

Rhiannon was already in her seat, in the first row in front of the stage, when Darius Simonides rose to preside over the council. He knocked his gavel on the podium twice, calling the room to order. Rhiannon looked around as conversation died down to whispers and then disappeared altogether.

The room was filled with vampires from every walk of life. Many were in film and TV in one way or another: producers, directors, actors, agents, sound men, electricians, costume designers, set designers, script writers, musicians and more. There were also bankers, ad execs, waiters and waitresses, shop owners and other businessmen and women. In a way, she mused, it almost looked like a PTA meeting, except that some in attendance were very young and some were very old.

"Welcome to this convention of our people," Darius said. "First, may I please have the minutes from our last meeting?"

The minutes were read. The last meeting—the last one her father had attended—had apparently been very dull. They had talked about sources for blood, most of which were slaughterhouses, and employment opportunities. A party was being planned for Halloween, and the discussion had centered on the date, since many vampires had previous commitments on the holiday itself.

Darius asked for old business, which was equally boring.

New business came next. A banker had ordered blood from a new venue and found it to be very high quality. A woman stood up and announced that she was purchasing land on the outskirts of Santa Barbara, and planned on cattle ranching. Someone else suggested a summer party.

Seriously, a PTA meeting would have been exciting in comparison, Rhiannon thought.

Except that it was very likely one of the seemingly normal vampires in attendance was a killer.

At last Darius brought up the most pressing piece of new business. "You all know that we've had to say goodbye to Piers Gryffald," he said, and his words were greeted with a groan. "But I'm happy to say that the new Keeper of the Canyon vampire society is here with us tonight, fresh, young, beautiful—and ready to take on her duties and become an integral part of our brother and sisterhood. I present Miss Rhiannon Gryffald."

She was greeted with hearty applause, but since it would have been rude of them to welcome her in any other way, she didn't read too much into that.

Rhiannon left her seat. Darius met her at the stairs and politely escorted her up.

"Thank you all for that cordial welcome, and thank you all as well for your show of warmth for my father. I know we'll all miss him while he serves the Otherworld in his new capacity."

Those words were followed by more applause. She lifted a hand.

"There is a grave matter facing our membership at this very moment," she announced, making sure that her voice rang loud and clear. "The police have found three bodies that show signs of vampire attack. We're lucky that, so far, the medical examiner who has handled all three autopsies is Dr. Anthony Brandt, a fellow member of the Otherworld. So far the press has taken very little interest in the case, though that may change soon, so we need to be prepared for rumors of a murderer imitating a vampire when he kills."

A man in a typical banker's suit stood. "Why haven't we heard anything about this before?" he demanded. "Why has there been no report of the murders at all?"

"There have been reports. But the dead were John Does, and their deaths were relegated to the back of the paper. Additionally, some details of the crimes have been withheld by the police," Rhiannon said. A discontented murmuring started, and she knew she had to nip it in the bud.

"So," she announced loudly, her voice ringing with authority, "as we all know, there are members of the human race who believe that vampires exist, and others who *know* they do, so it is certainly possible that a human being is using this method of murder to make the killings appear to be the work of a vampire. I want you to know that I'm your greatest champion. I know that you and the other members of the vampire community just want to survive and pursue your dreams. And I want you all to be aware that I *will* find out the truth of these murders in conjunction with other members of the greater Otherworld. If a vampire *is* guilty of these attacks—attacks that put the entire community in danger—that vampire will face the greatest punishment we are authorized to mete out." She paused and looked around the room. "Total extinction. Don't believe for a moment that I will not fulfill my duties to the letter of our mutual law, or that I will shirk in any way when it comes to protecting those who are innocent. I strongly suggest that anyone who knows anything tells me what they know, so they won't suffer along with the murderer."

She stood for a moment, staring out over the now silent crowd.

"It has to be a human!" someone in the audience said. "We're happy here. Why would we kill anyone?"

"As I said, it *is* possible that a human being is the killer," Rhiannon said. "And that possibility will be investigated. But a *vampire* attempted to attack my cousin at the House of the Rising Sun last night," she said. "That vampire is now ash. Be assured that I will not tolerate any attack on myself, my home or my family, and that transgressors *will* die without benefit of interrogation. If anyone knows anything about this attack, I need to know what you know. At the same time, if there is any threat to this community, I will just as aggressively seek to protect those of you who are innocent. But I will not forget what happened last night, and I won't stop until I have an answer." She paused again, looking around the room. "I am my father's daughter. Please don't believe that my justice will be any less swift. In the meantime, I am available whenever I'm needed by any one of you, just as my father was before me. In closing—if you find that you're missing a friend or acquaintance, please come to me. Because there is a pile of ash at my house that was once one of you."

She turned to Darius, who was staring at her, as stunned as the others. She smiled and said, "Thank you, Darius. I look forward to a long and mutually beneficial relationship with all of you—again, just as my father enjoyed before me."

Darius didn't offer her a hand back to her seat. It

didn't matter. She was perfectly capable of walking down a few steps on her own.

She was sure that Darius had originally planned to say more, but he seemed tongue-tied. Finally he banged the gavel on the podium. "This meeting of the Canyon vampire community is hereby dismissed!"

He came down the steps in a hurry. Rhiannon was certain he had a lot to say to her—no doubt he intended to chastise her for alienating the community from the get-go.

But she certainly hadn't alienated them all, because a lot of people came up to her to shake her hand and say they were glad she was going to take a firm stand. Others remembered her from when she was younger and spoke to her about her family, while some just wanted to welcome her.

Jerry Oglethorpe came over, studying her gravely. "Good start, Miss Gryffald."

"Thank you, Jerry. And while I have you, a magician who bills himself as the Count de Soir was performing at the Snake Pit the other night. He invited his entire audience here on Sunday night. Does that have any bearing on my case?"

"The Count de Soir—he's Elven," Jerry said.

"I know that. He told me that he saw Merlin—remember, Ivan Schwartz, the magician who owned the House of the Rising Sun—in a dream. And that Merlin told him to help me," Rhiannon said.

"Of course I remember Merlin," Oglethorpe said. "He was one of the finest magicians—and men—I ever knew. I don't know whether the count's invitation has anything to do with your case, though. He *is* performing Sunday night. I'll reserve a table for you."

"Thank you, Jerry. We'll be here—my cousins and I. And probably a friend," Rhiannon said.

Darius came up to her then. "My, my, Miss Gryffald. That was rather…hostile."

She shook her head. "I'm not being hostile, Darius. I am here to fight for the rights of the vampires, but someone out there is putting the entire vampire race at risk with these killings. If I don't find the truth, his actions will eventually bring down our entire house of cards. That's why it's so important that this community understand that I'm not a figurehead."

"You've certainly created a stir."

"Across all species in the Otherworld," she said. "The matter is being brought up at two other council meetings tonight, perhaps more." She paused. "Darius, my cousin was attacked last night in her own home. And it wasn't by any wannabe vampire. This was the real thing."

"Male or female?"

"I don't know—it was a very old vampire. No messy organ tissue left at all—except for a few bones, the intruder turned entirely to ash."

"Male, then, for the sake of conversation," Darius said. "Which of your cousins did he come after?"

"He attacked Sailor when she was sleeping."

"Sailor?" Darius said, sounding surprised.

He knows something! Rhiannon thought.

"Yes. Darius, if you know anything—"

"Don't you use that tone with me, young lady!" he said. "If I could prevent danger to anyone, I would. Especially Sailor. She is my godchild."

He turned and walked away from her. Jerry Oglethorpe looked at her and shrugged. "Rhiannon, Darius is old guard. He's not just powerful in our community.

He's extremely powerful in Hollywood and the entire film business. He's just huffy because you wounded his pride, saying what you did without consulting him first."

"Thanks, Jerry. Well, I guess I'm headed to the Snake Pit," she said.

He grinned. "I'll be there eventually myself. This is a big night for all of us Others. There's been a lot of anticipation and excitement about you and your cousins taking over as Keepers, you know. Anyway—" he smiled "—I'll see you there. Be careful on the drive over, okay?"

"Why?" she asked sharply.

"Okay, Rhiannon, now you're sounding paranoid. Be careful on the drive because it's late and this is L.A., where way too many people drive drunk, and drunk or sober, everyone drives at eighty and changes lanes without signaling. Okay?"

She smiled. "Yes, Jerry, okay. And thank you."

She left the House of Illusion and was approaching her car when she heard someone behind her. Instinct sent shivers up her spine, and she spun quickly to assess the threat.

It was the actress Audrey Fleur. She clapped as Rhiannon turned. "Bravo, Miss Gryffald. Wonderful speech."

"Thank you," Rhiannon said, even though she was well aware that the other woman was being sarcastic.

"Terribly distressing, of course," Audrey said. She walked over and leaned against Rhiannon's Volvo. "It was so upsetting last night when that poor man started asking about his lover. I'm assuming he's one of the dead?"

"Yes."

"Do you think that a rogue vampire would really defy your authority?" Audrey asked, her eyes wide, her voice scared—but a smile was playing over her lips.

"I don't actually *know* much of anything yet, Audrey. When I do, everyone will learn what *I* learn. I'll call a special session of the council if necessary."

"Wow! You really think you're that good?"

"I intend to be."

"Well, bravo once again. See you at the Snake Pit," Audrey said, pushing away from the Volvo and starting toward her own car. She turned back. "Oh, by the way, do be careful. Keepers have been killed in the past, and we would never want anything so horrible happening to you."

Rhiannon stared after Audrey and wondered if the woman really did hate Sailor for "stealing" her role. Because if she hated Sailor, she might hate them all.

But they'd killed the vampire who attacked Sailor last night.

And it obviously hadn't been Audrey, since she was definitely alive—or rather, undead—and kicking.

She got into her Volvo and looked at the clock in the dash. 1:00 a.m. The meeting had lasted nearly two hours, she noted. As she drove, she replayed events in her mind.

Last night they had killed a vampire. Maybe that had been *the* vampire, the one killing human beings and draining their blood. She needed to ask Brodie about that theory, see if maybe he thought they had come to the end of it. Of course, they didn't know who the dead vampire had been....

Or if he'd been working with anyone else.

She pulled onto the freeway. This being L.A., there were plenty of other cars; some sped by her, and some she passed. No big deal either way, since the Snake Pit was only a few exits away.

She had just taken the exit ramp when she felt a huge jolt on the roof, as if a pterodactyl had landed.

She fought with the steering wheel to keep the car under control, almost veering into the steel guardrail but managing to straighten the wheels just before she swerved into it.

She reached the end of the ramp and turned onto the street. Luckily the Snake Pit was just a few blocks ahead.

The thing slammed onto the top of the car again, sending her careening onto the sidewalk. She heard the undercarriage of the Volvo rip over the curb and managed to steer back onto the street just before crashing into a boutique.

Shaking, terrified, she delved desperately into her mind for some idea as to what to do, and then she knew. She had only one choice, and it was a choice she'd never imagined she would have to make.

She should have practiced more often, should have listened to her father.

Oh, Lord, she should have started as soon as this case began.

She slammed to a halt and sat there for a long moment. It would come again, she knew.

It could be anything, an Elven, a werewolf, a vampire, or, a shapeshifter, with its ability to become anything at all....

Shapeshifters lost strength when they shifted. Werewolves could only rip and tear when they changed into the beast they were at heart. Elven might be powerful, but they would always be Elven, the least aggressive of the races. And vampires…well, she could be a vampire, too.

And so she straightened and willed herself to change. She felt her fangs growing, her canine teeth elongating, and she felt the strength growing in her limbs.

She got out of the car and looked around, saw nothing.

A Buick drove by. The young couple in it stared at her, and the man hit the gas.

"I know you're out there!" Rhiannon cried. "You're out there, and you're a coward, attacking by night. Well, you won't get me. You won't get me, and you won't get my cousins. I will destroy you first, do you hear me? Your reign of terror is over!"

There was no sound at all then. Not even a car drove by.

Shaking, she got back into the driver's seat.

Had it been Audrey Fleur? Had Audrey been truly threatening her outside the House of Illusion?

She turned the key in the ignition and winced at the sound the car made as she started driving again, then cursed softly. Her car was going to need work.

For a moment it occurred to her that maybe her attacker was trying to frighten her into leaving L.A. or just cowering in her house, too afraid to perform her duties. And then…

Then, when she was weak and beaten, strike again and…

Take over the city? Could it be that simple?

She made her way the last few blocks to the Snake Pit, left her car with the valet and hurried inside.

She saw Brodie sitting in a booth with Sailor and Barrie the minute she arrived. The club was full; it seemed as if everyone from every race had shown up. Of course, since the shifters held their meeting there, they outnumbered everyone else. Piped-in music was playing in the background.

Brodie stood, frowning as she arrived. "What's wrong?" he asked her quickly.

"I'm fine," she said, feeling too shaken to talk about it. She slid into the booth next to Barrie. "How were your meetings?" she asked them.

"Mine was lovely," Sailor said.

"Everything went very well," Barrie said gravely. "And by the way, nice picture of you and Brodie in the paper today."

"Yes, the gnome came through," Rhiannon said.

"How was *your* meeting?" Barrie asked Rhiannon.

"Lovely," she said sarcastically. "I told them one of them might be a murderer. I went over really well. Although," she added, "some of them did seem to genuinely appreciate my honesty."

Barrie smiled. "I brought the situation up with the shapeshifters. They all swore they'd keep their eyes open."

"I spoke to Hugh on my way in," Brodie said. "He said that he talked to the werewolves, but they assured him that a wolf wasn't guilty—you wouldn't be looking at a few pinprick marks if a werewolf had gone rogue, you'd be looking at victims that had been torn apart."

"True," Rhiannon admitted.

"Did you tell them about last night?" Sailor asked her.

Rhiannon nodded.

"Wait, wait!" Barrie said, raising her hand. "Are we really supposed to be discussing our meetings? I thought we were supposed to keep some confidentiality going."

"Between *us?*" Rhiannon asked her.

"Yes, even between us," Barrie said.

"There are times when we're going to have to be open and brutally honest—especially with each other. When a situation might not involve the entire community, that's one thing. When what happens may have repercussions for everybody, that's different," Rhiannon said. "We're still learning here, of course. We were thrown into this situation. But that's the way I see it, and I think my view is logical."

"I don't really see—" Sailor began, but then she broke off. "There's Darius. And he's looking for me. He looks concerned. Excuse me, please, I'm going to go talk to him."

Rhiannon watched her cousin walk away, and then turned to Brodie and Barrie. "She doesn't seem to realize that she was attacked by a vampire last night, and if Merlin hadn't hit the alarm, we couldn't have stopped it."

"Do you think the attack last night was directed against *her*—or against her because of *you?*" Barrie asked.

"I don't know. I just don't know." Rhiannon looked at Brodie. "I had a wonderful moment tonight thinking that although we might never know his identity, we might have killed the killer last night. But now I don't think that's the case."

"What happened?" he asked sharply.

"Something kept attacking my car when I was on

my way here. And I'm pretty sure that Audrey Fleur threatened me," she told him.

He frowned. "Audrey?"

"You suspect her, too?"

"I wish to hell I knew—but she's the only vampire in the play," he reminded her. "Do you know if she's here?" he asked, looking around.

She set a hand on his and said quickly, "I don't know. But she was getting into her own car. If she drove here, then it certainly wasn't her."

"She could have parked somewhere and come after you," he told her.

Her hand still rested on his, and suddenly she wasn't thinking about being attacked anymore. She was far more afraid of something that Sailor had said earlier. *Once you go Elven...*

She drew her hand back. "I want to act as if nothing disturbing happened at all. Whoever is behind this, I want them to believe that I can handle whatever they throw at me."

"There's a story in this somewhere," Barrie said, and then her attention was caught by something across the room. "Your nasty little costar is here," she told Brodie. "She's right over there with Sailor and Darius. And look who's joining them. That shapeshifter doorman from the theater—what was his name? Bobby something? He looks as if he's hungering for Audrey, who's fawning all over Darius."

"Bobby Conche," Brodie said. "And see how he's watching Sailor, too? He just loves actresses. All the pretty ones, anyway."

Brodie looked as if he was about to walk over and confront Audrey.

"Wait," Rhiannon said. "Let's watch and see what she does."

They watched, but Audrey didn't do anything interesting. She just sat there chatting.

"I'll go join them," Barrie said. "And I'll watch out for Sailor. No one is going to try anything in here tonight, that's for certain."

"All right," Rhiannon said.

When Barrie had gone, Brodie looked at Rhiannon and said, "I don't like it. You're in serious danger."

She smiled at him. "Brodie, we Keepers are well able to defend ourselves and keep the law."

He caught both her hands, and his eyes met hers. "Rhiannon, someone else is dead," he told her.

She swallowed, lowering her head. Her guilt was choking her.

This was happening on her watch.

"Today? Someone was killed today?" she whispered.

He shook his head. "I had my tech go through the casting lists, and so far four of the five people he researched and couldn't find are dead. I found a woman today at the bottom of a pond in the back of an estate not far from the theater. So far Tony Brandt can't get a handle on when she was killed—could have been a week ago, could have been two. She was completely submerged and…well, you know what nature does to a body," he said quietly.

"Brodie, what do I do?" she asked miserably.

"We'll find the truth."

"But—it's my responsibility."

"No one works without help, Rhiannon," he told her. "And the thing is, now you know you're in danger, so now you know to protect yourself from it. And chances are your attacker is connected to our killer—if it's not the same person—and now we know for sure that our killer is connected to the play."

"I'm sorry to say it, but if we really are looking for a vampire, then we need to look at Audrey."

"And Darius," he added quietly.

"Why would Darius risk everything he has in order to gain…nothing?"

"I don't know, but we need to investigate them both. It's hard. We can't pin them down with a 'where were you on the night of whenever,' because we don't have a time of death." He was quiet for a moment. "I don't want you alone, all right? Tomorrow…during the day…"

"What?"

He sighed. "I'll keep you with me."

She grimaced. "You don't sound terribly happy about that. And frankly, I'm more concerned about Sailor. She could have been killed last night."

"And you could have been killed tonight. Anyway, Sailor told me she's having a costume fitting tomorrow. She'll be surrounded by people," Brodie said.

"That doesn't explain why you don't sound happy about having me with you."

He drew a deep breath. "Because I'm going to be searching for a fifth body."

Chapter 9

They stayed for another hour. At one point Rhiannon ended up in conversation with Audrey, but she didn't say a word about being attacked on the way in, and if Audrey was expecting her to be upset or afraid, she didn't show it.

Brodie spent some time off in a corner with Tony Brandt, and she knew by watching his face that they were discussing the case.

Finally even the denizens of the night began to head home.

Rhiannon joined up with her cousins and Brodie, and they walked together out to the valet stand. "We're good to go," Rhiannon told him. "The three of us can take my car. We'll be all right getting home."

He stared at her incredulously. "Rhiannon, I respect you, and I know how competent you are. Whatever you said tonight, all the vampires are watching you now, and they look as if they've had a good slap in the face, a wake-up call, like they realize suddenly that someone *is* watching. But come on. Last night there was a vampire attack basically in your *own home*. Tonight— *as you were leaving the vampire council*—you were attacked. Try to shake me all you like, but I'm following you home."

She stared at him silently, then turned to hand over the slip for her car.

"Rhiannon?"

"You just said that you're going to follow me no matter what. Is there something I should say?"

He grinned, that slow, lazy Elven grin that made her go a little crazy every time she saw it, and the blood surged warm and hot through her veins, making her fingers tremble, as warning bells went off in her mind.

"I guess not," he said.

An attendant brought Rhiannon's car around. She slipped into the driver's seat, and Sailor got in next to her. "I'll go with Brodie so he isn't driving alone," Barrie told her.

"Whatever you want," Rhiannon responded, giving in to the inevitable. Her tone, however, was sharp.

A few minutes later, with Brodie's car visible in her rearview mirror, she waited for the sound of something huge landing on top of her car. She was tense, but Sailor didn't seem to notice.

"This has been such a great night," Sailor said. "I think Elven are the wise men of the Others. They're so intelligent and…rational. They were so nice to me, too."

"I'm so glad," Rhiannon murmured. "Barrie sure clammed up earlier."

"She feels that her duty is to the shifters, that our

first duty is to our Others, rather than ourselves. You know Barrie. Not happy unless she's crusading for something."

Finally they arrived at the compound—and with no further incidents, which left Rhiannon feeling both grateful and relieved.

She opened the gate and she drove through. Brodie was right behind her, and despite the fact that she wasn't looking at him and certainly wasn't touching him, she could somehow *feel* him.

They parked and got out of their cars. Sailor immediately spoke up. "Look, I know you all feel like you have to guard me like a pack of Dobermans, but I won't have it. We've got the tunnels connecting the houses, and we know from last night that the alarm system is working perfectly. I'm not saying we should take stupid chances, but what we *are* doesn't last a week, it's a lifetime commitment. I say we go through the houses, make sure everything's locked up tight and then we all stay in our own places. I'll ask Merlin to stay with me. Of course, if *you're* frightened…"

"I'm not frightened," Barrie said quickly. "But I do think we should check out all three houses together."

"And everyone sleeps with a cross on," Rhiannon said.

"Does that really work?" Sailor asked.

"My father said it's not the cross per se," Rhiannon said. "If you were Jewish, it would be a Star of David, and if you were Muslim, it would be the crescent. The point is that you wear a symbol of faith in a power greater than yourself. Oh, and put up some garlic. Vampires really don't like garlic—it makes them sneeze. So let's get started."

Rhiannon glanced at Brodie, who had been silent. He smiled at her and nodded. She realized that he was being intentionally silent, letting her take the lead. She felt a surge of gratitude for his sense of faith in her.

With Brodie in tow, they went to work. Luckily Sailor was a vegetarian who made a lot of Italian dishes, so her kitchen was well stocked with garlic. They left cloves around the windows and doors of each house.

Brodie checked closets, cabinets—and the tunnels. Merlin stuck to the main house, and followed them around. "I don't need to sleep, so I'll stand guard," he said gravely. "I'll watch over Sailor."

"I'll stay on the couch at Rhiannon's," Brodie said. He looked at Barrie. "Maybe you should stay with one of your cousins."

She shook her head. "I have work I've got to do before I go in to work. I'll be fine." They all stared at her. "Look, it's almost daylight. Vampires don't have the same strength in daylight that they do in darkness. Plus I've been practicing my shifting. If anyone gets in, I'll turn into a dust mite and hide until one of you comes." She grinned.

"It really might be better if you all stayed together," Brodie said.

"No!" Sailor protested.

"We are *Keepers*. We'll always face danger, Brodie," Rhiannon said. "We need to live our own lives despite that."

He nodded, not happy, but resigned.

As he turned and they headed for Pandora's Box together, Rhiannon thought she heard her cousins giggling. She turned quickly and saw them staring at her like a pair of doting old nanas. She shook her head slightly and hurried toward home, trying to ignore them. Brodie was staying with her for safety's sake. This was business, not pleasure.

Right?

"I think your cousins want us to sleep together," Brodie said.

Startled, her face turning a half dozen shades of red, she looked at him. "They, um, can be a bit juvenile."

He lowered his head, hiding a half smile as they stepped into her house. She locked the door behind them, turned…and found that he was ridiculously close to her. She looked up at him. The breath seemed to rush from her lungs.

"It doesn't matter what your cousins think," he told her. "It *does* matter what *you* think."

"What *I* think?"

"About us sleeping together."

There was so much she could say, and even more that she *should* say.

But she was speechless.

He reached out, lifting a strand of her hair. "It seemed like such a wonderful strategy to explain your presence at the theater so you could watch what was going on there. But right after it started—I mean *right* after it started—I wanted it to be true."

"You did?" she whispered, then shook her head. "No, no, that can't be true. You didn't have any faith in me."

"Oh, it was worse than that! I thought you were an ineffectual, self-centered pain in the ass."

"How…rude," she told him. They were face-to-face, so close they were practically touching. His Elven magic seemed to wash over her in a tidal wave of staggering warmth and sensuality, and golden seduction.

She set her fingers on his chest, straightening the collar of his tailored shirt. "That's okay—I don't think I could even begin to describe my first impression of you."

He caught her hands. "But it's changed?" he asked softly.

"The jury is still out," she said. It wasn't, though. Not really. He was dedicated. He was...noble, even, she thought. He was Elven; she was a Keeper. Elven could be anything in life, and he had chosen, like her, to protect and serve.

There were a million reasons why she should back away. They were embroiled in a horrible situation together, surrounded by death and tragedy, by a threat to everyone and everything they knew, to the entire world of the Others and the city where they all hid in plain sight.

And yet the worst of it was that she was worried not for her world but for her heart and soul.

And not a drop of the fear tearing through her could save her.

Maybe it was everything in her life coming together in this one moment that aroused her need for him in that moment.

Or maybe it was because he was Elven, and as everyone knew, Elven radiated sensuality...sexuality.

Or maybe it was just that strangely ineffable something that was an innate part of existence, the unique chemistry that made one person more attractive and seductive than anyone else.

All she knew was that she'd never imagined wanting anyone the way she wanted Brodie McKay at that moment.

Alarms went off in her mind, her instinct for self preservation screaming a warning somewhere deep inside.

A warning that went unheard.

She moved closer to him, until her body was pressed against his. She placed her hand on his cheek and marveled at the strongly sculpted line of his jaw as she looked into his eyes, entranced by the blue that seemed to hold the ocean, the sky, the world.

"Right or wrong," she said huskily, "I say, let's do it."

He smiled, slowly, sensually, and heat suffused her body. At last she felt his lips on hers, his tongue teasing along her lips and then sliding into the depths of her mouth. Her knees threatened to give out, yet she felt ridiculously strong at the same time.

When her knees finally did give way, he picked her up. His eyes were fixed on hers as he walked toward the stairs, so focused that he bumped into Mr. Magician as he passed. Mr. Magician moved his gloved hand and dropped a fortune into the receptacle. Brodie balanced Rhiannon against his chest and reached for the card.

"What does it say?" she asked.

He grinned. "'Do it.'"

"You're kidding."

"I am not," he assured her.

"Then we've been blessed," she said softly. "So let's do it."

Laughing, he carried her up the stairs, then paused at the top.

"To the right," she whispered.

He used his shoulder to push open the bedroom door. The light from the hall drifted in, spotlighting the bed with its red and black cover. He fell to the mattress with her still in his arms, then paused, looking down at her for a long moment before he kissed her again.

Is this Elven magic? she wondered.

Or something more?

No kiss had ever been so deep, so erotic, such an irresistible promise of what was to come. So intimate—and becoming more so with every sweep and thrust of his tongue. When they broke apart, they were both breathless. He struggled out of his jacket; she worked at the buttons of his shirt. Her sweater hit the floor, and their shoes flew in several directions. It seemed to take forever to strip off their clothing, but each second felt precious and seductive. Finally he lay naked beside her, and she saw that his skin was golden everywhere, the heat from his body like liquid gold that rushed through her with the irresistible force of lava. Again they kissed, and then his kiss left her mouth, moving, sweeping golden fire along her skin. She clutched his shoulders, pressed her lips to them. And as he moved against her, she was compelled to move, as well, responding to every slight caress, every breathless touch of his lips.

His hands were large, his fingers long and his touch exquisite. She felt his caress and then his kiss, followed by the weight of his body as he moved lower. She arched against him until she had enough leverage to flip him over so he was lying beneath her, and then she leaned over him, her hair brushing along his flesh as she kissed her way lower, until he caught her in his arms again and they rolled together, entangled in each other's limbs. And then he was above her again and finally, *finally,* inside her. The room itself seemed to shimmer with each golden thrust of his body.

She was heedless of anything beyond the bed, yet

acutely aware of every sensual moment between them:
the feel of the satin coverlet beneath them; the vibrancy
of the hall light as it streamed across his skin; the very
air between them, which seemed visibly charged with
electric ions. But most of all she was aware of the way
his muscles rippled with his slightest movement, and the
way his body seemed to be a part of hers. The rhythm
between them grew frantic and strong, accompanied by
the beating of their hearts, the rasp of their breath and
the sweet, driving, near-desperate sensation growing at
her core. She arched, she writhed, she rose to meet his
every movement, their passion explosive and golden,
rising to a burst of searing fire that broke into a climax
as molten as the sun, as the power of their very existence. Finally she lay there feeling the sleek beauty of
his damp skin, feeling *him,* his heartbeat, his breathing, the touch of his flesh hot against her.

It was the most physically amazing thing she had
ever experienced, carnal and erotic. And then he was
above her again. He kissed her mouth with the greatest tenderness and reverence, and she realized that as
ridiculous as it might sound, as foolish as it might be,
she was in love…not lust, but love.

But whether it was the kind that could defy the
world and the ages, the kind her parents had shared, she
didn't know.

She did know that she would fight to hold on to what
she had…

Lest the world take it away.

He lay at her side, and she curled against him. She
worried that she might feel awkward after her climax
burned out and the flames of their lovemaking died
down to embers, but she felt as if she was right where

she should be. And her fascination with every inch of his flesh lingered. Would always linger, she was sure. Somewhere up in the hills a pack of coyotes started to howl, and she even heard the cry of an owl on the wind, the night itself beautiful and wild.

His hand was resting on her back, holding her gently near, and she winced at the thought that they had met only because people had died.

"Don't," he said softly.

She lifted her head, seeking his eyes, and realized that he had slipped past her guard and read her mind. For some reason that didn't even bother her the way it would have just a few days ago.

"We will find the killer," he said softly. "And neither of us can change what happened before we came on to the case." He moved, shifting to look more directly into her eyes. "Everyone, no matter what responsibilities they have to live up to, gets their time to live and their chance to enjoy that time. If we don't take that, then there's no sense to any of it."

She nodded. "I just... I was just thinking that it seems wrong to be so happy when..."

"I know. But you can't let yourself think that way," he whispered.

"But—"

"No."

He kissed her lips again.

Making love this time was slow. Deliciously slow, almost agonizing. The first time had been filled with desperation, while the second was filled with intimate foreplay and long moments in which desire spilled slowly into ecstasy, until finally the world filled with explosive golden fire again. Finally, when she lay panting in his arms once more, she realized that the world *was* golden. Morning had come, and a new day was beginning.

Brodie opted not to go in to the station that day. Rhiannon slept late, but when she finally came down the stairs, he was immediately aware of her, the sweet scent of her like a beacon in the air.

She walked over carrying an oversize cup of tea and sat on the corner of the desk in the corner of the living room, where he was using her computer.

"What've you been doing?" she asked him.

He leaned back. "I talked to the kid we met the other night—Nick Cassidy. He's sending Jordan Bellow's toothbrush and hairbrush to Tony Brandt, and making arrangements for his dental records to get to the morgue to confirm his ID." He was quiet for a minute. "I tracked down acquaintances of the other probable victims, looking for items for a DNA comparison, hunted for dental records. I'm checking their banking and credit card information, putting together a history of their last known movements."

"Do you still want to check out the lakes and stuff? I can be ready in about ten minutes," she said.

He nodded. "Yes, I have to. We're still missing one probable victim. I want to see if we can find her."

"Did you find any places they all frequented?" she asked.

"Yes. They all used the same gas station on Vine. Three of the five went to the same donut shop. All five used two places whose names are a bunch of letters and numbers. I was about to call the credit card company to find out what they are."

"Let me see," Rhiannon said.

He beckoned her closer, so she could see the computer screen. It was a mistake. Her hair fell and brushed his shoulder, and he was suddenly overwhelmed by the scent of her.

To his relief, she straightened suddenly.

"What?" he demanded, spinning the chair to face her.

"I know what they are!" she told him. "MC1888—that's the Magic Café. MC for Magic Café, and 1888—the year Hugh Hammond was born."

Brodie was suddenly deeply scared—for Rhiannon.

"What's the other one?" he managed to ask, but he already knew.

"MGHOI stands for Magic, House of Illusion."

Brodie turned and started reading through the credit card reports. "Add that to Nick Cassidy…three visits to the Snake Pit. Lila Mill, two visits the Snake Pit. Rose Gillespie, one visit." He looked over at Rhiannon. "Whoever the killer is, I have a feeling it's someone we see every day of our lives."

He heard a sudden whir.

Mr. Magician was doing his thing again.

He walked over to the machine and picked up the little card. He read it, then turned to Rhiannon, stunned. "It says 'Bingo,'" he told her after a long moment.

"I'll get ready. We'll go and search for the last victim."

He nodded glumly. "I'm going to get some patrolmen working on it, too. Even narrowing the search sites down to the general area of the theater, there's too much water to cover," he said quietly. He looked up at her, worried. "I shouldn't do the play tonight. I should go with you to the Snake Pit."

She smiled. "Thank you for worrying, Brodie, but we can't be together if being together means we can't do our jobs. I'll be fine at the club. You have to do the show tonight. When you're done, you can come and find me at the Snake Pit."

He sat back down at the computer and began typing hurriedly.

She stepped up behind him. "What are you writing in such a frenzy?" she asked him.

"I'm going to give your cousin a story to run in the paper. And then we'll see who—and what—comes out of the woodwork."

By four o'clock Rhiannon was exhausted. They'd checked out five bodies of water, two that were on private property and three that bordered various roads.

"Where now?" she asked Brodie as he slid back into the driver's seat.

He drew out his map, pointed north and said, "I have uniforms working up there, so…let's head over here, along Mulholland. There's a little man-made lake right in there, off a hairpin curve."

A hairpin curve? On Mulholland, that could mean anywhere.

Rhiannon nodded. "Wherever you want. I'm going to check on Sailor and Barrie," she said as she pulled out her cell. It didn't matter where they went. She was just along for the ride.

Barrie, who was at work, answered right away. "I'm working on an article using everything Brodie gave me. Don't worry, though. I'll be careful how I word things so I don't give away too much but I still draw out the killer."

They chatted for another minute or two, and then Rhiannon tried Sailor's number. It went straight to voice mail.

"I told her to listen for her phone," Rhiannon said crossly.

"It's Sailor, Rhiannon. You know how she is. She starts reading a script and loses track of the world," Brodie said.

Rhiannon left a message, trying to keep her voice level as she told her cousin to call her ASAP.

A few minutes later Brodie pulled off the road beside an empty lot. She looked at him. "I don't see any water," she said.

"It's over that little rise."

Brodie walked ahead of her, and she followed, not really giving him her attention. She was worried, and she needed to find Sailor. Brodie was right, of course. No matter what she said, Sailor would get involved in something and forget about her phone. In fact, she probably hadn't even heard it, because she was still at the costume designer's office. Barrie would be picking her up at the studio, and Barrie was still at work. Sailor was undoubtedly in the midst of a fitting, standing there all pinned together, unable to move.

In which case she was bound to call back soon.

They walked up the little hillock and then down. There was a small pond before them, longer than it was broad. It stretched toward several mansions on the right, a couple of which had docks extending into the water, and down toward a private road on the left. She wondered why Brodie had elected to park on the far side of the hill, then realized if he'd come in via the guarded entrance to the community, people would have started talking, and this was the kind of case he would want to keep quiet until he knew what he was dealing with.

Brodie started walking toward the houses, but she headed directly toward the water, her phone in her hand again. She hated to do it, but she put a call through to Darius. He would know how to reach the costumer, and even if she was being ridiculous, Rhiannon was desperate now to know that Sailor was all right.

Darius didn't answer his own phone, of course. Instead she got Mary.

"Hello, dear," the older woman said when Rhiannon introduced herself. "He's with a client, but you just hang on and I'll go see if I can get him for you."

Rhiannon walked along the shoreline, waiting.

Then she stopped, frozen.

About fifteen feet out she could see something that definitely didn't belong there. It looked like a cross between a blob and a mannequin, but she had a terrible feeling she knew exactly what it really was.

Brodie was quite a distance away at that point, so she waded into the water. It was shallow at first. Then she cursed as the bottom sloped abruptly away and she found herself in water up to her waist. She held her phone over her head and kept walking, seeing as she was already wet.

She reached for a piece of fabric, hoping to draw it nearer.

And an arm came free in her grasp.

She began to scream.

Chapter 10

They'd found her, Brodie thought dully.

The last of the victims. Or the last of the victims they knew about, anyway.

God help them. They had to stop the killer before he struck again.

The corpse belonged to a woman, though that wasn't easy to discern.

She'd been in the water for several weeks at least. She'd been weighted down with a cinder block—undoubtedly obtained from a pile in the vacant lot—until she grew too bloated with gas for it to hold her. The rope was a typical brand, found at any local hardware store. And after so much time, there was no evidence of any other sort left at the crime scene.

Tony Brandt had come out to the scene to inspect the corpse—the pieces of the corpse, at any rate. Fish had eaten away at the soft tissue, and once it had made its way to the surface, birds had been at it, as well.

"Fingers are missing again," Tony Brandt said.

"How are you doing with identifying the others?" Brodie asked him.

"Two out of four, and since one was Lila Mill, I'm assuming this is Rose Gillespie. I had her head shots sent over. She was a pretty girl when she was alive," Tony said. "Did you ever meet her, by any chance?"

Brodie shook his head. "I wasn't at the original auditions or the callbacks. I got the part when the original actor took off for home."

"Ah, yes, that's right. Well, I'll do my best with what I have. I'm taking her to the morgue now, but…" Tony's voice trailed off.

But…

But the body had been in the water awhile, plus it had rained in the past few weeks, washing away any evidence from the shore—even the damned weather seemed to be against them.

"Anyway, you know where to find me when you need me," Tony said.

Brodie motioned to Adam Lansky, who had come out with the crime-scene team.

Adam wasn't used to being away from his computer, much less coming face-to-face with a rotting corpse. He looked ill.

"You all right? You're green," Brodie said.

"I'm okay. Hey, if I'm ever going to get into the field, I've gotta learn, right?"

Brodie nodded. "I'm going to leave you here, because Rhiannon and I have to get ready for work. Just keep an eye on what's going on, and when they're done here, so are you. You've done good work, Adam."

"Thanks," the younger man said.

Brodie turned and stared halfway up the rise, where Rhiannon was standing with a police blanket around her shoulders. She was drenched from the lake, but she was calm now. In fact, she had composed herself quickly after discovering the corpse, which was tough. Even a seasoned detective might have screamed at finding himself at the business end of a decomposing arm.

Adam followed the direction of Brodie's gaze. "You're lucky. How many women look that pretty soaked in slime? And she's so talented."

"You've seen her play?" Brodie asked.

"Yeah," Adam said. "I went to the Mystic Café." He flushed. "I saw her last night. I was curious after I saw that picture of you and her. She's good."

"Yeah, she is," Brodie murmured. "All right, we're going. Call me if anything major turns up."

"Hey, Brodie!" Adam said. Brodie looked back, and Adam pointed toward the hill. "You might want to watch it. There are two news teams up there. The uniforms are keeping them out of the immediate area, but when you're leaving… And if you show up on the news, everyone at the theater is going to know you're a cop."

"Thanks," Brodie said. He looked up the hill. Rhiannon was still standing there in her blanket. There really was no way to get to his car without going by the news crews. He turned back to Adam. "I need you to get my car. Send Rhiannon down to me. We'll walk out by the road and meet you at the corner."

Adam grinned. "Pleasure, Brodie."

Adam watched as Brodie climbed the hill and talked

to Rhiannon, who quickly started down toward him. He had no idea what he should say to her. It was one thing to view a body on a coldly clinical autopsy table.

It was quite another to find one decomposing in a pool of algae-coated water and muck.

"You all right?" he asked her when she got there.

She nodded. "I'm fine now. Darius got hold of Sailor, and she just called me back. Brodie, this is all so horrible. The attack on Sailor, the dead woman—none of it seems real. And Sailor…she just doesn't realize her own danger."

"She's stronger than she looks," Brodie said. "Now come on. We have to walk around to where Adam is meeting us with the car. I really don't want to get caught on camera."

She nodded, but she still seemed lost in her own thoughts as they started walking.

"Rhiannon, Sailor is going to be all right."

"I hope so. She's the Elven Keeper, and the Elven—" she began, and then broke off, looking at him.

"You think the Elven are the weakest among the Others?" he asked her. "Let me tell you something. Elven have brought down vampires and werewolves—and more than once. We may not have fangs or claws, but we know all about stakes and silver bullets. And we have one asset that the rest of the Others tend to forget about when they're in full attack mode."

"What's that?"

"Brains—and the ability to think before we plunge in."

"Oh, Brodie! I didn't mean to offend you, it's just that I'm not sure Sailor has ever even tried to access her Elven qualities, other than teleporting."

"And you've had a lot of practice accessing your inner vampire?" he asked her sharply.

"No," she admitted. "But I'm going to get a lot of practice now."

They skirted close to the water at that point. He must have made a face, because she looked at him and almost smiled.

"You really hate water, huh?" she asked.

"I don't hate it. I can swim, and I've even gone diving a few times. We just can't be away from solid earth for any length of time," he said.

Adam pulled up at that point, so they stopped talking as they got in the car and Brodie thanked the tech for his help. They both waved as Adam walked away.

They were silent for most of the drive. Finally she asked, "Brodie, all these people were dead before you ever got the case, right?"

He nodded.

"Why would someone have targeted them? Hatred? Jealousy? Could it really be over a role in a play? It couldn't even be the *same* role, since the killer went after both men and women."

"Here's what we know. All the victims auditioned for *Vampire Rampage*. With the possible but unlikely exception of the one you found this morning, all the bodies have tiny puncture marks, but they could have been inflicted by a sharp instrument, but if that's true, the intent was to make the murders look like the work of a vampire. And Sailor was *definitely* attacked by a vampire, now deceased. You were attacked by someone or something that could have been a vampire. We don't know for sure that the attacks on you and Sailor are connected to the murders, but my gut tells me they are. One way or another, a vampire has to be in on this. The question is whether a human being is part of it or not. A human being who knows about the existence of vampires could be making use of one of them for his—or her—own purposes."

By then they had reached the compound, so she pulled her clicker out of her purse to open the gate, and they continued up the driveway.

"You can just drop me off, you know," she told him. "I know you have to be ready for your call, and I don't want to make you late."

He shook his head. "I'll wait. I'll take you to the Snake Pit and meet you there after the show."

"You don't need to do that. I was pretty shaken up before, but I'm all right now."

"I believe you. But there's not a soul out there who isn't *more* all right when someone else has their back. I don't mind *you* having *my* back," he said.

She smiled at that. "I like you having *my* back, too."

"I'm glad, but the way you just said that…probably not good for me to think about that right now."

"Or me," Rhiannon said. "Sorry, mental images and all that…" Her voice trailed off, and then she grew serious. "It's Sailor I worry about, Brodie. I mean, it is true—none of the three of us has had a lot of experience. Our dads were young—we didn't think we'd be taking over for years. But Barrie is dedicated to two things—journalism and being a Keeper. And as she pointed out to me, she can change into a dust mite and hide. Sailor…"

"Sailor is going to be all right. I don't think Sailor was the intended victim, I think *you* were. Whoever that vampire was, I sincerely doubt he intended to die in the attack. He could have killed Sailor long before you got there. He waited there for you, because his whole intent was to bring you into the fight."

"Maybe so, but all that means is that someone could use Sailor against me again," Rhiannon said, shaking her head in frustration. "I wish we knew where to start!"

"Why, Watson, that's easy," Brodie said.

"It is?" she asked. "Then why haven't we solved this already?"

"Process of elimination, my dear Miss Watson."

He was glad to see a real smile curve her lips. "Wait! I don't want to be Watson. I want to be Sherlock."

"No doubt, but I'm the detective," he reminded her.

Brodie waited in the living room while she hurried upstairs to shower and get changed. The temptation to join her was painful, but they had to remember who they were. And he was sure she was going to be scrubbing herself rigorously—trying to wash away the scent and feel of death.

There was a rap on the door, and he answered it. This time Merlin had knocked.

"Come in," Brodie said.

"I'm not interrupting?" Merlin asked.

"Not at all. Rhiannon is getting ready for work. I'm going to drop her at the club before I go to the theater," Brodie said.

Merlin nodded. "Have you seen the news?" he asked.

Brodie arched a brow and walked over to turn on the television. An attractive reporter was on the air at the scene of the crime. He stood silently watching with Merlin by his side, wondering just how much the press had figured out so far.

Luckily, while the cops had connected the victims,

the press had yet to do so. But tomorrow, after Barrie's story hit the papers, everyone would know they were searching for a serial killer. The details wouldn't be in the article, but a warning would be.

"Five," Merlin said woefully. He looked at Brodie. "How many more do you think there will be?"

"I don't know," Brodie admitted. "If we're lucky, none." He prayed that was true, and that he could keep L.A.'s newest Keepers safe.

Mr. Magician began to whir. Brodie turned just as the gloved hand dropped a card into the receptacle. "Again," he murmured in disbelief.

Merlin smiled. "Don't be so surprised. That's old Eli Wertner. He was famous for his coin-operated machines. Poor old Eli. I don't think he quite got the hang of being a ghost, but something of him remains in the machine. He was a good man. I'm sure he's only trying to help."

Brodie walked over to the machine to take the card.

"Well?" Merlin asked him.

Brodie looked over at Merlin. "'Everyone has an agenda. Charity begins at home.'"

Merlin shook his head worriedly. "Someone is out to hurt these girls," he said. "Whatever you do, please don't leave them alone."

"I don't intend to," Brodie said grimly. "Of course, it would be helpful if your old friend would make his messages a little clearer."

Rhiannon was really enjoying performing at the Snake Pit, a realization that surprised her after the day she'd had.

No amount of soap and water had made her feel any

better. Even though they were short on time, she hadn't been able to bring herself to get out of the shower, and after she'd scrubbed and shampooed for the fourth time she'd found herself wishing that Brodie had come up and joined her. She felt guilty for that, as she stood there with the stench of death still on her from a young life cut short, but she couldn't help the longing of her heart.

She knew she had to hurry, though, so she told herself it was a good thing he wasn't reading her mind at that moment. Besides, they had obligations. They were what they were, she a Keeper and Brodie Elven and a cop. They could never have a normal relationship, because their lives weren't normal. *They* weren't normal.

When she finally stepped from the shower, got dressed and went downstairs, she found that they had a visitor—Merlin—so it was a good thing Brodie had opted for responsibility over pleasure.

But now, having been at the club for a few hours, she was actually enjoying herself. She'd decided to mix things up and do something different from what she'd done with her band and at the café, opting for a mix of the classics and show tunes she'd always loved, and the piano instead of a guitar. The audience that night included werewolves, Elven, shapeshifters, vampires— even a tall, charming leprechaun and his girlfriend, an exceptionally pretty gnome. And of course there were plenty of human beings who had no idea of the true nature of the Others surrounding them.

Best of all—almost making her forget that she had discovered a decaying corpse that afternoon—Sailor was in the room.

Rhiannon was halfway through her second set when she saw Jerry Oglethorpe come in. He always looked like a magician, she thought, whether he was performing or not. He waved to her, then joined Sailor at her table.

At ten-thirty Hugh Hammond arrived and joined them. Rhiannon saw Sailor excuse herself and rise, and she felt a moment's panic, even missing a beat, as she watched her cousin leave the room. She didn't know why she was disturbed. Sailor was probably just heading to the ladies' room.

Rhiannon told herself that even though the killer had something to do with *Vampire Rampage,* so Sailor might be in danger on her own, too, not only because of her. But the cast couldn't possibly be there yet; the show had only just ended.

But she *was* unnerved, so she excused herself the minute she finished her song, taking her break a few minutes early. She saw Declan frown and look at his watch, but she didn't care. She rose from the piano bench and headed downstairs for the restrooms.

Everything at the Snake Pit was perfect. She entered an elegant lounge the minute she stepped through the door to the ladies' room, smiled at the attendant and called out, "Sailor?"

There was no answer.

"You looking for a friend, sweetie?" the attendant asked. "There's no one in here right now."

Rhiannon gave her a swift thank-you and hurried out, her speed increasing as she ran to the main entrance. She gasped in relief when she saw Sailor, who was heading over to the nicely landscaped area Declan had set up to one side to accommodate smokers, since the law now prohibited smoking inside.

The thing was, Sailor didn't smoke.
And someone was following her.

The play went well; the ensemble had grown tight, and Brodie thought wryly that he didn't mind acting. In fact, it was fun. The only downside was that he found himself constantly looking out at the audience, wishing that he knew whether anyone there had auditioned for the play. They'd found all the dead they knew about so far, but that didn't mean there might not be more to come.

He was determined that the Gryffald cousins would not be among those at risk. Not on his watch.

As soon as the show ended, he hurried to his dressing room to change. He was eager to get to the Snake Pit as soon as possible.

He'd just finished changing when Hunter Jackson came in, beaming and clearly thrilled with the way show was going. "Hey, Mac—we're heading out to the Snake Pit in a little while. Want to join us?"

"I was planning on it already, so sure," Brodie told him.

"I can't get over how well things are going," Jackson said. "We're at capacity every night, and we haven't even officially opened yet. The internet campaign is going great, and I've got a team already working on a game we can release when the movie opens."

"You've hit the jackpot."

"Yeah," Hunter said, and paused. "People are so strange, you know? They love vampires, think they're sexy. They don't get the dead and rotting part. Plus they like to be scared. You know, if there's news about a vampire cult meeting out in the woods, they want to go out in the woods. Me, I stay as far away as I can, but I thank God that most people aren't like me, at least when they go to the movies."

There was a tap at the door. Hunter opened it to find Kate Delaney.

"You guys coming?" she asked. "I feel the need for champagne!"

Lena Ashbury, in tight jeans and a sequined top, popped up behind Kate. "Did someone say champagne?" she asked.

"You sure did," Kate said, laughing. "Where's Audrey? Is she coming, too?"

"Oh, she took off already. She said she'd meet us at the club," Kate said.

Brodie surged to his feet and headed toward the door, feeling uneasy. Audrey was the only vampire in the cast, and she had gone on ahead.

There was no way to know for sure that the murders had taken place right after the show, but since he'd seen one of the victims in the audience, it seemed possible that the others had come to see the show as well, and been targeted on their way out of the theater.

And then there was the fact that Audrey had been talking to Rhiannon just before her car was attacked.

"See you all there," he said. A moment later he left by the stage door and looked out at the parking lot.

He saw Audrey getting into her car.

And there was someone in the passenger seat.

Because Declan Wainwright worked so hard to keep the club's atmosphere intimate, there was a particularly large amount of foliage surrounding the 'smokers' corner."

Rhiannon knew that if she didn't stop Sailor quickly, her cousin would be hidden by the ornamental trees and tubs of flowers—along with whoever was following her.

"Sailor!" she shouted as she hurried in her wake.

Sailor stopped and turned back to look, and so did the person following her.

Rhiannon frowned when she saw who it was.

"Rhiannon, hey," he said.

"Hey, Adam," she said. He seemed abashed as she approached, while Sailor just looked curiously from one of them to the other.

"Adam, what are you doing here?" Rhiannon asked.

He blushed. "I saw your cousin leave, and I was worried."

"You were sweet to worry about me," Sailor said, "but who are you and why do you care?"

"He's a cop," Rhiannon explained. "Adam Lansky, my cousin, Sailor Gryffald. Sailor, Officer Adam Lansky."

"Do you work with Brodie?" Sailor asked.

"Yeah," he said, blushing. "And I know that Brodie is seeing Rhiannon, and that he worries about her, so since you two are cousins…I thought I'd just come out and bum a smoke or whatever, so I could make sure nothing bad was happening."

Rhiannon wondered if her perceptions had been off. Was Adam a vampire?

She casually moved closer to check him out.

No, definitely not.

"I'm fine," Sailor said. "The door is twenty feet away."

"Why are you out here at all?" Rhiannon asked her. "You don't even smoke."

"I'm meeting someone," Sailor said.

"What the— Who?" Rhiannon asked sharply.

"I don't know." Sailor handed her a cocktail napkin bearing the words, *I have information that is important to the Gryffald clan. Please join me for a cigarette.*

"Sailor—you got this note and you just came out here—all by yourself?"

"Well, of course. We're right in front of the club. There are big hairy wer—um, bouncers standing at the door, watching everything that goes on."

"Who gave you the note?" she asked.

Sailor flushed. "I'm not really sure. One of the servers—I wasn't paying attention."

Rhiannon stared at her for a moment, but she wasn't going to say anything about the stupidity of answering such a summons—especially *alone,* when people were dead and Sailor herself had been attacked—in front of Adam.

Instead she hurried past her cousin and headed straight for the smokers' corner, rounding a Japanese maple only to find the area empty. Whoever had sent Sailor the note had obviously realized she wasn't alone and managed to slip away unseen. More proof that a rogue vampire was on the loose? Because a vampire could easily have taken bird or bat form and flown away into the darkness.

Rhiannon wasn't sure whether to be angry that they had missed an opportunity to gain information—assuming that there really had been any information to be gained, and that the offer hadn't simply been the bait to get Sailor alone—or just grateful that her cousin was all right. She was also forced to acknowledge the possibility that Sailor had been the real target the other night, just as she might well have been tonight.

"There's no one here," she called back to her cousin. "Let's get back in. Sailor, I don't care how safe you think the Snake Pit is—*please* don't answer a summons like that again. Not alone." She turned to Adam. All she needed was a young geeky cop who knew nothing of the Otherworld following them around.

"Adam, thanks, and I don't mean to insult you, but please don't follow us. We're pretty tough, and we could wind up kicking your ass before we realized you were one of the good guys."

He laughed. "Okay, backing off right now."

"Rhiannon?"

At the sound of her name, she swung around to see Declan standing just outside the door and looking at her curiously.

"Everything okay?" he asked. "The audience is getting restless."

Rhiannon turned back to her sister. "I've got to get back in there. Sailor, please?"

"I'm coming. And I won't leave again, I promise."

"You should give me that napkin," Adam said. "I can get it to the forensic experts."

Rhiannon had the napkin and she wasn't letting it go. "I want to show it to Brodie first, Adam, and then he can get it to you. Now let's go," she said. "I'd like to keep working here."

Sailor nodded and headed back toward the entrance. Adam followed her, and Rhiannon brought up the rear. Declan was waiting for her at the door. "Everything all right?" he asked.

"Of course. I just ran out for some air—and to see Sailor for a minute."

Declan seemed to sense that something was wrong, because when she started to follow the others he caught her arm. "Look—I know you're worried, so let me watch Sailor," he said. "I promise, I won't let anything happen to her."

"Thanks," she said, feeling backed into a corner. Declan might not be in the play himself, but the Snake Pit was involved with the film, which meant he was involved, too.

And Declan had been there the night she and her cousins saw the show.

Declan was a Keeper for the shifters. And that meant he could be anything he wanted to be.

She prayed that Brodie would arrive soon.

Everyone was looking like a suspect to her.

Back at her piano, she no longer saw the room as being filled with charming people who loved music.

They'd all suddenly become evil.

Chapter 11

"Audrey!" Brodie called.

She paused just before sliding into the driver's seat and looked back at him. "Hey!" she called in return. "You going to the Snake Pit?"

"Yes, I heard you were going, too," he said. He walked over and bent down to check out the young woman in the passenger seat.

"This is Penny Abelard," Audrey said. "Penny, Mac Brodie. He joined the cast when we were in production, after someone had to drop out. Brodie, Penny tried out for the role of Lucy, which is when we met. She made the callbacks, and Darius Simonides has talked to her about a role in one of the touring companies."

"Penny, it's a pleasure to meet you," Brodie said.

"Likewise," she said. She looked like so many Hollywood hopefuls: reed thin, blonde and very pretty, with huge dark eyes.

He focused his mind on her. It didn't take much effort—her thoughts were wide-open and easy to read. She was a little bit jealous of Audrey, but mostly she was just anxious, hopeful, focusing all her dreams on getting that role. There was nothing evil to be found in her thoughts, not that he'd expected there to be.

"I thought it would be good for her career to be seen with us at the club," Audrey said as Penny continued to stare at him, wide-eyed. Audrey gave her a little punch in the arm. "That boy is taken," she said teasingly. "He's got a girlfriend. But he's fun to hang around with anyway. Mac, we're going to get going, okay?"

"I'll follow you," Brodie said.

"Think you can keep up with me? I drive pretty fast, you know," she teased.

He tried to zero in on Audrey's thoughts. It was hard, even painful. But all she was thinking about was the strong desire to beat his driving skills.

He stepped away from her quickly, acutely aware that he needed to preserve his strength in case something dangerous happened later.

"No drag racing," he told her. "The cops will be on us like…like flies on a corpse."

Audrey grinned. "I'll drive safely. Let's get going."

He wished he could take Penny Abelard in his car, but that would be obvious. Audrey knew the cops were looking for a killer—a vampire killer—and he didn't want her to start wondering whether he was who he said he was.

At least she wouldn't act if she knew he was right behind her. If she was even the killer. Penny's presence in her car was strongly circumstantial, but it wasn't exactly proof.

He hurried to his car. Audrey was already pulling out onto the street as he slipped his key into the ignition.

She drove fast, but safely. She even used her blinker.

She drove straight to the Snake Pit and pulled up by the valet stand.

Both women got out of the car safely.

He gave his own keys to the valet and joined the women, who had waited for him. Before they even made it to the door another car pulled up.

"Look, there's Hunter," Audrey said with a smile. "And he's got Lena and Kate with him. We're all going upstairs, I take it?" She turned to Penny. "His girlfriend is a singer here."

"Well, I'm heading upstairs," Brodie said. "I don't mean to tell the rest of the crowd where to go."

The newcomers joined them, and Brodie led the way upstairs. The room was filled, not an empty table in sight. Rhiannon was at the piano, running her fingers over the keys and singing. He took a moment just to look at her, his body responding to the mere sight of her in a way that could quickly turn embarrassing if he weren't careful.

He was startled out of his fantasy when Sailor came up behind him, greeting him with a kiss on the cheek before turning to the others. "I've got a table we can squash into," she said. "Darius is the only one with me at the moment, and I'm sure he'll be happy to see you all."

"Thanks," Brodie said.

"Hey, I met one of your coworkers tonight," Sailor said as she led the way to the table. "Adam Lansky. I think he's trying to be you—he was trying to keep an eye on us. Sweet, huh?"

Brodie frowned, uncomfortable with what she'd just told him. Adam had always been a desk jockey, and he was excellent at what he did. Today he'd come out to a crime scene. He'd gone to the Mystic Café. And now he was watching the Gryffalds at the Snake Pit.

No one knew more about the murders than himself, Tony Brandt—and Adam.

He looked around and saw Adam flirting with a couple of twentysomethings at another table. So long as he was leaving Rhiannon and her cousins alone... And then he felt guilty, because what if the guy's motives were totally on the up-and-up?

He slipped in next to Audrey and thought, *Hail, hail, the gang's all here.* And for some gut-level reason he was certain that, though he still didn't know the rhyme or the reason for what was going on, the killer was in the room.

Declan and Hugh were at a nearby table, and he saw Jerry Oglethorpe across the room. The other man looked at Brodie gravely and lifted his glass.

He left the table and walked toward the stage, catching Rhiannon's eye and nodding toward the side of the room. She didn't miss a note as she smiled and nodded back. Confident that she'd read his intent, he headed back to the others.

As soon as she announced that she was taking a break, he stood and went over to the stage to meet her. She caught his hand, and for a long moment they just stood there, staring into each other's eyes. He could sense that the audience was whispering about them.

As she drew him out of the room, she slipped something into his hand. As soon as they were outside, he frowned and looked at it.

"Sailor received this tonight. I saw her leave the room and ran after her," Rhiannon said. "I asked her what was going on, and she gave it to me."

"Who wrote it?" Brodie asked.

"I don't know. I called out to her because someone was following her—which turned out to be Adam—and by the time I reached the smokers' corner no one was there."

"Who gave her the napkin?"

"She didn't know. One of the servers."

"Then I'll talk to them all," he said grimly.

He held her arm as they returned upstairs, then watched as she made her way back to the piano. Instead of joining the others, he walked over to the bar, where Declan was standing.

Declan lifted a glass to him. "I hear you're a hit as an actor."

Brodie shrugged. "I've had worse undercover work, that's for sure."

"How many of your cast know who and what you really are?" Declan asked him.

"Well, any Other knows that I'm an Other, too, but I'm hoping no one knows that I'm a cop and I'm there investigating them. All." He stared at Declan. "Why were you at the show the same night the Gryffald girls were there?" he asked point-blank.

Declan stared back at him in surprise, then offered him a bitter smile. "You think *I'm* the murderer?"

"I didn't say that."

"Read my mind, Elven. You'll see that my actions are pure."

Brodie gave him a dry grin. "If I tried to read your

mind, you'd do your best to block me, so I'd be wasting my energy. I was just asking."

Declan let out a sigh. "I wanted to keep an eye on Barrie, find a way to get to know her better. She's a brand-new Keeper, responsible for the shifters, just like I am. When you came to the Snake Pit with Hunter Jackson, I recognized you right away—I've seen you in the papers a few times—and I realized you were working undercover. I already knew something serious was going on in the Otherworld. Rumors fly—no matter how people try to contain social media these days, someone is always posting or emailing something. I figured you were on to the same thing. I knew you were in the show, so I figured there must be a reason for that—that it had to be connected to your investigation in some way—and when I heard that the Gryffald girls were going it seemed like a good chance to kill two birds with one stone. That's all there is to it."

Was he telling the truth? Brodie decided to chance a probe into Declan's mind, and he had to admit he was surprised to find out that the Keeper was being sincere.

Brodie nodded. "In that case, I need your help."

"How?" Declan asked. "I'll do anything."

"Someone sent Sailor a note on a cocktail napkin, asking to meet her outside. Rhiannon went after her, but she never saw who was waiting. The note referred to the Gryffald family, so it could have been intended for any one of them. I have to talk to your servers and find out where that note came from."

Behind him, someone cleared his throat. Brodie turned to face Jerry Oglethorpe, owner of the House of Illusion.

Vampire.

"You don't need to question people," Jerry said quietly. "I sent the note, and the server messed up. It was intended for Rhiannon."

Two hours later, after the club had closed, Rhiannon sat at a table with her cousins, Declan, Brodie and Jerry.

"I think I know the vampire killed at the House of the Rising Sun," Jerry told them. "It was Celeste Monahue. Do you remember her?"

They all looked at him blankly.

Jerry sighed. "She was the Gloria Swanson of the vampire set—an actress who was huge in the forties and fifties. We don't age, not much, anyway, but this is Hollywood. There's always someone younger coming up. She stopped getting the roles she wanted. Darius told her that she had to accept the motherly parts when they came along, and that didn't sit well with her. She wanted work in my shows, but…magicians' assistants tend to be young and leggy, as well as beautiful. Then one day she told me she was going to make a comeback. A big comeback. And now…well, now I haven't seen her in a few days. She wasn't at the council meeting the other night. I wanted to tell you my suspicions, Rhiannon, but I didn't want to be obvious, so I wrote that note and asked you to meet me." He looked at Rhiannon apologetically, and then at Sailor. "I'm so sorry. I didn't mean to create a problem."

Rhiannon set a hand on his. "It's all right, Jerry. No harm done."

"Jerry," Brodie said. "Did Celeste say anything specific about her big comeback? What the part was or who was offering it to her?"

Jerry shook his head. "Nothing, sorry. All I know

is she hasn't been seen since. I don't think she would have planned anything evil herself, but she longed to be famous again—known for her talent and her beauty. I can see how she might have been easily led astray by someone promising her that if she carried out a 'mission' she'd get everything her heart desired. I think she was your vampire and now she's ash."

"Did she ever say anything—even in casual conversation—that might have indicated that she had an in anywhere?" Brodie pressed.

Jerry was thoughtful for a minute. "Well, I don't know if it means anything, but…she seemed fond of humans lately—not in a bad way, not as a food source," he amended quickly. "She said she enjoyed discovering their talents."

"Thank you, Jerry," Brodie said, and looked at Rhiannon. He was convinced now that more than one person was involved. Someone—someone human, he suspected—was pulling strings and getting vampires to work for them.

"Come to the House of Illusion on Sunday night," Jerry said. "Brodie, your show will be dark, and Rhiannon doesn't work at the Mystic Café or here on Sunday nights. We get a real variety of Others and humans in the audience. Someone is bound to talk about Celeste going missing, maybe even make the connection that she was the one who was killed at the House of the Rising Sun." He looked at each of the three Gryffald cousins in turn. "I'd like to help. You girls were just tossed into the fray. We owe your fathers, and we owe you."

"Thank you, Jerry," Rhiannon said, and her cousins echoed her words.

Declan rose, impatient. "Like it or not, you three are in it now. You're in it up to your teeth."

He was staring at Barrie as he spoke, which made sense, Brodie thought. They were both shifter Keepers, Declan the Coastal Keeper and Barrie the Canyon Keeper. The Snake Pit actually fell under her jurisdiction.

Then Declan turned to Sailor. "Honestly," he said. "There's been a string of murders—possibly committed by a vampire—and you leave your window open?"

Startled, she stared at him, then shoved her chair back angrily and stood up. "I think we've done what we can do here tonight," she said. "Could we go home now, please?"

The others rose.

"My article will be in tomorrow's paper," Barrie said. "Which means a whole lot of evil may come crawling out of the woodwork."

"Good. Maybe that will help us solve this thing soon," Declan said. "All of you, out now. I need to lock this place up for the night."

When they left the Snake Pit, it was in silence. Everyone was exhausted.

Barrie drove with Brodie, and Sailor went with Rhiannon. Caught up in her own thoughts, Rhiannon didn't realize until they reached the estate that Sailor seemed to be seething.

She slammed the door when she got out of the car.

"Sailor?" Rhiannon asked.

"Sorry—I'm fine. I'm not angry with you."

"What's the matter?"

"That man is an ass!" Sailor said.

"What man?"

"Declan Wainwright."

"Ignore him," Rhiannon said. "He thinks he's all that and a bag of chips. Half the time he treats *me* like a servant, too, but I have to be decent to him. I made more money tonight than all week at the Mystic Café. And I think he really is trying to help Brodie and me."

Sailor shook her head. "He makes me so mad! He's not an Elven Keeper, he's a shapeshifter Keeper— and he lives in *Malibu,* for God's sake. I'm an Elven Keeper—if someone wants to be a jerk to me, it should be Brodie. But he's not, and do you know why? Because he's Elven. He's decent, intelligent. He doesn't prejudge people. And it's not like I can just avoid the damned Snake Pit! It's a hot spot for everyone in the industry… everyone I need to know."

"Ignore him, Sailor. Just ignore him."

Sailor nodded. "Yeah, all right." She gave Rhiannon a hug. "Thanks," she said softly. "Good night, and don't worry—I won't leave any windows open."

Rhiannon saw Brodie watching them as Barrie waved and went off toward Gwydion's Cave. Rhiannon was touched when Brodie came over to join them and gave Sailor a fierce hug. "Get in your house and lock up," he told her. "You'll be fine."

"I will. And if you see our ghost-pa, Merlin, send him over to me, okay? He's a great watchdog." Her brows rose. "Hey, that's what we need. A watchdog."

"I'd like a dog," Rhiannon agreed.

"Well, good night," Sailor said.

Rhiannon and Brodie watched until she was safely inside the main house. Then he slipped his arm around Rhiannon. "Night. Time to rest," he murmured.

"Rest," she echoed. "And wind down…"

"Wind down," he repeated, grinning. "Nice euphemism."

Rhiannon laughed, fitting her key into the door lock. Brodie was leaning against her, and she started to laugh, ready to swing into his arms the minute they got inside. Then she saw that they weren't alone.

Merlin was standing there looking impatient, as if he'd been waiting for them forever. "Well?" he demanded.

"Just the man I wanted to see," Brodie said, and Rhiannon stared at him.

Just the man he wanted to see? *Now?*

"Why, what's happened? Have you found the killer?" Merlin asked.

"No, but we know who attacked Sailor, or at least we're pretty sure we know. Celeste Monahue," Brodie said.

"Celeste?" Merlin was clearly surprised.

"You knew her? And she's been in the House of the Rising Sun before?" Brodie asked.

"Of course I knew her. Years ago she was quite the femme fatale. She was certain she could compete with the young crop that appears yearly forever. She was a real vixen in her day, and she'd attended many a party at the House of the Rising Sun."

"So she *had* been invited in," Brodie said.

"Yes. But…why would Celeste attack Sailor, much less kill a bunch of actors who hadn't even gotten a part?" Merlin asked.

"I think," Brodie said, "that we're looking for more than one person, and the person we're looking for—

who may or may not be human—is getting vampires who want to get into, or back into, the business to—"

"—to commit murder," Rhiannon said, then grimaced. "These killings took place before my father left, but I'm sure whoever's behind this isn't worried that the bodies have come to light. He thinks that I'm too young and inexperienced to catch him. But he's wrong."

Merlin stared at her. "Then you'd better find him quickly. Because he might just get away clean, because the actual killers will have vanished—into ash."

"Barrie's article will hit the street tomorrow," Brodie said. "With luck we'll force our puppet master out into the open."

Merlin looked ready to start ranting, so Rhiannon quickly cut him off. "Sailor doesn't want to be alone, Merlin. She asked if you'd go over there and watch out for her."

"Of course," he assured her, already walking to the door. "What you girls need is a good dog."

Rhiannon stepped forward to open the door for him, but he was too upset for courtesy. He walked right through it, and when she looked through the peephole, she saw that he was heading toward the main house with a purposeful stride.

She turned to find Brodie standing directly behind her.

It was amazing, the response that an Elven, *her* Elven, could arouse in the human body. She'd thought that the reality of their situation would weigh so heavily on her that nothing could distract her.

She'd been wrong.

All Brodie had to do was touch her and her only thought became that all time was precious, and their time together rarest and most precious of all. He swung her easily into his arms. "I think we're alone now," he said huskily, moving toward the stairs.

"You know, I really can walk," she told him.

"Why bother?"

Later she didn't remember being carried up the stairs or reaching the bedroom. All she knew was that they were suddenly just…there, on the bed together, urgently kissing and trying to struggle out of their clothing at the same time. As soon as she was naked, Rhiannon looked up at him breathlessly.

"Did we teleport?" she asked.

"No…but we did travel at the speed of light," he said, smiling into her eyes.

And then he was kissing her again. She kissed him in return, breathing him in, and even the scent of him seemed golden. When he moved against her, she moved against him, her body curving to echo his every shift. The taste of his kiss was sweet and suggestive and erotic, and when they finally broke away they were both breathless, staring at each other in wonder for a long moment. And then they were touching again. She pressed her lips to his shoulders while he ran his hands along the length of her back and down to her hips. Her fingertips seemed to streak with fire as she touched him. And where his kiss fell on her bare flesh, her blood felt as if it was boiling beneath her skin. They hungered, as if they could never have enough of the simple taste and feel of each other, until the urgency created by that longing become unbearable. They melted together, suddenly one, in a movement as natural as breathing….

Rhiannon felt as if she were soaring toward the sun, his every caress erotic, and the feel of his flesh, the thrust of his body, wickedly abandoned and so, so real. She felt everything acutely, each slightest brush of his fingertips, the pressure deep inside as he moved within her, driving her ever higher.

Her climax burst through her. She relished it, drifted on the wave, clung to the wonder that filled her, as molten and sweet as release itself had been. And then she saw that the sun had risen and the day had begun, golden light seeping in between the curtains.

"It's morning," she murmured, snuggling again him.

"Morning," he agreed, and groaned. "Matinee today."

"We need to get a few hours' sleep," she said huskily.

"We do," he agreed, cradling her against him.

Moments later she felt the liquid fire of his kiss moving along her back.

She turned in his arms, looking at him with a curious smile. "This is how you sleep?" she asked.

"I'll sleep...soon," he promised as he studied her, a slight smile on his face.

"Are you reading my thoughts?" she asked him.

"Not the way you're suggesting," he said. "But I'm reading what I can from the way you're looking at me. What's your *real* feeling about sleep?"

She smiled. "Soon..." she whispered. And then her lips met his and time lost all meaning.

Chapter 12

Is a wannabe-vampire serial killer on the prowl in L.A.?

Rhiannon started reading the story underneath the headline. Barrie had done an excellent job. Her story wasn't front page, but at least it was the lead story for the local section.

Barrie had included information on all five murders, information credited to an "anonymous source" at the police department. She listed the victims and the dump sites, and included the detail that every victim had been drained of blood. She listed the number for the police hotline, urging anyone who had any information whatsoever to please call.

There was a tap on the door just as Rhiannon finished the article. She jumped up and went to answer the summons.

Barrie was standing there looking decidedly nervous. "Well?" she asked.

"It was excellent," Rhiannon assured her.

"Where's Brodie?" Barrie asked.

"On his way to the theater—matinee today. Have you seen Sailor?"

"I was just over there—she and I are going for a run," Barrie said.

"Wait," Rhiannon said. "I just need a minute to grab some sneakers, and then I'll go with you."

"I'm warning you," Sailor said when they joined her, "I'm not slowing down just so you can keep up with me."

"We'll struggle along as best we can," Rhiannon said, laughing.

Twenty minutes later Rhiannon was regretting her words. Sailor was in excellent shape and had no trouble with the hills, while Rhiannon was appalled to realize that she was quickly panting and sweating.

"Have mercy!" Barrie cried at last, saving Rhiannon from having to be the one to cry uncle.

Sailor paused, and Rhiannon bent over, gasping for breath. As she did so, she realized that they had reached the area where she had found the body in the pond.

"Cops walking around—look," Barrie said, breathing heavily between words.

Rhiannon looked. There were two patrol cars parked on the private road, and she could see two sets of officers knocking on two front doors.

Then she noticed that someone was standing on the sidewalk, a notebook in his hands, watching as the officers went door to door.

"Isn't that Adam—the guy from the club last night?" Sailor asked.

Rhiannon nodded and straightened. A pain shot through her rib cage, and she gasped.

They had to find the killer fast, she thought, or she would perish just from trying to keep up with Sailor.

Adam must have heard them talking, because he looked up and saw them, then smiled, waved and started in their direction. "Morning, ladies," he said cheerfully.

"Hi, Adam," Rhiannon said. "You working the streets now?"

He nodded, then looked at Barrie. "I guess I don't have to wonder who your source is, but don't worry, I won't tell anyone. Your article got the phones ringing, at least. We got an anonymous tip that someone saw a pair of lovers out here a few weeks ago, walking down toward the water. We're trying to find the tipster, see if he can't tell us more." He shook his head glumly. "It's just hard, you know? If coyotes could talk, we might get better information."

"If coyotes could talk," Rhiannon agreed.

"Well, ladies, have a beautiful day. I'm going to get back to work," he said, then met Rhiannon's eyes. "I'm surprised to see you out here. Yesterday must have been hell for you."

"It wasn't pleasant, that's for sure," she said. "Well, time for us to get going."

She waved and was about to start jogging again when something on the sidewalk caught her attention. She didn't want Adam to see, so she quickly paused to do some stretching, keeping an eye on him until he was safely out of range.

"What are you doing?" Sailor asked her.

"Stretching to pick up…this."

She reached down for the bit of white cardboard

that had attracted her attention. It turned out to be a matchbook.

"House of Illusion," Barrie said aloud.

"Want to have a late lunch there?" Rhiannon asked.

"I don't know. We're going tomorrow night anyway, and Brodie will be with us then," Sailor said.

"We're just going to have lunch, not storm the place," Rhiannon said.

"All right," Sailor said. "Race you home!"

As soon as he finished with costume and makeup, Brodie stepped outside to the parking lot to call the station. He was surprised when he got Adam's voice mail and a message saying he was out for the day. Brodie hit "0" for the switchboard and asked to be transferred to Bryce Edwards, his werewolf friend in Vice.

"Hey, Brodie."

"Bryce, sorry, I was trying to reach Adam Lansky in tech assistance, and I thought you might know where he is."

"He's out on the streets, with the uniforms, going door to door by that pond you were at yesterday," Edwards told him. "The kid is trying to earn some brownie points with you, I think. So, how are you really doing on this case, Brodie? Do we need to start worrying that it's going to blow up on us?"

"I promise you, I won't let it get to that. Can you get me patched through to Adam? I don't have his cell number, since he's never away from his desk," Brodie said.

"I'll make it happen. That article in this morning's paper has brought out the crazies. Are you going to get in here to help sift through the tips?" Edwards asked.

"First thing tomorrow morning," Brodie promised.

"And if anything comes in that you think I should know about…"

"I'll call you, anytime, day or night," Edwards promised. "Okay, hang on. I've got Lansky for you."

A minute later he was connected to Adam.

"Hey, Brodie," Adam said.

"What are you doing?" Brodie asked.

"Helping."

"That's great, Adam, but I need you on the computer."

"It's Saturday, you know. I'm working on my own time," Adam said. "I came in this morning to print out pictures for the patrol teams to show around. Head shots of the victims, stuff I found online. I know I'm a geek, but I'd like to make detective one day."

Brodie wasn't sure why he felt uncomfortable. Adam had been a godsend many times in the past, digging up all kinds of information on the internet.

He'd also followed Sailor the other night at the club. For her safety? Or for some other reason entirely?

"All right," Brodie said, seeing that he wasn't going to get Adam to back off, at least not today. "I'll give you a call after the matinee, okay? You can catch me up on what's going on."

"Sure. I'll do that. You going to the Snake Pit tonight?"

Brodie frowned, thinking quickly, and said, "Yes, I'll be there to watch over Rhiannon. I've got friends watching her, too, keeping her safe 'til I can get there."

"Good to know. Well, I guess your show is about to start. Break a leg. I'll talk to you later," Adam promised.

Brodie hung up, not happy with the situation. He'd

worked with Adam a long time. He'd seemed a good enough kid. But now...

Everybody wanted something. The kid didn't want to be a geek all his life. But how would that turn into a compulsion to kill?

"Hey, Mac!"

He looked up. Bobby Conche and Joe Carrie were standing at the cast entrance.

"Getting late," Bobby warned him.

"Places in five," Joe called, then added, "You all right, Mac?"

"Yeah, I'm great, thanks. I'm coming," Brodie said.

He was afraid it was going to be a long performance.

The story had broken, and something was going to happen—he could feel it.

Adam wasn't the killer. Brodie had been convinced from the beginning that the killer had something to do with the play, and he was even more certain of that than ever.

The killer was here.

But the killer had accomplices—he was convinced of that now, too.

But how many? That was the question.

Jerry was in the entry hall, chatting with one of his magicians when the cousins arrived. He seemed surprised to see them, but also pleased.

"How nice to see you," he said. "There's not much going on, but the lunch buffet is still open. Or I can give you a tour," he suggested.

"We'd love to have some lunch, Jerry," Rhiannon said. "And a tour would be great."

"Wonderful. I'll call ahead, have a nice table set for

you—I'll make sure you have a view of the valley." True to his word, he pulled out his cell phone and called the hostess. Smiling, he hung up, but then his smile wavered. "I saw the paper today. Are you sure that was the right move?"

"We need help, Jerry, and that article could bring in crucial information. And thank *you,* by the way, for everything you're doing for us," Rhiannon said.

Jerry was visibly pleased. "All right, ladies, follow me."

The castle had been built in the late 1890s, and the generously proportioned main-floor rooms had been converted to both large and small showrooms, the dining room and what Jerry called the Magician's Cave, an intimate space where a magician was currently staging a demonstration for a group of his peers. There was even an outdoor stage with a patio seating area that stretched right to the lip of the canyon, with only a low concrete wall to stop the unwary.

"Downstairs, we have our staging area," Jerry said. "You know, trapdoors, secret passageways…all the good stuff. Would you like to see it?"

"The hidden underbelly? You bet," Rhiannon said.

"No spilling secrets," Jerry warned Barrie.

"My typing fingers are sworn to silence," Barrie promised.

Jerry smiled and led them through a small unmarked door. A sign on the other side read Magicians' Staging Area and pointed the way to a set of stairs next to an elevator.

"We need an elevator, and you'll notice it's quite large. Needless to say we can't make a 757 disappear in a venue like this, but some of our performers use large boxes, tall glass tubes—like the one the Count de Soir used at the Snake Pit the other night," Jerry explained, then gave them a wicked grin. "Come, enter my den of mystery!" he said teasingly.

They followed him down the stairs to a basement with a definite dungeonlike feel—at least until she looked around and saw the electrical outlets everywhere, not to mention the huge LCD monitors on the walls, each screen showing a different view of the rooms just above, most of them various angles of the stage in the large showroom.

He pointed out a series of dressing rooms to the left, and then Sailor asked, "What are those doors to the right?"

"Guest room for visiting performers, complete with coffins for beds. We get a lot of vampires, along with all sorts of Others," he said quietly.

"Is the Count de Soir on the program Sunday night?" Rhiannon asked, changing the subject.

"Yes, he is," Jerry said.

"Interesting," Rhiannon said. "We'll look forward to seeing him."

Jerry nodded. "I hope I can help you. You'll come here, you'll see who you see and you'll ask all the questions you want to ask." He smiled suddenly. "And now lunch!"

The audience loved the show. Every Saturday they ran a fund-raiser for the local animal shelters, and that went well, too. As he stood with a basket and greeted people, Brodie thought about how much he'd learned by going undercover as an actor. Take the fund-raiser, for instance. He loved seeing how willing people were to donate to support creatures who desperately needed the help.

He found himself thinking about dogs, wonderful creatures with a sixth sense about who was trustworthy and who wasn't, and an ability to be useful in any fight against the kinds of danger a stone wall couldn't keep out. The Gryffald cousins definitely needed to get one, maybe more.

As soon as he could, he put a call through to Adam. "Found out anything useful yet?" he asked.

"A couple of things, starting with a couple you may want to talk to yourself. They live in the house nearest to the pond where the last body was found. They saw a car parked out in front, some kind of dark sedan. They didn't think anything of it at first, thought it must've been someone visiting a neighbor. A couple came out, and they were laughing, seemed happy. Another car came along a few minutes later, but they didn't see it, they just heard the motor. They heard a lot of laughter coming from down by the water, loud enough that they were going to call the police."

"So did they?"

"No, the laughter stopped, and they didn't hear anything else. When the husband finally went out to look, both cars were gone," Adam said.

Brodie was silent. Yes, more than one killer. Someone calling the shots. Someone else carrying out commands. And one of them able to glamour the guard to let them through. But…what was the underlying motive?

"So, Brodie, more than one killer, right?" Adam asked eagerly.

"Yes, Adam, more than one killer." He took a deep breath. "So, you said you said you had a couple things."

"Yeah, I have a name for you. That newspaper article really got things going. We got a tip from a woman named Shirley Henson. She was friends with our last victim—Rose Gillespie. The last time she saw Rose was about ten days ago. They met for lunch at the Mystic Café. Rose told her that she was going to go to see *Vampire Rampage*. She'd heard they were going to be casting the touring companies, so she wanted to see it again. Which means you were right—she most likely disappeared right after the play."

"Please, Sailor, I know it isn't a hardship for you, hanging out at the Snake Pit," Rhiannon said to her cousin. "Now that Barrie's article is out, I'm really afraid. The killer is either going to be gloating because his work has been noticed or afraid because of it. Please, stick with us tonight?"

Sailor sighed. "Rhiannon, I'm just tired of Declan Wainwright being a—a dick. I'll be perfectly safe at home with Merlin. And all my windows closed, of course."

"Sailor, please? Can we just stick together for the next few days?" Rhiannon asked.

"What if you and Brodie don't find out anything in the next few days?" Sailor asked.

"We have to," Rhiannon said, desperation in her tone. "So, what do you say? Will you come?"

Sailor sighed dramatically. "All right. But you're both coming running with me tomorrow morning."

Barrie and Rhiannon looked at each other.

"Well, it is good for our health," Barrie said. "Though I'd rather be hiking or rock climbing, or…well, you know—doing something a little more interesting."

"And I'd rather be in an air-conditioned gym with earphones and a little television screen showing something entertaining," Rhiannon said. "But tomorrow we run."

Sailor grinned. "Then I'll go with you tonight."

Brodie took the few free hours between performances to talk to Shirley. She seemed unusually surprised to see him.

"You're...a detective?" she asked. "I could swear I saw you in that new play, *Vampire Rampage*. I'm an actress, too. I saw it about two weeks ago—I'd heard they would be casting the touring companies soon."

Brodie offered her a rueful smile. "I'm undercover. I believe someone associated with the play is responsible for Rose's death, along with the others you read about in the paper this morning. I'm even more convinced because of what you told Adam. Tell me about the last time you saw Rose Gillespie."

Tears instantly filled Shirley's eyes. "It was a Saturday—two weeks ago tonight."

Brodie felt as if there were rocks in his stomach. That had been his first show. He hadn't really known anyone, and he had tried to watch them all as they left. He hadn't seen any of them leave with an audience member.

The couple next door to the pond had said there were two cars, so presumably Rose had been in the first, part of that happy couple, and the other had arrived after. She had been lured to her doom and then killed...by the second party?

He stayed with Shirley a little while longer, listening as she rambled on. She obviously needed to talk about the friend she had lost.

But there was nothing else he could gain from her. When he left her house, he called Adam again, this time getting him at the station.

"I need you to go through the victims' credit card receipts. I want to know how many times they saw the play, and the dates."

"Once might not have been enough, huh?" Adam asked.

"Just find out for me, please," Brodie said.

He headed back to the theater for the night's performance. As he parked, he called Rhiannon, anxious just to hear her voice.

"We're fine," she assured him. "We went to the House of Illusion for lunch and got a tour of the place."

He frowned at that. "Rhiannon, I'm not sure that was safe. We'd agreed we would all go together tomorrow night."

"We were fine. We stayed together. And now we're home, getting ready to head to the Snake Pit. We'll stay close there, too. Oh, I had to promise to go running with Sailor tomorrow, so make sure you have sneakers," she said lightly.

"Stay safe," he cautioned her.

"I swear I will."

"Everything is all right at home?" he asked, feeling anxious, though he told himself there was no reason for him to be afraid. The woman were together, and Merlin was there to play watchdog.

He just didn't have a sense of smell—or teeth.

"You need a dog," Brodie said, and thought about the ones that had been at the theater that afternoon, looking for homes.

"I would love to have a dog, I told you that," she said. "But let's get through this first, huh?"

"I'll be at the Snake Pit when the show lets out," he promised.

The minute he hung up, his phone started to ring. He picked it up and checked the caller ID. Adam, and he sounded excited.

"Brodie, you won't believe this. They all saw the play three times. Every one of them went three times. Strange, huh?" Adam asked.

"All right, do your computer magic. Check out a woman named Penny Abelard. Find out how many times *she's* seen the show," Brodie said. "And check out Shirley, too."

"Will do," Adam said.

Brodie parked the car and saw that Joe and Bobby were at the stage door entrance. They waved, smiling, as they saw him. He waved in return.

As he started to get out of the car, his phone rang again.

It was Adam. "Penny Abelard has seen the show twice. She has a ticket to see it tonight for the third time. The dates of the performances are on the sales receipts."

Brodie felt an icy chill run up his spine. He didn't know why three was the magic number, but it clearly was. He thanked Adam and hung up.

Nothing seemed unusual. Joe and Bobby greeted him as he entered. Hunter Jackson arrived, and he and Brodie chatted as they did their makeup. Places were called. The show began.

Brodie saw Penny Abelard immediately; she was sitting in the first row, looking enthralled.

He couldn't wait for the play to end. When it did, he

dressed with record speed and was ready before Hunter even made it to their dressing room. He ran past the director on his way out, dimly aware that he'd agreed to meet everyone at the Snake Pit later.

He found Penny waiting backstage.

"Well, hello," he said, pretending to be surprised by her presence.

"Oh, hey! Great to see you. You were brilliant tonight," she told him.

Wide-eyed hope and innocence, he thought. It was such an L.A. look, at least for so many new arrivals. All too often it was followed by a dull look of weariness, of exhaustion and lost hope, as the young and the hopeful became the drained and hopeless.

"Thank you," he said. "Who are you here to meet?"

"I'm hoping to see Audrey—she's been so nice to me, and so has Lena Ashbury."

Lena! How the hell could he have missed it?

Penny was still smiling and talking. "I'm hoping to bum a ride with Audrey again, maybe get a chance to hang out with some of her friends at the club, like Declan Wainwright, and maybe even Darius Simonides. She knows all the cool people."

Cool people who might be murderers.

He didn't know what to do. Take her with him so he could keep her safe?

Or wait to see who was anxious to give her a ride?

Audrey Fleur, Kate Delaney and Lena Ashbury came out of their shared dressing room, laughing together.

"Hey, Brodie, Snake Pit?" Audrey called.

"Definitely," he said.

"Penny!" Lena called in greeting. "I saw you out in the audience."

"Hey, Lena," Penny said, flushing happily.

Hunter emerged from the dressing room just as Bobby Conche came walking over. He looked as hopeful as Penny. "You all heading to the Snake Pit?" he asked.

"Absolutely, and I hope you're coming, too," Hunter said.

Bobby seemed to bask in the glow of Hunter's words.

"Hey, where the hell is Joe?" Audrey asked. "If we're going, he should be going, too."

"On three," Kate said playfully. "One, two, three…"

"Joe!" they all cried as one.

Joe popped his head out from behind the curtain. "What? What did I do?"

"Heading out to the Snake Pit! I'm taking the sheet music for the show. Maybe Miss Gryffald will play it for us."

"It's a plan," Joe said

Brodie gritted his teeth. With everyone there, he didn't know what his next step should be.

But he couldn't risk an innocent woman's life. "Penny, why don't you ride with me?"

"Don't be silly, Brodie. Penny can come with us," Audrey said. "You're taken, remember?"

"And Rhiannon trusts me completely. Stick with me, Penny. Audrey thinks she's filming *The Fast and the Furious* every time she gets in a car."

"Who cares who drives with who?" Hunter asked. "Let's just go."

Brodie took Penny's arm politely but firmly. "It will be my pleasure to give you a ride," he said.

Oh, yes, my pleasure—if I can just keep you alive.

Chapter 13

If it weren't for the possibility of a vampire serial killer and the attack on her cousin—okay, and the attack on her own car, too—Rhiannon thought, life would be pretty great. She was making a living playing music, and then there was Brodie. She didn't know where that relationship was heading or how long it might last, but she intended to enjoy every minute of it while she had the chance.

She noticed Brodie the minute he arrived with the cast and crew from the show, along with a young woman she didn't recognize, and she smiled at him, nodding toward the table where Sailor and Barrie were sitting. Sailor waved as he approached with the woman, while Barrie didn't notice him until Sailor nudged her—she was engrossed in reading something on her tablet.

Even from a distance, she could see that he looked troubled. She couldn't desert the stage, but she suspected Brodie would find a way to join her as soon as he could.

He did, sliding onto the bench next to her when she paused between songs.

"Sorry if I'm acting distracted, but I'm trying to keep my eye on a woman," he said.

"I don't think you're supposed to tell me that you're watching another woman while we're sleeping together," she told him with a sexy grin.

He grinned back. "Rhiannon, I found out that all five victims disappeared after having seen *Vampire Rampage* three times. And this woman—Penny Abelard—also auditioned for the show, and she saw it for the third time tonight."

Rhiannon nodded. They both had a clear view of the table where Penny was now seated. "I'll try to keep an eye on her, too. Plus you have help here, if you want it." She started playing again, but this time she let the piano speak for itself, so she and Brodie could keep talking.

"Who?" he asked, frowning.

"Well, Declan is walking around looking like an eagle on the hunt. Hugh's here, too, but mostly he's just staring at me as if I were a caged wolf someone suddenly set loose. I meant your tech buddy, Adam Lansky. He's at a table a couple of rows back from where my cousins are sitting. He's alone. See him?"

"Thanks," he said, but he was getting more and more curious as to why Adam was suddenly showing up in a lot of places where he didn't need to be. "I'd better get back to the table. Our murderer intends to kill again tonight, and I've got to— Damn! She's leaving the room."

Worse, Adam Lansky was following her.

Without even taking time to say goodbye, Brodie stood and hurried off the stage in Adam's wake.

The minute Rhiannon reached the end of the song she announced that she was taking a break. Not even caring what people might think, she went racing through the club and out into the night.

She didn't see any of them.

Then she heard a groan coming from behind some bushes.

It might be a trap, she realized, but she had to do something.

Plunging into the bushes, she gasped.

"Rhiannon! Is that you?" It was Brodie's voice, coming from somewhere off to the left.

"I'm over here!" she called.

Brodie thrust his way through to her. "That little rat bastard. I was two steps behind. I can't find Penny—Adam has her somewhere."

"No, Brodie," she said. "Adam doesn't have her. Adam is here. Call an ambulance. He's bleeding."

Brodie had his phone out even as he hunkered down over the tech, who, judging from the blood, had been bashed on the head.

"Son of a bitch," Brodie cursed. "Get Humphrey out here until an ambulance comes. Then you get back inside with your cousins."

"I can't hide from what's going on, Brodie. I'm a Keeper. Finding a vampire killer is what I'm supposed to do."

He grasped her by the shoulders. "The killer isn't out for you tonight. He's out for Penny Abelard. I have to find her—quickly. It might already be too late. Please, watch out for your cousins. There's more than one person involved in this, and for all I know at least one of our killers is still inside. Rhiannon, please, go now."

Rhiannon called for the bouncer as she ran for the door. The minute she had his attention she sent him over to help Brodie with Adam, then hurried back inside.

"Rhiannon, I know there's serious stuff going on, but you can't just disappear every few minutes and keep your job here," Declan said, catching her as she entered the room.

"A cop was attacked just outside, and a woman is missing. I think that's a good reason for taking a break, don't you?"

Declan paled. "Go back to the piano. I'll go out and see what's happening."

Rhiannon scanned the room as she headed back onstage.

The entire cast of *Vampire Rampage* was now gone, except for Lena Ashbury, who was sitting with Darius and laughing. Then, to her surprise, she spotted Audrey, who was flirting with a tall attractive stranger at the bar. But everyone else was among the missing.

She sat down and started to play, glad that her fingers could find the keys by rote, because her mind was racing.

Declan found her on her next break and told her that she needed to give a statement to the police.

"Is Adam hurt badly?" she asked the officer who sat down to talk to her.

"He was still unconscious when the ambulance left," he told her. "But the paramedics said his pulse was steady, so with luck he'll come out of it soon."

"Have you seen—" She broke off before finishing

the question, remembering just in time that Brodie was undercover.

The officer smiled, then lowered his voice and spoke close to her ear. "Detective McKay is still looking for the young woman Officer Lansky was following."

He took her statement and her number in case of additional questions, then let her return to the stage.

Finally she saw that the crowd was thinning out. Eventually the only other people remaining at the club were Sailor, Barrie, the workers who were closing up and Declan Wainwright.

"I'll follow you girls home," Declan told her.

"We're together—we'll be fine," Rhiannon assured him.

Declan smiled. "I don't doubt it. I just don't want Brodie on my case, okay?"

Rhiannon nodded. "All right. And I'm ready to go. I'm exhausted. Of course, I probably won't be able to sleep after all this," she said.

"But you'll be home. I still have to drive to Malibu," he reminded her.

"Good point," she said, feeling guilty. They all stood, and she noticed that Sailor seemed a little unsteady. "What's with you?" Rhiannon asked, slipping a supportive arm around her cousin.

"Five cosmos. I mean, hell, we've been here for hours," Sailor said.

"Can she make it?" Declan asked sharply.

"Of course," Rhiannon said indignantly. "All she has to do is walk to the car." The man owned a bar, and now he was being insulting because Sailor had actually been drinking there.

Barrie moved around to Sailor's other side, and together they walked out to Rhiannon's car. Just as they got there, Rhiannon's phone rang. It was Brodie. "Hang on," she said as she pulled her keys from her purse.

"Toss me the keys," Barrie said. "I'll drive, you talk."

"Thanks," Rhiannon said, handing them over. She balanced the phone between her shoulder and her cheek while she got Sailor settled in the backseat. "Brodie?" she asked a moment later as she slid into the front.

"You okay?" he asked anxiously.

"We're fine. Declan is going to follow us home."

"I'll be there soon," he told her.

"Did you find her?" Rhiannon asked.

He sighed. "Oh, yeah, I found her."

Penny Abelard was alive. Just barely.

And she still had her fingers.

The killer—or killers—must have known he was on the trail, Brodie thought.

He'd headed for the nearest body of water—a lousy little rock pit beside the ramp to the 101. She'd been attacked, but the killer hadn't had time to finish the job.

He'd found her facedown in the water, and his heart had dropped—it had felt as if it were sinking right into the mud—but when he dragged her out and started to perform CPR she had spewed water into his face, then begun to cough and wheeze.

For a moment, a brief moment, her eyes had opened and she'd stared at him. They'd been wide and filled with terror.

"It's all right. I'm here to help you," he'd said.

Her eyes had closed again then, and he'd called 911, then sat by her, waiting. Soon he heard sirens, and in moments the medics were there.

"She needs a transfusion—quickly," Brodie told them.

They were good at their jobs, and one of them was a vampire who opened his mind to Brodie.

I'll see that she gets blood, McKay. She'll be okay.

"I'm going to follow you guys," he told them.

He waited at the hospital. After forty-five minutes a doctor came out. "Miss Abelard is a lucky young woman. You found her in the nick of time. We've transfused her, and her condition is serious but stable."

"Is she conscious?" Brodie asked.

"No, and I don't expect she'll come around for hours. Why don't you get some sleep? I'll have someone call you the moment she comes to," the doctor promised.

Brodie decided to read the man's mind.

It's going to be days, at best, 'til that poor girl comes to.

Brodie's head ached; he was soaked, muddy and exhausted.

"I'm calling for a uniformed officer to watch over her, and then I'm going to get some sleep, just as you suggested," Brodie said. "I want to be informed the minute she wakes up."

He checked on Adam while he waited for the uniform to arrive, and he had better luck there. Adam was conscious, and the doctor told him he could have five minutes.

The kid had a black eye and a bandaged head. He looked contrite and utterly dejected.

"Who was it?" Brodie asked him.

"Someone taller than me, that's all I know. That girl—Penny—she got a call and nearly ran out of the place. That seemed weird to me, so I ran after her. I made it outside, I got hit and the next thing I remember, I'm here. I'm pretty sure it was a man who hit me, but that's all I know. I'm sorry. I suck."

Brodie grimaced, shaking his head. "You're all right, kid. But maybe you should stick to computers for a while."

"For the rest of my life," Adam vowed.

Brodie decided that he wanted someone watching Adam, too, and made another call. He waited until both uniformed officers arrived, and then he left, driving well over the limit to the Gryffald compound.

Rhiannon must have been watching for him, because the gate swung open as he drove up. She was waiting for him in the driveway, and ran toward him the minute he parked. "Is she still…?"

"Alive, yes," he said. "But in a coma."

"Adam?"

"Awake and aware, but he doesn't know anything other than that his attacker was tall."

"I know who wasn't involved," Rhiannon said.

"Who?"

"Audrey. She was flirting with some guy at the bar the whole time. And Lena Ashbury was talking with Darius."

"What about Joe, Hunter and Kate?" he asked.

She shook her head. "No idea where they were. Which may not mean anything, but…"

"It might mean everything."

"Oh, and you know who else was missing?" Rhiannon asked. "Bobby. You know—the security guy."

"Shapeshifter," Brodie noted. "I get the feeling we're being led in circles."

"Maybe. But we have to follow, don't we? At least, I do."

"Rhiannon, I'm a cop *and* an Other. *I* have to solve this."

"*We* have to solve this. *We*."

He stroked her cheek gently. "We," he agreed.

She nodded, smiling at him sympathetically. "You look like hell. No insult intended."

"A shower would help a lot. May I?"

"Of course. And how about some tea?"

"So long as you lace it with whiskey." He grinned.

Twenty minutes later he collapsed on her bed. The tea had helped, the shower even more so. She lay by his side, just there, supportive. He felt so drained, so tired.

She stroked his hair, then his cheek. He felt as if her energy was pouring into him, and he turned to her and smiled. "You can be a little more…energetic, if you want."

"You need to rest," she told him.

The scent of her seemed to invade his blood. The feel of her created life in limbs and loins. He pulled her to him. "Um, not so sure what I need right now is rest," he said, his voice husky.

She smiled, a beautiful slow smile that lit her eyes and seemed to brighten the night. The very air seemed alive with sensuality.

She kissed his lips and drew her shirt over her head, baring the fullness and beauty of her breasts.

"I'll sleep…soon," he whispered as he reached for her.

In the end, it wasn't really all that soon. But with her in his arms, when he slept, he slept deeply, and when he woke it was to find himself feeling fully restored.

* * *

Rhiannon managed to get out of running with her cousins, because Brodie needed to get to the hospital, and she wanted to be with him.

He didn't want Sailor and Barrie running around the Canyon alone, though, so he arranged for a couple of officers-in-training to go with them. Both women were more amused than upset. After the events of the previous night, it seemed no one wanted to take any chances.

Rhiannon and Brodie visited Adam, who was still feeling down and looking forward to getting back to the safety of his computer.

Penny Abelard was still unconscious, though the doctor on duty told them that he believed she would recover. Her vital signs were growing stronger, but he couldn't predict when she would wake up.

Brodie seemed uncharacteristically depressed, and it hurt Rhiannon to see him so down, but even the reminder that he'd saved Penny's life didn't seem to help. "Brodie, we're close, so close, to figuring this thing out," she said.

"Joe Carrie, Kate Delaney and Hunter Jackson," he said. "They're my friends, Can it really be one of them?"

"I think that has to be the answer," she said. "I don't understand, though—why? Joe's a vampire, but this play, the film, the video game…they're going to make him rich. And Hunter Jackson, he's already famous and he's only going to get more so. Kate Delaney…she's human, like Jackson, but this play is going to open doors for her. And there's Bobby, too. One of them must be involved, because they were all missing in action when Adam and Penny were attacked, and the circle always comes back to the theater and the play."

"Or the movie," Brodie said.

"Jerry Oglethorpe is convinced we can learn something tonight at the House of Illusion. Who the hell else is involved in this?"

"It could be a trap," Brodie pointed out. "Maybe I should go and the three of you should stay home. It's as if your arrival, in particular, has been some kind of catalyst."

"The murders started before I took over," she reminded him.

"Yes, but your father's…promotion was already in the works, and the bodies were pretty well hidden, as if the killer knew they wouldn't resurface—literally—until your father was gone."

"A vampire is involved somehow, maybe more than one, but I don't think a vampire is pulling the strings. We'll find out something at the House of Illusion, Brodie. I know it."

"Then we'll go early, for dinner," he said. "But we have to be prepared for anything—including the possibility that you're wrong and it really is a trap. Call Sailor and Barrie, tell them we want to get there by six." He looked at her consideringly. "Three," he said. "Why three? Why did the killer wait until each victim had seen the show three times?"

Rhiannon shook her head. "I have no idea."

"What about Jerry Oglethorpe?" he asked.

"Jerry *is* a vampire, but he has nothing to do with the show. And the first magician who said we should go to the House of Illusion, the Count de Soir, is Elven, and he has nothing to do with the play, either. Getting back to vampires, though, the House of Illusion is where they meet, so maybe that's the connection to tonight. Have you ever been through the entire mansion?"

"No, I haven't," Brodie said. "I've been to shows there, but that's it."

"There are bedrooms in the basement for guest performers to use. And the beds are all coffins. I know it's a cliché, but a lot of vampires like that kind of thing."

"Interesting. We really need to be on the alert tonight, especially you, because I think the killer would like nothing better than to make you the next victim. Rhiannon—"

"Oh, Brodie, I love that you want to protect us—protect *me*—but it's our job to fight when there's trouble among our charges. You know that. I have to face this."

He drew her close to him and he held her for a moment, then kissed her tenderly. "I know you do," he said at last.

"Everything was peaceful out here for so long. But now, when we—when *I*—have just arrived, all hell had to break loose."

"And that's exactly why it did."

"And why we have to prove ourselves," Rhiannon said.

At six o'clock, they arrived at the House of Illusion. Jerry Oglethorpe had reserved a prime table for them, right in front, and they had plenty of time to eat before the featured performance started. In the meantime, while the audience waited for the main act—the Count de Soir—a series of young magicians took the stage.

Rhiannon watched them, but mostly she tried to keep track of everything that was going on *off* the stage. All the while she could sense Brodie's tension as he, too, made a point of watching everything while trying to appear not to.

As soon as he finished his meal he leaned over and whispered to her that he wanted to take the tour and see the basement bedrooms, then excused himself and went in search of Jerry Oglethorpe.

Thirty minutes later he was back, but before he had a chance to share his thoughts with her, the Count de Soir took the stage.

He performed some rather ordinary tricks at first, using scarves, rabbits and doves. But then he built up to a major routine, the music growing louder and a bevy of beautiful assistants gesturing dramatically as a huge glass case, something like the water tanks Houdini used to perform his amazing escapes, was wheeled onto the stage.

"First," the count announced, "I will turn a beast into a beauty!"

And then, with great fanfare, he introduced a large wolf to the stage.

Jerry Oglethorpe, who was standing near their table, bent down to whisper, "Don't worry, it's real. Not a werewolf. Actually, it's a hybrid. Most magicians use dog/wolf crosses. They're not as volatile."

The Count de Soir continued with his act, ushering the wolf into the glass case before covering it with a red velvet drape and tapping his wand lightly on the top. When he pulled away the drape, one of his assistants was inside the case.

"But that was child's play," he said. "Watch." A second glass enclosure was wheeled on. "Beauty to beauty.

In the blink of an eye, one beauty will become another. I will need a volunteer. You!"

This time he was looking at Sailor and not Rhiannon.

"Don't go," Rhiannon whispered. "He could be using us for some reason—baiting us."

"What's wrong with you, Rhiannon?" Sailor said. "You helped with one of his tricks."

"That was different. Something is happening here tonight, and we can't take any foolish risks."

"Rhiannon, the man hasn't done anything at all to make us suspicious."

"It's just that we have to be very careful. It's dangerous to trust anyone we don't really know. He's just… an unknown entity."

"I'll be careful, Rhiannon, so stop talking to me like I'm an idiot. Besides, he's the one who suggested we come here. Maybe he's afraid of something. Maybe he's trying to help us."

Without creating a massive scene—and perhaps sacrificing their chance to learn the truth—Rhiannon couldn't stop her, so she exchanged a worried look with Barrie, and then, with her heart in her throat, she watched her cousin go up onstage.

The three of them were ready. As ready as they could be.

Three!

The number three had to mean something. There were three new Keepers in the Canyon because three had been called to the council.

"I don't like this," she whispered to Brodie. "He's got her onstage, where there are all those trapdoors that lead down to the basement."

"I'll go down there, just in case," he said, but he looked worried.

"Before you go," she said, "I just thought of something. You said the victims all saw the play three times. And there are three of us. Sailor, Barrie and me. Three new Keepers."

"Interesting," he said, nodding thoughtfully. "But now I have to get down there. You need to watch up here." Jerry Oglethorpe was still standing nearby, and Brodie beckoned him over. "I'm going downstairs, Jerry. I just want to make sure nothing is going on down there, in case the count sends her down there as part of the switch."

"Whatever you want. But I'm sure Sailor will be all right. The Count de Soir is an Elven, after all."

"I know. Still…"

Jerry nodded, and Rhiannon watched as Brodie left, then returned her attention to the stage. The Count de Soir was escorting one of his assistants into one of the glass enclosures and Sailor into the other.

He did his bit with the draperies, waved his wand and pulled off the draperies.

The two women had changed places.

"And now…"

Once again Count de Soir covered the cubicles, but this time, when he whipped off the drapes, there were wolves in both cases.

Her heart pounding, Rhiannon jumped to her feet.

Barrie caught her hand and pulled her back down. "Wait—let's just see what he's doing," she advised.

"He's got Sailor in the basement," Rhiannon said. "Anyone could be doing anything to her down there."

"Just hang on."

The drapes went over the cubicles. The wolves turned back into the two women.

"See?" Barrie said smugly.

Rhiannon saw, but something wasn't right. She didn't know what, and she didn't know how she knew, but she did.

The count thanked his beautiful volunteer as he let Sailor out of her glass box. She walked down the steps from the stage, but instead of returning to the table she started to walk out of the room.

"What the hell is she doing?" Barrie asked, her eyes narrowing suspiciously.

"I don't know— Yes, I do!" Rhiannon exclaimed, staring at Barrie. "That isn't Sailor! Come on."

By then "Sailor" was heading out the back door, toward the outdoor stage—and the sheer drop-off into the canyon below. Rhiannon, with Barrie close behind, raced after the shifter impersonating their cousin.

Outside, Rhiannon burst into motion and grabbed the faux Sailor, who turned to face her, looking startled.

"Rhiannon!" the shifter said in Sailor's voice. "Why do you look so worried? I just needed some air. Come on, let's walk."

"You're not Sailor," Rhiannon said. "And I'm not going anywhere with you."

"Sailor" stared at her, trying to wrench free and hissing. And then...

In seconds Sailor became Bobby Conche.

She dropped her hold, and Bobby Conche swung a fist right at her head. She ducked just in time.

She vaguely registered Barrie catching up to them as she felt adrenaline pulsing through her and her teeth... becoming fangs. She leaped on Bobby, slamming him to the ground and baring her teeth, ready to rip his throat to shreds.

"Rhiannon, stop!" Barrie said. "He has to tell us where Sailor is."

Bobby began to laugh. "The count? He's an innocent pawn. He's busy congratulating himself on a great show. We rigged the setup. It's so easy to manipulate people."

Rhiannon struck him—hard. "Keep it up and I just might kill you. You're a shifter, Bobby. And a vampire bite is pure poison to an Other. So tell me where my cousin is."

He started to shift again, squirming beneath her, thrusting her aside.

Barrie pounced on him, holding him firm as he changed from form to form, until finally he was Bobby again, staring up at them.

"He'll kill me! Don't you understand? He'll *kill* me!"

"Who?" Rhiannon demanded. "Bobby, damn you, who? I can stop this, but you have to tell me—who?"

Brodie reached the basement just as the last of the young magicians was leaving. He raced toward the guest rooms—and their coffins.

The first yielded nothing.

The second was the same.

He could feel time ticking away.

He threw open the door to the third room and stopped, stunned. There was Sailor, lying motionless, eyes closed, in a coffin, arms crossed over her chest as if she were…dead.

Three. Three new Keepers. Destroy them one by one, and in the process destroy the entire system they repre-

sented and the laws that governed an Otherworld so-
ciety whose members possessed legendary strengths.

"Sailor!" he shouted, and hurried toward her. She
was breathing; she had a pulse.

He heard the sound of clapping and turned.

Three people stood in the doorway: Kate Delaney,
Joe Carrie—and Hunter Jackson. Hunter and Kate were
armed, their guns pointed at him.

Joe kept applauding as he walked toward Brodie.
"We've got you just where we want you—cop." He practically spat the last word.

"Where? In a basement?" Brodie demanded.

"That's right. In a basement—where no one will ever
think to look for you. As you've noticed, we already
have Sailor here. And we'll have the other two within
minutes. You were a bit of a fly in the ointment, Elven,
but we have you now, ready to be packed into a magician's box, transported down to the port and sent on a
long ocean voyage."

Brodie crossed his arms over his chest, staring at the
three of them. Kate? Human. He could take her with
one swipe of his hand. Hunter Jackson? Human—he
wouldn't take much more. The guns might pose a bit
more of a problem, but still, he could teleport.

Joe Carrie...

Vampire. Taking him out might require a little more
effort.

"I'm armed, you know. If I shoot Kate and Hunter,"
he told Joe, "they're dead."

"They can shoot you, too, Elven."

Brodie smiled. "They don't have my speed. I can kill
them before they even begin to pull a trigger."

"Whatever. Then it will be you and me," Joe told him.

"Joe!" Kate protested. "What are you saying?"

She and Hunter were both staring at Joe, dismayed.

They hadn't realized they were pawns, Brodie thought. Of course, neither had he and Rhiannon. They'd gotten everything backward, thinking a human was controlling the vampires instead of vice versa.

In the second when they were distracted, Brodie pulled his own weapon.

"Now, that's going to be interesting. You—shooting two civilians," Joe said.

"They're armed. Trust me, I can find a way out," Brodie assured him, trying to appear completely calm. They had a plan—he had to know what it was.

And quickly. He had to find Rhiannon and Barrie. He didn't fully understand it yet, but Rhiannon had been right. Three new Keepers. It meant something.

Before anything else, though, he had to rescue Sailor.

"Rhiannon and Barrie will be down here any second," Brodie said.

Joe started to laugh. "I told you—she and her cousin have been taken care of. And now I have both the Elven Keeper and the Elven cop. Give up, Brodie. Give up, and maybe, when I've gotten you boxed up for a nice sail, you'll figure out a way to escape before the sea kills you."

"Where is Rhiannon, then?" Brodie asked, playing for time. He had to believe that Rhiannon and Barrie would figure out what was happening and save themselves. And then there was Jerry. He knew where Brodie was…but when would he suspect that something was wrong?

"Rhiannon is busy dying," Kate said. "Your little Keeper and her other cousin are out chasing Bobby

Conche—who, at this moment, looks just like that im-
becile Sailor. And once he has them somewhere out of
sight, he's going to turn into a grizzly or something."

"I wouldn't count on Bobby beating Rhiannon," Brodie said, praying that he was right. Then he turned to
face the two humans. "Meanwhile, I want to know one
thing."

"What's that?" Joe asked.

"Why? Hunter, you have Hollywood in the palm of
your hand. Kate, you're beautiful. Your career is just
taking off, thanks to *Vampire Rampage*."

Kate laughed. "Are you kidding me? The only way I
even got this role was by agreeing to help Joe."

"Same here," Hunter said. "I was actually on my
way downhill. It just hadn't hit the gossip columns yet.
You really don't understand yet, do you? There's going
to be a new world order, and Joe is going to make us
part of it."

"Joe is ready to sacrifice you at any time for his own
ends," Brodie said. "I thought you'd just figured that
out. And…what new world order?"

As he spoke, he felt something creeping along his
shoulder. He allowed himself a split-second glance. It
was some kind of caterpillar.

Instinctively, he knew. Barrie was here. And that
meant Rhiannon couldn't be far behind.

"I'm bringing down the Keepers—all of them," Joe
said. "This has been ridiculous for decades now…all
of us hiding what we are. There will be a new world
order, and the vampires will be at the top. I couldn't
have asked for a more perfect opportunity for starting the revolution. They took away the men who had
strength for their grand World Council and gave us

three inexperienced girls, no opposition at all. And, I must admit, it was fun watching you try to figure it out. Three, Brodie. Three new Keepers. So we threw you bread crumbs. Trace that number three. Don't kill people unless they've shown up three times. It's poetic justice, don't you see? Now, destroy the three new Keepers. Rid the world of the new international council and the annoying local ones all at once. Strike down the ridiculous order."

"What's wrong with order, Joe? Everyone just wants to live and let live. Elven, vampires, shapeshifters, human beings, you name it. We all want the same things."

"You're wrong. And this…hierarchy hasn't been natural. We should be able to dine on human chattel as we choose."

"Human chattel?" Brodie repeated, laughing. "That's you," he reminded Kate and Hunter.

"Shut up!" Kate screamed. She raised her gun and fired.

He moved in a flash, knocking the gun from her hand. "You're supporting the beast who would like to drink your blood," he warned her.

"The Keepers are going down," Joe told him. "By tomorrow morning I'll be ruling the Canyon." He walked toward Brodie. "A council? A world council? To rule over us? Oh, no. We are powerful, and we will rule the world. And I'm going to show you now just how powerful we vampires really are."

Joe suddenly grabbed Kate and shoved her away so that he could face Brodie. He hissed, his fangs lengthening, and flew at Brodie.

Brodie threw him, saying, "Get Sailor out of here. Wake her up—make her teleport."

"Who are you talking to?" Hunter cried out, backing away.

"He's not talking to anyone," Joe said. "It's a ploy. Now quit being such a sniveling coward or I'll kill you myself." He laughed. "Distract him, at least, you pathetic human beings!"

Kate rushed at Brodie head-on at the same time that Hunter attacked from behind. Brodie backhanded Kate hard; she crashed against the door and went limp. Then he spun and easily sent Hunter flying.

Both were out stone-cold, flat on the floor.

But when he turned, Joe was standing over Sailor.

"Get away from her!" Brodie roared, throwing himself at Joe.

They were locked in battle, but finally Brodie managed to trip Joe, and they both went down, rolling.

Joe broke away and ran toward the coffin, his fangs dripping.

But before he could reach her, Sailor opened her eyes.

"Teleport!" Brodie shouted to her.

And she disappeared.

Joe let out a roar of fury, turned and ran toward Brodie again just as Brodie felt himself being kicked savagely in the ribs. He looked up from the floor to see Audrey Fleur staring down at him.

In a flash, he weighed his options.

Teleport himself? Stand his ground and fight?

"Enough!" The voice was strong, full of authority.

For a moment they all stopped.

Rhiannon, tall, confident and furious, had entered

the room. She drew her lips back, displaying long fangs, as she came closer.

Audrey blocked her way. "I'll take you down in a heartbeat," she vowed.

"I don't think so," Rhiannon said, reaching out, clutching Audrey by the collar and throwing her to the side of the room. Joe flung himself furiously at Rhiannon, but she evaded him and rushed to Brodie's side.

"Trust me?" she begged him in a whisper.

He met her eyes and nodded.

"Then stay down."

"Bitch!" Joe screamed at Rhiannon. "Stop now, and maybe I'll let you live. But first I have an Elven to rip to shreds."

"I want to live," Rhiannon said. "I'll do anything. Let *me* kill him. I'll rip him to shreds for you."

"Really?" Joe said. "How fascinating."

"Don't trust her!" Audrey cried.

"Don't trust me?" Rhiannon asked. "Why not? You have the power—you have the numbers. I want to live, and it's obvious I have no choice but to answer to the strength of a real vampire. I'll help you overthrow the Keepers. I'll be your servant, Joe," she said. "I don't want to die."

"And you'll really kill your lover?" Joe asked her. "That I would like to see."

"I'll drain his blood and find him delicious," Rhiannon said.

Brodie knew he could fight her off, or he could teleport. But it was equally true that the last fight had taken a heavy toll on his strength. What was she playing at?

Trust me, she had said. She had a plan, even if he didn't know what it was.

She opened her mind to him, and he read her thoughts. *Trust me,* she pleaded again.

He nodded his acknowledgment.

To his amazement, she sank her fangs into his throat. And then, carefully hiding her actions from the others, she ripped a gash in her own wrist with her nail and forced the wound to his lips.

A vampire bite could be poison to an Other. And drinking vampire blood…he had no idea what that might do to him.

Inordinate strength seemed to rip through him. He leaped to his feet just as Joe came at him again, enraged.

"I warned you!" Audrey screamed. "She's done… something!"

Ignoring her, Brodie teleported, smashed the coffin, grabbed a shard of wood and thrust it into Joe's heart.

Audrey screamed and turned to run, but Rhiannon stopped her, picking up another makeshift stake.

"No!" Audrey shrieked.

"You're a killer," Rhiannon said. "I am the vampire Keeper—and I condemn you to die for your actions."

She impaled Audrey with a single thrust, never faltering.

Brodie looked at Rhiannon. "We've won," he told her. "But, Rhiannon, I'm Elven. A vampire bite will kill me. And if not the bite, the blood I drank."

She shook her head, beautiful beyond measure as she seemed almost to float over to him. "No," she told him. "Bobby thought the same—that I could kill him. But a bite from my fangs really isn't the same, and drinking my blood isn't the same at all. Because it's not real vampire blood. It was a *Keeper* bite. It won't kill you, and the power will fade from you just as it will from me."

He drew her into his arms, and they were both shaking.

But they were together….

And the enemy had been defeated.

A moment later Jerry burst into the room. "What's going on? Barrie came for me, and… Oh, Lord, what happened? I don't understand."

Before either of them could explain, Sailor and Barrie came running in.

"You did it," Sailor breathed to Rhiannon.

Rhiannon smiled and let go of Brodie to draw her cousins into her arms. "*We* did it," she said. She turned to Jerry, still holding tight to her cousins. "It's complicated, and we'll explain later, but let's just say it's a good thing we have Barrie at the paper. She'll see to it that everything's explained in a way that…makes sense."

"Sense?" Jerry asked. "In Hollywood? Is that really going to matter?"

Epilogue

Sailor found her new friend right away.

Or perhaps he found her.

As they walked through the kennels, their hearts bleeding for the unwanted animals waiting at the shelter in hopes of finding love and a home, a massive mix of golden retriever and…something jumped against the fence just as Sailor was passing. She jumped and then laughed, looking at the big yellow mutt.

"Well, hello," she said.

"That's Jonquil," the kennel volunteer said. "His owner died. Sad story, really. He sat by her bedside until a neighbor finally came in, worried because he hadn't seen the old lady in a week. The poor woman had no family, so there was no one to take Jonquil. He looks like a bruiser, but he's a kitten inside."

Sailor hunkered down by the kennel, slipping her fingers through the wire. Jonquil proceeded to slobber on her fingers, and that was it, she was in love. She looked up at Rhiannon, Barrie and Brodie. "I've found my true love," she told them.

"He's beautiful," Rhiannon assured her, and kept walking. She paused near what she thought was an empty kennel, then realized that a huge dog was huddled against the back wall. "Who's that?" she asked the attendant, who had come up behind her.

"Wizard," the woman said. "He's mostly Scottish deerhound, I think. Kind of wiry, kind of gray and he doesn't trust people easily."

Brodie joined Rhiannon then, and she looked at him and smiled. "Hmm. I don't trust people easily, either." She knelt by the kennel. "Hey," she said softly.

The dog stared back at her with wide eyes, hunching a little closer to the wall.

"Rhiannon, he might not be the right dog," Brodie warned.

She looked up at him. "His name is Wizard. He's the right one."

He shrugged and hunkered down beside her. "Come here, boy. Come on."

"Wizard?" Rhiannon called softly.

At last the dog moved away from the wall. He was mammoth, Rhiannon realized. Standing on his hind legs, he would be her height.

He came slowly toward them.

"I promise you, he doesn't bite," the attendant said.

"If only I could say the same about me," Rhiannon said, looking sheepishly at Brodie.

"The occasional bite can be a good thing," he assured her with a grin.

Just then she felt something wet touch her fingers,

and she turned to look back at Wizard. His big brown eyes were on her, and she could have sworn that she saw hope in them.

"I guess you've found your dog, too," Brodie said.

"Looks like we've got two dogs," Barrie said, coming over to see Wizard. "I'm going to find a cat."

"Right this way," the attendant said.

An hour later, animals in tow, they were back at the compound. On the ride home they'd decided to have a barbecue later. By evening the summer heat would slack off, but it would still be warm enough for everyone—even Brodie—to enjoy the pool.

But with the barbecue a few hours off, Brodie and Rhiannon were busy making Wizard comfortable, setting out his bowls and making him a bed in the kitchen out of an old comforter.

"I wonder if I should make him a bed upstairs in my room, too," Rhiannon said.

Brodie set his hands on her shoulders and said, "No. We already need to lock the door and hang up a do-not-disturb sign, what with your cousins and Merlin. We'll give Wizard plenty of love, and he'll be fine with that and enjoy his bed in the kitchen." He smiled knowingly at her. "In fact, I think we should give him a chance to try out his own bed in privacy right now."

He swept her off her feet into his arms, strong and secure. There really was nothing like an Elven for romantic gestures, she thought.

Wizard began to bark.

"It's okay, boy," Brodie said. "Your mama and I may be looking at a future together, so you'd better get used to me."

Wizard sat and wagged his tail.

Rhiannon stroked Brodie's cheek. "It's hard to know *where* we're going," she said. "An Elven and a Keeper."

"True—even with fortune-teller machines all over the house," he agreed. "I do know that I've never been happier. We are what we are—but I know I want to be with you more than anything in life, even if it's going to be a journey strewn with obstacles."

"Yeah, vampires, shapeshifters, werewolves, Elven, even some gnomes and a fairy or two," she said drily.

He nodded. "But I believe we can avoid them all. As long as you're game?"

She smiled. "There's nowhere else I'd rather be than where I am right now. In your arms." Lest she get too sappy, she added quickly, "Especially since you're Elven and very unlikely to drop me."

"Not a chance," he told her. "And I can scale staircases with a single bound."

She laughed, and he set out to prove it.

In seconds they were falling on the bed together, wrapped in each other's arms. Rhiannon was certain that the future that lay ahead would be hard, but equally certain that it would be worth it.

Then she forgot about the future, because she was too busy living in the present.

There was nothing in the world like making love with an Elven.

No.

There was nothing in the world like making love with *Brodie*.

* * * * *

THE KEEPERS

To Connie Perry, my extremely dear friend and cohort in many an endeavor. Thank you for all you do—and especially for New Orleans!

Also, for Daena Moller and Larry Montz and the ISPR. Thank you for some great adventures, too!

Prologue

When the world as we know it was created, it wasn't quite *actually* as we know it.

That's because so much was lost in the mists of time, and the collective memory of the human race often chooses what it will hold and what it will discard.

But once the world held no skyscrapers, rockets did not go to the moon—in fact, the wheel had barely been invented, and families lived together and depended upon one another. The denizens of the world knew better the beauty of waterfalls, of hills and vales, sun and sunset, shadows—and magic.

In a time when the earth was young, giants roamed, gnomes grumbled about in the forests and many a creature—malignant, sadly, as well as benign—was known to exist. Human beings might not have liked these creatures, they might have feared them—for a predator is a predator—but they knew of their existence, and as man has always learned to deal with predators, so he did then. Conversely, there were the creatures he loved, cherished as friends and often turned to when alliances needed to be formed. Humankind learned to exist by guidelines and rules, and thus the world went on, day after day, and man survived. Now, all men were not good, nor were all men bad, and so it was also with the giants, leprechauns, dwarfs, ghosts, pixies, pookas, vampires and other such beings.

Man was above them all, by his nature, and he prospered through centuries and then millennia, and learned to send rockets to the moon—and use rockets of another kind against his fellow man.

When the earth was young, and there were those creatures considered to be of light and goodness, and others who were considered to be, shall we say, more destructive, there was among them a certain form of being who was human and yet not human. Or perhaps human, but with special powers. They were the Keepers, and it was their lot in life not only to enjoy the world as other beings did, but they were also charged with the duty of maintaining balance. When certain creatures got out of hand, the Keepers were to bring them back under control. Some, in various centuries, thought of them as witches or wiccans. But in certain centuries that was not a healthy identity to maintain. Besides, they were not exactly the witches of a Papal Bull or evil in the way the devil in Dante's *Inferno,* nor were they the gentle women of pagan times who learned to heal with herbs and a gentle touch.

They were themselves and themselves alone. The Keepers.

As time went by, anything that was not purely *logi-*

cal was no longer accepted, was relegated to superstition, except in distant, fog-shrouded hills or the realm of Celtic imagination, which was filled with Celtic spirits other than those of which we speak. But some of the beliefs of the past were not accepted even there. Man himself is, of course, a predator, but man learned to live by rules and logic, or destroy all the creatures upon which he might prey. Too late for some, for man did hunt certain creatures to extinction, and he sought to drive others to the same fate. But those other creatures learned a survival technique that served them well: hide. Hide in plain sight, if you will, but hide.

As human populations grew, as people learned to read, as electricity reigned, and the telephone and computer put the world in touch, the earth became entrenched in a place where there were things that were accepted and others that were not. Oh, it's true that the older generations in Ireland knew that the banshees still wailed at night. In Hungary and the Baltic states, men and women knew that the tales of wolfmen in the forests were more than stories for a scary night. And there were other such pockets of belief around the globe. But few men living in the logical and technological world believed in myths and legends, which was good, because man was ever fond of destroying that which he feared.

All creatures, great and small, wish to survive. We all know what humans are like—far too quick to hunt down, kill or make war on those they didn't fully understand. Many people are trying, as they have tried for centuries, to see the light, to put away their prejudices. But that's a long journey, longer than the world has lasted so far.

Even so, those who were not quite human found various special places of strange tolerance to live their lives quietly and normally, without anyone paying them too much attention. Places where everyone was accustomed to the bizarre and, frankly, walked right by it most of the time.

Places like New Orleans, Louisiana.

Since there were plenty of people already living there who *thought* they were, or *claimed* to be, vampires, it seemed an eminently logical place for a well-behaved and politically correct vampire society to thrive, as well.

As a result, that is where several Keepers, charged with maintaining the balance between the otherworldly, under-the-radar societies of *beings* who flocked there, came as the twenty-first century rolled along.

And thus it was that the MacDonald sisters lived there, working, partying—this was New Orleans, after all—and, of course, keeping the balance of justice in a world that seldom collided with the world most people thought of as real, as the only world.

Seldom.

But not never.

There were exceptions.

Such as the September morning when Detective Jagger DeFarge got the call to come to the cemetery.

And there, stretched out on top of a tomb in the long defunct Grigsby family mausoleum, was the woman in white. Porcelain and beautiful, if it hadn't been for the delicate silk and gauze fabric that spread around her, she might have been a piece of funerary art, a statue, frozen in marble.

Because she, too, was white, as white as her dress, as white as the marble, because every last drop of blood had been drained from her body.

Chapter 1

"Sweet Jesus!" Detective Tony Miro said, crossing himself as he stared at the corpse.

The cemetery itself had already been closed off, yellow crime tape surrounding the area around the mausoleum. Jagger DeFarge had been assigned as lead detective on the case, and he knew he should have been complimented, but in reality he just felt weary—and deeply concerned.

Beyond the concern one felt over any victim of murder or violent crime.

This was far worse. This threatened a rising body count to come.

Gus Parissi, a young uniformed cop, stuck his head inside the mausoleum. The light was muted, streaks of sunlight that filtered in through the ironwork filigree at the top end of the little house within the "city of the dead."

Gus stared at the dead woman.

"Sweet Jesus," he echoed, and also crossed himself.

Jagger winced, looking away for a moment, waiting. He wanted to be alone with the victim, but he had a partner. Being alone wasn't going to be easy.

"Thank you, Parissi," Jagger said. "The crime-scene crew can have the place in ten minutes. Hey, Miro, go on out and see who's on the job today, will you?"

Miro was still just staring.

"And get another interview with Tom Cooley, too. He's the guide who saw her and called it in, right?" Jagger asked.

"Uh—yeah, yeah," Tony said, closing his mouth at last, turning and following Gus out.

Alone at last, my poor, poor dear, Jagger thought.

The dust of the ages seemed to have settled within the burial chamber, on the floor, on the stone and concrete walls, on the plaques that identified the dead within the vault. In contrast, the young woman on the tomb was somehow especially beautiful and pristine, a vision in white, like an angel. Sighing, Jagger walked over to the body. To all appearances, she was sleeping like a heavenly being in her pure perfection.

He pulled out his pocket flashlight to look for the bite marks that had to exist. He gently and carefully moved her hair, but there were no marks on her neck. He searched her thighs, then her arms, his eyes quick but thorough.

At last he found what he sought. He doubted that the medical examiner—even with the most up-to-date technology available—would ever find the tiny pinpricks located in the crease at her elbow.

He swore out loud just as Tony returned.

His partner was a young cop. A good cop, and not a squeamish one. Most of the crimes taking place these days had to do with a sudden flare of temper and, as always, drugs. Tony had worked a homicide with him just outside the Quarter in which a kid the size of a pro linebacker had taken a shotgun blast in the face. Tony had been calm and professional throughout the grisly first inspection, then handled the player's mother with gentle care.

Today, however, he seemed freaked.

"What?" Tony asked.

Jagger shook his head. "No blood here at all, no signs of violence. No lividity, but she's still in rigor.... Is the M.E. here?"

Tony nodded.

"Send him in," Jagger said. "Have you interviewed the guide yet?"

Tony, staring at the body, shook his head. "One of the uniforms went to find him."

"He can't have gone far. Stay out there until they find him and interview him. And anyone who was with him. Then meet me back at the station, and we'll get her picture out in the media. I want uniforms raking the neighborhood, the Dumpsters, you name it, looking for a purse, clothing, anything they can find."

Tony nodded and left.

The M.E. the Coroner's Office had sent out that morning was Craig Dewey. Dewey looked like anything but the general conception of what a medical examiner should: he was tall, blond, about thirty-five. Basically, until they found out what he did for a living, most women considered him a heartthrob.

Like the others, he paused in the door. But Dewey

didn't stand there stunned and frozen as Tony and Gus had done. He *did* stare, but Jagger could see that his keen blue eyes were taking in the scene, top to bottom, before he approached the corpse. Finally that stare focused on the victim. He looked at her for a long while, then turned to Jagger.

"Well, here's one for the books," he said, his tone matter-of-fact. "On initial inspection, without even touching her, I'd say she's been entirely drained of blood." He looked around. "And it wasn't done here."

"No. I'd say not," Jagger agreed with what appeared to be obvious.

"Such a pity, and so strange. Murder is never beautiful, and yet…she *is* beautiful," Dewey commented.

"Dewey, give me something that isn't in plain sight," Jagger said.

Dewey went to work. He was efficient and methodical. He had his camera out, the flash going as he shot the body from every conceivable angle. Then he approached the woman, checked for liver temperature and shook his head. "She's still in rigor. Other than the fact that she's about bloodless, I have no idea what's going on here. I'll need to get her into the morgue to figure out how and why she died. I can't find anything to show how it might have happened. Odd, really odd. A body without blood wouldn't shock me—we seem to attract wackos to this city all the time—but I can't find so much as a pinprick to explain what happened. Hell, like I said, I've got to get her out of here to check further. Lord knows, enough people around here *think* they're vampires."

"Right, I know," Jagger said. "When did she die? I was estimating late last night or early this morning."

"Then you're right on," Dewey told him. "She died sometime between midnight and two in the morning, but give me fifteen minutes either side."

"I want everything you get as quickly as you get it," Jagger said.

"I have two shooting deaths, a motorcycle accident, a possible vehicular homicide—not to mention that the D.A.'s determined to harass an octogenarian over her husband's death, even though he's been suffering from cancer for years—" Dewey broke off, seeing the set expression on Jagger's face. "Sure, Defarge. I'll put a rush on it. This is the kind of thing you've got to get a handle on quickly, God knows. We get enough sensationalist media coverage around here. I don't want to see a frenzy start."

"Thanks," Jagger told him.

He looked around the Grigsby family tomb one more time. It was what he *didn't* see that he noted. No fingerprints in the dust. No footprints. No sign whatsoever of how the girl had come to lie, bloodless and beautiful, upon the dusty tomb of a long-dead patriarch.

He wanted the CSUs, Tony and the uniforms all busy here. He had some investigating to do that he needed to tackle on his own.

He lowered his sunglasses from the top of his head to his eyes and walked back out into the brilliant light of the early fall morning.

The sky was cloudless and brilliantly blue. The air was pleasant, without the dead heat of summer.

It seemed to be a day when the world was vibrant. Positively *pulsing* with life.

"Hey, Detective DeFarge!"

It was Celia Larson, forty, scrubbed, the no-nonsense

head of the crime-scene unit that had been assigned. "Can we go on in? I've had my folks working the area, around the entry, around the tomb…but, hey, with the cemeteries around here being such tourist hangouts, folks had been tramping around for an hour before we got the call. We've collected every possible sample we could, but we really need to get inside."

"It's all yours, Celia. And good luck."

She leaned into the mausoleum and said accusingly, "You and Dewey have tramped all over the footprints."

"There were no footprints."

"There had to be footprints," she said flatly, as if he was the worst kind of fool.

He shrugged and smiled.

"None, but, hey, you're the expert. You'll see what we missed, right?" he asked pleasantly. Celia wasn't his favorite civil servant with whom to work. She considered every police officer, from beat cop right on up to detective, to be an oaf with nothing better to do than mess up her crime scene. She didn't seem to understand the concept of teamwork—or that she was the technician, and the detectives used her information to put the pieces together, find the suspect and make the arrest. Celia had seen way too many CSI-type shows and had it in her head that she was going to be the detective who solved every case. Still, he did his best to be level-tempered and professional, if not pleasant. He did have to work with the woman.

"Get me a good picture of the face, Celia. We'll get her image out to the media."

She waved a hand dismissively, and he walked on.

This wasn't going to be an ordinary case. And he

wasn't going to be able to investigate in any of the customary ways.

He made it as far as the sidewalk.

Then he saw real trouble.

He groaned inwardly. Of course she would show up. Of course—despite the fact that he'd only just seen the corpse himself, word had traveled.

She didn't look like trouble. Oddly enough, she came with a smile that was pure charm, and she was, in fact, stunning. She was tall and slim and lithe, mercurial in her graceful movements.

Her eyes were blue. They could be almost as aqua as the sea, as light as a summer sky, as piercing as midnight.

Naturally she was a blonde. Not that brunettes couldn't be just as beautiful, just as angelic looking— or just as manipulative.

She had long blond hair. Like her eyes, it seemed to change. It could appear golden in the sun, platinum in moonlight and always as smooth and soft as silk as it curled over her shoulders. She had a fringe of bangs that were both waiflike and the height of fashion.

And naturally she was here.

Sunglasses shaded her eyes, as they did his. The Southern Louisiana sun could be brutal. Most people walked around during the day with shades on.

"Well, hello, Miss MacDonald," he said, heading for his car. Officers had blocked the entry to the cemetery and the borders of the scene itself with crime-scene tape. But the sidewalk was fair game. The news crews had arrived and staked it out, and the gawkers were lining up, as well.

Before Fiona MacDonald could reply, one of the local

network news reporters saw him and charged over, calling, "Detective! Detective DeFarge!" It was Andrea "Andy" Larkin. She was a primped and proper young woman who had recently been transferred from her network's Ohio affiliate. She was a fish out of water down here.

She was followed by her cameraman, and he was followed by a pack of other reporters. The local cable stations and newspapers were all present. And, yes, there came the other network newscasters.

He stopped. Might as well handle the press now, he thought, though the department's community rep really should be fielding the questions. But if he dodged the reporters, it would just make things worse.

He held his ground, aware that Fiona was watching him from a spot not far from the cemetery wall. He wasn't going to escape the reporters, and he definitely wasn't going to escape her.

"Detective DeFarge?" Andy Larkin had apparently assigned herself to be the spokeswoman for the media crew. "We've heard a young woman has been found— drained of blood. Who was she? Do you think we have some kind of cultists at work in the area? Was it a ritual sacrifice?"

He lifted a hand as a clamoring of questions arose, one voice indistinguishable from the next.

"Ladies, gentlemen, please! We've just begun our investigation into this case. Yes, we *have* discovered the body of a young woman in a mausoleum, but that's all that I can really tell you at the moment. We'll have the preliminary autopsy reports in a day or so, which will answer any questions about the state of the body. We don't have an identity for the victim, and it's far too early for me to speculate in any way on whether this is a singular incident or not. However, at this time I have no reason to suspect that we have a cult at work in the city. As soon as I have information, you'll have information. That's absolutely all that I am at liberty to say at the moment."

"But—" Andy Larkin began.

"At any time that I *can,* without jeopardizing our investigation, I will be happy to see to it that the news media is advised."

"Wait!" A man from one of the rags spoke up; he was probably in his early twenties, taking the best job available to a young journalism graduate. His hair was long and shaggy, and he was wearing jeans and a T-shirt, and carrying a notepad rather than an electronic device of any kind. "Shouldn't you be warning the citizens of New Orleans to be careful? Shouldn't you be giving them a profile of the killer?"

Jagger hoped his sunglasses fully covered his eyes as he inadvertently stared over at Fiona MacDonald.

She had a profile of the killer, he was certain.

"We don't know anything yet. I repeat—we've just begun our investigation. I'm going to give young women in this city the same warning I give all the time—be smart, and be careful. Don't go walking the streets alone in the dark. Let someone know where you're going at all times, and if you go out to party, don't go alone. People, use common sense. That's my warning."

"But aren't serial killers usually young white men between the ages of twenty-five and thirty-five?" shouted a tiny woman from the rear. She was Livy Drew, from a small local cable station.

He reminded himself that he had to stay calm—and

courteous. The public affairs department was much better at that, though, and he fervently wished they would hurry up and get there.

"Livy, there's nothing to indicate that we have a serial killer on our hands."

"You're denying that this is the work of a serial killer?"

"I'm not denying or confirming anything," he said, fighting for patience. "One more time—our investigation is just beginning. Yes, young women should take special care, because yes, a young woman has been killed. Now, if you'll let me get to work, I'll be able to answer more questions for you in the future. Though we have no ID on her yet, we may make a hit with fingerprints or dental impressions, and we'll have a picture available for you soon. And, as always, the department will be grateful for any information that can help us identify the victim—and find her killer. But no heroics from anyone, please. Just call the station with any information you may have."

Someone called from the back of the crowd. "Detective, what—"

"That's all!" Jagger said firmly, then turned to head for his car, parked almost directly in front of the gates. He looked for Fiona MacDonald, but she was gone.

He knew where he would find her.

He got into his car and pulled away from the curb, glancing expectantly in the rearview mirror. She was just sitting up. Her expression was grim as she stared at him.

"What the hell is going on, DeFarge?" she asked.

He nearly smiled. If things hadn't been quite so serious, he would have.

"I don't know."

"Well, *I* do. You have a rogue vampire on your hands. And you have to put a stop to this immediately."

He pulled up the ramp to a public parking area by the river. He found a quiet place to park along the far edge of the lot and turned to look at her.

Fiona was young, somewhere around twenty-nine or thirty, he thought. Young in any world, very young in *their* world.

They knew each other, of course; they saw each other now and then at the rare council meetings in which several underworld groups met to discuss events, make suggestions, keep tabs on one another and keep the status quo going.

He suddenly wished fervently that her parents were still alive. The savage war that had nearly ripped through the city had been stopped only by the tremendous sacrifice the couple had made, leaving their daughters to watch over the evenly divided main powers existing in the underbelly of New Orleans, a world few even knew existed.

Naturally the war had been fought because of a vampire.

No, not true. A vampire and a shapeshifter.

Vampire Cato Leone had fallen deeply and madly in love with shapeshifter Susan Chaisse, who had fallen in love with him in return. The two had been unable to understand why they weren't allowed to fall in love. Frankly Jagger didn't understand it, either. Old World prejudice had done them in. It had been a *Romeo and Juliet* scenario, a Southern *West Side Story,* a tale as old as time. Young love seldom cared about proper boundaries. Man and every subspecies of man seemed prone to prejudice, and it was usually born of fear and or economics. Either way, the outcome was almost always the same. In this case, just as in Shakespeare's tale, it had been cousins of the young lovers who had caused the problems. Susan's first cousin Julian had taken on the form of a monster being, half vampire, half werewolf, and attacked Cato. Shapeshifters were truly gifted; they could take on whatever shape they chose, and mimic not only another's appearance but take on their powers, as well. Cato hadn't even known who he was battling, and in the thick of the fight his own cousin jumped to his aid and was killed by the shapeshifter. That raised an uncontrollable rage in Cato, who in turn killed his attacker, and because the shapeshifter had taken on a guise that was partly werewolf, Cato's family had attacked the werewolves, and the violence had threatened to spill over into the streets. The power that Fiona MacDonald's parents had summoned to defeat the warring parties had cost them their lives. No Keeper, no matter how strong, could exert that much power and survive.

They had known what they were doing. But they had known as well that if the battle had erupted into the human world, it would have brought about the destruction of them all. Humans far outnumbered the various paranormal subspecies, not just here, but across the world, though the largest concentration of any such creatures was right here, in New Orleans, Louisiana, commonly referred to locally as NOLA. History had decreed that they all learn how to coexist. Werewolves learned to harness their power at each full moon, and vampires learned how to exist on the occasional foray into a blood bank, along with a steady diet of cow's blood. The shapeshifters had it the easiest, subsisting in their human form on human diets. Hell, half of them were vegetarians these days.

"Fiona," he said quietly, "I can only repeat what I've said to the media. I don't know anything yet. I have to investigate. God knows there are enough idiots living here, and more coming all the time, who want to *think* they're vampires. You can't deny that this city does attract more than its share of would-be mystics, cultists, wiccans, psychics and plain old nuts."

"I heard that she was entirely drained of blood," Fiona said flatly.

He wished that he were dealing with her mother. Jen MacDonald had lived a long life; she had been a fine Keeper, along with her husband, Ewan. The two—both born with the marks of each of the three major subspecies—had been fair and judicious. And wise. They had never jumped to conclusions; they had always done their own questioning, conducted their own investigations. They had loved those they had been born to watch, never interjecting themselves into the governing councils of their charges but being there in case of disputes or problems—or to point out potential problems before they became major bones of contention.

Jagger took a deep breath. He had become a police officer himself because he didn't want history to keep repeating itself. Most of the underworld—Keepers included—had come to NOLA after years of seeking a real home. The church's battle against "witchcraft" had begun as long ago as the 900s, and in 1022, even monks—pious, but outspoken against some of the doctrines of the church—had been burned. Witchcraft had become synonymous with devil worship, and the monks were said to cavort with demons and devils, indulge in mass orgies, and sacrifice and even eat small children. In 1488 the Papal Bull issued by Pope Innocent III set off hundreds of years of torture and death for any innocent accused of witchcraft. Jagger found it absolutely astounding that any intelligent man had ever believed that the thousands persecuted through the years could possibly have been the devil worshipping witches they were condemned for being. If they'd had half the powers they were purported to possess, they would have called upon the devil and flown far away from the stake, where they were tied and allowed to choose between the garrote or burning alive.

Sadly thousands of innocents had perished after cruel torture. The Inquisition had thrived in Germany and France, and many of those who truly weren't human left to escape possible discovery. Many of the main subspecies, as well as the smaller groups, came to the New World from the British Isles. Pixies, fairies, leprechauns, banshees and more fled during the reign of James VI of Scotland, also known as James I of England. Before 1590, the Scots hadn't been particularly interested in witchcraft. But in that year James—as a self-professed expert—began to enforce the laws with a vengeance and impose real punishment. He was terrified of a violent death, and certain that witches had been responsible for a storm that had nearly killed him and his new wife at sea. His orders sent the witch-finder general into a frenzy, torturing and killing for the most ridiculous of reasons, using the most hideous of methods.

When the Puritans headed for the New World in the early 1600s—intent, oddly enough, on banishing anyone from their colonies who was not of their faith, despite the fact that they had traveled across the ocean in pursuit of religious freedom—the various not-quite-human species began to make their way across the sea to a new life, as well.

There were other witchcraft trials in the New World before Salem, but it was the frenzy of the Salem witchcraft trials that caused another mass migration. The French in America had little interest in witchcraft, and French law allowed for a great deal more freedom of belief.

By the time of the Louisiana Purchase, most Keepers and their charges alike had made it down to New Orleans. And there, though not particularly trusting of one another, they had still found a safe home.

Until the elder MacDonalds had been killed. Their deaths, their sacrifice, had been noted by all clans and families. And not only had peace been restored, there had been a sea change in the way the different species felt about each other. There had been a number of intermarriages since that time. Of course, there were still those who were totally against any intermingling of the bloodlines, those who thought themselves superior.

But overall, there had been peace. America was a free country. They were free to hold their own opinions about sex, religion, politics—and one another. They obeyed the laws, the countries and their own. And their most important law said that no one was to commit crimes against humanity—and bring human persecution down upon them.

"Yes," he said quietly, "she was drained of blood."

"And a vampire did it?" Fiona demanded.

"Fiona, I'm trying to tell you—I've only just begun to investigate," he said.

"Oh, please. I'm not with the media."

He looked at her in the rearview mirror. "And you haven't the patience, knowledge or wisdom of your parents, Fiona."

Maybe that hadn't been a good thing to say. She stiffened like a ramrod. But, somehow, she managed to speak evenly.

"My parents died to keep you all from killing one another and preying upon the citizenry of the city in your lust for power and desire to rip each other to pieces. My parents were unique—both of them born with all three of the major signs. But that was then, and this is now. My sisters and I were born without the full power of my parents, but you know that I was born with the sign of the winged being, Caitlin with the mercurial sign of the shapeshifter and Shauna with the sign of the fang. But here's where we do have an edge—I have all the strengths of the vampire, and the vampires are my dedicated concern, just as Caitlin must watch over the shapeshifters and Shauna is responsible for the werewolves. Don't you think I wish my mother were here, too? But she's not. And I will not let the vampire community start something up again, something that promises discovery, death and destruction for hundreds of our own who are innocent. Do you understand? Whoever did this must be destroyed. If you don't handle it, I will."

He swung around to face her. "Back off! Give me time. Or do you want to start your own witch hunt?"

"You need to discover the truth—and quickly," she said. "And trust me—I will be watching you every step of the way."

"Of course you will be," he said, regaining his temper. He couldn't let her unnerve him. "Damn it! Don't you think I realize just how dangerous this situation is? But these *are* different times. Hell, I'm a cop. I see violence every day. I see man's inhumanity to man constantly. But I also see the decency in the world. So let me do what I do."

She was silent for a minute.

"Just do it quickly, Jagger."

"With pleasure. Now would you be so kind as to get out of my car so I can begin? Or should I drop you off at the shop?" he asked icily.

"I'll get out of your car," she said softly.

Oh, yes, she would get out. She wouldn't want to be seen around her shop in a police car—even an unmarked car. Especially *his* car.

The rear door slammed as she exited. She paused for a moment by his window, staring at him through the dark lenses of her glasses.

So fierce.

And so afraid.

Yes, whether she wanted to admit it or not, she was afraid. Well, she had a right to her fear, as well as that chip on her shoulder. She'd been nineteen when her parents died, and she had fought to prove that she could care for herself and her sisters, who'd been only seventeen and fifteen at the time. She had taken on the mantle of responsibility in two worlds, and thus far she had carried it well.

The wind lifted her hair. Despite himself, he felt something stir inside him.

She was so beautiful.

She was such a bitch!

"Good day, Fiona. I'll be seeing you."

"Good day, Detective. You can bet on it," she said, and turned to walk away, the sunlight turning her hair into a burst of sheer gold.

Chapter 2

New Orleans was her city, and Fiona MacDonald loved it with a passion.

She tried to remember that as she walked away from Jagger DeFarge's car.

The parking area was new and paved, and sat on an embankment right at the edge of the river.

She paused to look down at the Mississippi. It really was a mighty river. The currents could be vicious; storms could make it toss and churn, and yet it could also be beautiful and glorious, the vein of life for so many people who had settled along its banks.

The great river had allowed for the magnificent plantations whose owners had built an amazing society of grace and custom—and slavery. But even in the antebellum days before the Civil War, New Orleans had offered a home for "free men of color." Ironically, black men had owned black men, and quadroons had been *the* mistresses of choice. In Fiona's mind, the city was home to some of the most beautiful people in the world even now, people who came in all shades. God, yes, she loved her city. It was far from perfect. The economy was still suffering, and, as ever, the South still struggled to gain educational parity with the North.

But everyone lived in this city: black, white, yellow, red, brown and every shade in between. Young and old, men and women.

And the denizens of the underworld, of course.

She took a deep breath as she stared at the river. She was furious, yes. She was afraid, yes. And what might have been bothering her most was the fact that she didn't think Jagger DeFarge had actually intended to wound her with his words.

God, yes! Her parents would have handled this much better. But they were dead. They had known what they were doing would cost them their last strength, their last breaths. But they had believed in a beautiful world, where peace could exist, where everyone could accept everyone else.

She walked down to Decatur Street and paused. St. Louis Cathedral stood behind Jackson Square, its steeple towering over the scene before it, including the garden with its magnificent equestrian statue of Andrew Jackson. Café du Monde was to her right—filled with tourists, naturally. It was a "must see" for visitors, perhaps something like the Eiffel Tower in Paris, even if it wasn't nearly so grand. It was a true part of New Orleans, and she decided to brave the crowd of the tourists and pick up a nice café au lait for the three block walk back to the shop on Royal Street.

Though an actual drink might be better at this mo-

OFFICIAL OPINION POLL

Dear Reader,

Since you are a book enthusiast, we would like to know what you think.

Inside you will find a short Opinion Poll. Please participate in our poll by sharing your opinion on 3 subjects that are very important to all of us.

To thank you for your participation, we would like to send you **2 FREE BOOKS** and **2 FREE GIFTS!**

Please enjoy them with our compliments.

Sincerely,

Pam Powers

YOUR OPINION POLL
THANK-YOU FREE GIFTS INCLUDE:

▶ **2 PARANORMAL ROMANCE BOOKS**
▶ **2 LOVELY SURPRISE GIFTS**

OFFICIAL OPINION POLL

YOUR OPINION COUNTS!
Please check TRUE or FALSE below to express your opinion about the following statements:

Q1 Do you believe in "true love"?

"TRUE LOVE HAPPENS ONLY ONCE IN A LIFETIME."
○ TRUE
○ FALSE

Q2 Do you think marriage has any value in today's world?

"YOU CAN BE TOTALLY COMMITTED TO SOMEONE WITHOUT BEING MARRIED."
○ TRUE
○ FALSE

Q3 What kind of books do you enjoy?

"A GREAT NOVEL MUST HAVE A HAPPY ENDING."
○ TRUE
○ FALSE

YES! I have placed my sticker in the space provided below. Please send me the **2 FREE books** and **2 FREE gifts** for which I qualify. I understand that I am under no obligation to purchase anything further, as explained on the back of this card.

237/337 HDL FV55

FIRST NAME

LAST NAME

ADDRESS

APT.#

CITY

STATE/PROV.

ZIP/POSTAL CODE

TF-PAR-13
Printed in the U.S.A.
© 2012 HARLEQUIN ENTERPRISES LIMITED.

⊕ HARLEQUIN READER SERVICE—Here's How It Works:

Accepting your 2 free books and 2 free gifts (gifts valued at approximately $10.00) places you under no obligation to buy anything. You may keep the books and gifts and return the shipping statement marked "cancel." If you do not cancel, about a month later we'll send you 4 additional books and bill you just $21.42 in the U.S. or $23.46 in Canada. That is a savings of at least 21% off the cover price of all 4 books! It's quite a bargain! Shipping and handling is just 50¢ per book in the U.S. and 75¢ per book in Canada.* You may cancel at any time, but if you choose to continue, every month we'll send you 4 more books, which you may either purchase at the discount price or return to us and cancel your subscription.

*Terms and prices subject to change without notice. Prices do not include applicable taxes. Sales tax applicable in N.Y. Canadian residents will be charged applicable taxes. Offer not valid in Quebec. Books received may not be as shown. All orders subject to credit approval. Credit or debit balances in a customer's account(s) may be offset by any other outstanding balance owed by or to the customer. Please allow 4 to 6 weeks for delivery. Offer available while quantities last.

If offer card is missing write to: Harlequin Reader Service, P.O. Box 1867, Buffalo NY 14240-1867 or visit: www.ReaderService.com

BUSINESS REPLY MAIL
FIRST-CLASS MAIL   PERMIT NO. 717   BUFFALO, NY

POSTAGE WILL BE PAID BY ADDRESSEE

HARLEQUIN READER SERVICE
PO BOX 1341
BUFFALO NY 14240-8571

NO POSTAGE
NECESSARY
IF MAILED
IN THE
UNITED STATES

ment. A Hand Grenade or a Hurricane, or any one of the other alcoholic libations so enjoyed on Bourbon Street.

But she couldn't have a drink. She couldn't drink away what had happened—or everything she feared might be about to happen next.

She made her way through the open air patio to the take-away window, ordered a large café au lait to go, then headed on up toward Chartres Street and then Royal. Her love for the city returned to her like a massive wave as she walked. She returned a greeting to a friend who gave tours in one of the mule-drawn carriages, and headed on past the red brick Pontalba Building. She passed shops selling T-shirts, masks, the ever-present Mardi Gras beads, postcards and sometimes, true relics, along with hand-crafted art and apparel.

Some of the buildings along her path were in good repair, while others still needed a great deal of help. Construction was constant in a city that was hundreds of years old, where the charming balconies often sagged, and where, even before Hurricane Katrina, many had struggled through economic difficulties to do what was needed piecemeal.

But there was something she loved even about the buildings that were still in dire need of tender care.

The French Quarter's buildings were an architectural wonderland. The area had passed through many hands—French, Spanish, British and American—but it had been during the Spanish period in 1788 that the Great Fire of New Orleans had swept away more than eight hundred of the original buildings. And then, in 1794, a second fire had taken another two hundred plus. The current St. Louis Cathedral had been built in 1789, so it, like much of the "French Quarter," had actually been built in the Spanish style.

She reached her destination, a corner on Royal, and paused, looking at the facade of their shop and their livelihood.

A Little Bit of Magic was on the ground floor of a truly charming building that dated back to 1823. She ran the shop with Caitlin and Shauna, her sisters, and she supposed, in their way, they were as much a part of the tourist scene as any other business. When you got right down to it, they sold fantasy, fun, belief and, she supposed, to some, religion. She remembered that, although they attended St. Louis Cathedral regularly, her mother had once told her, "All paths lead to God, and it doesn't matter if you call him Jehovah, Allah, Buddha, or even if you believe that he is a she."

She knew that her parents had always believed in two basic tenets: that there was a supreme being, and that all creatures, including human beings, came in varying shades of good and evil. The world was not black-and-white. Like New Orleans, it was all shades in between.

And so, in A Little Bit of Magic, they sold just about everything. They had expansive shelves on Wiccan beliefs, voodoo history and rights, myths and legends, spiritualism, Native American cultures, Buddhism, Hinduism, Christianity and Judaism and more. She ordered the books for the shop, and she loved reading about different beliefs and cultures.

Caitlin, however, was their reigning mystic. She was brilliant with a tarot deck. Shauna was the palm reader, while she herself specialized in tea leaves—easily accessible, since they had a little coffee and tea bar of their own.

They also sold beautiful hand-crafted capes, apparel, masks—this was New Orleans, after all—jewelry, wands, statues, dolls, voodoo paraphernalia and, sometimes, relics and antiques. The shop had always done a good business, and despite occasional disagreements, the sisters got along extremely well.

She sipped her café au lait, hoping it would give her what she needed: patience, wisdom and strength.

In a way, at the beginning, it had been easier. She'd been nineteen, an adult. Caitlin had been right behind her at seventeen, but Shauna had been only fifteen. It had been quite a fight to get the family courts to allow her to "raise" her sisters, but she had managed. She'd had help from a dear old friend, August Gaudin—a werewolf, of all things—but he had a fine reputation in the city, and he'd been her strength. At first, her sisters had been young, lost, so what she said was the law. But she had never wanted to hold them down, and now they were women in their own right, with valid thoughts and opinions.

And they were both going to be in a state of extreme anxiety now!

Squaring her shoulders both physically and mentally, Fiona entered the store. Caitlin was behind the counter, chatting with a woman who was selecting tea. She eyed Fiona sharply as she entered, but continued her explanation of the different leaves.

Fiona saw that Shauna was helping a young couple pick out masks.

She nodded to both her sisters and walked through the store to the office in the rear, where she pulled up the chair behind her desk.

First things first. Then, tonight, a trip to the morgue.

A minute later, Caitlin burst in on her.

"Is it true? A dead woman in the cemetery, *drained of blood?*"

Fiona nodded. "I saw Jagger DeFarge. He's lead detective on the case. Naturally I told him that he has to find the killer right away, and obviously we don't care if it's one of his own, the murderer must be destroyed."

Caitlin sank into the chair on the other side of the desk. Fiona knew that the three of them resembled one another, and yet there were also noticeable differences. Her sister had the most beautiful silver eyes she had ever seen, while Shauna's had a touch of green and hers were blue. Her own hair was very light, Caitlin's a shade darker and Shauna's had a touch of red. Their heights were just a shade different, too. She was shortest at five-seven, while Caitlin had a half an inch on her, and Shauna was five-eight.

Right now, Caitlin's eyes were darkening like clouds on a stormy day.

"He admits the killer has to be a vampire?"

"No, of course not. He didn't admit anything."

"But we all know it has to have been a vampire."

Fiona hesitated. The last thing she wanted to do was defend Jagger DeFarge.

She had kept her distance from him, for the most part. Keepers were not supposed to interfere with everyday life. They did have their councils—kind of like a paranormal Elks Club, she thought with a smile—but as long as the status quo stayed the status quo, each society dealt with their own.

She knew, however, that Jagger did well in life passing as a normal citizen of the city. He was a highly respected police detective and had been decorated by the department.

She'd seen him a few times on television when he'd been interviewed after solving a high profile case. She remembered one interview in particular, when Jagger and his squad had brought in a killer who had scratched out a brutal path of murder from Oregon to Louisiana.

"Frankly, most of the time, what appears on the surface is what a perpetrator *wants* us to see. Any good officer has to look below the surface. In our city, sadly, we have a high crime rate much of it due to greed, passion or envy, not to mention drugs and domestic violence. But in searching for those who murder because of mental derangement or more devious desires, we can never accept anything at face value," he had said.

Before she could reply to Caitlin's question, Shauna came rushing into the office breathlessly. "Well?"

Her youngest sister's hair was practically flying. She was wearing a soft silk halter dress that swirled around her as she ran, and even when she stopped in front of the desk, she still seemed to be in motion.

"Jagger won't admit that it was a vampire. Maybe I'm phrasing that wrong. He said that he has to investigate. He reminded me that this is New Orleans—that we attract human wackos just the same as we attract those of us who just want to live normal lives. He didn't insist that it wasn't a vampire, he just said that he needs to investigate."

"Vampires!" Caitlin said, her tone aggravated, as if vampires were the cause of everything that ever went wrong.

"What are you going to do?" Shauna asked.

Fiona frowned. "I don't know. But look, we can't all be back here. We can't leave the shop unattended."

"I put the Out for Lunch sign up in the window," Shauna said.

"Out for lunch? It's ten-thirty in the morning!" Fiona protested.

"Okay, so we're having an early lunch," Shauna said with a shrug.

"What do you intend to do?" Caitlin asked. "And don't say you don't know, because I know that's not true."

"Investigate myself," Fiona said with a shrug. "Vampires. It's my duty. I *will* find out the truth, and I *will* fix the situation." She sighed. "Obviously I'll be out most of the day. Oh, and even if we have to have 'lunch' several times in one day, never leave the shop unattended with the door open. We need to be especially careful now, all right?"

Her sisters nodded gravely.

Fiona rose. She had to get started. The situation demanded immediate action.

"Where are you going first?" Caitlin asked her.

"To see August Gaudin," Fiona said grimly.

Usually werewolves were not her favorite beings, though she tried very hard not to be prejudiced and stereotype them. It was the whole transformation thing that seemed so strange to her—so painful. And the baying at the moon.

Vampires were capable of certain transformations, as well, though it was far more a matter of astral projection and hypnotism. A vampire could take on a few legendary forms, such as a wolf and a bat, but they were weakened in such states, and since no vampire wanted to go up against an angry werewolf, for example, in the creature's own shape, the legendary transformation seldom happened.

Like vampires and shapeshifters, werewolves lived among the human population of the city, controlling themselves—with Shauna as their Keeper. But August Gaudin had fought alongside her parents, and in his human shape he was a dignified older man with silver hair, a broad chest and broad shoulders, and benign and gentle powder-blue eyes. He was an attorney by trade, and he had been elected to the city commission, and also worked with the tourism board. He had been genuinely wonderful to Fiona and her sisters, helping them when they truly needed a friend.

His offices were on Canal Street, and she walked there as quickly as she could, not wanting to call ahead, because trying to explain on the phone or, worse, leave a message would be too difficult.

August would see her. He always did.

The office manager stopped her when she would have absently burst right through to see him, but they had met before, and the woman knew that August wouldn't turn Fiona down. Still, the woman pursed her lips and said, "Please, sit, and I will let Mr. Gaudin know that you're here."

"I'll stand, thank you," Fiona said. Silly. The woman was just wielding her power.

August Gaudin came out to greet her, reaching out to take her hands. "Fiona! Dear child, come on in, come on in. Margaret, hold my calls, please."

Gaudin's office was a comfortable place. He had a large mahogany desk, and leather chairs that were both comfortable and somehow strong. The office conveyed the personality of the man.

He sat behind his desk as Fiona fell into a chair before it.

"I was expecting you," he told her.

"I suppose the entire city has heard by now," she said. She leaned forward. "August, the girl was murdered by a vampire. I'm sure of it. She was drained of blood. Completely. The wretched creatures are at it again!"

"Now, Fiona, that's not necessarily true," August told her. "First, we all know that—"

"Yes, yes, there are ridiculous human beings out there who think they're vampires, who even cut each other and drink each other's blood."

"It *is* possible that such a lunatic killed the woman," August said.

"Possible, but not likely."

"I take it that Jagger DeFarge is the investigating officer?"

"Yes. Imagine," she said dryly.

"That's good, *cher*. He'll know how to investigate properly, and he won't get himself killed in the process," he told her.

"August, this is my fault," she whispered.

"Now, stop. It's not your fault. It's your duty to see that the perpetrator is caught and punished. But it's not your fault any more than it's your fault when some crackhead falls on top of his own infant and kills him, or when drug slayings occur on the street. Crime exists. And it's unreasonable to expect that crime will never exist in our world just as it does in the human world," he said softly.

She stood and began pacing the room. "Yes, but…

if the vampires respected me as their Keeper, they wouldn't have dared attempt such a thing."

"Not true. There will always be rogues in any society."

"August, you've always helped me. What should I do?" she asked.

He leaned back. "You tell me."

"All right. Tonight, I make sure that the victim isn't coming back, that…that she rests in peace. I'll go as soon as the morgue is closed, and hopefully before… well, before. Then I'll go to see David Du Lac at the club and make sure he's ready to deal with what's happened."

"The perfect plan. Here's another," August told her.

"What?"

"Trust in Jagger DeFarge. He's a good cop. He became a cop to make sure he regulated things that happened among our kind. He's thorough in every investigation. He'll be especially vigilant on this one."

"He's a vampire."

"He's proven that he has integrity and honor."

"He won't want to destroy another vampire."

"He'll do what is right. You have to trust in that."

"I'd like to," she said.

"But?"

"He's a vampire," she repeated.

Jagger headed straight to Underworld, the club owned by David Du Lac, the head of the vampire population of the City of New Orleans. His rule stretched farther, but the city was his domain. He was essentially considered the vampire mayor.

And he did a better job than some of the human beings who had been entrusted with the city's human citizens, Jagger thought.

Naturally Underworld was frequented by vampires. But David Du Lac prided himself on running an establishment where everyone was welcome. He brought in the best bands and kept the place eclectic, and the human clientele never had any idea just who they were rubbing shoulders with.

Underworld was located just off Esplanade, on Frenchman Street. The edifice was a deconsecrated church. Beautiful stained-glass windows remained, along with a cavernous main section, balconies and private rooms. The old rectory, David's home as well as a venue for jazz bands and private parties, was right behind the old church. There was a patio, too, open during the day, and a jazz trio played there from 11:00 a.m. to 3:00 p.m. every day, while the clientele enjoyed muffalettas, crawfish étouffée, gumbo and other Louisiana specialties—along with the customary colorful drinks served in New Orleans and a few designer specials, dryly named the Bloodsucker, Bite Me, the Transformer and the Fang.

Jagger paused for a minute after he parked just down the street from the club. David took good care of the place. The white paint sparkled in the sunlight. The umbrellas in the courtyard were decorated with pretty fleur-de-lis patterns—naturally boasting the black and gold colors of the home football team, the Saints.

He got out of his car and walked through the wrought-iron gate to the courtyard, where a crowd had already gathered, and where the jazz trio was playing softly pleasant tunes.

"Detective Jagger!"

He was greeted by Valentina DeVante, David's hostess. She worked all hours, although she was almost always at the club at night. She was a voluptuous woman, with a way of walking that was pure sensuality. She had the kind of eyes that devoured a man.

He didn't actually like being devoured, so he'd always kept his distance.

"Valentina, is David up and about?"

"Actually, he's over there in the courtyard, toward the back. Tommy, the sax player, is sick, so the guys brought in a substitute. You know how David loves his jazz. He's making sure he likes the new guy so he can fill in again if he's needed. Come on. I'll take you to him."

She turned. She walked. She swished and swayed. Half the men in town, especially the inebriated ones, would trip over their tongues watching this woman. He was surprised to find himself analyzing his feelings toward her. Too overt. He liked subtlety. Sensuality over in-your-face sexuality. He liked a woman's smile, a flash in her eyes when she was touched, amused, or when she flirted. He liked honesty, an addiction to decency…

Fiona MacDonald.

God, no.

Yes. She was sleek and smooth, and she never teased or taunted; she was simply beautiful, and even when she was angry, there was something in the sound of her voice that seemed to slip beneath his skin. Her hair was like the sunlight, and her eyes…

"David, Jagger is here," Valentina said, leading him to David's table and pulling out one of the plastic-cushioned patio chairs. As he took the seat and thanked her, she leaned low. Her black dress was cut nearly to her navel, displaying her ample cleavage right in front of his face.

But then, since Valentina was a shapeshifter, she could shift a little more of her to any part of her body she desired.

"Hey, Jagger, I was expecting to see you," David said. He had half risen to greet Jagger, but Jagger lifted a hand, silently acknowledging the courtesy and assuring him that he was welcome to keep his seat.

"David…" Jagger said in greeting.

Since they were both wearing dark glasses, there was nothing to be gleaned by seeking out honesty in David's eyes, though Jagger knew from past encounters that they were fascinating eyes, almost gold in color. David was Creole, mainly, with additional ancestors who had been French and Italian, so his skin was almost as golden as his eyes, complemented by dark lashes and dark hair. He was a striking man and had always been a friend.

He couldn't tell what his friend was thinking right now but…

David tended to be a straight shooter.

"Obviously, yes, I've heard about the body," David said quietly.

"Any suspects?"

"You think it was one of us?" David asked. He didn't have to keep his voice low; the music was just right, and the courtyard was alive with the low drone of conversation. They wouldn't be heard beyond the table, even if Jagger did note that customers—most of them women—did glance in their direction now and then.

"David, the body was bone-dry. Not a drop of blood."

David nodded, looking toward the band. "They're good, don't you think?"

"Yes, very good. Your taste in music is legendary. Listen, right now the investigation is wide-open. Obviously no one but me suspects anything…out of the ordinary. But we've got a serious problem, because it certainly looks to be the work of a vampire. And pretty soon it's not going to be just me hanging around here and questioning people."

David groaned.

"The Keeper?" he said quietly. "Oh, Lordy."

"She found me right after I made it to the crime scene."

"That one has some attitude, too," David said with a sigh, then shrugged. "Oh, well, comes with the territory, I guess. She had a hell of a lot to contend with at a very young age, and, so far, we've all kept the peace. She hasn't had the time—or the need—to acquire the wisdom of her parents. And she's got that strict code of ethics thing going on, too. Guess it comes with being the oldest." David grinned suddenly. "Beautiful little thing, though, huh? If we were back in the old days… yum. And I wouldn't have let anyone interfere with her birth into a new existence, either. Hell, she's the kind who might have made me monogamous. For a century or so, anyway."

Jagger wasn't at all sure why he immediately felt protective. Fiona MacDonald certainly wouldn't expect or even want him to defend her.

Maybe David's words irritated him because they had touched a little too close to home.

"Well, she is nice eye candy," David continued. "And

everyone is welcome at my club. She has to do her job, right, Jagger?"

"No, *I* have to do *my* job. I have to find a murderer. I hope that it doesn't prove to be a vampire, but if it does…well, we have to handle it as a community."

David looked away. "It's against nature," he said softly.

"Our lives are against nature. We drink blood that's inferior to what our ancestors craved, but we've evolved, we've adapted to it. Louisiana has the death penalty. And since we don't have any vampire prisons, we have no choice. Rogues die, and it's a community affair."

"What do you want me to do?"

"Call a meeting."

"All right. And I'll make it known that everyone's presence is required, though I can't guarantee that we'll get everyone."

"I think most of our kind will be extremely concerned, since they know the other races will be breathing down our necks. This is frightening, David. Frightening for everyone. A young woman was killed, drained of blood. The whole city will be up in arms. And you can guarantee our friends in the underworld of New Orleans society will all be staring at us."

"I'll call the meeting," David assured him. "You'll be presiding?"

"You bet."

"I think I can manage it by late—*late*—tomorrow— the following morning, really. Make it 3:00 a.m. Those who are still hanging out here will probably be three sheets to the wind, not likely to interrupt. The rectory, 3:00 a.m."

"That will work. Thanks, David."

"So, will you have some lunch? As my guest, of course."

"I appreciate the offer, but it's going to be a long day."

"Where are you off to now?"

"The morgue," Jagger told him.

Fiona arrived at Underworld while lunch was still being served. She walked up to the hostess stand, and the woman standing there looked up at her with patronizing patience. She looked Fiona up and down, and would have sniffed audibly if it weren't against all sense of Southern courtesy. She was dressed in black, and had long black hair, black eyes and enormous breasts.

"Yes? A table for…one? I'm afraid there's a wait," the woman said.

Shapeshifter, Fiona thought.

And she probably knew damned well who she was, and what she wanted.

"I'm sorry, I'm not here for lunch at all. I need to see Mr. Du Lac," Fiona said.

"Ah," the woman said, just looking at her.

Fiona wasn't in the mood for a staring contest.

"If you would be so kind, I would deeply appreciate it if you would tell Mr. Du Lac that I'm here."

"Do you have an appointment?"

"I'm quite certain that he's expecting me," Fiona said.

"He's a very busy man. Perhaps you could leave your card."

"Perhaps you could inform him that Fiona MacDonald is here. In fact, I strongly suggest that you do so right now."

The woman lifted her chin. Fiona could tell that she was about to stall again.

Fiona hated *changing*. She seldom had to do so, but she was adept at the art that was her birthright. She could do so in an instant, and change back so quickly that anyone seeing her who didn't *know* would assume it had been a trick of the light. So…

She *changed*. She gave something that was a warning growl, fangs dripping and bared.

And then she changed back instantly.

"You don't need to get huffy," the woman told her. "Right this way."

She led Fiona past the scattered tables in the courtyard. Beneath one of the lovely umbrellas with its fleur-de-lis in black and gold, she saw David Du Lac comfortably seated.

He had been leaning back, eyes shaded by his dark glasses, hands folded, toes tapping to the sounds of the jazz band.

His pose was casual, but he had seen her coming. He rose, extending his hands to her, a broad smile stretching out across his features.

"Fiona, my dear, welcome, welcome to my club."

She accepted his hands, along with the kiss he gave her on each cheek. "Valentina, be a dear and see that Miss MacDonald receives a libation right away. What will it be, my dear? A Bloody Mary is always a lovely concoction for lunchtime."

"I'm fine, really."

"You must accept my hospitality," David insisted.

"Iced tea, please," Fiona said.

She noticed that Valentina, the bitchy shapeshifter,

as she would always think of the woman from this moment forth, did sniff audibly then.

"Certainly, David," the woman crooned.

"David, you know why I'm here," Fiona said, watching the bitchy shapeshifter swish away.

"Don't mind her. She's a jealous vixen if ever I've seen one."

"She's a triple D with feet," Fiona said. "Hardly likely to be jealous of me."

"Ah, my sweet child, what you don't know about your own sex!" David said, then grew serious. "But never mind. I do know why you're here."

"David, this wasn't just someone who went insane and attacked a woman, then tried to hide her body. It wasn't someone trying to create his eternal love. This was an act of…war, really. She was left where some city guide with tourists in tow would find her. She was put on display, stretched out… David, this is extremely serious."

"I do know that, my child," he said.

"I'm not a child, David," she reminded him quietly. "I'm the Keeper."

"Fiona, no offense meant. But you're supposed to step in when we can't police our own."

"This was the action of a rogue, David."

"Yes, yes, of course. And I promise you, if we'd known he—or she—was out there, we would never have let it happen. But have some faith, Fiona. Please. Jagger DeFarge is working the case and—"

"He's a vampire, David. He doesn't want to believe that he's hunting down one of his own."

David leaned back, stretching his arms out as if to encompass not only his club but the entire city. "Fiona,

I love my life. Or death. Or afterlife. However one chooses to refer to this existence, I'm a good man."

"David, I wasn't accusing you of anything."

"My point is that I don't want anyone taking this away from me. I enjoy the money, frankly, not to mention the beautiful creatures of all kinds who cross my threshold. I revel in the music. Would I risk losing this? If I knew who had done this, I promise you, I would see to it that Jagger DeFarge knew, and that our own council handled the matter immediately. You must believe me."

A friendly ash-blond waiter with a broad smile delivered her iced tea and asked if she wanted anything else.

"The crawfish étouffée is to die for today," David told her.

"Thank you, but—"

"Please," David said.

She *was* hungry, and she had to have lunch somewhere. "Fine, thank you," she said.

David grinned broadly, delighted, as the waiter moved on to place her order.

"David, you know that I will follow this all the way through, that I'll be in everyone's face everywhere," Fiona said.

"It will be charming to have you here," he assured her. "Fiona, I swear, I will do my utmost to help you in any way that I can. But I am asking *you* something, too. Give Jagger DeFarge a chance."

"I have to give him a chance, don't I? He's with the police—he'll be front and center in the investigation," she said dryly. "But here's what I won't get from Jagger, David. I don't believe he'll tell me when he's suspicious of someone. He'll protect his own until the very end—

and he may cause more deaths by his unwillingness to believe the killer is a vampire."

"That's not true," David said.

A throat was cleared behind them. "Crawfish étouffée," the young waiter announced, giving Fiona a fascinated smile. She thanked him as he refilled her tea and handed David another Bloody Mary.

"Who do you suspect?" she demanded, when the waiter had left them at last.

"No one," David said.

"You're a liar. But if you point me in a certain direction, I will be discreet as I investigate," Fiona said.

"No one, really...."

"Liar. Who is the most belligerent? Who wants to go back to the old ways?"

David looked away.

She followed his line of vision toward a tall man across the courtyard, just on the other side of the small stage reserved for the jazz band. He was flirting with a woman seated at his table. She was middle-aged, slim and elegant, with fingers that dripped jewels. She was laughing delightedly at something the man was saying.

"Who is he?" Fiona demanded, staring at David. "He's a newcomer to the area, but a vampire, I can smell him a mile away."

David sighed. "Well, of course, you can," he murmured. "All right, all right. That man is Mateas Grenard, and, yes, he's not been here long. He immediately sought out the council, though, before anyone had to find him and 'welcome' him to the city. He has openly disagreed with some of our rules, but isn't that the American way?"

* * *

"There's not much else I can tell you," Craig Dewey said. They were in autopsy. The corpse of the beautiful blonde still looked as angelic as when it had first been discovered. "I haven't opened her up yet—we'll get to that tomorrow. We've done the death photographs and taken what blood we could for tests—which was hard, since she's been drained almost completely dry. If there's a quarter of a pint left in her body, I'd be surprised. Cause of death—well, I could be wrong, but it looks pretty obvious that she bled out. It's as if it was siphoned from her body. We've tried to find semen stains, and we ran a rape kit…with intriguing results, particularly given what we just found out in the last few minutes. Determining sexual assault has been almost impossible."

"What? Why? Was there evidence of semen? Or condoms?"

"At least seven different brands," Dewey said dryly. "We're taking it step by step. I'm sorry, but it's the only way, even though—I know you want to catch this killer before panic fills the city."

There was something that seemed eternally sad about the snow-white body on the table, though the white gown had been replaced by a morgue sheet.

"You said you found something out in the last few minutes," Jagger said. "You know who she is?"

"Got a match on her prints. The results posted to your office and mine about five minutes ago," Dewey told him, an odd look on his face.

"What is it?"

"Snow White here isn't what she appears to be. Her name is Tina Lawrence. She worked at Barely, Barely,

Barely, which is a pretty lowbrow establishment across Rampart from the Quarter," Dewey said, offering him the report folder.

Jagger scanned it quickly.

The angelic Miss Tina Lawrence had a rap sheet a mile long. Drugs, prostitution and assault and battery.

"Wow," he said.

"Not a nice young lady," Dewey said.

Jagger winced. "She knifed a college student for being four dollars short," he said quietly.

"Keep reading. She tried to cut the balls off another john. Get this, she *admitted* she wanted to kill him. Amazing she wasn't in jail," Dewey said.

"We can pick people up, but we can't always get them past the legal systems and the pleas and the deals," Jagger said. "Seems she got off that because she had some drug connections and the D.A. offered her a plea in order to pick up a few of her friends who were higher up in the drug chain."

"Not a nice girl. Actually a *deadly* girl—and now a dead one," Dewey commented. "Well, anyway, there you have it. I guess you'll be heading off to the strip club," Dewey said, punching him lightly on the arm. "Have fun."

"Thanks."

Jagger walked out of the autopsy room and left the morgue. He called Tony Miro, and told him where to head to start questioning Tina Lawrence's friends, co-workers and employer, and to pull the credit card receipts and find out who had been in attendance at Tina's last show. He needed to hang around near the morgue.

Waiting for the sun to fall.

As Dewey had said, Tina Lawrence hadn't been a nice girl. She'd been a deadly one.

He could only begin to imagine the horror that would be Tina Lawrence as a vampire.

Chapter 3

The coroner's office never closed. It employed all manner of forensic specialists, along with financial and clerical staff. Under the Napoleonic Code of Law still in effect in Louisiana, the New Orleans coroner's office was responsible not only for the classification of death, but also the evaluation of sex crimes and the overall general health of the citizens of the city, specifically recognizing serious threats from disease. It was a busy place. By day pathologists, forensic psychiatrists, patient liaisons, nurses in charge of sexual assault exams, forensic anthropologists, forensic odontologists and more clogged the corridors.

Death didn't stop at any particular time of day, so naturally a morgue couldn't close.

But by nightfall the accountants, assistants and usually even the experts in such fields as toxicology, entomology and more had called it quits for the day, and

only a skeleton crew—if the pun could be forgiven—
were on duty. The dead, after all, were dead.

Usually.

Fiona headed down Martin Luther King Boulevard
and arrived outside the building's entrance while it was
still early; she watched as people came and went, and
then kept on watching as they mainly went.

There was no choice then but to go through the
change, to concentrate and enter as a vampire would,
in a shroud of mist.

The guards never suspected a thing as she went by;
the outer offices, where a few doctors were still working, were easily breeched; and she breezed by the night
attendant sitting outside the morgue without being noticed. Because several people had died in recent days,
she took a chance and searched through the records to
find the right body.

Then she headed into the dim, chilly room.

To her surprise, the body of Tina Lawrence had not
been slid away neatly into a refrigerated slot but she
was stretched out on an autopsy table.

The room smelled heavily of antiseptics and chemical compounds, not so much of death itself, yet the very
antiseptics made it seem that the scent of death was
prevalent in the air.

She slipped in and concentrated hard on regaining
her customary form, aware that during the good times
she should have been practicing her transformations
techniques. But all the while she couldn't help wondering why they had left Tina Lawrence as she was.

Fiona knew that the tenor of the investigation had
changed; the news media had released the woman's

identification and touted her past record. Reporters had a knack for finding out what the investigators had barely discovered themselves.

While the media had no doubt thought that releasing the victim's background was a good thing—a reassurance to most citizens that they were safe—Fiona was certain that Jagger considered the knowledge to be dangerous. It was hard to catch a killer when everyone knew too many details about the victim and the crime. Cranks, crackheads and anyone else looking for a little notoriety might decide to confess to the crime. But New Orleans was still raw, still learning painful lessons after Katrina's devastation, and Fiona was certain that most of the media believed they had done a good thing by releasing the information that the victim had led something much less than a blameless life. A majority of the city's women would be able to think, *I'm safe. I'm not a stripper or a prostitute, and I've certainly never been arrested.*

On the other hand, the news about the victim's past had made Fiona incredibly nervous. Tina Lawrence must *not* be allowed to go through the change. Fiona had known what she had to do from the beginning; the information about Tina's past had only made it all the more urgent.

And so, as she retook her human form there in the autopsy room, she worried that the medical examiner assigned to the body might come back any minute to begin working on it still, that the assistant she'd passed in the hall might step in at any time, or that she might be caught by someone else entirely unanticipated who could enter any second.

A sheet covered the body, and all she had to do was

pull it back and use the stiletto-sharp stake she had
brought, making sure that she pierced the heart.

She wasn't surprised that Tina Lawrence wasn't yet
marked by the Y-shaped incision of autopsy. Given the
circumstances, Fiona was certain that it had taken some
time to transfer the body to the morgue, and then the
victim would have been fingerprinted, photographed
and...

She wasn't sure what else.

She actually didn't want to know what else.

All she had to do was make sure that Tina Lawrence
did not wake up.

But as she approached the corpse, she heard a noise
in the hallway and the door started to open, so she dived
behind a stainless-steel table holding an array of instruments, most of them totally unfamiliar.

The night attendant stuck his head in, looked around
briefly, then closed the door and left.

She started to breathe a sigh of relief, then realized
that she was hearing something in the room. No, some-
one. She glanced quickly up at the table, but the corpse
hadn't moved. She held her ground, listening, her heart
pounding.

Nothing. She looked around in the dim light and
waited. Still nothing. She started to rise and saw a flurry
of motion behind her.

Instantly alarmed, she started to change, but she
wasn't quick enough.

Someone tackled her hard and forced her down to
the ground.

She instantly went into combat mode, lashing out
with her arms and legs, delivering one solid punch that

brought out a startled "Oomph" from her attacker before he caught and secured her arms, straddling her.

She found herself looking up into the eyes of Jagger DeFarge.

"Fiona!"

"DeFarge!" she lashed back angrily. "Get off me."

He didn't comply, though he released her arms as he remained straddled over her, staring down at her angrily.

"What the hell are you doing here?" he demanded.

"It's obvious what I'm doing here—cleaning up the mess," she replied.

"It's my concern," he told her.

"No, it's *mine*. I'm responsible in circumstances like these, and I have no guarantee that you'll do the right thing," she replied.

"Well, I'm here, and I'm handling the situation," he said, crossing his arms over his chest and staring down at her.

"Will you please get off me?" she inquired.

Before he could respond, the door opened. The young night attendant walked in, flicking on the bright overhead lights.

Jagger and Fiona stared at one another as the attendant let out a startled cry.

Jagger rose instantly to his feet, shushing the man with authority. "It's all right. I'm Detective DeFarge, just looking for Dr. Dewey and the results of this autopsy."

"I'm about to put her on ice for the night," the attendant said. "Dr. Dewey will be in first thing in the morning to start the autopsy."

As he spoke, the corpse on the gurney jackknifed

into a sitting position, the sheet falling to reveal her naked torso.

The young man opened his mouth to let out a scream, but Jagger leaped over the table in an instant, slipping behind him and silencing him with a hand over the mouth, pulling the door shut with his other hand.

Tina Lawrence glared around, a hissing growl coming from her lips.

Then she parted those lips to reveal dripping fangs.

Despite her calling in life and the way she'd died, Tina Lawrence was still beautiful. Her blond hair cascaded over the white flesh of her shoulders, and despite the terrifying distraction of her fangs, she had lovely wide blue eyes, which settled on the attendant with hunger.

He spoke from beneath Jagger's hold, his words muffled but audible. "She's alive. She's alive!"

Jagger stared at Fiona. "Take him—quickly. Silence him."

She hurried over to where Jagger was struggling with the attendant—both to hold him still *and* to keep from hurting him. She grasped the young man's arms, staring into his eyes. "Quiet now, quiet. It's all right. You're dreaming this. You're asleep at your desk, and you know that you have to wake up, that you have a job to do...."

She kept speaking softly. Jagger apparently assured himself that everything was fine and turned toward the corpse of Tina Lawrence, but as he did, the corpse leaped naked from the table, ready to pounce on Fiona and the young attendant.

Jagger slipped between them just in time.

As she continued trying to calm the attendant, Fiona saw that Jagger had taken a weapon from his jacket.

It was far superior to her own, a long stake, honed to a sharp point, even narrower than hers. He took Tina Lawrence into his arms, and, just before her newly grown fangs could tear into his throat, he struck hard, delivering the lethal blow directly through the wall of her chest and straight into her heart.

The corpse collapsed against him.

Despite her prowess with hypnotic mind control, Fiona began to lose the young morgue attendant.

He began to emit a low moaning sound and started to slip lower in her arms.

She had a feeling then that he must be a football player—a blocker or a tackle—with Tulane or Loyola, because she simply didn't have the strength to stop him from falling. Though she tried to hold him upright, she began to slip to the floor.

She heard Jagger swearing softly as he shoved the corpse of Tina Lawrence quickly back onto the table and came to help her.

But by then the attendant had passed out cold.

"We've got to get him back to his desk," Jagger told her.

"What if someone else is in the hallway? There are still people in the building," she warned.

"Get out there and make sure no one is coming," he told her. "Quickly."

"Why me?"

"Well, you obviously can't lift him."

"All right, all right, I'm going," Fiona said, and pointed an angry finger at him. "But you don't give me orders. I am the Keeper!"

"And you're going to have a hell of a lot to keep if you don't get moving," he told her.

She wanted to reply; she wanted the last word. But they needed to hurry. She rushed out into the hallway.

It was clear.

"Now," she told Jagger, sticking her head back into the autopsy room.

Luckily the attendant's desk was just down the hall. She rushed toward it, ready to fend off anyone who might come by.

Jagger had lifted the attendant as if he were no more than a ten-pound lapdog and was hurrying toward the desk. Just beyond the desk, Fiona saw a door opening. She rushed toward it just in time to see an older man in a lab jacket about to come through.

"Oh!" she said, staring at him, trying to lock her eyes on his and demand his attention.

Apparently she succeeded, because he stared curiously back at her.

"Hello," he said weakly.

She smiled. "You're so tired—you've been working very hard. Go and get your things, then go on home and have a nap. You're hallucinating, you're so tired."

"I'm so tired," he echoed. "You're a lovely hallucination."

"Thank you."

He was of average height and weight, with close-cropped white hair. He was usually very dignified-looking, she was certain, but right now he was staring at her with wide-eyed wonder.

"You're daydreaming, sir. You have to go home. You need some rest."

"Yes, yes, but…why don't you come, too, and make this a really good daydream? An erotic daydream, maybe. Please?"

Fiona groaned inwardly.

"That wouldn't be a very good idea. You probably have a wife, and I think *she's* your daydream."

"All right."

He stepped back the way he had come, closing the door.

As she turned, she almost screamed herself. Jagger had come up quietly behind her.

"He's at his desk. He'll wake up confused. Poor boy may never be the same. He'll have some memory...but he'll just think that he imagined everything," Jagger told her. He was staring at her with amusement, and she could tell that he must have heard her conversation with the middle-aged man in the lab coat.

She pushed against his chest. Like a rock, but he moved back. "This is a disaster," she said, her voice a low and angry whisper. "You need to let me handle things."

"With what? A sledgehammer? So you could let the whole world know something was going on in here?"

Fiona ignored that. It was true that he had definitely...taken care of things.

But he was a vampire. And a vampire was normally loath to kill another vampire.

"The corpse?" she asked briskly.

"The corpse will have nothing but a tiny hole through the heart. If you had done this, it would have been obvious that someone had been here. Do you understand?"

"Your weapon is the right one. I'll see that I improve on my arsenal," she snapped.

"We need to finish up quickly," he said.

He hurried back to the autopsy room, checking the hallway after she followed him in, then closing the door.

"The sheet," he said, which irritated Fiona, since she was already returning Tina Lawrence to her original position on the table and covering her with the sheet.

Jagger just had to straighten it.

"Now let's get the hell out of here," he said.

He changed in a split second, appearing to be no more than mist, and headed out. Cursing silently, she did her best to make the change as quickly and efficiently.

Still, he looked impatient when she met him back on the street, though she couldn't have been more than a few seconds behind him.

"You could have caused a real problem in there tonight," he told her.

They had met on the street corner, beneath the shadow of a giant oak that dripped moss. He was tall, dark, lean, strikingly handsome—and deadly—in the glow of the flickering electric streetlight. Powerful in a way that was frightening, that stole her breath.

She wasn't afraid of him, she told herself.

She was the Keeper.

"I was there to see that the right thing was done," she said with dignity. "And I would have managed just fine—if you hadn't come in and messed everything up."

"I'm a cop, and I know how to manage any situation—especially one that has to do with vampires."

"I repeat. I am responsible. I am the Keeper. *Your* Keeper."

He bristled at that, and took a step closer to her. He used a body wash or aftershave that was subtle and masculine, and despite herself, she took a step backward, not sure if it was because she was intimidated—or because she found herself too attracted, too tempted to lay her hands on the broad expanse of his chest.

She forced herself to stay still as he took a step closer to her, pointing a finger and touching her just above her cleavage.

"You *are* the Keeper. But you're overstepping your bounds. You're supposed to step in when we can't handle a situation ourselves. In this case, I was handling the situation just fine."

She shook her head. "I can't trust you to kill a vampire," she said, her words soft.

"You *have* to trust me."

"A vampire has committed murder," she reminded him.

"That's not proven," he insisted. "Look—we're on it. Give us a chance, Fiona. Good God, learn from your parents. They were amazing because they understood delegation."

"My parents are dead," she reminded him angrily.

She was surprised when he seemed to soften, when something in his eyes became gentle, almost tender.

"I'm sorry. Please, give me a chance…as a cop—and as a vampire. I *will* get to the bottom of this, but none of us will be in good shape if we get the city abuzz with rumors, and all the underworld starts getting edgy and worried. Please."

She nodded. "I don't want a panic erupting, either, but that's the point. I have to keep watching—that's what Keepers do," she reminded him. She was overwhelmed by the sense that she needed to get away from him. She didn't want to be this close, didn't want to be noticing his physique or realizing that his scent was extremely evocative. She wanted to be irritated from a distance; she wanted to solve the problem herself, because she was the Keeper.

"I have to get home," she heard herself say a little nervously.

"I'll drive you."

"I have my own car," she told him quickly.

"I'll walk you to it," he told her.

"I'm all right. This is my city."

"And like every city, it has crack houses, drug addicts and plain old thugs. I'm a cop—I do my job even when the denizens of the underworld *aren't* out causing trouble. I'll walk you to your car."

"Honestly, Jagger, I'm a Keeper."

"And a Keeper—just like a vampire, werewolf, shapeshifter, pixie, pooka, leprechaun or even a lamia—can be taken by surprise. Why the hell do you think our kind had to escape the old world, then flee places like Salem, to find a place where we could blend in? We're all vulnerable, Fiona, despite whatever strengths we have. We're all vulnerable —in so many ways."

He took her arm as they walked down the street. She wanted to wrench from his touch, but...

The lady doth protest too much, methinks, she thought.

But she was so acutely aware of him!

They reached her car.

"Good night, Fiona," he said, as he opened her door for her.

"You'll keep me apprised—of everything going on? From a cop's standpoint *and* a vampire's?" she inquired.

He nodded.

"I have to follow up and investigate. You know that."

"Have some faith in me, please," he said.

"I'm having faith. But I'm using what I've got, too, that's all."

"I'll report in daily," he said.

"Yes, you will."

He smiled suddenly.

She frowned, looking at him. "I don't see anything to smile about in any of this, Jagger."

"Oh, certainly not. Not in the situation."

"Then?"

"You just have to have the last word, don't you?" he asked.

She didn't reply, just slid into the seat, and he closed the door. She stared at him and turned the key in the ignition. He stepped away quickly as she gunned the engine, then started to ease out onto the street.

A good exit, she told herself.

Except that she could hear his husky laughter even as she drove away.

Chapter 4

Fiona had just slipped into the long, soft cotton T-shirt she loved to wear to bed and crawled under the covers when she heard the tap on her door that announced Caitlin's arrival. Her sister knocked, but didn't wait for an invitation.

"Well?" Caitlin demanded.

The room was dark, but with the hall lights on, Fiona could see her sister's anxious face.

"It's done," she said.

"Thank God," Caitlin breathed. "For some reason the media have been trying to hide the details of Tina Lawrence's life, but finally one of the anchors started reading her police sheet, and…I literally shivered. Can you even imagine? The best vampire is a bloodthirsty beast and—"

"Caitlin, please. We know plenty of vampires who are fine citizens. And let's get serious. There's no more violent beast out there than man, when he chooses to be," Fiona argued.

Caitlin sighed softly. "Look, I know that they're your charges, but...well, I just don't believe there's ever been a truly good vampire."

Jagger DeFarge.

The name came unbidden to Fiona's mind.

She realized that despite her earlier misgivings, she believed that he was a force for good. After all, was anyone really all good or all bad? Everyone, every being, every creature, came with a form of free will, and free will led to behavior that was good, bad and everything in between.

"Jagger DeFarge was there," she told her sister. "He was already attending to the matter, as he should have been."

Caitlin sniffed. "Was he? Or did he decide he had no choice, once he saw you?"

"Caitlin, please. I have to have some faith in his ethics and his commitment to our laws. The vampires, like all creatures, are supposed to police their own, and I believe that they will do so. I also went to see David Du Lac, and I know that the higher-ups among the vampires are deeply concerned. Caitlin, they like their lives. They're not going to risk everything they have, all to protect a rogue."

Caitlin looked at her gravely, the softly glowing hall light making her appear angelic.

"I'm just worried," she said. "Worried...for you."

Fiona rose and walked over to the door, where she took her sister into a warm hug. "I understand."

They stayed close for a minute, sisters who had seen the worst. Then they broke apart, and Fiona smiled. "I'm fine, honestly. Have some faith in me, if not the vampires. The truth is, I need your help."

"My help? We're talking vampires. Not my thing, remember?" Caitlin said.

Fiona nodded. She had been born with the sign of the bat, a tiny birthmark at the base of her spine. Caitlin had been born with the sign of the mist, shape-shifting. She loved her sister's birthmark, which was magical, changing continuously, though most who saw it thought it a trick of the eye.

Shauna bore the mark of the werewolf Keeper, the wolf, howling at the moon. No tattoo artist had ever created a work of such perfection.

Their friends had marveled at the marks on those rare occasions when they'd been revealed by a low-cut bathing suit. They hadn't tried to hide them, had merely shrugged them off, leaving their friends to wonder how and when they'd come by them.

Before Fiona could reply, Shauna popped up behind Caitlin.

"So? What's going on? Do you know who did it?" she demanded.

Fiona gave up and turned on her light. "Come in. Actually I don't know—yet—but I do have a plan for finding out."

The three of them sat cross-legged on the bed as Fiona went on.

"I want to attend the luncheon at the Monteleone tomorrow."

"The lunch to honor Jennie Mahoney?" Caitlin asked, frowning.

Jennie Mahoney was the untitled queen among the shapeshifters. She was a beautiful woman, a socialite and a member of the local literati. If it was happening in New Orleans, Jennie was in on it.

She was going to be honored for the work she had done in soliciting funds to redo a coffeehouse just outside the Quarter. The place offered open-mike nights to poets at least once a week, along with hosting up-and-coming musicians and decorating its walls with works by local artists. Since Jennie and several of her friends considered themselves poets, Fiona wasn't sure that all the effort Jennie had put in wasn't a little self-serving, but the coffee house had been a local landmark that was completely ruined by Katrina, and the fact that it was now open again was a big boost for a city in need of every boost it could get.

"Are you going?" Fiona asked Caitlin.

"Of course. It would be incredibly rude of me not to attend," her sister said.

"Can we all go?"

"If I'd known you wanted to go, I should have gotten tickets ages ago," Caitlin said.

"Do *I* want to go?" Shauna asked, frowning as she looked at Fiona.

"I think all three of us should be there. I'd like to talk to Jennie," Fiona said.

Caitlin was frowning. "If you talk to Jennie, she's going to think you're suspicious of her—and her kind."

Fiona shook her head. "Not at all. I'm hoping *she* can tell *me* about anything suspicious going on."

Caitlin nodded slowly, staring at Fiona. "But you know this was the work of a vampire," she said.

"Certainly not a werewolf," Shauna said. "A werewolf…well, a werewolf kill is never subtle or pretty, you know?"

That was true, beyond a doubt.

"Caitlin, I really need your help," Fiona said.

Caitlin nodded slowly. "All right. I'll text a few people right now. The lunch was sold out weeks ago, but… there's always someone who has to cancel."

"Thank you."

"It's late. We should get some sleep," Shauna said as she rose and yawned. "Boy, what a relief."

"What's a relief?" Caitlin asked.

"That it wasn't a werewolf."

Fiona glared at her.

"Sorry…" Shauna apologized. "I'm not saying…I mean, I'm not accusing anyone. For all we know, it might have been some drugged-out weirdo who *wants* to be a vampire."

"No," Fiona said.

They both looked at her.

"Tina Lawrence…she started to rise from the dead."

"But you said Jagger DeFarge was there to handle the matter," Caitlin pointed out.

"Yes," Fiona said, meeting her sister's eyes. "I'm afraid it's in our jurisdiction. She was definitely killed by one of ours."

Caitlin stared at her steadily. "Good night," she said finally, then turned and left.

"What's wrong with her?" Shauna asked softly.

"She thinks I'm accusing a shapeshifter. I'm not. I just have to keep my mind open, and if it wasn't a vampire, then it had to have been a shapeshifter. No other creature could take on—or pass on—the abilities of a vampire."

"It probably *is* the work of a vampire," Shauna said softly.

"I know," Fiona assured her, then smiled with what she hoped was reassurance. "It's our first real challenge. We will meet it."

Jagger spent his time checking out the city's streets.

Bourbon was crawling with tourists, as usual. He heard excited conversations, visitors talking about the "vampire murder," girls teasing boys about taking care of themselves in strip clubs—and boys teasing girls about the same.

A stripper-slash-prostitute had been killed. It was worthy of gossip, not of great concern.

Walking along, he came upon mounted officers, Reginald Oaks and Vickie Gomez. He slowly patted Gomez's horse, Enrique, and questioned his fellow officers about what was going on.

"Seems like a regular night in Boozeville," Vickie told him.

"Frat boys are singing karaoke, dancing in the streets, throwing beads around… It's not Mardi Gras, but it's busy. Nothing to suggest anything going on," Reginald told him. "Have you been up past Rampart?"

Jagger nodded. "I've been everywhere tonight. Uptown, Garden District, Frenchman Street…you name it. I even cruised the Central Business District. But that's the way it's going to have to be until this is settled. Anything, anything at all unusual, you have me on speed dial."

"Yes, sir," Vickie assured him, flashing a quick smile. "Sir, there's a weaving group behind you looking for a picture with the mounted cops and the horses."

He turned away just as a group of inebriated tourists came weaving over, looking to take a picture with the horses. He started to step away.

"Oh, please. Stay," one girl told him.

"Sorry—official business," he said, flashed his badge and quickly moved away. His partner, Tony Miro, was supposed to be meeting him at Barely, Barely, Barely, the strip club up past Rampart where Tina Lawrence had worked. He hurried down the cross street to where his car was parked by the station on Chartres.

Tony Miro was waiting for him in front of the club when he pulled up a few minutes later.

It was odd to think that the club was really only a degree below plenty of the other clubs in town. Even on Bourbon Street, you could find some truly sleazy down and dirty places, but...Barely, Barely, Barely seemed even more worn around the edges, and he knew the girls working the poles in the place were going to be a little harder, a little more beat-up by life, physically and mentally.

He had met strippers who only worked the clubs to get through college—it was good money and, sad but true, good money that seemed like easy money often twisted people, and led to worse ways of making more money, and plenty of bad things to spend it on. Not that all strippers were prostitutes. But in his time on the force he'd seen far too many girls who started out stripping on the weekend, only to discover they enjoyed the drugs they often started taking to give them the courage to strip in the first place. Drugs cost money, and prostitution paid better than stripping.

He left the car on the street, his police insignia evident. Tony approached him with a long-legged stride.

He was wearing a work suit, and when he eased a finger around his collar, Jagger realized he was uncomfortable.

"Everything all right?" Jagger asked.

"I questioned everyone in the place, and I got a list of their charge customers," Tony told him. "Some of the girls weren't working last night, so I've listed them at the end. I highlighted a few names—" he pointed to the list he was offering to Jagger "—because those two were bartenders, and those two were the girls who went up right before and after Tina Lawrence, and that name—Trisha Bean—belongs to the cocktail waitress who was working the floor while Tina Lawrence was working the pole."

"Thanks. Did you see anything, hear anything, among the workforce? Do we have a reason to compel a search warrant and start looking for blood?" Jagger asked.

"No. And I don't think she was killed here," Tony said. "But then again, I don't seem to have your nose for blood."

Jagged nodded dryly and said, "It's acquired. Let's go on in."

Tony opened the door, wincing. "Back into Dante's Inferno."

It wasn't really Dante's Inferno. It was a strip club where very little was spent on a cleaning crew and every effort was spared when it came to the decor. Animal-print upholstery that looked to be from the sixties or seventies covered the ratty sofas and chairs. There was a main stage, along with a number of small circular tables cum stages with their own dance poles, surrounded by C-shaped couches covered in the same retro animal prints.

The place was dark, filled with smoke, and what seemed like a miasma of pain and loneliness that stretched back through decades of human existence. Two girls were dancing on the main stage, while the small stages Tony said were for "private screenings" were all empty.

"The bar?" Tony asked.

"No, let's check this one here, in the back," Jagger said, heading toward one of the tables with its own stripper pole.

Tony, wide-eyed, looking torn between fascination and repulsion, joined him, groaning softly as he sat down.

"What?"

"Something sticky—I just sat in it," Tony said.

"Is it blood?"

"Some kind of fruity drink," Tony said.

"Then ya just gotta live with it a bit," Jagger told him, grinning. "Who's on stage now?"

"The one girl over on the left is called Rosy Red. Her real name is Martha Hamm. And the other one, the blonde, is Jamaka-me, real name Tammy Curtis. Jamaka-me was on stage just before Tina Lawrence—who was known as Ange-demonica when she was working. They all have stage names," Tony explained. "Hers was pretty grotesque, if you ask me."

Jagger grinned at his partner. Tony was twenty-eight. Both his parents had been born to Italian immigrants in an area of Boston where Italian was still the most commonly heard language. Tony had gone to Loyola here in town and fallen in love with New Orleans.

He was still a good Catholic Italian boy, though. He had grown up quickly working New Orleans' rough streets, but he had a pure heart that seemed to be something of a birthright.

A tired, skinny cocktail waitress wearing some kind of a costume—Jagger wasn't sure what, but both the tail and the ears were drooping—came up and asked them what they'd like. She noted Tony's badge hanging from his breast pocket and said, "Oh. Cops. You want some coffee...?"

"Are you Trisha Bean?" Jagger asked her.

She nodded glumly.

He was sure she'd never worked the stage. Trisha Bean, who worked with coffee beans, he thought dryly, and she even looked a bit like a string bean, she was so thin.

"Yeah, Bean's even my real name. Go figure, huh?" she said. She was clearly long past seeing any humor in the situation. "Coffee? Speak up. Believe it or not, I'm busy, and I need the money. I've got a kid to feed."

"We're actually off duty, so I'll have a beer," Jagger said. "Something in a bottle, please," he added, as Tony held up two fingers to tell her to double the order.

Trisha Bean laughed. "Good call. Don't think the beer taps in here have been cleaned since year one. Be right back."

"Don't you want to question her?" Tony asked.

"I will. Let her get the drinks first." Jagger loosened his tie and set a foot on the coffee table. "Chill. Keep your eyes open. Watch everyone in here. I would bet money that the killer came in here to find Tina Lawrence. I'm not sure where he'll go next, but I think it was a conscious decision to go with a stripper."

Tony looked at him with surprise, then gave serious attention to the room.

Jagger laughed. "Tony, casually, or these guys will make us for cops and be out of here in two seconds flat. Ease it back."

Tony flushed and relaxed as Trisha Bean returned with their bottled beers. "Here you go," she said.

Jagger set a large bill on her tray, telling her to keep the change.

"They're paying cops well these days," she commented, but he saw the smile of appreciation in her eyes.

"I have to confess, family money," he told her.

"'Family money?'" she said. "I'd be living the life of luxury. A little pad dead center in the Quarter, no crack whores banging around the building at all hours of the night. Anyway, what can I do for you? I wasn't holding out on you before," she told Tony. "I just didn't see anyone being any more of an ass than usual in here the night Tina was taken and killed. You think she went with the murderer willingly?"

"I think she met him here, yes," Jagger fudged.

Trisha was thoughtful. "Oh!" she said suddenly. "There *was* one guy I noticed…." Clutching her tray to her, she spun around and pointed to a private-screening table that was a few rows closer to the stage. "He wasn't being a jerk, though. He was in here alone, sitting right there. He was drinking, but he wasn't smashed, and he tipped me and the girls pretty good. I remember now, because Tina…went to that table. Here's the thing I noticed most, though. He was young, and really good-looking."

"Young. How young?"

"Twenty-five, thirty…maybe thirty-five. And he was almost…pretty. Beautiful skin. Thin, tall…pretty."

"Dark? Light?" Jagger asked.

"Dark hair, nice cut, lean face."

"What color eyes, do you remember?" Jagger asked.

"You know, I don't remember his eyes at all," she said. "Kinda dark in here."

"How about I get you to see a sketch artist?" Jagger asked her.

"Can I do it in the morning?"

He nodded. "Give me your address, and I'll pick you up and get you home after. Thank you," he said.

She nodded. "I just gotta get my kid to school first, you know?"

"Of course. I really appreciate all help," Jagger assured her.

She walked away, and Tony turned to stare at Jagger. "I talked to her at least twice today. She didn't remember the guy then."

Jagger shrugged. "You were being a cop then, looking for someone who'd made a stink. She was nervous. Now you're being human. You're having a beer. People think better when they don't feel threatened."

As Jagger spoke, Jamaka-me did a flying leap onto the main stage, spun around the pole athletically and leaped down to the floor.

Her action was greeted by whoops and catcalls and applause.

She moved through the audience, accepting tips stuck in the string that passed for a thong but managed to hide nothing at all.

Finally she leaped on their table and stared at Jagger before doing a slow, sultry spin around the pole.

Jagger met her eyes.

Werewolf, he thought.

At 3:00 a.m. Fiona was still wide-awake. She gave up tossing and turning, threw her covers off and walked to the windows that led to her balcony.

She loved this house, as did her sisters. It was huge and old, filled with memories of their family. Its long hallways were hung with photos of the three of them and their parents. Skiing in Aspen—and meeting up with other Keepers. A holiday to Jamaica—and a meeting with another Keeper family from New York City. The father was in charge of Leprechauns, which weren't nearly as plentiful in New Orleans as they were in Boston and New York. But then, no one had the workload her parents had always managed, except those working in places like Transylvania, Edinburgh or the true home of all the magical creatures of the earth: Ireland.

Out on the balcony, she looked across to her sisters' rooms. Shauna had the middle bedroom, and Caitlin's windows were just beyond.

Shauna's room was dark, but Caitlin was pacing. Her light was still on, and Fiona could see her walking back and forth, back and forth, behind the curtains.

Caitlin despised vampires. She believed that they were the eternal troublemakers, and she blamed the deaths of their parents on vampires.

Fiona wished that she could ease some of the hatred in her sister's heart. It wasn't that she didn't know that her own reason for existence was to keep the vampires' bloodlust in check or that she thought her job was easy. In truth, all the beings of the underworld were so much stronger and, often, craftier than humans, or at least they came with talents that allowed them to carry out feats of tremendous deceit.

But Fiona had realized at an early age that evil came in all sizes, shapes and races. Human beings were capable of as much cruelty and torture as any paranormal being, and though she had suspected from the first that they were looking for a vampire, she knew that a human being was perfectly capable of the murder, even if not the method.

She had to stay on top of the situation, had to investigate as if she had been trained at Quantico. This was her responsibility.

And yet…

She was paradoxically glad to be sharing that responsibility.

With Jagger. Jagger DeFarge.

She left the balcony, locking the double doors behind her once she was back inside. This was a time to be careful, and she didn't intend to be taken unaware by anyone.

Or any*thing*.

She had to get some sleep.

She lay back down, closed her eyes and wondered if anyone had ever really managed to fall asleep by counting sheep. She tried. It didn't work.

Instead she kept seeing Jagger DeFarge. The rugged and yet ascetic lines of his face. His eyes, gold and entrancing. The richness of his dark hair. The sense of security she felt when he was near. Surely, she told herself, that was only because he was tall and strong.

At last she began to drift to sleep.

But even then, she kept seeing his face, hearing his voice. She saw his smile of gentle amusement when he looked at her, the hardness that locked his jaw when she annoyed him. She felt his hand, touching her.

When she drifted to sleep at last, she was imagining his voice, husky in her ear, and his fingertips, stroking her. His lips were coming closer to hers as he whispered words she couldn't quite comprehend.

He was a vampire. She knew vampires. He was probably getting ready to sink his fangs into her throat and drink her blood.

No…

She was imagining what it would be like if his lips touched on hers and he drew her close to him. He wouldn't be cold to the touch—that was a myth. He would be warm, maybe hot as fire. He would draw her into an embrace that was secure with vibrant warmth, hot and edgy and erotic. His kiss would be filled with passion, searing and wet, and crushed against his body, she would feel the electricity of his being.…

The alarm suddenly rang, persistent and irritating. Fiona bolted awake, jerked from the arms that had seemed so real.

She was drenched in sweat. Swearing, she leaped from her bed and headed for the shower.

The ballroom where the luncheon was being held had seating for approximately a hundred and fifty people. The room was beautifully decorated with flowers everywhere, and a large banner stretched across the top of the small stage area boasted, In Honor Of Jennie Mahoney, Philanthropist Extraordinaire.

A jazz trio had played while they were seated and served their salads, followed by a main course of jambalaya, which was delicious. The hotel had always boasted top-notch food, even when serving hundreds of meals for a formal function.

After the entrée, there had been several speakers. Some talked about Jennie's humanitarian work. Others spoke about her talent for poetry. Then Jennie herself spoke, reminding them all that New Orleans was unique, a breeding ground for art in all its guises. The coffeehouse they had managed to get back on its feet recognized new talent, from poets to visual artists, violinists to drummers to jazz musicians, as well as those who hoped to one day climb the pop and rock charts.

Her speech drew thunderous applause.

"Son of a bitch," Caitlin, seated to Fiona's right, suddenly muttered.

Fiona looked up to see Jennie Mahoney welcoming Jagger DeFarge to the stage.

She hadn't even seen him here.

Admittedly, the attendees were mainly women, but she had noticed a number of men there, as well. A few of the city commissioners were there, including their old friend August Gaudin. He was at their table, in fact, along with Jill Derby, Sue Preston and Sean Ahearn, who were a couple, and Mya Yates, shapeshifters like Jennie, and supporters of her philanthropic efforts.

The only vampire she'd noticed was Lilly Wayne, an octogenarian and philanthropist in her own right, well-loved by everyone, human and supernatural alike.

Fiona realized now that Jagger had been seated at Lilly's table near the stage, but her view of him had been blocked before he rose to take the microphone.

"How very odd," Shauna, at Fiona's left, said softly. She didn't sound suspicious or angry, just curious.

"What in God's name is *he* doing here?" Caitlin asked.

"Well, since he's about to speak, I'm assuming he was invited," Fiona told her dryly.

Caitlin's lips were pursed; she didn't answer, only looked on with disapproval.

"He's so cute," Sue, a pretty redhead, whispered to Mya.

"Dreamy," Mya agreed.

Dreamy? Who used that word these days? Fiona wondered, annoyed.

Like it or not, Jagger DeFarge was a presence. His height gave him an immediate advantage, and he had such dark hair. His shoulders were broad, making him stand out in any room. He moved with impressive agility for such a large man, and his smile could only be called compelling.

Because he was a vampire. A vampire with the innate ability to seduce his victims.

But to the best of her knowledge, Jagger DeFarge lived his life like a man. A human being. He worked for the city, a city he truly seemed to love.

They had that in common.

Caitlin made a sound of distaste. Fiona glared at her sister, who looked away, but her cheeks were touched with color.

Just then Jagger began to speak.

"Jennie, I'm here as an officer of law, one who speaks for us all, all of us who love this city and work for all the good things that make up the Crescent City, the Big Easy—our New Orleans. We honor you for the beauty and the creativity you tirelessly work to promote, and we thank you from the bottom of our hearts. We've been through bad times in this city, but bad times teach us how we must cherish all that is fine in life, and for that we thank you. Now, I believe I'm the last speaker, and I think I'll stop here, so we can hear the Mountjoy trio spin their magic again—and enjoy the bourbon-pecan pie."

His words were met by thunderous applause, and Jennie went over to give him a big hug.

"Detective!" someone cried as he started to leave the stage.

He paused, then returned to the mike.

"Yes? Miss Chase, is it? Julie? What is it?"

"Do you have any leads on that bizarre murder?"

"Unfortunately, no, we don't have the answers yet. But we're pursuing the case twenty-four hours a day."

"Do you think there's a killer going after the…fallen women of this city? Are the rest of us safe?"

"Julie, I don't know yet, but we're pursuing any and all leads, and I promise you, we won't stop until this killer is caught."

Another woman stood up.

"Detective—is it true she was drained of blood?"

He didn't hesitate. "Yes. And before everyone starts running for cover, my advice to all of you is the same advice I always give. This is a big city, full of very fine people, along with some very unusual ones and, yes, an admitted criminal element. Ladies, be smart. Go out at night in groups. Lock your doors. Don't let strangers in. If you're at work late, make sure you don't walk to your car alone. Think. Always think. And be smart at all times. And now I'm leaving this luncheon to go back to work on the case—rejoining my partner, along with a team of top-notch officers and forensic investigators. As for you, go about your lives, just be smart, including street-smart."

His words were met by another round of applause. Jennie Mahoney took his arm, waving a hand to indicate that there would be no more questions as she walked with him off the stage.

"Oh," Mya sighed, watching him flash a smile at Jennie as he seated her back at her table, then drew out the chair next to hers.

He'd not only been invited, he'd also been given a place of honor.

"I'd feel safe if *he* was sleeping with me at night," Sue said, grinning.

Caitlin made a sniffing noise. Fiona kicked her beneath the table.

Sean Ahearn laughed, having noticed the exchange, and reached across the table to cover Sue's hand with his. "Honey, please. I *am* right here, you know."

They all laughed then. "And you know I love you," Sue told him.

"I'm not in a relationship," Mya pointed out.

August Gaudin spoke up then. "Ah, my dear, I hear that a handsome young football player has his eye on you."

Mya flushed. "Randy Soames. Yes."

"And he's your kind," August said softly, as aware as Fiona and her sisters were that their table was filled with shapeshifters.

Sue flicked her hair back. "That, Monsieur Gaudin, sounds both prejudiced and archaic, though I'm sure you didn't mean it to."

"He's right," Caitlin said, her tone hard. "Certain… aspects of society should simply remain separate."

"Oh, look! The pie is coming," Fiona said, wanting to hush them all. Her tablemates might be denizens of the underworld, but there were well over a hundred other people in the room, emphasis on "people."

Fiona rose as the pie was brought to the table, acutely aware that Jagger DeFarge was rising, too—ready to go back to work, if what he had said on stage was true.

"Excuse me," she murmured. "I'll be right back."

She hurried out to the hallway, managing to get there just as Jagger did—with Jennie Mahoney right behind him.

"I'm so sorry, but I should have expected the question to come up," Jennie was saying. She stopped short when she spotted Fiona.

"Hello, dear. I'm so pleased you were able to come today." She was a very attractive woman, somewhere in her mid- to late-thirties, with flashing green eyes, deep auburn hair and a slim, shapely build.

Of course, she could have any build she wanted, but changing required effort, and most shapeshifters were consistent in the appearance they donned in their day-to-day lives.

"It was my pleasure, Jennie," Fiona said.

"I knew your sister was coming," Jennie said. "But—"

"I'm afraid I have to get going," Jagger said, interrupting. "I'm praying we can catch the killer before the city falls into a state of panic."

"How intriguing that you're in such a hurry to be off," Jennie said, "Since, quite honestly, I'm assuming that Fiona is here today not as a friend, but because she is willing to entertain the idea that a shapeshifter is the guilty party rather than a vampire."

"Actually, Jennie," Fiona said, "I'm here because I want to ask you for your help."

"My help?" Jennie said, her ruffled feathers smoothing over almost visibly.

"Yes. Jennie, you know everyone… I'm hoping that you'll be on the lookout and let us know if you see anything that might be a clue, or anyone behaving oddly in any way."

Jennie arched her brows. "But Jagger is on the case." She lowered her voice, looking around to be sure she wouldn't be overheard. "And he's a *vampire*."

"A vampire who has to be on his way, Jennie…." He gave her a kiss on the cheek, and then his eyes met Fiona's. She was sure she saw a sizzle of amusement. "Miss MacDonald."

He didn't touch her.

She hated that she wished he had.

He walked away down the hall, his strides long and sure.

"Jennie, I'm really sorry if I gave you the wrong impression by being here," Fiona said. "I really do think we need all the help we can get."

Jennie sighed. "Well, I can assure you, this isn't the work of a shapeshifter." She looped arms with Fiona, leading her back into the ballroom. "Why don't I join you at your table for a few minutes?" she suggested.

As they approached the table, Sean quickly went to find an extra chair for Jennie. There was gushing all around as she sat, her fellow shapeshifters congratulating her, Caitlin mentioning her pride in her and August Gaudin announcing she was a wonderful example for everyone in the city.

Jennie thanked them, then glanced around quickly, making sure no one was nearby.

"Listen, we all have to focus on solving this murder. It looks like we have a rogue vampire among us, though I do have to acknowledge that Fiona may be concerned because the only other entity who could have pulled this off is a shapeshifter."

"It was obviously a vampire, it's just that I'm afraid neither my sister nor DeFarge wants to admit that," Caitlin said.

Fiona controlled her anger; Caitlin should never betray a breech between the three of them.

"We know it wasn't a werewolf," Shauna said happily.

"And I'm quite certain it wasn't a shapeshifter," Jennie said. "You have to understand our kind, Fiona. We're pranksters, not violent at all."

"It's true," Sue said. "I love to shapeshift into some hot movie star and tease the paparazzi."

"Or a rock star," Mya said, giggling. "I've met the most interesting people that way."

"You two are wicked," Sean said.

"Hey, you like to impersonate politicians," Mya reminded him.

"My favorite, ever, was being Tom Cruise," Jill Derby announced in a whisper, grinning.

"You didn't!" Mya said.

"I did," Jill said.

Fiona forced herself to laugh along with the rest of the group. "I'm just asking all of you—help us out, please."

"None of us want another war," August Gaudin said quietly.

"No," Fiona said, rising. "We don't want a panic, and we don't want a war. And we have to live by the law, just like everyone else. The difference being, of course, that we have to handle our own criminals. If a vampire *is* guilty, I guarantee you he will be brought to justice."

She looked at her sisters.

"Whoever is guilty, he will be brought to justice. I swear it."

Chapter 5

David Du Lac groaned audibly.

Jagger, standing at the head of the table, looked up and saw that Fiona MacDonald had arrived.

Of course, she had.

He wanted to stride over to her, take her by the shoulders and shake her.

She had to give them some space. She had to give them a chance to police their own.

"Gentlemen, ladies, please proceed, I'm not here to interrupt," she assured the assembled group.

There were about fifty people there, including several vampires who held positions in the highest echelon of city politics. There were also two football players, a local DJ, a TV anchorwoman, a singer, a float designer, a costumer, a woman who worked at the city's most successful wig shop, several restaurateurs and others who weren't well-known but were still important in their own right.

"Fiona!" Gina Lorre, the anchorwoman, said, smiling. "How lovely to see you."

"Thank you," Fiona said, as gracious as if she'd just been welcomed by the queen—or at least the voodoo queen. This *was* New Orleans, after all. One of the football players rose, insisting she take his chair. She thanked him, giving him a patented Fiona smile.

He smiled back, smitten. Their Keeper *was* a stunning young woman, Jagger admitted to himself. She was also capable of radiating confidence. Not arrogance— just confidence. Along with her beauty, her manner, her silken voice and her undeniable grace meant she was not just accepted but, he saw, truly welcomed.

Was he the only one who didn't want her there?

"I didn't mean to interrupt. I'm so sorry," Fiona said. "Please, Detective DeFarge, go ahead. I'm just here to keep abreast of what's going on. I have complete confidence that you'll quickly and efficiently solve this problem by yourselves."

Like hell! he thought, not believing her for a moment.

But he smiled. "Of course. And naturally we're all pleased that you're *keeping abreast,* and that you have *complete confidence* in our ability to handle this situation."

He looked from her to the assembly and made a point with his next words. "As of yet, there's no proof positive that this is the work of a vampire rather than a shapeshifter. However, since the evidence does point in our direction, I want to make sure that we're all aware of just how deeply this may affect our lives. We've worked extremely hard around the world—and especially here in New Orleans—to be a part of society. We work, we play, we fall in love. Right here in this city, we enjoy our jazz, our homes, our world—and when that world needs protecting, we come out and fight natural disaster alongside everyone else. We have proven that we are among the city's finest citizens."

"Jagger, that's just it," Billy Harrington, a college student, said. "I don't understand why any of us would have done this and put everything at risk. It just doesn't make sense."

"Billy, in a way it does," Jagger said. "Take human beings. Everyone's born with a capability for good and evil, and with natural instincts that drive them toward one rather than the other. People can be almost unbelievably evil toward each other, practicing torture and murder—sometimes for love, sometimes for hatred, sometimes in passion and often for greed. We have the same instincts as humans do, but we try harder to control our baser impulses—we have to, because our natural craving is for blood. Why couldn't there be one among us whose instincts are baser than most, who is weary of the restraints we put on ourselves so we can live something approaching normal lives? We have to bring that person to justice. Each of us has power and strength, but together we are less than half a percent of the population, and we can be brought to extinction, even though each of us would take down dozens of 'them' if it came to a fight. That's the reality—even beyond the fact that most of us *like* our lives and enjoy our neighbors, human and other, making it imperative that we police our own."

"We do police our own," David Du Lac said firmly.

"I know that. And we're not alone in this," Jagger

said. "Jennie Mahoney intends to keep watch among the shapeshifters, and August Gaudin has always been a friend, and a supporter of peaceful coexistence among all the races. We've had a decade of ease, with any disagreements being solved quietly among our own, but now we must be vigilant. Rumor and suspicion can lead to hurt and bitterness, and I don't want us all to start looking at our neighbors and suspecting them of being responsible. But I do ask that if anyone among you find something suspicious, you bring it to me. It's easy to cause a world of hurt by casting accusations without solid evidence, so we all need to stay calm and be discreet at all times. First, because we don't want to sow suspicion among ourselves, and second, we don't want to cast blame where it doesn't belong and drive our fellow races to see us as monsters."

"I'm sure they already do," Billy said dryly.

"Why not? We *are* monsters."

The comment came from a relative newcomer at the end of the table, Mateas Grenard.

"Mateas, would you care to speak?" Jagger asked. If the man wanted the floor, it was better to give it to him now than listen to subtle barbs that would get beneath everyone's skin.

Grenard stood. He was a hair shorter than Jagger, a little stockier, but he bore himself with confidence and a certain charm.

A man who could easily influence others, Jagger thought. A vampire to be noted.

"We are monsters—that's why we have a Keeper," Grenard said, smiling and nodding toward Fiona. She watched him without expression, waiting for his words.

"When I arrived, I was amazed at the self-control

you—*we*—exercise here in New Orleans. I love being here, but I've often wondered why we don't do as they do in other places and feast on occasion upon the dregs of society. How often does the murder of a prostitute really get noticed? And this state has a death penalty— why waste the blood? There are drug lords and gangs out there. I keep thinking that an organized kill now and then—especially one supervised by an officer of the law—would not be out of order."

"I don't know about that," Gina Lorre said. "Someone would be bound to notice that even a hooker or a criminal was drained of blood. I don't know exactly what happened, but when we were looking into this murder, our reporter found out that the young man working the graveyard shift at the morgue quit the day after the body of Tina Lawrence was brought in." She looked worried for a minute. "Jagger, she's not out there, is she?"

"No, she's not out there," Jagger said quietly.

"Even if she were, this is a forgiving city, and we all know that dozens of human beings in the area *think* they're vampires," Mateas Grenard pointed out.

Fiona stood. "That may be true, sir, but no human being is capable of taking blood as a vampire takes blood. As Detective DeFarge has pointed out, we don't know for a fact that a vampire is guilty—but suspicion falls that way. And to address your other point, if the vampires justified the taking of a human life, no matter how seemingly worthless, then the shapeshifters would want to kill, and the werewolves would be hungry, and those three groups are just the largest and strongest of the underworld. What if every race decided it had a right to take a life now and then?"

"Excellent point," David Du Lac commented.

One of the city commissioners stood. "More than an excellent point. I can tell you that the city government is already up in arms, arguments have started with the tourist board, and there's trouble brewing, despite the fact that the victim was hardly an innocent and there are plenty who claim she only got what she deserved. Luckily for us, because of the way she was displayed, so far the majority opinion is that some nut case psycho committed the murder. But I know for a fact, the department brass are breathing down Jagger's back, wanting to know where she was killed, and how, not to mention how all her blood was drained…. We need to work to keep the status quo. Everyone has to help by doing exactly as Jagger has asked and bringing anything odd, any suspicion, to his attention and only his attention, so we can retain the peace among ourselves."

A murmur of approval rose from the group.

"Ah, well, then I fear I am in the minority," Mateas Grenard said.

"That's fine," Jagger told him. "Discussion is always welcome."

"Open discussion, yes," David Du Lac said. "Mateas, we thank you for speaking candidly."

"Yes, and I thank you for understanding our position here in New Orleans," Fiona told him.

"I bow to wiser heads," Grenard said.

"All right, ladies, gentlemen, I thank you all for coming," Jagger said. "David will call for another meeting, if need be. For the time being, please be on the alert, and come to me with anything you feel might be relevant."

Murmurs of consent went all around, and the group began to break up. David Du Lac, always the perfect host, had arranged for refreshments and a table at the rear of the room was set with food and wine.

Jagger greeted friends, nodded to acquaintances and made his way to the table, procuring two glasses of wine.

Fiona was still at the rear of the room, talking to David and Gina, when he walked up and offered her one glass. "Thank you for coming, Fiona."

She flashed him a quick glare. He knew what it meant: *thanks for inviting me.*

"David told me about the meeting. I thought it was important for me to be here," she said.

"Well, of course it is, sweetheart," Gina said, walking up and giving her a hug.

Jagger met Fiona's eyes and raised his own glass in a toast. "To all involved doing their best to find a speedy solution to our problem," he said softly.

Fiona stared at her wine suspiciously.

David laughed softly. "It's nothing but merlot, and an excellent vintage, I swear."

Fiona blushed and drank.

"I promise you, I will be totally vigilant," Gina said. "I have to go, my darlings, David, Fiona…Jagger, you handsome hunk of…well, whatever." She looked at her watch. "Goodness, I have to be at the studio in a little over an hour. See you all soon."

"Take care, Gina," Jagger told her.

She laughed softly. "Just hope the killer, who and whatever he is, doesn't come after me, or he'll be sorry."

Others were filing out. There were pleasant good-byes all around.

It might have been a late-night buffet thrown by the tourist board.

Jagger offered David his hand, and the two men shook. "Thank you," Jagger told him.

"I am always ready to serve," David said graciously.

Billy came by. "Fiona, thank you," he said. "I think it's cool that you're our Keeper."

He was so young and cute and sincere that even Fiona could ignore his blatant admiration.

"Thank you, Billy. Will you be okay this late? Aren't you living in a frat house?"

He grinned. "I am, but don't worry. I'm great at sneaking back in. Oh—and guess who's the new late-night morgue attendant?"

"You?" David asked him.

He grinned. "Seemed perfect for me. I start tomorrow night."

"I just hope you get nothing but the elderly dying of natural causes," Jagger told him. "I don't want to have to come in and see you anytime soon."

Mateas Grenard left right behind Billy. He, too, stopped to thank David for his hospitality.

Then the man looked at Fiona with a twinkle in his eye and took her hand, planting a kiss lightly on it. "Miss MacDonald, a sincere pleasure. And, DeFarge," he said, turning to Jagger while still holding Fiona's hand. "I speak my mind, but I didn't make the kill. I swear it."

"Did you think that I was suspicious of you?" Jagger asked. He wanted to wrench Fiona's hand away from Grenard's hold.

Grenard chuckled softly. "I'm a newcomer and not shy about expressing my views—and I'm not stupid. Of course I would fall under suspicion. But I didn't do it. Don't waste your time on me."

"I never waste time, and I always discover the truth," Jagger told him, then turned to Fiona. "Miss MacDonald, are you ready for me to see you home?"

"If you've business to attend to, DeFarge, I can see our Keeper home," Grenard offered.

"That won't be necessary, thank you. I have a few matters to discuss with Fiona," Jagger said, but he didn't look at her, afraid she might say that she preferred to go with Grenard.

But she didn't.

"I'm ready whenever you are," she said.

"Alas, well, then, good night, my friends," Grenard said, and departed.

Jagger doubted that she was going to let him see her home for the pleasure of his company. Maybe she distrusted Grenard. Or maybe she was hoping that he had something to say.

"Good night, David, and thank you," Fiona said, kissing him on the cheek. "Thank you very much."

"Don't be a stranger, sweetie," David told her.

She shook her head. "I won't be. Just, please, tell Dragon-lady to let me in when I come."

He laughed. "Consider it done."

"Dragon-lady?" Jagger echoed, and was surprised to see Fiona flash a smile.

"Bitchy shapeshifter," she said.

"Valentina," David explained. "She seems to have claws when she sees our dear Keeper." He smiled. "I shall inform my hostess that you are always welcome here, Fiona. Come back some night, when the music is sweet and the 'joint is a hoppin' and a poppin'.'"

Fiona promised him that she would. Then Jagger

nodded to David and led Fiona toward the door, steering between the tables in the courtyard to reach the street.

It was the rare hour of "tween" in New Orleans. The clubs often stayed open until five, and a few of the late-night pizza, chicken or burger joints boasted twenty-four-hour service. But, for the most part, the last partiers had finally called it quits, and it was too early for the workaday world to have begun stirring.

The streets were quiet.

And beautiful.

"You walked?" Jagger asked.

"Yes."

"Alone?"

"Yes."

He sighed deeply. "Don't you ever listen to intelligent advice?" he asked her.

She lifted her hands. "I'm a Keeper," she told him.

"And you're vulnerable. Any vampire could take you by surprise, and a werewolf could be on you before you blinked. Not to mention that a shapeshifter can be and do pretty much anything. And let's not forget our normal run-of-the-mill crackheads, heroin addicts, thieves, rapists and murderers."

She had the grace to flush.

"I can change pretty quickly myself, you know. And anyone can be taken by surprise."

"Right. So don't let that anyone be you," he said.

She glanced up at him with her beautiful, opalescent eyes, a dry grin curving her lips. "I'm glad to hear that you genuinely seem to want me to survive."

"Protect and serve, that's my motto," he said.

"And you resent my intrusion," she said.

He shook his head. "No, I don't resent you. I just

don't understand why you won't believe that I'm not shirking my responsibility, that I *am* policing my own, that I *will* act when necessary—even against my own breed. My…people are committed to the 'lives' we lead here, Fiona. For the most part, we're extremely good citizens. If someone is guilty, they will be brought to justice. And I won't be acting alone. The entire vampire community will be behind me."

"Get real," she murmured.

"Pardon?" he asked.

She squared her shoulders. "What have you discovered?" she asked. "Anything?"

He looked ahead as they walked, weighing his answer. They were into the Quarter, and the moonlight and soft glow of the street lamps hid anything that might mar the perfection of the buildings, with their balconies and decoration. He thought there was little in the world as picture-perfect as the architecture in the French Quarters. People loved their balconies, and ferns grew profusely in pots and planters, along with flowers in an array of colors, and insignia plaques that held the city's symbol, the fleur-de-lis, adorned more than one building. Banners still proclaimed the city's pride in the New Orleans Saints, and beautifully fashioned signs advertised various shops and restaurants.

"Jagger?" she asked.

"I spent part of last night at Barely, Barely, Barely—the club where Tina Lawrence worked. I met a woman there, a waitress, who came in this morning and worked with a police artist to create a sketch of a man she thought was suspicious. I met a werewolf who worked with her, and verified that Tina carried on a conversation with the man and intended to meet him after work.

I don't know if he's the one who killed her, but I didn't recognize him."

"Do you have a copy of the sketch on you?" Fiona asked.

"Of course," he said. "I didn't want to show it tonight, because I didn't want anyone to go off half-cocked, but it will run in tomorrow's paper, and they'll show it on the local newscasts. No one at the club had ever seen the man before, so we're not putting it out that he's under suspicion, just that we're hoping he may have some information regarding Tina Lawrence. Thing is, if he's a married man, he'll probably be afraid to come forward, won't want to admit where he was. But, one way or another, someone out there must have seen him. And if we find him, with luck he will lead us somewhere."

He paused beneath a streetlight on St. Ann's and took out his phone, then brought up the picture.

Fiona stared at it for a long minute.

"Anything?" he asked her.

She shook her head. "No, I've never seen him before."

He slid the phone back in his jacket pocket as they started walking again. "Before the meeting, I went back to the club, and the girls who'd seen him all agreed that it's a good likeness of him."

"I hope it leads us in the right direction," Fiona said.

A moment later they had reached her house, which was surrounded by a ten-foot brick wall, with a wrought-iron gate that led to the front walk.

She hovered before opening it. "Do you want to come in? Can I get you anything? Although after that wine, we should probably get some sleep."

Mixed signals. Did she want him to come in? Or was she just being polite?

He shrugged. "It will probably be another hour or so before I wind down."

"Do you only sleep when it's light?" she asked him.

He laughed. "I long ago learned to sleep whenever I get the chance. And, yes, I wear sunglasses, and slather on the sunblock, but in general my 'life' is as normal as anyone else's."

She smiled. "I'm sorry, I wasn't implying anything, just pointing out that we all must be tired."

"Are *you* tired?"

She looked away from him. "I'm...keyed up, I guess." She grinned suddenly. "Want to watch a movie? Pay-per-view has everything—adventure, horror, thriller, you name it."

He laughed. "I can actually sit through a chick flick, you know."

She grinned again, pulled out her key and opened the gate. "Please, come in, then."

"Thank you, Miss MacDonald, I believe I will."

He had never been in the MacDonald house, though he had heard it was spectacular.

He'd heard right.

The front path took them through a small garden to the door, which led up one step to a tile entry. There was a small mudroom before the grand foyer, which offered two hallways, one to the left and one to the right. Straight ahead, a grand stairway led to the second floor.

Fiona walked down the hallway to the right.

"We've basically divided the house," she explained. "I'm in this wing, Shauna is in the center upstairs and

Caitlin has the left wing. There's a huge dining-room-slash-ballroom at the back of the first floor, and the kitchen is back there, too, though we all have little kitchenettes of our own. There's a third floor, a little garret, above Shauna's rooms, so the division of space is about even. We live and work together, so we have to give one another a little privacy where we can."

"Nice," he murmured.

They had reached what was clearly Fiona's living room. He quickly saw that she liked antiques and eclectic art. There was a huge fireplace against the wall, all done in red brick, with a pink marble mantel. Books were everywhere, and pictures of her family and New Orleans adorned several of the tables and the mantel, along with small sculptures of cats, dogs and other animals, gargoyles, ornate wands and more. She was clearly fond of Rodrigue, judging by the many prints of his Blue Dog pictures.

"The TV's upstairs, sorry," she said, her words a little awkward. "Does that make you uncomfortable?"

"Does it make *you* uncomfortable?" he asked.

She hesitated. "I don't think so."

They were caught there together in the soft glow of the few night-lights she'd left burning when she went out, and everything was quiet around them, as if they were alone in the world.

He suddenly found himself speaking the truth. "Any man in creation would want to be with you anywhere," he said softly.

Soft color suffused her cheeks, but she didn't blink, and she didn't turn away.

"Isn't it forbidden?" she asked.

"Only if we forbid it," he told her.

"But…before…what happened…the war when the races mixed…"

"We would never allow that to happen again," he said.

She continued to stare at him. He wanted to move closer, but he wouldn't allow himself to. He drew upon his every reserve of strength to keep his distance from her. He imagined holding her, really holding her, inhaling the scent of her hair, feeling the warmth of her, feeling her heart beating, the rise and fall of her breath, her skin, so silky, crushed against his…

He had to go or he would be screaming in frustration in a matter of seconds.

Then, to his astonishment, *she* moved toward him.

In a second—no, less than a second—she had crossed the few feet that separated them. She was in his arms, against him, and instinct demanded that his arms tighten around her, that he bury his face against her sun-colored hair to inhale the sweet feminine scent of her. He didn't know if he was dreaming at first, if his imagination hadn't been taunting him so completely that he was hallucinating the wonder of the moment. But it was real.

She was real.

And more than his imagination could ever have predicted. She trembled slightly in his arms, and he felt her warmth, her vitality, the heartbeat that had so fascinated him. Her skin was as soft and smooth as silk, and even more tempting than he'd imagined. For seconds that felt like an eternity, he just held her. Then he drew away far enough to lift her chin, to look into her eyes and whisper to her, "Fiona…I don't…I'd never…"

"You'd never hurt me," she said softly.

"Never," he swore.

She smiled. "I believe you."

"But…I am what I am."

"I know what you are."

"Others may…talk."

"Let them."

"Are you sure?"

She nodded, staring up at him with a beautiful honesty, heart and soul bared, something he'd never imagined he would receive from her. "Truthfully I didn't want to feel this way. I didn't even want to like you," she told him.

He had to laugh softly. "Sorry about that."

"I am the Keeper, after all," she whispered.

"What better way to keep me?" he teased.

"I dreamed about you," she told him.

"I hope I can live up to the dream."

Then he touched her lips gently with his own. Hers were soft and welcoming, parting beneath his tender touch. And then he was locked with her in the soft light, his tongue reveling in a wealth of sensation, heat that led to slow-burning fire, something that wasn't just beautiful and angelic, but deeply passionate, as well. Stepping backward, her lips still locked with his, she drew him toward the staircase. Step by step they went up, never breaking the kiss. The stairs led to a large room where he glimpsed the promised TV, and on the back wall, a door. They made their way to that door.

He closed it behind him when they entered her bedroom. Gentle, pale light streamed in through the soft white curtains that covered the doors to the balcony without blocking the moonbeams or the artificial light from the street. As they broke apart at last, he saw a room that felt instantly welcoming. Her bed was large and covered with a homemade quilt, her shelves were filled with more bric-a-brac, and there was local art on the walls, a rocking chair by the fireplace…everything warm and individual, and uniquely the woman who had demanded his attention, and seduced his senses and his heart.

Fiona never hesitated. She kept backing up until they reached the bed, and there she studied his eyes, as if she could see into his soul. Perhaps she could. If so, she would know he was trembling inside.

His existence had gone on for more years than she could probably imagine, and he had known battle and peace, family, friends…and enemies. But he had seldom, if ever, felt so in awe, so touched, and all from a woman's eyes upon him. Eyes that promised honesty and an exploration of the heart, eyes that he could never, not even in the full span of his near-eternal lifetime, betray.

He kissed her again—hard and passionately—feeling as if he were drowning in nothing but a kiss. His lips traveled to her collarbone and, impatiently, he began to undo the tiny buttons of her blouse. At the same time, he felt her hands on him. Her fingers were like pure magic, moving down his spine, slipping beneath his waistband.

She shrugged impatiently, letting the blouse slip from her shoulders, then slipping her hands beneath his jacket. He stood up, shedding the jacket, along with his holster and gun. And then she was against him again. A dream. Silk in his arms. He pressed his lips to her breast, felt the intake of her breath, the press of her body against his. He eased her skirt down, found the tiny line of her string panties, let them fall. A second later he'd shed the rest of his clothes and was with her at last. Naked flesh to naked flesh. Feeling the play of muscle beneath her smooth skin, as she arched against him.

It hadn't been that long since he'd had sex.

But it felt like forever since he'd made love.

His desires seemed to burst instantly and almost savagely to the front the instant they came into contact, but he brutally willed them under control. Being with her in this moment, this seemingly impossible moment, was something to cherish and savor. And he did. He stroked her flesh in wonder. Kissed her with reverence and wanton need. He explored the length of her body with his touch, with his lips. She was not to be outdone. Her hands moved along his back, teasing his spine, his buttocks. Her lips found his chest, his abdomen, below. Soft groans escaped him, and he took the lead again, bearing her beneath him to the mattress, finding her breasts with the pressure of his mouth, the teasing touch of his tongue, then moving lower, down to her ankles, her knees, the luxurious length of her thighs…and between.

She cried out, dragging him to her. Their lips met again as he entered her, drawing her long legs around him, sinking together so completely that he felt as if they were sharing their very beings. All that had been slow became desperately fast, subtle became bold, and they seemed to both give way before something so urgent it was almost cruel, and yet there was still time for kisses of liquid fire, caresses and whispers as tender as the softest breeze.

He held himself in check as he held her, felt her shudder and jerk and climax, and at long last he allowed himself to release the shattering volatility that he had

held in check, the entire world darkening and then exploding along with him. She fell against him, drenched
and liquid, spent and limp, and he held her, feeling as
if he actually had a heart himself, one that hammered
along with hers as they both eased down from the pure
carnal ecstasy of incredible sex.

Together, they lay entwined on the bed, with the soft
white light slowly bringing the world into focus again.
He didn't want to leave—ever.

She stirred against him. He slipped an arm around
her, drawing her head down to his chest, gently thread-
ing his fingers through the tangled mass of her hair,
marveling at the color in the light. Where she went, he
thought, there was sun. A sun that didn't burn or hurt,
just brightened the world.

She could be the most infuriating individual in the
world. Stubborn. Pig-headed, actually. But being with
her was amazing. Making love with her was even more
amazing. Lying beside her, just being near her…

He must be insane. Being with her was the most
wonderful experience in his memory, in his life, in his
death…in his entire existence. But he needed to be careful. His emotions were running rampant.

He didn't care. He didn't think all the powers in
heaven or hell could have stopped him from making
love to her tonight.

And then he stopped, amazed at the tenor of his own
thoughts. He was a *vampire*.

And he was falling in love.

She moved slightly, getting more comfortable against
him.

He wondered if she realized just what they might

have to face as he continued to stroke her hair in silence. Then, he couldn't stop himself.

"Are you sorry?" he asked softly.

She shook her head. "No...actually, I haven't felt this...I don't know...so..."

"So...what?" he asked, setting a finger on her chin to lift her face so that she had to look at him.

She was smiling. "I was about to say 'at peace.' I haven't felt so at peace in years. But I didn't want you to think that your lovemaking was peaceful. I mean, I'm not sure that would be a compliment, and I wouldn't want to insult you. At all." She was suddenly flushing, but he laughed, not in the least bit offended.

"I won't take it as an offense against my masculinity, I promise," he assured her.

Her smile suddenly faded. "I want you to know...I mean, I have no expectations. I...don't think I meant to do this when I let you walk me home tonight. I...I don't mean to intrude on your life. I mean...I *do,* as far as discovering what happened goes. So far..."

"So far," he said firmly, wrapping his arms around her, "so far, there's nothing we can do until morning. Tonight...tonight, I'm in awe, and I don't want to give up a minute of the time that's left."

"I think it's already starting to get light."

"Then hush, and let me love you."

Fiona awoke with his words echoing in her mind.

Of course, he hadn't meant it as "love." He'd meant it as "make love." But still, she believed with her whole heart that there was something between them more than sex. She really hadn't wanted to want him.

But she had. And she did.

She'd dreamed about him.

She'd felt a pang when others had talked about him. She had admired him.

But he was a vampire, and she shouldn't have been with him.

Why not? It wasn't forbidden. Just because her parents had died to stop a war because beings from two different societies had fallen in love...

Hadn't they learned from that war? People were people, even when they were creatures of the night or the underworld. Surely they had learned that society's dictates could never control the heart.

After all, look at her. She was lost in a whirlwind over him. Falling deeply. She didn't have affairs; she had never been the type. Sex was the most intimate act possible between a man and a woman, and she had never taken it lightly.

But...

She didn't even know how old Jagger DeFarge really was, or how long he had existed, or...

If he knew how to feel emotion.

She started to roll over, certain that he would still be there, when she was stunned as her door flew open.

She pulled up her covers, suddenly self-conscious.

Jagger was gone.

But Caitlin, wearing a look of pure fury was standing in her doorway.

Chapter 6

"Oh, my God!" Caitlin said. And then again, "Oh, my God!"

"Excuse me, what happened to knocking?" Fiona demanded.

"When did we ever knock?" Caitlin said, then gave her anger free rein again. "I would think, if there was a need to knock, *you would have told me!*"

"Would you excuse me?" Fiona said, ignoring her and wanting only to get away to think—about Caitlin's words, Jagger's absence. "I'd like to grab a shower."

"A shower? You need to be decontaminated," Caitlin snapped.

"What?"

"You were with—you were with Jagger DeFarge!" Caitlin said.

How did she know? Fiona was certain that her sister hadn't seen Jagger. She was positive. He never would have put her into that position. He could be far faster than any speeding bullet. Even if he had been sound asleep, with his acute hearing, he would have known when Caitlin twisted the knob, and he would have been gone, rather than let her sister catch him there.

"Caitlin, this isn't really any of your business," Fiona said.

Caitlin stared at her, her jaw clenched. Finally she spoke icily. "I'm afraid that, because of who we are, it is very much my business."

Then she slammed the door and was gone.

Ruing the situation—but never the deed—Fiona hurried into the shower. Afterward she brushed her teeth, dressed quickly in a soft knit halter dress, grabbed her sandals and sped down the stairs. A glance at her watch assured her that she hadn't missed opening time at the store—again—and that her sisters would be at the breakfast table.

Caitlin might have been angry, but Shauna was just amused.

"Ah, there she is at last. The fallen woman. Thank God! I've thought for a very long time that you needed to get in bed with somebody," Shauna said.

"But a vampire!" Caitlin said, almost spitting out the word.

"Does somebody want to run up to the roof and announce it to the city?" Fiona asked.

"Honestly, Fiona. I can't believe that in the middle of everything going on, you brought a vampire into our home," Caitlin said.

Fiona sighed and walked over to the coffeepot on the buffet. Antonia—a shapeshifter—came and helped them out three days a week. She was a natural housekeeper and a warm mother figure. She'd been with them for over five years, after coming into the shop one day and overhearing them admitting that even between the three of them, they were having trouble keeping up with the house and the store.

Antonia made the best coffee in the world. It was strong and bracing, with a slight touch of pecan.

Fiona got her coffee, then turned to face Caitlin. She loved her sister so much, and she knew that Caitlin loved her, too. She hated it when they were at odds.

"August Gaudin has been coming here forever. Antonia is a shapeshifter and she might as well live here. They're good...beings. So is Jagger DeFarge."

"How can you say that? You hardly know him," Caitlin said.

"One way or another, we've known him forever, actually," Shauna said in Fiona's defense. "Caitlin, come on. The city trusts him. We might as well, too."

"None of us should become involved," Caitlin said quietly.

"Perhaps we shouldn't," Fiona said, walking over to where her sister was sitting at the dining room table. "I'm sorry. Maybe I should have...maybe I should have told you both how I was feeling, but I didn't really know myself until... Look, that's not the point. We have to worry about the real problem here, not whether or not I choose to have sex, or with whom."

Caitlin inhaled a deep breath. "I'm trying not to overreact. Honestly." She took another deep breath and stood, her hands on her hips. "But the vampires started the war, the war that killed our parents, Fiona."

"They—they didn't start it alone," Fiona said.

"They started it over an affair—a love affair—between a vampire and a werewolf," Caitlin reminded them grimly.

"Well, there you go," Fiona said quietly. "I'm not a werewolf. And no one's going to war."

"Everyone will start to think that mixed affairs are all right," Caitlin said accusingly.

"Would that really be such a bad thing?" Fiona asked.

"Let me tell you why it's a bad thing," Caitlin said. "It's not you or me or Shauna—it's not Jagger. It's the rest of the underworld. It's people. It's the world around us. I'm sorry, but the world is filled with prejudice, and that's simply the truth."

"Then shouldn't we work to change things?" Fiona asked.

Caitlin looked at her and sighed. "I don't want you to feel the hurt the world can dish out," she told her sister.

Fiona hugged her, suddenly at a loss for words.

"Get serious. Half the shapeshifters were drooling over him at that luncheon," Shauna said. "I think things are going to be fine. When is the wedding?"

"Wedding?" Caitlin gasped.

"Shauna! Stop, I beg you. There *is* no wedding," Fiona said. "Seriously, there's a killer out there, and catching him is my only focus at the moment."

"Except for having sex with a vampire," Caitlin noted sourly.

"Yes, I'm sorry, forgot to throw that in. I'll probably have a few meals and sleep for a few hours in the midst of all this, too. Caitlin, please..."

Caitlin bit her lower lip, looking away. "I'm sorry. I do love you, and you know it. I don't mean to be difficult. It's just that Jagger is..."

"Jagger is a vampire. Yes, I am aware of that. And

I'm the oldest of the three of us, and I need to act responsibly. And I will. I swear, I would never do anything to risk the two of you or myself—or anyone else, for that matter," Fiona said.

"Responsible, intelligent and aware—and sleeping with a vampire," Caitlin said, then lifted a hand when Fiona would have spoken. "And vulnerable. We're all vulnerable. That's life. Just don't let it be your death."

The artist's sketch of the man from Barely, Barely, Barely who had probably met up with Tina Lawrence after her last night at work was everywhere.

It was shown on every local news channel. It was in the newspapers.

In some neighborhoods the residents printed up flyers and plastered them all over trees and poles and shop windows.

But not a soul called in to say that they had seen the man.

Jagger had returned to the scene where the body had been found, though with very little hope that he would find anything, but he had to start somewhere.

Of course, it was still early days, he told himself. The sketch had just started making the rounds. They could still hear something.

Meanwhile, he was standing in the tomb in the old cemetery just on the edge of the Quarter when the call came that a body had been discovered in a cemetery in the Garden District.

In ten minutes' time he was standing in the Alden family vault, last interment 1921. He noted everything about the vault as he went in, the architecture and the inhabitants. The first interment had been in 1840, soon after the cemetery was established in 1833. The gated door was guarded by two angels, now minus their heads. That detail fit in well with the asymmetrical rows of little stone houses in this particular city of the dead. As for the Alden mausoleum itself, there was an altar at the far end, a small table in the center of the room and rows of divided shelving for bodies, most of them sealed in. A few of the oldest had broken—or been broken—open, but not even bones remained. The heat in New Orleans provided for burial of another family member or loved one in the same space in "a year and a day." In that time, the corpse was basically cremated by the intense heat alone, and what was left of the remains could be raked to a "holding cell" at the end of each tomb so that someone else could be interred in the first body's spot.

This tomb itself was slightly different from the one where Tina's body had been left, so this time the killer had left his victim on the altar that stretched across the back wall.

She was beautiful—blonde and beautiful. Her face was perfect, like porcelain. Her hair was almost platinum, and curled over the edges of the stone. She was laid out in a white halter-necked gown, as if she had just been to a dance. Maybe a prom. This one was young.

There didn't appear to be a mark on her.

"Oh, God," Tony breathed.

Jagger turned to him. "Apparently she was also found by a tour guide. Can you head out and talk to him? I don't think he found her until eleven, and the first tours go through around nine, so maybe we'll get lucky and someone saw our killer. Can you find out just how he stumbled on her?"

Tony nodded, looking almost as ashen as the corpse.

When he was gone, Jagger slipped on his gloves and began his intense search of the corpse.

As before, the marks he was looking for were there.

He sighed softly. This time the killer had gone for the major artery in her left thigh.

"Now we're in serious trouble," a voice said from the entryway.

He turned around.

Craig Dewey had arrived. He was standing in the doorway, caught in the dust motes that played against the rays of sunlight seeping into the tomb.

Dewey laughed dryly. "Hey, buddy. You look like a character out of a movie, standing there all 'Son of Dracula,' bending over his last meal."

Jagger didn't laugh. He knew Dewey wasn't trying to be funny.

The other man strode on in, stared down and shook his head.

"They have an ID on her yet?"

"Nothing certain, but she matches up with a missing co-ed call that came in this morning. Abigail Langdon, last seen at a frat party last night. One of the uniforms is getting me her college ID picture. If it's her, we'll have to bring someone in to make a positive ID. One of her friends, maybe," Jagger said.

Dewey slipped on gloves and stepped closer to the body. "Skin as white as snow. The killer seems to like blondes. And he's bold. Wants his victims found, and found by ordinary citizens. This is considered one of the safest cemeteries in the city to visit."

"I'm not sure any cemetery is safe at night," Jagger said. "There are too many places for someone to hide.

We call them the cities of the dead, and the dead don't call the cops when you run in to escape observation."

Dewey looked at the victim's eyes, turned her, touched her and took her body temp, then turned to Jagger. "Well, we're looking at exactly the same kind of killing—late last night, very late. Can't say much about lividity, because there was no blood left to pool beneath the skin. Again, I can't help but think she was killed elsewhere, since I'm not seeing a drop of blood around the body anywhere. What a shame. This one looks like a kid."

"Rape?" Jagger asked.

"I'll need a kit, but no obvious signs of violence or trauma…." He looked at Jagger. "I'm not a vegetarian, and I don't avoid leather, but I'd never buy fox fur. They electrocute the poor little things with a rod up the rectum. Quite gruesome."

"She wasn't electrocuted," Jagger pointed out.

"Just don't ever buy fox fur," Dewey said, stabbing a finger at him. "The point is that she looks as pure as the day she was born. The killer didn't leave a mark on the body that I can see so far. I'm not even sure she suffered. It's almost as if she were hypnotized and told to go to sleep or something. Poor child, so beautiful."

"Well, we've got to let the crime-scene unit in, and then you can take her to the morgue," Jagger said. "How soon can she be scheduled for autopsy?"

"Not right away, I'm afraid. First thing tomorrow. I'll have her photographed, bathed…set for first thing tomorrow morning."

"I thought she'd be a priority."

"You would think so, right? But a city bigwig—potential candidate for mayor—died in his home last night, and his children are making waves against the stepmother."

Jagger groaned inwardly. Another night he'd have to head for the morgue. Slip in. Maybe traumatize a few employees.

Then he remembered that Billy Harrington had taken the job of night attendant. He could just call Billy and ask him to handle the matter.

No, he couldn't. This was his responsibility.

He stepped outside and saw that Officer Gus Parissi was standing at the gate, patiently waiting, presumably for him.

He saw, too, that the media were already there, being held on the far side of the gates. Tour groups were being sent away.

"Parissi, you waiting for me?" Jagger asked.

The other cop nodded. "The brass are keeping the same group of uniforms working both murders," he said, then winced. "This that missing college kid?"

"Looks to be," Jagger said.

"I brought a yearbook," Gus told him.

Jagger took Parissi's elbow and led him behind one of the tombs. A winged cherub set to guard an ironwork-covered window stared at them balefully.

"Let me see the missing girl," Jagger said.

Parissi silently opened the book to a marked page.

She was a junior, a nursing major. She was in the chess club.

She was the latest victim.

"Family?" he asked Gus Parissi.

"The sisters at the convent," Gus said. "She was orphaned at seven and never adopted. They say only babies stand a chance to—"

"Gus?"

"Sorry. She doesn't have a family. Just the sisters."

"All right. I'll let them know. Parissi?"

"Yessir?"

"Keep the mob out. Let the M.E. and the crime-scene unit take their time in here. The Catholic Church still has control of the cemeteries just outside the Quarter, but this place is managed by a historical foundation. See that it isn't reopened until tomorrow. Understood?"

"Understood."

Jagger turned away. Celia Larson, her bag in hand, was headed toward the tomb. She glowered at him. "How can you think that we'll turn anything up when the crime scene has been trampled by hordes of tourists?" she demanded.

"Celia, if I knew where a crime would be discovered, I'd be there before the damned thing happened," he said, trying to maintain his temper. "Come on, surely you've been briefed. She was discovered at eleven. The first tours are at nine. What do you think I could have done?"

She sniffed and walked on past him. Dewey was standing at the door to the tomb. He rolled his eyes toward Jagger as she approached, and Jagger shrugged.

He had to go see the nuns.

"Oh, God, there's been another one!"

So far the three of them had been doing well, considering the way the day had started.

But Fiona knew the minute her sister spoke that there was real trouble ahead.

Caitlin was behind the desk, focused in on the news on the store's computer. So far, the identity of the victim hadn't been released to the public, but from what the news media had been able to gather, the method of murder and the disposal of the body matched the first, just a different cemetery.

Fiona felt as if her stomach pitched down to her feet.

She moved to stand behind her sister. Jagger was on the news, caught by the media as he exited the Garden District cemetery.

"The police will not lie, nor will we hedge," he said. "Yes, we have discovered a second body. We have formed a task force, and every officer will be on overtime, following every possible lead. We will not stop. We ask the citizens of the city to help us, and we ask the women of New Orleans to be especially vigilant. We will be working tirelessly to find this killer. Please, don't panic, but be smart. That's all that I can say right now. We have to let our crime-scene unit and our coroner's office do their work."

Gina was at the head of the crowd.

"Detective DeFarge, we've heard that the dead woman was a blonde, and that she was drained of blood. Should the blonde women of New Orleans be dyeing their hair?"

"The women of New Orleans need to be vigilant and not go out alone after dark. Don't walk through parking lots alone, don't leave a party alone, stay with friends and family. We've released a sketch of a possible witness to the disappearance of Tina Lawrence, so please, if anyone has seen the man, notify the police. If anyone sees anything out of the ordinary, notify the police. We need your help. Thank you. Now, please, I have work to do."

Despite the barrage of questions that followed him, Jagger made his way out of camera range.

Caitlin glared at Fiona. "There's a rogue vampire out there, Fiona. You have to stop him. This will turn into a panic and create a mess in more ways than most people in this city can possibly expect."

"She's right," Shauna said. "I'm going to a meeting tonight of the were clans. I'll do my best to keep them from flying into a fury, but…two murders, Fiona. This is bad."

"We need to call a general assembly," Fiona said, forcing herself to remain calm. "All the races need to be invited—and the voodoo priests and priestesses, as well. And Father Moran."

Father Moran was a priest, and a human being. But like the city's most powerful voodoo priest, Antoine Geneset, who would also be invited, he had an instinct for all creatures and often attended the general assemblies, which were usually held no more than twice a year.

This was an emergency, however.

"I'll stop by and see David Du Lac. He'll make the arrangements," Fiona said.

It was a terrible duty, informing people someone that someone they loved was dead.

Jagger felt out of his league, even though he'd had to perform the same sad duty before.

The sisters who had raised Abigail Langdon had loved their charge dearly, and caught in the midst of their grief, he felt as if he had been overwhelmed by a flock of penguins.

But the sisters had a powerful faith, and eventually their tears gave way to prayers. Listening to those prayers, Jagger felt his resolve doubled. He *would* see to it that their beloved Abigail was allowed to rest in peace, to return to the tender hands of her Maker.

Sadly, the sisters were unable to help him in his quest for the killer. Abigail had been living in a dorm. She had a roommate, and they had talked to the roommate just before the girl had called the police, which was how they had found out that she was missing to begin with. The roommate, Linda McCormick, had called them to tell them that she had last seen Abigail at a frat party. When Linda was ready to head home, Abigail was nowhere to be seen. Linda assumed her roommate had headed out without her, but when she reached the dorm and found no sign of Abigail, she had begun to worry. But she had known that Abigail was an orphan, and where she had been raised, and she had called the sisters.

Jagger's next stop was the dorm, where he met up with Tony Miro and went to speak with a teary-eyed Linda McCormick.

"It was a party, just like any other party," she told him. "Yeah, there was beer. There's always beer… we *are* in college, and this *is* New Orleans," she said, sounding a bit defensive.

"What about drugs?" he asked.

"Sure, some kids do drugs. But I don't, and Abigail didn't."

"What about the kids at the party? Was there anyone there you didn't know?"

"No, I don't think so."

"Can you give me a list of names?" Jagger asked.

She started crying again, and he took her gently by the shoulders. "Linda, we need your help. I know you cared about your roommate. I need you to be strong, though. I need a list with the name of every person who was at that party. No one is going to get in trouble for underage drinking, I swear. Okay? I need every name."

Linda stopped crying long enough to shudder and nod. Tony provided a paper and pencil, and she went to work.

They headed out of the dorm as soon as she was done. Jagger called in the ten officers he'd been given as his "task force," so that they could all begin questioning the frat boys at the house where the party had been held, before starting to track down the other attendees. Before long Celia Larson and her team showed up to search for trace evidence.

Jagger wasn't sure what they thought they were going to find. Even if the entire fraternity and all their guests had been full-on inebriated, he was sure they would have noticed if a murder had taken place right in front of them.

The sketch of their possible suspect from the strip club was passed around, but no one had seen anyone who resembled the "pretty" man who had waited for the first victim, Tina Lawrence.

Something big—and bad—was going on.

It was while he was talking to a frat boy who claimed to have been in love with Abigail that he found a possible—and troubling—suspect.

"Hey, have you talked to Billy Harrington?" the boy asked. "He and Abigail were friends."

Jagger frowned and looked at his list. Billy's name wasn't on it.

"Billy was here?"

The young man wiped his wet cheeks and frowned as

well. "Come to think of it, Billy wasn't going to come. Said he had to be somewhere else."

That rang true; Billy had been at the meeting at David's last night.

The murder could have taken place in the hour right before the meeting.

"All right, he wasn't supposed to be here. But you saw him?"

The boy suddenly seemed confused. "Did I see him? I don't remember him coming in, and I was by the door. But…I thought I saw him. No, maybe I didn't. But… oh, I don't know!" Fresh tears streamed down his face. "I had a lot of beer."

The kid went on.

It didn't matter.

Jagger knew that he would be seeing Billy that night.

Valentina—apparently chastised by David—was icily cordial when Fiona stopped by the club. She led Fiona right to David, who was in his private quarters, thoughtfully sipping a cup of something when she arrived.

Once they were alone, he lifted a hand before she could speak. "I heard, of course," he said softly.

"We have to call a general assembly, David," she said. "I'm afraid that things will start getting ugly. Everyone—every being—is going to be up in arms."

He nodded. "Let's try for 3:00 a.m. again. Tomorrow-night-slash-morning," he said. He looked at her sadly. "Who would do this? Who would risk everything?"

"I don't know. We have to find out," Fiona said. "And we have to keep the peace while we find the killer, and I think an assembly is going to be the best way. The others have to believe you when you say you want the killer as badly as they do. You have to be beyond convincing."

"You got it, kid," he said softly. "Tomorrow night."

She thanked him, said goodbye and left.

She hoped the next night was going to be soon enough, but there was no way to meet any sooner. It wasn't as if they could broadcast this particular meeting on the airwaves.

Back out on the street, she saw that the sun was setting. She got in her car and headed for Martin Luther King Boulevard.

Darkness was falling, but it seemed as if the entire morgue staff was working late.

Jagger waited, watching the entry, watching the sky. Finally he could wait no longer.

He turned to mist and entered, aware that some people felt *something* as he passed by. A chill. "Footsteps walking over their grave." Bad expression for New Orleans—there weren't many graves to actually walk over.

He headed to the autopsy rooms, certain that Abigail would be in the same situation as Tina Lawrence. With the autopsy scheduled for first thing in the morning, a tech would have prepared the body. He wondered what thoughts had accompanied the process. Anyone in their right mind would have felt sad at the sight of one so young, with so much hope for a future, lying dead on a cold gurney at the morgue.

He passed the desk where Billy Harrington should have been working, stopping anyone who came to that part of the morgue and requiring them to sign in, but Billy wasn't there.

As Jagger stood there for a moment, he realized that

the place had gone very quiet. Most of the day workers had left at last.

He strode down the hall, quietly opening the door to the room where he'd so recently seen Tina.

And there she was: the beautiful young victim.

He entered silently, and there he found Billy.

The boy was standing in front of the gurney, holding a stake. It wasn't nearly as efficient as Jagger's own weapon, but it was apparent that Billy had intended to carry out what he saw as his duty.

Or his necessity?

Was Billy the killer?

Jagger glared at him. "You were seen," he said. "One of the frat boys saw you, Billy."

The look Billy gave him as he turned in surprise was one of sheer astonishment. "What?"

"You were seen at the party. The frat party. The last place Abigail was seen."

"I wasn't there!" Billy protested. "You know where I was. I was at the meeting."

"She could have been killed as much as an hour before the meeting."

Billy shook his head, astounded. "Jagger, I'm telling you, I wasn't there. I swear it. I swear it on my soul and any hope of heaven! I've never killed anything, except for a rat here and there. And they're awful! I get my blood the same places you do. I wasn't even born into *human* life before the peace was made, much less reborn as a vampire. And I remember the war. Good God, Jagger, I don't want anything like that happening again. It wasn't me, I swear it!"

"You'll have to appear before the council, Billy,"

Jagger said. "For now, you need to step aside. I'll take care of this matter."

Billy didn't move.

"No," he said softly.

"Billy—"

"No. Jagger. I knew her. Abigail was a sweetheart. She'd never hurt anyone, alive or…dead. She might not even need to be—"

"Billy, the girl was murdered. The entire city knows she was murdered. The medical examiner has seen her. She's been photographed and bathed. Her time of death has been listed."

"She hasn't been cut yet," Billy said. "There are medical miracles."

"Stop this!" a woman's voice said, one Jagger had come to know well.

He turned as Fiona MacDonald stepped into the room.

Billy stared at her and groaned softly. "I…I love her. I'll fight you both. I'll die for her if I have to, and they'll find me here, because—I'm not old enough to turn to dust. I mean it—I *will* die for her."

"Billy, you're already dead, technically," Fiona pointed out gently.

Before he could reply, a sound drew their attention, and the body on the gurney suddenly jackknifed into a sitting position. The sheet fell away.

Abigail, in all her glory, stared at them with huge blue eyes.

"Where am I?" she asked, and looked around. Her mouth fell open; she was going to scream.

Fiona started forward as Billy clamped a hand over

the girl's mouth. "Please," he whispered, meeting Fiona's eyes beseechingly.

Fiona stared at Jagger. *You have to do something,* her eyes told him.

"Billy, you have to step away," he said gently.

"Why? She didn't wake up screaming and hungry," Billy demanded.

"I *am* hungry," Abigail said, still so confused. Then she gasped. "I'm naked! I'm naked and I'm—I'm in a morgue!" She opened her mouth to scream again.

Billy put his hand over her mouth again as both Fiona and Jagger moved forward.

"Look," Billy whispered urgently. "She's a nice kid, a good kid—raised by nuns, for God's sake. She'll follow our laws, she'll…she'll be a good citizen. Please, give her a chance."

"Billy, she doesn't even understand what happened," Fiona said.

Billy's hand slipped from Abigail's mouth. "Please, be quiet, okay?" he begged her.

She let out a little whimpering sound and leaned against him. "Billy, I really *am* hungry. Starving. For a rare steak. Or for…"

She stared at Fiona.

At the pulse in Fiona's throat.

Abigail lowered her head and started to cry. "I'm hungry for blood."

Jagger stepped close to her, showing her that he had his stake at his side, not ready to strike.

"Abigail. My name is Jagger DeFarge. I'm a cop. I need to know what happened to you. You went to a party, and then…?"

She stared at him, confused, humiliated. She suddenly realized that she had a sheet and pulled it over her breasts.

"There was a lot of beer," she whispered.

"Think, Abigail. Please."

Billy moved between Jagger and Abigail, and shook his head angrily. "No! You can't try to use her and then… You can't. For the love of God, Jagger!"

"Someone is going to hear us soon," Fiona pointed out.

"They'll hear us when I fight you!" Billy promised. "I don't want to hurt anyone, but don't you see? I love Abigail."

"Oh, Billy, really? I've been in love with you for ages, too," Abigail cried softly. "I was just too afraid to say anything."

Jagger stared at Fiona. She was not untouched.

"Look," Billy said quickly. "We'll just say she wasn't really dead. There have been mistakes before, medical miracles."

"Dead?" Abigail's voice shook with horror.

"Shh," Billy pleaded.

"Billy, this is the real world," Fiona pointed out gently. "A team of doctors will start performing tests. At best, she'll become a freak, and there won't be anyone who can tend to her, who can make sure she gets the nourishment she needs." She touched his shoulder gently, looking like a caring angel. "Billy, a lot of people would wind up dead."

Billy whipped out the stake he had brought, intending to kill the love of his life.

He aimed it toward Fiona. "No, please," he pleaded.

Jagger grabbed Fiona, drawing her behind his back.

"Billy, don't you dare threaten her," he whispered fervently.

Billy paused for a moment, staring at him, and understanding entered his eyes.

"So that's the way it is," he said softly. "The powerful old vampire is in love with the Keeper."

"Billy, don't be ridiculous. And step away from the girl. I can make the change in a split second, and when I do, I'm powerful," Fiona said. "So don't threaten Jagger, and don't threaten me."

"Please," Billy entreated. "You have to understand. I'm not threatening you. I'm *begging* you. I'll do anything, anything at all. And how can you?" he demanded. "You're the Keeper—can't you see that she would be an asset to our community?" When Fiona didn't say anything, his shoulders sagged and he lowered his stake. "Fine. Kill us both," he said in resignation.

"Billy…" Abigail protested, putting a hand on his arm.

If the situation weren't so dire, Jagger thought, it might have been amusing. There was the lovely Abigail, hiding in back of Billy, clutching the broad young shoulders of the one she loved.

And facing Billy—him. With a rock-hard determination that he would die for the woman *he* loved as willingly as Billy had vowed to do. Was she in love with him, as Abigail was in love with Billy? He didn't know. He did know that there was something between them. He did know that he felt as if he had waited several lifetimes to feel for someone the way he did about her.

"There is no easy solution," Fiona said softly, sadly.

Jagger was electrically aware of her standing behind him. Felt the length of her body against his own. Felt her whisper against his skin and trembled inside at the sound of her voice.

Love.

Was it real? Something growing, something more precious than life, that went far beyond death?

Fiona groaned softly. "What do we do?" she whispered. "In the name of God, what do we do?"

Jagger sighed, hanging his head for a moment.

"I guess we steal a corpse," he said at last.

Chapter 7

During the following hours, Fiona decided that she was insane.

She kept wondering what her parents would have done.

Handled it. They would have handled it. Gotten there earlier, they would have made sure Abigail was dispatched before...

Maybe. Or maybe not.

Billy had probably hovered over the corpse from the moment he had reached the morgue, maybe even proclaimed his love.

Would her parents have been so uncertain? So hesitant to act?

Maybe. They had certainly believed in love. They had known all about evil, along with good, and they had coped—because they'd always had each other....

As she—maybe?—had Jagger now.

She stood guard at the door as Jagger and Billy started explaining the situation to Abigail. The girl was still in shock, still whining that her stomach hurt, as if rats were gnawing at it.

Billy tried to explain that the faster she paid attention, the faster they could appease that hunger. Jagger was a stronger personality, and he dispensed with the preliminaries and demanded that she listen to him, which she finally did. He explained the process changing into mist, and how it was imperative that she listen, so they could get her out of there. Quickly.

Finally she tried it herself. At first, she was so bad at it that Fiona began to regret their decision to let the girl "live."

But finally Abigail got it.

"Billy, you can't come with us. Fiona will have to knock you out," Jagger told him.

"But…"

"Billy, do you want me arresting you in a matter of hours for stealing Abigail's corpse—and maybe for having killed her in the first place?" Jagger demanded.

Billy understood. He clutched Fiona's arm. "You're the Keeper," he whispered to her. "You'll—you'll take care of her, right? Keepers don't lie, not to anyone they're responsible for."

"I promise I'll watch over her," Fiona said.

"I'll get her out of here," Jagger told Fiona. "Follow as soon as you can."

She nodded, knowing he was far more prepared than she was to handle the situation if Abigail panicked or something went wrong.

"Meet at my place," he said softly.

She nodded, wincing inwardly, certain that her sisters would be expecting her to come straight home from the morgue. They might not like it, but they might even be expecting her to come home with Jagger.

But she couldn't bring a freshly turned and completely ignorant vampire home.

Once Jagger and Abigail had turned into mist, Fiona followed Billy out to the desk. She'd put on surgical gloves before she entered the building, not wanting to leave fingerprints, and now she looked around for a weapon. Finally she picked up the computer keyboard from the desk and creamed him with the flat side.

Mist herself, she left the morgue, and she didn't regain her shape until she reached her car. She drove away, praying that no one saw her, and headed for the French Quarter.

Though she had never been inside Jagger's home, she knew where it was, two blocks in from Rampart, halfway between Canal and Esplanade.

It was one of the few houses that had survived the great fires in the early 1800s, standing on a man-made rise, the better to display its charming facade. He lived behind a wall and gate almost as tall as hers, but his courtyard was in front of the house, rather than behind, and his property stretched from street to street.

The gate opened as she arrived; obviously he'd been looking for her car. She drove up to the front of the house as the gate closed and locked behind her.

When she got out of her car, Jagger was already there.

"Come, quickly, I'm afraid to leave her alone for long," he said softly.

She nodded.

Though he'd said he wanted her to move quickly,

for a moment he paused and stared down into her eyes. Then his lips touched hers with a kiss that was tender and yearning...and brief.

Then he caught her hand and hurried her into the house. The entry was large and impressive, leading into a tiled foyer, with a curving stairway to one side.

They hurried past the stairway toward the dining room and kitchen, moving through both rooms so quickly that she had no time to note a single detail. At the rear of the kitchen there was a door, and when he opened it she saw a stairway heading down, and she realized that the lot had been built up to allow for a small basement in an area of the country that was prone to serious flooding, because most land was—barely at sea level.

As he led her quickly downward, she expected dank earth—with a coffin in the middle of the room.

But what she saw was nothing like her expectations. There was a canopied bed instead of a coffin, the floor was redbrick with a Persian carpet, and there were attractive paintings on the walls, along with a massive entertainment center.

There was also a small kitchenette, complete with refrigerator.

Abigail, still wrapped in her sheet, was greedily drinking from a large pitcher.

Of blood.

Fiona could feel her eyes widening

"Don't look at me like that," Jagger said to her. "It's pig's blood. You eat bacon, right?"

"I wasn't staring at you," she said. "I'm used to blood. I'm the Keeper, remember?"

He nodded and touched her cheek. He didn't say anything, but the look in his eyes seemed to wrap around her heart.

What the hell had they done? she wondered. There were going to be terrible repercussions from tonight. She was sure of it.

"I have to ask you to stay here, to…teach Abigail," he said.

"No! You…have to teach her," Fiona said.

"I've already been called about her corpse being stolen," Jagger said. "I'm the detective on the case, remember?"

She opened her mouth, desperately wanting to protest, but then Abigail made a slurping sound, and she knew someone had to do something.

"But I'm not a vampire."

"Make the change. It will help you," he advised. "Please, Fiona."

She nodded jerkily. "All right. And, Jagger, an assembly has been called for tomorrow night."

"Good. It will definitely be necessary."

"My sisters will be calling me soon."

"I'll be back as soon as I can," he swore.

With that, he pulled her to him and kissed her, hard. And again, quickly.

Then he was gone, and she was left with a naked young woman slurping blood in the center of the room.

Billy was good. If Jagger remembered correctly, his major was engineering, but he might as well be majoring in theater arts, he was playing his part so well.

Tony was already there at the morgue, along with two beat cops, a few night-shift employees and a city security officer. Tony had started questioning Billy Harrington, but he took a break and pulled Jagger aside the minute he arrived.

"He was hit on the head with a computer keyboard. He doesn't know how or why someone took the body. Why the hell steal a corpse?" Tony asked.

Jagger jerked his head in a manner that suggested he couldn't fathom the question himself. Then he pulled up a chair across the desk where Billy Harrington was sitting, an ice bag pressed against his temple.

"What happened, son?" he asked.

Billy looked at him and shook his head gravely. "I was doing paperwork. The next thing I knew, I woke up on the floor with a cop standing over me."

Jagger stood up and turned to the remaining morgue personnel. "No one saw anything?" he asked.

"Nothing," said a buxom middle-aged clerk. "Nothing at all. And the door was still locked."

"There must be other doors," Jagger said.

Looking embarrassed, people ran to check other possible means of entry.

To his astonishment and vast relief, someone had actually forgotten to lock one of the doors where the bodies were wheeled in from the ambulances that brought them to the morgue. As accusations began to fly among the workers, guilt bit into Jagger.

He lifted a hand, stopping the flow of conversation, and sighed. "The crime-scene unit will be here shortly. We'll do our best to settle this as quickly as possible, but meanwhile, be prepared. The press are going to have a field day."

Several people urged Billy to go to a hospital, but he adamantly refused. Jagger offered to take him home, and Billy agreed.

"You're going to take the kid home?" Tony asked him, incredulous.

"Maybe I can get him to remember something," Jagger suggested. "My guess is that something might come to him after a while, and I'll be right there to find out what it is. Go home, Tony, and let the night guys handle the scene. Get some sleep tonight. Tomorrow is going to be hell."

A few minutes later Jagger led Billy out to his car.

As soon as they were inside, Billy let out a sigh of relief. "Sweet Jesus, bless you," he whispered, his eyes closed.

Jagger marveled at the fact that so many vampires were religious; in fact, they were often some of a church's best attendees. They were always praying that they really did have souls.

"You're one hell of an actor," he told the boy.

"So are you." Billy frowned then, and shook his head. "Look, you can't still believe I'm the one who did this, can you?"

"Billy, if my thoughts were running in that direction, you'd be dead, along with Abigail. Dead—as in stone dead. Staked through the heart. But I do want to talk to you about that night. That frat boy really thinks he saw you, though he admitted he was drunk. But he also said you didn't originally intend to go to the party because you had something else to do."

"Yeah, I went to the meeting," Billy said, and he sounded genuinely lost. He twisted in the passenger's seat to stare at Jagger. "She's all right, isn't she? Abigail. You didn't whisk her away and—and stake her, did you?"

"No, we didn't stake her. I left her with Fiona."

"She's going to be so confused," Billy said.

"Fiona is the Keeper," Jagger said. "She'll manage just fine."

"Dead?" Abigail said, staring at Fiona. "What are you talking about? Vampires don't exist. They're just a myth. They're not real."

"Abigail, you woke up in a morgue, remember? You escaped by turning into mist," Fiona pointed out.

The girl strenuously shook her head. "No. No, no, no. They made a mistake. They thought I was dead, but I wasn't. I'm alive. You can see that."

"Abigail, you're a vampire now. You just drank a gallon of blood, and you'll have to keep drinking blood to stay…alive."

"I will not run around killing people!" Abigail exclaimed, horrified.

"No, you definitely will not. If you make a single kill, I'll consider it my responsibility to stake you through the heart and end your existence."

The girl stared at her, then leaped to her feet in horror, letting the pitcher she'd been holding slip to the floor. "You…you want to kill me." She gasped, pointing a finger at Fiona. "I know you—you're…you're some kind of a witch or a voodoo priestess or something. You own that shop that sells potions and things. You do tarot-card readings—"

"That's my sister, I read tea leaves," Fiona said wearily. "And I'm not a witch."

"You are! You want to hurt me. Where—where's Billy?"

"Billy will be here soon. Abigail, I know this is really hard to comprehend, but please, think. You woke up in the morgue. Billy, Jagger and I were there, and we got you out. But you are not alive. You have become a vampire."

Abigail shook her head, looking as if she were about to burst into tears. "No! It can't be true. They just made a mistake."

She rushed forward, clutching her sheet to hold it in place as she fell to her knees at Fiona's feet. "I'm alive. They made a mistake. I'm a college student, for the love of God. Let me go home to the sisters! They raised me. They know me. They'll tell you I'm alive."

"No! Of all places you can't go now, number one is home," Fiona told her. "Come on, let's get you something to wear." She looked around and spotted a folding door. "That must be Jagger's closet. At least we can get you a T-shirt or something." She opened the closet door, and just for a second, she closed her eyes and inhaled deeply. She must be falling in love with the man. Just the clean scent of his aftershave, lingering lightly in the air, seemed to seep right into her. To remind her that she wanted to be with him. That she could be with him. That he wanted to be with her…

She pulled herself back, reminding her that she had a dead girl on her hands.

"All right, here's a shirt," she said and turned around.

Abigail was gone.

Jagger drove into the French Quarter and down his street. As he neared his gate, he hit the electronic opener on the dash. The gate slowly opened inward, allowing the car access.

He drove in, parked and got out of the car. Billy did the same.

As Jagger looked toward the house, he was astounded to see Fiona, who'd made the change, perched atop the wall toward the rear of the house. As he watched, she made a leap down to the street.

"Oh, hell," Jagger muttered.

"What?" Billy demanded.

"They're out!" Jagger said.

Moving faster than the human eye could follow, with Billy on his heels, he made a flying leap up to the wall himself. He was just in time to see Fiona adeptly landing on the sidewalk, and for a moment he paused to thank God that he didn't live on Bourbon Street, where a hundred tourists would have been there to see.

He jumped lightly to the street himself, searching the road, the houses, the darkness.

Then he saw her.

Abigail, stark naked, a block away and just walking down the street, looking lost.

He swore softly.

Fiona reached her before he could, catching her by the shoulders and quickly wrapping her in one of his long-sleeved tailored shirts.

A woman walked by, leading a yappy Papillon.

"Well, I never!" she declared. She was about sixty, dignified, plump, with graying hair.

The dog wouldn't shut up.

Jagger quickly walked over to her. "Good evening, ma'am."

"That's indecent exposure," she declared.

The dog kept yapping.

Ten feet away, Fiona and Billy were urging Abigail off the street.

Jagger stared at the dog first, and the animal went silent.

"Do something, or I'll call the police myself," the woman began.

"It's fine, ma'am. It's all fine. That young lady is supposed to be in the hospital. We're here to take her back."

"Oh?"

Jagger smiled and stared hard into her eyes. "You won't remember this in the morning," he said quietly.

She blinked. The commotion behind him had quieted; they had gotten Abigail off the street and, hopefully, back into his house without further notice.

"That's all right, then," the woman said, smiling. The dog wagged its tail.

"Good evening," he said pleasantly.

"Just getting off work, Detective?" she asked.

"Yes, ma'am." If he knew the woman, he didn't remember her.

"You shouldn't be out this late, you know," he added. "Not walking your dog alone."

"Mrs. Beasley needs her constitutional, Detective."

"Then walk her in your yard. Please, don't wander in the dark alone. There's a killer out there."

She laughed. "I'm old, plump and gray. Not his type at all."

"Please, for me, will you stay inside once it's dark?"

The woman flushed. "When such a handsome young man asks a favor, I do my best to oblige," she said, and winked at him.

"Where's your house?" Jagger asked.

She pointed.

"I'm walking you back," he said, and offered her his arm.

She gave him a bountiful smile and turned to walk with him.

When they reached her house, she thanked him, gushing, and gave him a kiss on the cheek.

The dog yapped.

He bade her good-night and hurried back to his own place, wondering why on earth human beings couldn't have the common sense to lock their doors when there was a murderer on the loose.

Chapter 8

"How on earth did you let her get away?" Jagger demanded, still unnerved by everything that had been happening that evening.

"I didn't *let* her get away. Did you notice that she was *naked?*" Fiona protested. "I was getting some clothing for her!"

Thankfully, Abigail was at long last clothed—still blonde and beautiful, and now cute, as well, in one of Jagger's shirts.

"I'm so sorry," Abigail said. "Oh, my God. What would the nuns say? I was running around naked." She looked at Billy with her huge blue eyes.

"What would the *nuns* say?" Fiona asked impatiently. "You're a *vampire*." Fiona turned to confront Jagger. "You'll have to excuse me. I have to get back home or my sisters will be calling a city-wide meeting, wondering if I'm alive or dead. You chose this course of action, so you—"

"Wait just a minute," he said. "*We* chose this course of action, and you're just upset because you let her escape."

Fiona stiffened. "Then I'm sure you'll find it a relief to manage the rest of the evening on your own, Detective DeFarge. I leave everything in your capable hands." She spun on Billy and Abigail. "You two! Get it right or I will have no choice but to handle the situation—and you know what that means."

She had started for the stairs when Abigail suddenly tore after her. For a moment Fiona felt a rush of fear, sure she was about to be attacked.

But Abigail only touched her arm, and she turned to look into the young woman's anguished eyes.

"I'm so sorry. I understand that you've shown me incredible mercy. It's just that I was so terrified, so confused…and it's still so hard to believe. I went to a party, and now… Please forgive me. I swear, I'll stay here and do anything and everything Detective DeFarge tells me to do."

Lovely. You'll listen to him—now that you've made a fool of me, Fiona thought.

She told herself not to let her own hurt and humiliation affect her handling of the situation.

Before she could speak, Billy Harrington strode over to stand behind Abigail.

"We'll never be able to express our gratitude. We'll both do anything Detective DeFarge says, I promise," Billy told her.

"If you really mean that, then Abigail has to disappear. The world thinks she's dead, remember? So no one can see her. *No one*. Perhaps David Du Lac will be able to discover that she has a long lost identical twin, but setting that up will take time. And, Billy, you have to go to your classes. You can't spend your days hanging out here with Abigail. If you want this to work, you *have* to do these things, or else leave the city. And this isn't a good time for you to leave the city, Billy. Not unless you want to look guilty of murder. Do you understand what I'm saying?" she demanded.

The two of them nodded in fervent agreement.

She looked back at Jagger. His golden eyes had a glitter in them that told her he was angry with her, but he didn't say anything. Apparently he had chosen not to argue any further, at least not then.

She hurried up the stairs, trying to make a dignified exit.

Then she realized she couldn't get through the gate without Jagger's help, so she waited at the door, arms crossed over her chest, trying not to admire the warmth of the large fireplace in the living room, the masculine and inviting…decor that was earthy, warm and secure, and spoke volumes of the man. She didn't want to fight with him. She just wanted to touch him and be touched by him.

Tonight, however, they had taken a dive into a serious situation that could bring nothing but hardship to either one of them.

Jagger arrived and hit a button on the console by the door. Then he held the door open for her as she watched the massive gate swing open. She started toward her car without a word.

His eyes met hers when she turned back for a moment. "Don't worry. I'll see that everything gets done—just as you demanded."

She didn't answer him, just slid into the driver's seat, wondering how they had managed to agree on a course of action, only to arrive at such a cold impasse.

All in the name of love, she thought dryly. And hadn't some of the greatest tragedies and travesties in history taken place in the name of love?

She drove the few short blocks home, then breathed a sigh of relief as she entered her quiet house.

She walked directly up to her bedroom and opened the door.

And found both her sisters, Shauna curled up on the bed reading a magazine, Caitlin pacing.

They both stopped what they were doing and stared at her.

"A stolen corpse?" Caitlin demanded, practically hissing. "Did you think we wouldn't hear the news?"

Fiona tossed her shoulder bag onto the chair by her dressing table, pressed her fingers to her temple and, ignoring Shauna, flopped backward on her bed. It was a big bed, and there was room.

"She was just a college kid, huh?" Shauna said sympathetically.

"Where is the body?" Caitlin asked.

"Risen," Fiona said dryly.

"You let her get up? What in the world were you thinking?" Caitlin cried, striding over to the bed, arms crossed over her chest, eyes filled with a tempest of emotion.

"I am so tired. If you came here just to lash into me—"

"We're here to find out what's going on," Caitlin said.

Shauna cleared her throat. "This is a real mess, Fiona. All the races are up in arms. Since you've been… busy, I'm assuming you didn't hear about the altercation in Jackson Square. Mateas Grenard was attacked in the park. He's new, and he's not exactly politic about what he says. He fought back, of course. The attacker was one of mine, a werewolf named Louis Arile, who owns a T-shirt shop over on St. Peter's. Anyway…"

"Anyway, Shauna was there, she calmed Louis down, and the cops ended up giving them both a slap on the wrist. It was only Shauna who kept the whole thing from turning into a real disaster," Caitlin said.

Fiona looked thoughtfully at Shauna. Her little sister was coming into her own.

Shauna shrugged casually. "Louis isn't a bad guy, just scared, like everyone else. He loves his shop, and he really loves Jazz Fest, and he doesn't want to be forced out of New Orleans if these murders end up alerting the humans to the existence of the underworld."

"The police didn't figure out that there was something…different about them? Neither of them…made the change?" Fiona asked, concerned.

"No. Shauna got there in time," Caitlin said. "She convinced the cops that they were fighting over a sports bet."

"Clever," Fiona said.

"Maybe, but something tells me that was just the start of our problems," Caitlin said.

Fiona stood. "There's another general council meeting tomorrow night. We'll nip this in the bud."

"Nip it in the bud?" Caitlin said quietly, almost gently. She touched Fiona's cheek. "You're my older sister. I love you, and I admire you. You've held us together.

You've done everything for us. But this has gone way past the 'nip it in the bud' stage. I understand how you might have fallen under Jagger DeFarge's spell. He's sex on legs. But you can't forget who and what you are. You're a Keeper. And this is serious. The races will be up in arms—they're not stupid. They'll figure out that you made the choice to let that girl rise, and they'll know she's young, that she's almost certain to make serious mistakes that could ruin things for everyone— like going out in public and being recognized, when she's supposed to be dead. And if one of them, just one, decides to take matters into his own hands... Frankly, Fiona, I'm terrified. We've seen what a war can do."

"There won't be a war, Caitlin." Fiona sat down at the foot of her bed. "There won't be a war," she repeated, trying to sound convincing. "It was easy to see that Tina Lawrence had to be...dispensed with. Even as a human, she was frightening. She'd hurt people. She was dangerous. But this girl...she was eighteen and raised by nuns. She's a college student."

She saw that Caitlin was about to protest and raised a hand. "*Was* a college student. The girl hasn't a whiff of evil in her. She'll be fine."

Shauna shook her head, scooting closer so that she was sitting next to Fiona. "How is she going to be fine?"

Fiona was quiet for a moment, surprised by the tide of emotion that swept over her.

"David Du Lac. He'll make it fine. Mom and Dad went to him a few times over the years. God only knows all the places he's lived during his...existence, but no one loves this city more, and no one's better at creating new identities. We'll bring Abigail to him. He'll take care of everything."

Caitlin laughed. "And when will that be? After the funeral? Don't forget that everyone out there thinks you've stolen a corpse."

"No one thinks I've done anything," Fiona said firmly. "People may know her corpse was stolen, but I wasn't seen."

"What about DeFarge?" Caitlin asked.

"No one saw him until he went to the morgue after the report that the corpse had been stolen and the attendant had been knocked out," Caitlin said. "Look, both of you, I beg—no, I demand—that you both show me some respect and faith here. I fought hard, really hard, to keep us all together—and I managed it. Now we're facing our first real crisis, so please, remember that I came through for you before and just trust me."

Both of them stared at her for a long moment. Then Shauna leaned over and kissed her on the cheek. "Of course. And we're here, ready to do our part," she promised.

"I love you, you know that," Caitlin said.

"Yes, I do, but how about some faith, too?" Fiona asked.

Caitlin nodded. "Right." She turned to leave, then paused at the door. "Vampires. It's just—well, vampires," she said, and walked out.

When she was gone, Shauna looked at Fiona. "I'm sorry. You know Caitlin adores you."

"Yes, I do."

"But—she really doesn't like vampires," Shauna said.

"I've noticed. Hey, kid, good work tonight," Fiona said.

Shauna grinned, but her grin faded quickly. "Thanks. I do think there are some scary times ahead."

"No doubt," Fiona agreed.

"Good night," Shauna said, then kissed her cheek again and left the room, closing the door quietly in her wake.

Fiona was exhausted, but she had been at the morgue. She was afraid she would never sleep with the smell of formaldehyde—real or imagined—in her nose.

She headed into the shower, turned on the spray and reached for the large container of coconut-and-almond shampoo.

The tropical scent rose around her, and she inhaled deeply as she massaged the shampoo through her hair, wishing that the pressure of her fingers could make the whirlwind in her mind come to a halt. Did she know that she had done the right thing?

No.

Would she feel any better now if she had been coldly efficient and dispatched Abigail and Billy both?

No, definitely not.

Admittedly they were stuck working around the disappearance of a corpse, but it could have been worse.

They could be dealing with a dead morgue attendant.

She rinsed her hair and groped blindly for the soap, then nearly screamed when the container of body wash was placed in her hand.

Her eyes flew open, and she gasped.

Jagger was standing there outside her shower, grinning in admiration.

He had no right.

She wanted to yell at him for scaring her, when she was already feeling like an incompetent fool.

She wanted to yell and scream and beat her fists against his chest.

Because she was afraid.

But more than all that, she wanted him there.

The water beat down. The steam rose.

He looked at her without moving. And then he spoke softly.

"I'm sorry, Fiona. I'm so sorry."

Had he really just apologized?

Suddenly her eyes were stinging.

To hide the rising tears, she turned back into the spray.

"All right, I understand," he said.

He was going to leave, she realized.

She groped blindly again, catching his arm, soaking the sleeve of his immaculate jacket.

"No, no…it's just my eyes," she said.

In a second, a dry washcloth was in her hands.

And then he was in the shower, naked and standing behind her, holding her close to him and whispering against her ear, above the rush of the water,

"I really am so sorry."

She turned in his arms, as if she had been starving for years for a human touch. In a way she *had* starved, of course, because she had always been a Keeper, never allowed to forget her responsibilities.

And *he* wasn't human.

He was more than human. Better.

It was true that neither of them really understood the complete ramifications of the extraordinary lives they led. The secrets of heaven and hell were not in their possession. What they did know was that kindness and cruelty, good and evil, were natural attributes of all living things, represented in greater or lesser degrees in everyone.

But Jagger seemed to contain more of the best than anyone she knew, and his strength was greater because it could bend.

And the way he held her...

She turned into his arms.

"Forgiven," she said softly.

It was deliciously erotic, making love in the water, the slickness of soap lubricating their flesh, the steam hot and luxurious, and his hands...

Touching her. Holding her. Making her feel as if she were completely savored and cherished, as if he worshipped every part of her.

His lips, hot and slick. His tongue, teasing.

His whispers echoed in the close confines of the shower....

He held her against the tile, oddly cool against the heat, and the complex mix of emotions and sensations seemed to heighten every touch, every movement. When she fell against him in release, she could still feel his lips against her shoulder, his arms around her, his body against hers. She reveled in the security of his support and her immersion in another—a man, no matter that his heart didn't beat.

He fumbled for the faucets, turning the water off at last, and lifted her easily to the bathroom rug, following her out and wrapping a large fluffy towel around her, then reaching for one for himself. She smiled as she met his eyes, longing to tell him how glad she was that he had come, how much it meant to her that they stood together. And more than anything, how it made her tremble to realize that he was willing to ask her forgiveness when he felt he'd been wrong.

He pulled her to him, cradling her against him, and looked into her eyes.

"It's frightening, what we've done," he said.

She nodded, then grinned slowly. "Yes, but I realized we only had one other choice. A dead morgue attendant."

"True."

"Where are the young lovers?"

"Sound asleep."

"What if they wake up?"

He laughed softly, gently stroking her wet hair.

"Billy is back in the frat house. And I took Abigail to David Du Lac, who welcomed the challenge and is ready to forge ahead. He thinks we made the right decision, said we did what was right."

"There will still be hell to pay," she said.

"I know."

"My sister broke up a fight tonight between Mateas Grenard and a werewolf named Louis Arile."

Jagger was quiet. "And unless I catch this killer quickly, we're going to see a lot more of the same."

"My sisters are up in arms."

"I tried to make a hasty exit and not get you in trouble with them."

"Excellent work. But they're not fools."

"Of course not. They're Keepers."

"I'm so worried about this. We can't let it come to another war."

"We won't."

"Then…"

"Then," he said, pulling her closer to him by tugging on the towel, "we learn to make each precious moment that we have alone together count."

She smiled, closing her eyes, savoring the simple feel of being close against him.

"Even the seconds…" she murmured.

"Exactly."

He lifted her, his eyes locked on hers, his every movement both romantic and excruciatingly sensual as he carried her to the bed and laid her on the mattress, then moved the towel as if he were unwrapping something exquisite and fragile. He made her skin burn with the intensity of his gaze before his lips skimmed her body with a slow, liquid touch that burned and yet was still somehow tender, awakening an array of incredible desire. She lay still for a moment, in simple awe of the way he could make her feel, and then she burst to life, desperate to return every caress.

The sun was coming up when at last they lay exhausted and spent, entangled in one another's arms.

Fiona drifted to sleep on a dream more wonderful than any other.

When she awoke, he was gone.

Only mist and memory remained beside her.

But even they were beautiful, and more than she had ever dreamed she would find.

There were certain matters of police procedure that Jagger had to follow—no matter what he knew to be true.

The dorms had to be searched. All the dorms in the city, all the frat houses—even all the sorority houses. With the new morgue attendant being a college kid, the police had immediately theorized that the corpse might have been stolen as some kind of sick college prank.

There was also no way to keep the media from

becoming a major presence. And once they got wind of the fact that the missing body looked like the stereotypical victim of a vampire attack, the less responsible papers ran with the story.

Has Beauty Arisen?

Co-ed, Drained of Blood, Seems to Have Walked Out of Morgue!

To make matters worse, a recent cable documentary had focused on vampire cults in the city of New Orleans. One group in Uptown that had been given special attention had taken to walking reporters around their communal home, explaining their rites—and need for blood.

Jagger hoped against hope that the entire city hadn't seen the show. He hadn't, but Tony had, and happily told him all about it.

His first order of business once he became aware of what was happening had been to send a couple of black-and-white cruisers out to protect the residents of the house. Didn't those idiots realize they were courting an attack?

He was in his office, having just arranged a press conference for early that afternoon, when he received a call from August Gaudin.

"What on earth is going on?"

"August, I can't share privileged information with you, but I can assure you that no one is more concerned than I am about the situation."

"And let *me* assure *you* that I am not a fool. If a new vampire is walking, you and Fiona know something about it."

"There's a meeting tonight, August."

"And you had better be prepared to keep the peace."

Jagger looked around. There were three other vampires, two werewolves and one shapeshifter on the force. Only the shapeshifter, Michael Shrine, was on the day crew, and he'd sent him out to the vampire cult house.

They also had one of the largest leprechauns he'd ever met on the force, also working days, and he, too, was out of the office, leaving only human beings surrounding him now.

But no matter who was around, Jagger was always careful to keep this kind of discussion out of his office.

"Got time for an early lunch, councilman?" he asked now.

"Do you?"

"Gotta eat. I'll make time."

"Sure. How about the Napoleon House?" Gaudin asked.

"It will be busy," Jagger warned.

"Which is fine. I want us to be seen together, but it will be noisy, so we can talk—and not be overheard. Oh, and they make a po'boy I really like," August said.

A little while later, seated in the historic restaurant, they ordered quickly—they were, after all, working men just grabbing a bite.

"You've seen the papers?" Gaudin asked immediately.

"Of course."

"I know that Gina is trying hard to keep the media from going crazy, but she can't ignore the obvious, and she can't protest too much—that's always a dangerous course. So...I want the truth."

Jagger nodded, meeting Gaudin's eyes. "Okay. You were right. No new vampire would be walking without Fiona and me knowing. The girl was eighteen, August. *Eighteen,* raised by nuns and as pure as the driven snow."

"Doesn't snow much in New Orleans," Gaudin noted, his innuendo obvious.

Jagger ignored him and went on. "She's being given a new identity, of course."

"Are you ready to face an argument from the assembly?" Gaudin asked.

"Of course."

"Would you have made the same decision, do you think, if we had been looking at a werewolf or a shapeshifter?"

"You know me, August. You know that I'm always fair."

"I know it. I'm just trying to warn you that everyone else may not be so understanding."

"Warning gratefully noted," Jagger told him.

"I'm sorry to say, I think it's obvious now that a vampire is guilty."

"The only thing I'll admit is that it's obvious a werewolf isn't," Jagger said dryly.

"We also know that no human being, no matter what occult kick he's on, was the killer."

"Yes." Jagger took a long swallow of sweet tea. "The timing of that documentary was really unfortunate."

"I won't argue with you," Gaudin said, then frowned. "I wonder if they realize how much danger they're in. Have you—"

"Officers are watching the house. And I've called a press conference for this afternoon."

August Gaudin nodded thoughtfully. "This is a very tenuous situation we're in. How close are you to finding the killer? Was the girl able to tell you anything useful?"

Jagger shook his head. "She was drinking at a frat party. That's the last thing she remembers. She's with David Du Lac, and he knows to inform me right away if she remembers anything else."

"All right, then. I'll be there to support you—and the peace. Three in the morning. Damn. These old bones could use more rest than they're getting these days," Gaudin said, shaking his head.

Rest would be nice, Jagger thought. But the time he spent with Fiona was infinitely more precious.

"Well, well, gentlemen," a soft, feminine voice said from right beside them.

Jagger turned and almost groaned aloud.

Jennie Mahoney, stunningly and sophisticatedly dressed—no touristy T-shirts for her—was looking down at him.

He rose, pulling out an extra chair so she could take a seat beside him.

"Jennie. What a pleasure."

"I'm sorry, but I'm not here for pleasure, Jagger."

"It's still always a delight to see you, my dear," August Gaudin assured her.

"And you, August, of course," she said, and gave him a gracious smile. Then she turned on Jagger. "Explain yourself, Detective."

"I intend to, I promise. Tonight."

"You saved her, Jagger," Jennie said, studying him. "Why?"

"Innocence," he said.

"No excuse."

"Actually it was, Jennie."

"The Keeper will see that she doesn't join society."

"The Keeper is in agreement with me."

Jennie frowned severely. "Jagger, this is dangerous."

"Not if we all keep our own counsel."

Jennie shook her head. "I'm perplexed. Why hasn't the girl fingered her murderer? She was at a frat party, according to the news. She must know who she was with."

"No, I'm afraid not. All she remembers is a lot of beer."

"Jagger, you need to get out and grill those boys mercilessly. Isn't one of your kind a student? He was at the meeting…was he at the frat party, too? What was his name? Billy…? That's it! Billy Harrington."

"Billy Harrington wasn't at the party, because he was coming to the meeting at David's," Jagger explained.

Jennie made a sound of distaste. "From what I've heard, there would have been plenty of time for him to kill that girl first."

"There was just enough time, yes," Jagger agreed. "But trust me, Billy didn't do this. I don't see any vampire doing something like this, frankly. It would be a blatant challenge to the rest of us. He'd have to know we'd come after him, that he couldn't get away with it."

"Well, if it wasn't a vampire, the only other possibility is… Jagger! My God. I didn't expect much from the vampire Keeper, but really! You, too? You're accusing a shapeshifter."

"I'm not accusing anyone, Jennie, I don't have enough evidence yet," Jagger explained.

Jennie straightened regally. "You need to get moving then, Detective. You don't have time to be sitting here enjoying a leisurely lunch."

"Jennie, I asked him here," Gaudin said.

Jagger stood, laying money on the table. "August, we'll talk more later. Jennie, I know what I'm doing."

He leaned down and spoke softly.

"And yes, I'm a vampire as well as a detective, but I take my commitment to keep peace in the city very seriously. I *will* discover the truth. When I have evidence, I'll see that the killer is brought down—whether he's a vampire, a shapeshifter or something none of us has ever seen before. I'll see you both at the meeting."

He heard Jennie's indignant gasp as he left, but he wasn't in the mood to give a damn.

It rankled him that Jennie was right about one thing.

He needed to be out on the streets. He belonged at that frat house, asking questions.

Billy Harrington had indeed had the time to kill the love of his life and put her body on display. As for a motive, he was madly in love. Now he could be madly in love forever.

Billy had sworn that he would never harm Abigail. And the truth was that none of them knew what awaited a vampire once his existence on earth was over. Many of them believed in the power of God and the devil.

Would Billy have risked the possibility of sending the object of his devotion to a fiery hell?

Jagger didn't think so, and he was a good detective—vampire or not—because he had gotten to be very good at reading people and their emotions. It wasn't impossible, and he wasn't ruling anything out, but he would need actual evidence before he was willing to even consider it likely.

Then there was the killing of Tina Lawrence.

Billy had no motive in her death. And they hadn't gotten a single call from anyone who had seen anyone who even remotely resembled the police artist's sketch of the man from the strip club.

And in his mind, that could only mean one thing.

Shapeshifter.

Chapter 9

"Shauna, you still have friends in grad school, right?" Fiona asked her youngest sister, while she brewed herself a cup of her favorite English breakfast tea behind the counter in the shop. She spoke softly, because Caitlin was in the back, giving a tarot-card reading.

"Yeah, sure, why?"

"I'd like to talk to some of the kids who were at that frat party," Fiona explained.

"Sure—when? The major emergency assembly is tonight."

"How about early this evening?"

"What about Caitlin?"

"She's welcome to come, too," Fiona said.

Shauna was thoughtful for a moment. She joined Fiona behind the counter and absently began brewing a cup of her favorite tea, white peach.

"Fiona, I'm afraid of what will happen if you receive

information that puts…well, casts *you* in an unflattering light," Shauna said.

"What do you mean?"

"Okay, let's face it, you've been bowled over by a vampire."

"I've been bowled over by a *man,*" Fiona protested quietly.

"Yes, and I can definitely see the attraction. I think that Caitlin would, too, if…I don't know. It might be different if she were the Keeper for the vampires, but… she still blames that vampire for the fact that Mom and Dad are dead. She blames the vampires for the war."

"And you don't?"

"I blame everyone. I blame intolerance everywhere," Shauna said. "And another thing—the one who helped us through everything was August Gaudin. A werewolf. There's never been a reason for her to trust a vampire." She lowered her voice. "Now come on. We all know you're not telling us everything about letting Abigail the student survive the change. What really went on?"

Fiona hesitated, but it was probably all going to come out eventually, and she felt she owed it to her sisters to be completely honest.

"Billy Harrington—you remember him from the meeting? The college student? He had just started working the night shift at the morgue. They knew each other. In fact, they were madly in love with each other, though neither one had had the guts to tell the other. Anyway, he was willing to fight for her."

"So? You didn't back down from a fight. I know you," Shauna said.

"No. But he offered to do it for her, and we chose to respect his…feelings. Besides, think about it. She was raised by nuns. She's a good kid, with a good soul and I believe in the existence of the soul."

Shauna looked as if she were about to speak, but just then Caitlin and Mrs. Vickery, her client, came from the back room into the shop proper.

"My dear, you are the most insightful reader I have ever met," Mrs. Vickery was saying. She was one of those people who seemed to have been sent into the world just to make it pleasant. She was about sixty, gray hair always coiffed, plump figure attractively attired. She loved children and animals, and was active in the community, constantly giving to others. She was always smiling, and she always came with her tiny Papillon in a designer bag. The dog was as sweet as her owner. Her hairy little head popped out the top of the bag as they neared the counter.

"Thank you," Caitlin said.

Mrs. Vickery smiled at Fiona and Caitlin. "Your sister is so wise. She sees what others don't." She looked down fondly at her dog.

"I *will* find a mate for my little Mrs. Beasley here," she said, delighted.

Caitlin laughed softly. "You didn't need a tarot reader to tell you that, Mrs. Vickery. You're going to find a mate for Mrs. Beasley because you're so determined."

Mrs. Vickery flushed happily. "Well, yes, there's that, too. Fiona, dear, one day next week, would you read the tea leaves for me? They tend to show such different possibilities."

"Of course. I'll fit you in wherever you like," Fiona assured her.

"I've just been so worried lately," Mrs. Vickery said.

"And," she added, looking at Shauna, "I'm looking forward to another palm reading, young lady."

"I'll give you a freebie right now," Shauna said, taking the older woman's hand. A look of concern briefly crossed her face, and she seemed to force a smile. "See this little line? It's new. It means that you're going in a new direction with a pet project, that you're going to do well, and others will embrace your ideas."

"Oh, how lovely. And it *is* a 'pet' project," Mrs. Vickery said. "I have a friend who owns one of those old plantations who's agreed to open up the old kennels as a shelter where no animal will ever be put to sleep."

"That's wonderful," Fiona approved.

"And it's so reassuring to know others will embrace the idea," Mrs. Vickery said happily.

"Kindness begets kindness," Fiona said.

Mrs. Vickery flushed. "Well, I inherited a fortune. In all honesty, with so much money at my disposal, I owe it to others to help them, at least in my own mind."

"It's a beautiful mind," Fiona assured her.

"I do worry these days," Mrs. Vickery said. "All this horrible business with women being killed, their bodies drained. And now that second girl's body was stolen. What on earth have we come to? I bet it's those cultists in the old Brewer mansion."

"What?" Fiona asked sharply.

"There's a group of so-called vampires living in Uptown, in the Brewer mansion. Can you believe it? They were in a documentary that aired just the other night! If the police don't deal with them, I'm sure someone will," she said knowingly.

Fiona groaned inwardly. Great. Just what they needed at a time like this.

"They're probably just a group of confused kids," Caitlin said reassuringly, glancing over at Fiona.

Mrs. Vickery sighed softly. "All I know is that too many frightening things are happening. And I'm having dreams. I saw a girl turning into a vampire—a real one, like in the movies—and walking down the street naked." She gave an exaggerated shudder. "Well, we'd best get going, my little one and I. Next week, girls."

As soon as the woman had left the store, Shauna turned to Fiona. "A dream, huh?"

Fiona frowned and asked, "What did you really see in her palm?"

"Probably the same thing I read in her cards," Caitlin said.

"What was that?" Fiona asked sharply.

"She's in danger," Caitlin said.

Fiona's heart sank. She hadn't realized that Mrs. Vickery was the woman on the street when she had been trying to corral Abigail back into Jagger's house.

"You…you didn't see her *death,* did you?" she asked.

"A jagged line," Shauna said.

"Danger—that could lead to death," Caitlin told her.

Fiona groaned aloud. "All right, I've got to get going. I need to see what's going on with that cult. Listen for your cell phones. I might need help at any time."

As she grabbed her bag, Shauna went over to the computer and logged onto a local news site.

"Hey!"

Shauna called, and turned up the volume.

Fiona and Caitlin ran to join her.

Jagger was speaking to the press, and Fiona's heart practically stopped. How was he going to explain things to the public when he didn't know who the killer was but he did know *what*.

And when that "what" wasn't human...

"It's unfortunate for our city that a certain documentary that was shown recently seems to have put some strange ideas in people's heads. Only concrete evidence can lead us to the perpetrator of these heinous crimes, and the police are working diligently to find that evidence," Jagger assured the media.

"But this group claims to drink blood!" one of the newscasters shouted.

"Claiming and doing are two different things," Jagger pointed out. "Listen, please. Protecting these people from a potential lynch mob is costing us police man hours. I'm begging the public to work with us, not against us."

"What about the corpse that was stolen?" another reporter asked, thrusting a microphone closer to Jagger.

"The police are investigating that, as well, I assure you. All I'm asking is that you and everyone in this city stay calm and help us do our work. Don't become an accusing mob, and do inform us if you see anything out of the ordinary, anything that looks dangerous. The police are trying to help the city, and we ask that you all do the same. And now I thank you for your attention, but you'll have to excuse me. I'm needed on the streets."

Jagger walked away, followed by a barrage of questions, but he was firm, politely lifting a hand until he could make it to his car. Fiona saw that his partner was waiting behind the wheel as Jagger slipped into the passenger seat.

The press conference was definitely over.

"I've got to get moving," Fiona said, and hurried out of the store.

"Wait," Caitlin said. "Shauna, cover for us, please. Fiona, I don't want you going alone. I'm coming with you."

Jagger and Tony drew up in front of the cult house. Sean O'Casey—the world's largest leprechaun—was partnered with shapeshifter Michael Shrine as part of the task force that had been assembled to deal with the murders and the possible rise of violence in the city. They were parked by the entry to the cult house.

Michael Shrine, six feet four of muscle in his human form, was leaning against one side of the car. Sean O'Casey, stretched to his top height of an amazing six even, was just as implacably entrenched on the other side of the car, arms crossed over his chest.

Both men looked grim.

Jagger didn't blame them.

There wasn't a city employee who wasn't worried about the possibility of violence. Of course, most of them were worried that human beings—Baptist, Catholic, nondenominational Christian, Jewish, Hindu, atheist, alien-worshipping or even run-of-the-mill New Orleans voodoo practitioners—would attack other human beings.

Those who haunted the city's underground knew that the situation might be far worse.

"Any trouble?" Jagger asked, approaching the car, with Tony a step behind.

"Well, a truckload of high school kids went by— looked as if they were going to hurl eggs, but they saw us and drove on by," Shrine said.

"Then there was the crazy woman," O'Casey told them. "And her crazy followers."

"What? Who?" Tony asked.

Sean shook his head. "Skinny woman, walked from that way—" he pointed "—to get here, had about ten people behind her. They were all carrying Bibles and saying that disbelievers would burn in hell."

"Scarier than our would-be vampires, if you ask me," Shrine said.

"Fanatics are always scary," Jagger said. "But no one attempted to go to the house, or attack the residents in any way?"

"Not yet. No one in, no one out," Shrine assured him.

"Thanks," Jagger said. He started toward the front door, then turned around so quickly that Tony almost crashed into him.

"Go on, I'll be right along," he told Tony.

Tony headed for the door as Jagger walked back to Sean O'Casey. "How the hell did you get to be so tall?" he asked.

Sean O'Casey shrugged. "Must be the hormones in the milk over here. I've two brothers back home who aren't a full four feet. And my sisters are tiny little things."

Jagger grinned, asked the two of them to be sure to write up full descriptions of everyone who'd come by, then thanked them again and headed back to the door.

Tony had already knocked.

A woman with dyed black hair opened the door.

She was wearing a black dress and looked like a younger Elvira, Mistress of the Dark.

"Hello. I'm Detective Jagger DeFarge, and this is

my partner, Detective Tony Miro. We'd like to talk to you and your…group for a few minutes, if we could."

The woman smiled. She had just a touch of bloodred lipstick on her teeth. "Of course. Come in. We're already entertaining guests, so please join us."

"Oh?" Just how long ago had those guests arrived? he wondered, making a mental note to check with the officers who'd been on duty before Shrine and O'Casey.

He stepped in. The house was a basic grand colonial, with a huge entry hall, doors to the left and right and a massive staircase leading up from the middle of the room.

The banisters were adorned with garlands of black roses.

The walls were painted black. Black curtains hung over the windows.

The walls held movie posters celebrating Hollywood's fascination with werewolves, mummies, vampires, witches and every conceivable monster, from a giant lizard that had just crawled out of a swamp to King Kong.

The woman offered him a hand, long fingers, with longer fingernails painted in bloodred, dangling.

"I'm Lucretia. Real name. It goes with Brown. Please, come in. I'm the titular queen of our little group."

She led them to the door on the right and into the next room. For a moment the scent of blood was strong, and Jagger steeled himself against it.

The living room added red to the black of the entry hall, and instead of movie posters, the paintings that hung on the walls qualified as erotica at least as much as art. A man was seated in a claw-foot chair by a huge fireplace, and side by side on a massive sofa covered in plush red velvet were Fiona and Caitlin MacDonald.

He groaned inwardly. "Fiona, Caitlin, I didn't expect to see you here."

"You all know each other?" Lucretia asked pleasantly.

"I've known these ladies quite a while, yes," Jagger said. "Tony, have you met my friends, Fiona and Caitlin MacDonald?"

Caitlin apparently realized in an instant that Tony was human and decided to be nice to him.

"It's a pleasure," she murmured.

"Fancy finding you here," Jagger said, staring at Fiona. He bent close and said for her ears only, "How the hell did you slip in? The men outside didn't see you. No, wait. Don't tell me. She shape-shifted into a mouse or something, and you went to mist. You just made my officers look like fools."

Fiona flushed, looking away momentarily.

"I thought I should come. I wanted these people to understand that they could be in serious danger. I explained about the shop, and how we know the mood of the city."

Jagger knew his smile looked glued on as he took a seat next to Fiona and said softly, "Great."

"Your officers aren't in trouble. No one knows," she said.

"Tony knows now, doesn't he?" Jagger asked.

"Is everything all right?" Lucretia asked worriedly. "Detectives, can I get you something to drink?"

Yes, a nice cup of the blood I can smell would be great, Jagger thought dryly, wondering why the man in the chair was there. Muscle in case things got out of hand, he supposed.

"We have a full liquor cabinet, soda, tea...coffee?" Lucretia continued.

"No, we're fine, thank you," Jagger said. "We need to talk."

Lucretia's bloodred lips pursed. "As I've been explaining to Fiona and Caitlin, we believe that blood is life. We're not murderers. We drink animal blood. We're no worse than someone who has a nice steak—served rare."

"There's human blood in this room somewhere," Jagger said firmly.

Lucretia looked startled.

"Um...actually, yes, we do keep a few vials—all from our members, and all given quite voluntarily." She sighed, extending her arms. "We've joined together because of our shared beliefs. We...we believe that love-making is enhanced by a sip of blood. None of us is on drugs, and in case you've forgotten, the United States offers freedom of religion. I'm a legally ordained minister."

"Did you get your credentials online?" Tony asked.

Lucretia flushed. "Yes," she snapped. "And they're perfectly legal."

"What's the name of your...church?"

"We're the Church of Elizabeth Báthory," Lucretia told him.

Tony stared at Jagger, then turned back to her. "Really?"

"Really and legally," Lucretia said icily.

Jagger lifted his hands. "Look, here's the problem with your current situation, and it isn't legal, it's human.

First, you admit to drinking blood—to using it for religious purposes?" he asked. She nodded, frowning. "The city has two bloodless corpses—"

"One," Lucretia reminded him. "You lost one, remember?"

"The point is that everyone in New Orleans knows that two women were killed and drained of blood. Therefore, I or one of my officers will need to speak with every one of your members. Personally I don't think you're guilty. I *do* think you're going to cost me man hours I can't afford. And frankly, I'm not sure how worshipping Elizabeth Báthory counts as a respectable religion."

"Hey! People worship aliens. And cows—and cats, so I've heard," Lucretia said indignantly.

"Whatever. This isn't a good time to be drinking blood," Jagger said. "And you and your members have to start being careful about what you say and do, all right? This is a...delicate time in the city. All right? Once we catch the killer, knock yourselves out. Go on every news show out there. But until then..."

He noticed that Fiona and her sister had risen. Tony rose, too, and he followed suit.

"I think we should leave you to your police business," Fiona said.

"How kind of you," Jagger murmured.

"Thank you so much for coming," Lucretia said, rising, as well.

"Tony, you stay here and talk to Lucretia. I'll see the sisters to the door," Jagger said, taking each of them by an elbow and steering them in that direction.

"What are you doing here?" he asked Fiona when they reached the door. "This is police business."

"Jagger, they needed to be warned. And we were doing a better job than you did of explaining that they shouldn't run around right now announcing their devotion to a fifteenth-century countess who bathed in blood," Fiona said.

"And," Caitlin added, her glare icy, "when the police can't seem to handle police business, I think we need to lend a helping hand."

Jagger looked at Fiona. "I really don't want to arrest your sister," he said.

"Jagger, don't be ridiculous! I'm the Keeper—"

"And she's not. Not *my* Keeper, anyway," he said. "Get out of here—both of you. Oh, Caitlin, you might want to apologize to the tall fellow at the car—Michael Shrine, shapeshifter. He's going to feel like an ass for letting you walk in right under his nose."

He saw them both out the door and closed it with a bang. Irritated, he headed back to the living room, with its choking red-and-black decor, and wretched paintings.

Hell.

He wanted to be anywhere but here.

He sat on the sofa and pulled out his notebook. Tony did the same.

"We're going to need the names of everyone who is involved in your religion in any way. Now, let's start with you, Lucretia. We'll need to know where you were on the nights of both murders. And I'm going to pray that you aren't all each other's alibis."

This was a total waste of time, he thought. A killer was out there, and he wasn't some deluded wannabe. This killer was the real thing.

* * *

"Oh, man, it was terrible. I haven't had a drink since." Standing on the lawn in front of the frat house, Jude Andre gave a sudden, fierce shiver.

Fiona stared at him, certain it would be a while before he had another drink. His tone had been sincere.

She was with Shauna. Caitlin—who had actually apologized to Michael Shrine, and even to the leprechaun, Sean O'Casey—had gone back to the shop, muttering about Jagger being rude, unappreciative of the role of a Keeper and an all around...vampire.

Shauna had joined Fiona for their planned visit to the frat house where Abigail had attended her last party, but they'd split up after arrival so they could talk to more people in less time.

The long-haired and lanky young man with the sax case and book bag stared at Fiona and Shauna, shaking his head. "What a party, you know? It was great. The booze was good—no cheap beer. We were jamming, you know? A bunch of music majors, just having fun."

"Sure," Shauna said. "But here's the thing. No one remembers Abigail leaving. I'm trying to get everyone to tell us about the last time they saw or talked to her that night."

He scrunched up his face, thinking. "About twelve. I was in the old parlor, playing my music. I was pretty drunk. She came by and led me to a chair, told me I was about to fall down."

"Okay, you saw her around twelve. Did you see anyone else with her?"

The boy narrowed his eyes in deep thought. "No, she was alone then. I thought it was kind of odd."

"Really? Why?" Fiona asked him.

"Well, hell, everyone knew that Billy Harrington was crazy-mad for her. She was pretty nuts for him, too. They just never figured it out about each other, you know? Went around together all the time like they were just friends. I didn't think I'd see her at a party without him. Hey, wait!" His face wrinkled as if he were a Shar-Pei.

"What is it?" Fiona asked.

Jude looked at her, shaking his head. "He wasn't at the party because he said he had some big shindig in the Quarter he needed to attend. He said he didn't want to come to the party and get started drinking and all, since he had to drive to the Quarter later."

"So you saw him during the day, but not at the party."

"Right. I think," Jude said. "Don't know why, but I have an impression of Billy in the house, but I know I didn't see him at the party." He gasped suddenly. "Oh, God! You think Billy Harrington…that's crazy! You think he murdered Abigail and then stole her body. That he loved her so much he murdered her. You think he's a necrophiliac!"

It sounded as if he thought the latter would be far worse than murder.

"No. No, that's not what I mean at all. I'm just trying to find out what happened, that's all," Fiona said firmly.

"Are you a cop or something?" he asked.

"No, my sister and I are just concerned local businesswomen with an interest in keeping our city safe," Shauna said, walking up to join them.

"Hey, Jude, Shauna!"

The call came from the steps of the frat house, breaking into the awkward conversation. The young man who walked over to join them had long dark hair, neatly kept, and a slender, attractive face. He was tall and lean, and Shauna greeted him with pleasure.

"Jimmy!" she called.

Werewolf. Fiona knew it instantly.

Jimmy smiled and shook hands when Shauna introduced him to Fiona.

"Jimmy, Fiona thinks Billy Harrington is a necrophiliac," Jude said with horror.

"I did not say any such thing," Fiona said firmly.

"Come on, I'll show you two the house," Jimmy offered, drawing them away from Jude.

"Thanks," Fiona murmured in gratitude, grateful for the chance to get away from Jude Andre, as well as the chance to see the house.

"Wrong dude to be talking to if you want useful answers," Jimmy explained to the two of them once they were out of earshot. "Jude is an all right guy, but he loves two things—his sax and his weed. He's not exactly living in the real world, if you know what I mean."

Jimmy had a nice grin—it dimpled his cheeks.

"Were you at the party?" Fiona asked him.

He nodded gravely, pushing open the door. The frat house was painted white, and the door had a beautiful cut-glass oval that sparkled in the light of the setting sun.

Fiona noticed a strange dark substance coating the door.

Jimmy shrugged. "The crime-scene people kind of got carried away…dusting for prints."

"They had to. They're looking for the prints that don't belong," Fiona said.

"Well, they have their work cut out for them. There were a lot of people at that party. And did you know we all had to go down to the station for an interview today? We're all missing classes, and we didn't even do anything."

"Jimmy Douglas, you know it's imperative that the police find the killer," Shauna said.

Jimmy lowered his head and spoke quietly. "We all know the killer's a vampire, so Jagger needs to be interviewing vampires, and that's that. And I intend to say so at the meeting tonight. Anyway, come on upstairs—I see Nathan, Billy's roommate. I'm sure you'll want to talk to him."

Fiona glanced at Shauna, and then they hurried up the stairs in Jimmy's wake. Nathan was sitting on the floor, his back against the wall, a book in his hands. As they approached, he looked up, saw the two women and smiled.

"Hey, I know you two. You run that supernatural shop in the Quarter. I was there with about ten guys a couple of weeks ago. They sure don't have anything like that in Indiana, where I come from."

"Nathan, these are my friends, Shauna and Fiona MacDonald," Jimmy said.

Nathan struggled to his feet. He looked like he was from Indiana. Corn-fed and strapping, with wheat colored hair and bright blue eyes. "Nice to meet you formally."

"They're here about Abigail," Jimmy said.

"Oh." He looked at them gravely. "What happened to her was…horrible."

"Did you see anyone with her? Was she flirting with anyone, or was anyone trying to flirt with her? Did she leave with someone, and do you remember when she left?" Fiona asked.

"The cops asked me that, too. I saw her and all, but I don't think she was flirting. She wasn't the type."

"Did you see Billy Harrington that night?" Fiona asked.

A strange expression crossed his face. "The cops asked *that*, too. He said he wasn't going to be here, but somehow…I have the impression that he was, only I don't actually remember seeing him or talking to him. Bizarre, huh? He's in our room. Poor guy—he's all ripped up over this."

"I'll go see him," Fiona said, and turned to Shauna. "Can you talk to Nathan? Thanks." Then she walked over to Billy's door and tapped gently.

"Yeah?" She heard Billy's muffled voice.

"It's Fiona."

The door opened, and he practically dragged her into the room.

Billy was clean and neatly dressed, the complete antithesis of a man in deep mourning. "Fiona, oh, my God, they think I'm in mourning. I'm crawling the walls. I have to see her. I'm terrified. I don't know what she and David are doing, what the police are doing…. I'm going insane here."

"I'm sorry," she said. "But you'll just have to pull yourself together and keep going. Listen, this is serious. A lot of people *think* you were at that party—even though you said you had to go into the Quarter and wouldn't make it."

He was indignant. "I told you—I wasn't at the party!"

She sighed. He sounded so sincere.

"Even your roommate, who certainly doesn't seem to be out to get you, has the impression you were there."

"And I just told you, I wasn't there," he insisted. "Damn it, Fiona! You know how I feel about Abigail."

"Do you love her enough to want to keep her by your side for all time?" It was the only motive for murder she'd been able to come up with for him, but she had to admit, it made a certain amount of sense.

He drew himself up stiffly. "I would never have turned her. Ever. I swear it. And you know why? Because I would never damn someone I love to the uncertainty every vampire faces every day."

He sounded so sincere.

Then again, she'd seen him act.

An impression. The other kids had an *impression*.

No one knew for a fact that they had seen him.

"I'm innocent. I swear it."

"All right, Billy. Just stay in here as long as you can—alone," Fiona said. "I'll see you at the meeting tonight."

He nodded, and she slipped back out.

She and Shauna spent another hour talking to the kids from the party, but except for a few more who had the vague sense that they'd seen Billy, they didn't come up with anything useful. Finally they decided to call it a day and left.

As they walked across the yard toward their car, they saw a pretty girl heading toward the frat house.

Fiona stopped her. "Hi. Mind if I ask you a few questions?"

The girl, who had blond hair and big blue eyes, stopped, a sad and slightly weary expression on her face.

"Are you undercover cops here to ask about Abigail?" she asked. "Sorry, I don't mean to be rude, but

I've been asked the same questions over and over again, and it just…hurts. Abigail was a friend. A bit of an airhead, but a friend."

"Did you see her with anyone at the party?" Fiona asked.

"No one in particular. She was just mingling, talking to people, having fun. You know how, when you start out in college, every boy is a mystery waiting to be explored? But then after a while the boys are just boys, except maybe for one you really like."

"Right," Fiona said. "And Abigail really liked Billy Harrington."

"Yes, exactly," the girl said, then frowned suddenly.

"What is it?"

"I had a weird dream that night. Maybe I was worried about her."

"What was your dream?" Fiona asked.

The girl laughed, looking a little embarrassed. "I dreamed that I saw her walking down the steps and out toward the street, looking tired—but happy, too." She shook her head, as if to clear it.

"I could see the veins in the leaves on the trees. It was really freaky. And then…there was some boy, hurrying to catch up to her."

"Did you tell that to the police?" Fiona asked.

The girl laughed again. "Hell, no! You don't tell the police about a *dream*."

"Did you recognize the boy who was about to catch up with her?"

"Yes, of course."

"And who was it?" Fiona asked.

"Billy Harrington."

Chapter 10

The staff had been apprised that Underworld would be closing early that night, with last call being given soon after 2:00 a.m. The ostensible reason was that the place was set for a massive cleaning. Since David was known for the high standards he applied to the place, it wasn't a stretch.

Earlier, Jagger had left most of the conversations with the cult members to Tony Miro and the other officers, and moved on to the frat house.

He'd been irritated to discover that Fiona and Shauna had been there ahead of him. And he'd been genuinely disturbed to learn how many people thought they might have seen Billy Harrington that night.

No doubt Fiona and Shauna had heard the same information—and maybe more. He could certainly see how a bunch of hormone-addled teenage boys might have opened up to a pair of gorgeous sisters who were so concerned for the safety of the community, and who were ignoring the fact that people shouldn't have been opening up to them at all. They didn't have any right to question anyone.

At 10:00 p.m. he'd called Tony and told him to go home at last. His partner was going above and beyond, and he was sorry that, to maintain appearances, he was causing his partner to waste hours of work that he knew would bring them no closer to finding the killer.

He rationalized the situation by telling himself that at least now they had a lot of information on record that might be of use in the future.

He was heading back to the French Quarter, planning to arrive at Underworld well ahead of time when he picked up a sound, some kind of a thud, coming from the cemetery off Canal.

Jerking his car to a halt, he looked around carefully. Seeing no one, he got out of the car and leaped effortlessly to the top of the wall, where he hunkered down, searching the rows of mausoleums and monuments in the darkened city of the dead.

Another thud.

His eyes quickly darted in that direction, and then he jumped down and started running toward the location of the sound.

Suddenly he crashed into someone hidden in the shadow of a massive—and armless—weeping angel.

Instantly on the alert, he drew back, reaching for the gun in his shoulder holster.

"*Stop*," came a woman's urgent whisper. "Please."

He was startled by her near hysteria, but even so, he recognized the voice. It was Sue Preston, a shapeshifter friend of Jennie Mahoney's.

He caught her hand as he hunkered down by her. "What is it? What's going on?" he asked.

"They're fighting—and it's terrible," Sue said. She was a pretty young thing, but right now she had giant tears in her eyes. "I saw Georgio Tremont on Chartres Street when I was having dinner, and then Ossie Blane. We started talking, decided to kill some time before the assembly, so we came out here to go walking, and the next thing I knew, they were tearing into each other."

Georgio Tremont was a vampire.

Ossie Blane was a werewolf.

This could be trouble.

"Stay here," he told Sue quietly.

He rose and slipped around the side of the small family vault where he'd found Sue. Another thud. Someone—or some*thing*—had crashed hard into the wall right beside him.

He didn't let who—or whatever it was—rise. He shot out an arm and reached, and found himself grabbing the scruff of a furry neck.

It was Ossie Blane. He'd changed, and was in rare, snarling form.

Werewolves were very powerful. Their teeth were merciless.

Jagger knew he would have one chance before winding up in a literal fight for his life.

He kept his grip hard and shook Ossie with all his strength. "Ossie! It's Jagger, Jagger DeFarge. Stop this now!"

Ossie was, at heart, a decent guy, and to Jagger's relief, that guy hadn't sunk too far beneath the surface. Ossie went still. Slowly the snout became a face. Hair dissolved.

Claws and fangs retracted.

The sleek shape of the wolf elongated and straightened into an erect position.

Gasping for breath, Ossie stared at him.

A wing of perfect, menacing darkness came gliding toward them both. Jagger stepped forward, using the full brunt of his body as a bulwark. The vampire came flying into him with so much force that Jagger had to take a step back to absorb the blow.

Bend and you'll never break.

He didn't think his martial arts teacher had been thinking vampires when he'd said it, but it had turned out to be true nonetheless.

Georgio dropped to the ground after slamming into him. For a moment Jagger was reminded of a commercial he'd seen, in which two birds laughed at a man who hit the ground after walking right into a newly cleaned and completely see-through glass door.

With a stunned cry, Georgio started to make his way to his feet.

Jagger helped him up. "What are you two idiots up to?" he demanded.

"DeFarge, what are you doing here?" Georgio asked. "That walking furball attacked me!"

"I didn't attack you!" Ossie protested, stepping forward belligerently. "I said that it was obvious that the killer's a vampire, and that no one should be attacking innocent college students."

Jagger interposed himself between them. "Look, we're all in a bad situation right now, and we have to keep calm. The last thing we need, if you'll pardon the pun, is some kind of witch hunt."

To Jagger's amusement, the other two pointed fingers at each other at the same time and said in unison, "He started it!"

Most of the time they were both average citizens, interesting conversationalists over a meal or a drink. Ossie loved animals and worked at the zoo, and Georgio was a middle-school teacher.

"Both of you," Jagger said quietly. "Look at what you're doing. Myths and movies call us monsters. This is why."

Sue emerged from behind the angel-topped mausoleum at last.

"You scared me," she accused them. "I thought you were my friends."

They might have been a comedy act when they spoke in unison again.

"I'm so sorry, Sue."

Jagger leaned back, crossing his arms over his chest. "All right, time to kiss and make up. I ought to knock your heads together. Damn it! We need to get through this together or the whole city's going to turn on us. We need to find a killer—and I don't give a damn what race he is. To do that, I need help, not a couple of hotheads trying to rip each other to shreds."

Ossie hung his head. "I'm sorry, Jagger—Georgio. And Sue. Really."

"Maybe we could keep from mentioning this?" Georgio asked, looking across the darkened cemetery, worry creasing his brow. He turned back to Jagger. "All the Keepers will be at the assembly, right?"

"Just about everyone will be at the assembly. There are a few people working in emergency services or other jobs where their absences would be noted, but I'm expecting a showing of at least two hundred," Jagger said.

"I'm planning to get there early. In fact, I was on my way when I got sidetracked by your fight. Speaking of… You all need to clean up and get there on time, and you had both better do something really nice for Sue." He turned his attention to her. "You okay?"

She nodded, linking arms with the two men. "Thank you. We're fine," she assured him.

He left them making their apologies, making it back to his car in time to see two thugs were trying to break in.

They were wearing ski masks.

In New Orleans.

"Hey!" he shouted.

One of the men looked at him, and then they both took off.

He could have caught them. Maybe he should have.

But he was looking for a killer who was going to take more victims if he wasn't stopped.

Soon.

"I'm sure of it. Billy is the killer," Caitlin said. She, Shauna and Fiona were in their communal living room, watching the clock, discussing the events of the day.

"I just don't believe that," Fiona said. She was pacing, she realized. Arms crossed over her chest, walking back and forth in front of the fireplace like the depressed polar bear in the Central Park Zoo that had needed therapy, because all it did was swim back and forth, back and forth….

She stopped pacing and realized both her sisters were staring at her, waiting for her to speak.

"Are you even listening? I said if Jagger won't put him down, you'll have to," Caitlin said.

"We don't have any proof that it was Billy," Fiona said. "Look, for one thing, we're all concentrating on the second murder and forgetting about the first. Billy has no connection to Tina Lawrence, who was last seen at a strip club. The police have a sketch of a man who was there that night, and not a single person has come forward to say they recognize him, *think* they recognize him or even know anyone who even slightly resembles him."

"Could there have been two separate killers?" Shauna wondered aloud.

"I don't think so. Too many similarities," Fiona said, and took a deep breath. "Here's where we are right now. Tina Lawrence, last seen at the strip club. A man was watching her—he's never been seen again. We've actually questioned Abigail, but she doesn't remember anything. She was at a party, she was drinking beer. Someone might have slipped something in her drink—frat boys have been known to do that—but we don't actually know, since there was obviously no autopsy. No one from the party remembers actually talking to Billy, though a lot of people got the impression he was there. They all knew he had plans in the Quarter—which he did. He was at the meeting with the three of us."

Caitlin had been curled up on the sofa. Now she stood, walked up to Fiona and placed a hand gently on her shoulder. "Look, I know I've been a bitch. It's just that I can't forget that vampires caused all our problems—caused Mom and Dad their lives. But I want to help you, want to be a good sister and a good Keeper. And I don't want to upset you, but I do need to point out two things. First, both victims were drained of blood, vampire style. And this wasn't the act of a human being.

A human being might have pulled off the blood draining, but both victims woke at dark. Only a vampire can create a vampire."

"Or a shapeshifter—posing as a vampire," Shauna pointed out.

"I think you're forgetting one thing. Shapeshifters can take on many forms, but when it comes to masquerading as another supernatural, they don't have the strength of the real thing," Caitlin said.

"That's true," Fiona agreed. "But," she asked quietly, "how much strength would a shapeshifter have needed to attack two women? Tina Lawrence had a violent streak, true, but she was still only human. A shapeshifter might not be as strong as a vampire or werewolf, but he would still be more powerful than a human being."

"You just don't want to accept that it was a vampire," Caitlin told her.

"*You* just don't want to accept the possibility that it might have been a shapeshifter," Fiona countered.

They stared at each other. Then they both started to smile at the same time.

"All right—it was most likely a vampire," Fiona said.

"And, I admit, there's a possibility it was a shapeshifter," Caitlin said.

"What a relief," Shauna said. "Now we can go to the meeting and present a united front."

"We have to," Fiona said. "We have to make the entire paranormal community understand completely that we're not only judicious but strong—and we *will* keep the peace."

Shauna jumped up from the sofa.

"Group hug!" she cried.

Laughing, Fiona let herself be dragged into her youngest sister's exuberant embrace.

"All right—enough," she said finally, taking a step back. "One for all, and all for one. Now, let's get over to that meeting."

Despite the time it had taken to break up the altercation, Jagger arrived at David's early. A little while later, from his seat in the front row, he watched the attendees filing in and realized everyone seemed to naturally group together with the other members of their own race.

Ossie and Georgio had made up, but even so, they split up when they entered, Ossie to sit with the werewolves and Georgio with the vampires. Even the Keepers separated on arrival and sat with the races they were charged to protect.

Jagger was grateful when August Gaudin came down the aisle and sat next to him, breaking up the divisions.

He thought back to the war—and the peace. The peace motivated by the deaths of the elder MacDonalds had forced them all to learn patience and tolerance, and to obey the unwritten laws that allowed them to maintain their place in society. Their laws, like the Constitution of the United States, mandated equal rights for all.

But laws didn't always end old hatreds or prejudices.

Even Caitlin MacDonald couldn't let go of her belief that the vampires alone had caused the deaths of her parents. But the vampires hadn't caused the war all by themselves.

It took two to fight. And once two were fighting, everyone wanted in on the brawl, or so it seemed.

He found it especially sad that the war had been started on behalf of perhaps the finest emotion of all: love.

"Shall I open?" August asked Jagger.

"That would be fine," Jagger said, taking another look around the room. It was filling up. It was almost like a wedding where no one got along with anyone else. Vampires to the left, shapeshifters to the right, werewolves in between, the others finding space where they could.

Sean O'Casey came in, nodded to him and took a seat between the vampires and the werewolves. Leprechauns were not in large supply in New Orleans, but as far as he was concerned, they were as welcome as anyone else. Sure, they tended to drink and get in bar brawls now and then, but most of the time they were cheerful, and a big presence in the local art and culture scene.

A well-respected voodoo priestess known as Granny Caldwell, one of the few human beings welcome at a major assembly, came in, greeting friends and chose to sit next to Sean O'Casey.

Granny Caldwell had to be about eighty, but she had the bearing of a young woman. Her skin was a beautiful copper hue, and she wore a blue turban that emphasized the aristocratic bone structure of her face. She wore a dress in shades of green and the same blue as the turban.

She nodded at Jagger, and he smiled in return. Her eyes sparkled, but she wasn't going to smile back.

"Are we about ready?" David said.

Jagger turned to see their host at his side.

"Yeah, thanks, looks like we're about set to go. You'll introduce us, then August will speak first, and Jennie Mahoney is here—she'll want her turn at the microphone." He turned to August. "Let's make that the order—David, you, Jennie, then me. I have a feeling I'll be trying to hold the peace together by then."

David must have seen Jagger's frown of concern and known what unspoken question lurked behind the expression. He bent down to whisper, "It's okay. Abigail is here—and safe." Then he nodded and went to the podium, where he cleared his throat and tapped the microphone. "Welcome, everyone, to this emergency meeting of our peoples. We all know that we have a dire and escalating situation not only in our community but in our beloved city as a whole. We're here for two reasons. First, to discuss what has happened, all the possible explanations and how we proceed. Second, to see to it that we remain strong among ourselves. To that end, we'll have three speakers, one for each of the most populous, but we're not attempting to exclude anyone, so if…anyone else…wants a say, they're more than welcome to come to the podium."

He paused, looking around the room. When no one seemed inclined to comment or object, he went on.

"First let us welcome August Gaudin."

August was greeted with massive applause.

He flushed and began to speak.

"First, I'd like to sincerely thank all of you for your commitment to keeping the peace between the races. Some of us are young and don't remember what it was like when war broke out among us. The death toll was excruciating, and if two of the finest Keepers I've ever known, the MacDonalds, hadn't used their last strength—indeed, their very last breaths—to subdue the violence, things might have escalated to a point where we became visible and the human population not only felt threatened by our very existence, but determined to erase us from the face of the earth. The MacDonalds have left us their daughters, fine young women in their own right. We *must* take our grievances to them—not fight each other in the streets."

His words were greeted with more applause.

"I'm calling out now to my own people, the were-wolves and all the were-creatures. Thankfully, due to our very nature and powers, we're not suspects in these heinous crimes, but that doesn't change the fact that we're called upon to remember that we are all brothers in a special and tight-knit society that demands we respect one another. I ask you, my brethren, to keep the peace at all times and no matter the costs. Shauna MacDonald is here tonight, not only our Keeper but our mentor and our guide. If one of you has any problem at all, please come to me or to Shauna. Whatever you do, don't let a petty squabble lead to teeth and fangs and more bloodshed."

Shauna nodded gravely to him from her seat in the audience as more applause greeted his final words.

When the applause died down, he said, "And now I give you Jennie Mahoney."

Jennie, as regal as ever, rose and walked to the stage. The shapeshifters applauded her loudly, and the rest of the room politely followed suit.

"I, like my dear friend August Gaudin, am here to ask that we remain calm and rational in these trying times. These are the facts. Two human women were murdered and drained of blood. We are all aware that they rose as vampire, and we are all also aware that only the bite of a vampire—or a shapeshifter in vampire form—could be the cause. Therefore we must take great care not to look at each other with suspicion, or let our fears lead us to violence. We must put our faith in our own Keeper, Caitlin MacDonald, along with her sister Fiona, Keeper for the vampire community, and Jagger DeFarge, not only one of this city's most respected vampires but an upstanding officer of the law. I hope you'll all join me in being grateful that Jagger DeFarge was put in charge of the investigation into these murders, because we know he won't let personal bias get in the way of his search for the truth. He's lucky, because he'll have the help of the entire New Orleans Police Department, including several members of the underworld who also carry a badge. I want to finish by asking all of you to be open minded, to recognize the fact that we all have weaknesses and emotions but can't let ourselves act on them. In particular, I'd like to ask my fellow shapeshifters to understand that we may fall under suspicion. We must not let ourselves fall back on resentment, but instead answer any questions willingly and honestly, out of our desire to end this horror as quickly as possible."

After the applause that followed her speech, she said, "And now Jagger DeFarge would like to speak."

Jagger stood, grateful to realize that the explosion of applause came in equal amounts from all the races.

He looked around the room when he reached the podium, then started to speak.

"Like you, I've listened to my colleagues' words, and they've spoken the same truth that I see. We have to take the high road now. We can't be afraid of each other, and we can't blindly attack each other. However, I believe we have to go even further. I would bet that every one of you can say with complete honesty that you have at least one friend whose race is different from yours. But what hasn't happened since the war is a real combining of the communities, and I think that's going to prove crucial now. We need to mix, to mingle, to merge into one whole with the same goal in mind: apprehending the killer whose viciousness has put all our lives in jeopardy. And the easiest way to become a community is simply to act like one. Vampires, go to werewolf restaurants. Werewolves, I charge you to shop at shapeshifter-run stores. We need to get past looking at one another for what we are biologically and embrace one another as if we were all the same."

He was pleased to see the attendees start looking around, to see realization on their faces as they noticed that they had come into the room and automatically segregated themselves by race.

"At the same time, feel free to just dislike someone now and then. We have to get past the idea that somebody doesn't like so and so, it has to be because of what they are. Sometimes you just think someone is a jerk—and maybe the rest of us have to learn that you just might be right."

He was glad to hear the rise of real laughter at his words. Their situation was serious, but that only made laughter more necessary.

After that he went on to recap what little the police knew about the two murders, with the additional information that, as all those in attendance already knew, both women had risen from the dead, and the revelation—greeted with a gasp—of the real fate of Abigail's corpse.

"Now I'm going to open the floor to questions and

comments," he said when he was done, wincing inwardly at what he knew was to come.

Jennie Mahoney stood immediately. "Jagger?"

"Yes, Jennie?"

"Frankly, I can tell by looking around that most of us are disturbed about your decision not to stake Abigail. Would you care to explain yourself?"

He took a deep breath. "When Abigail rose at the morgue, I was faced with a swift decision. She was a student, bright, sweet—raised by nuns. I chose not to end her existence."

"And what does Miss MacDonald say to that?" Jennie asked primly.

Fiona stood. "I was there," she said. "And I approved the decision."

"Really?" Jennie said, sounding doubtful. "I don't mean to find fault—"

"Then don't," Fiona said pleasantly.

Mateas Grenard stood up, and Jagger wondered what was coming next.

"I'm new to this community, so I don't know most of you yet," he said, addressing the room. "But the longer I'm here, the more amazed I am at how much a part of the city you are, not just as businesspeople, but in government and, of course—" he nodded toward Jagger "—in the police force. Which does make me wonder, Detective DeFarge, since you're in charge of the investigation, doesn't it concern you that you have to make a show of searching for a corpse you know doesn't exist when you should be searching for a murderer?"

"Of course. Obviously that's made my workload more difficult," Jagger said.

"Aren't you worried about bringing the city's suspicions down on us?" Grenard asked.

"I'm up to the challenge, I assure you. My top priority is finding the killer, not the corpse."

"What about Billy Harrington?" Jennie demanded.

"What about him?" Jagger asked.

"First, why isn't he here?"

"Because he's doing what I told him to do. He's staying in his room at the frat house and acting like a teenager who's depressed over losing a friend," Jagger said.

August Gaudin stood, clearing his throat apologetically. "Jagger, I believe that Jennie is hedging around something that must be said. We're suspicious. It's evident that Billy was very fond of this young woman. I believe that the natural question—question, not accusation—is whether the young man might have been fond enough of the young woman to want to make her his for eternity, whether she agreed or not."

The room fell silent, and Jagger was certain everyone was waiting for him to deny the possibility.

He didn't.

"We have certainly considered that theory," he said.

There was a murmur in the crowd.

"However…" Jagger lifted a hand and waited for the noise to die down. "However, in my position, I've learned to consider all the facts. Have we forgotten Tina Lawrence already? Billy was at the frat house, with witnesses, when Tina was murdered."

"He could have moved quickly, could have left and returned before anyone noticed he was gone," Mateas Grenard said quietly.

"Yes, he could have," Jagger conceded. "But he has no history of frequenting strip clubs, and he did—

does—feel a fondness for Abigail. It's doubtful that a man in love—human or vampire—would suddenly start spending time in a strip club. Additionally, as you all know, we found a witness who gave us a good description of a man who talked to Tina that night, though we have yet to find that man."

Jennie gasped indignantly. "Are you implying that he was a shapeshifter?"

Jagger spoke quickly and loudly before her words could sow dissension. "No, Jennie, I'm doing no such thing. I'm simply saying that all the evidence isn't in yet. And in fact, I expect help from this community that no one else can provide, because the rest of the world doesn't even know that we exist, much less what to look for. But I've also been a cop long enough to know that what we see is not always what it seems. Therefore, as we've all made a point of saying tonight, I'm not casting suspicion in any specific direction. We know the killer wasn't a human being, because both women rose. So yes, I'm saying the killer had to be either a vampire or a shapeshifter. An *individual* shapeshifter or vampire. And we *all* want that person apprehended—don't we, Jennie?"

Jennie opened her mouth, but she had to agree— she had just given a speech about doing exactly what he was asking—and after a moment of hesitation, she finally did.

Sean O'Casey suddenly stood.

"Sean?" Jagger said.

"I just want to add that peace is the most precious thing in the world. I come from a land that spent hundreds of years in battle. To this day we still fight prejudice—and the hatreds of the past. It's ugly. Innocents get hurt, and the good die with the bad. I pledge my support to you, Jagger. And so will everyone who's seeking the truth and wants to see this murderer caught."

Sean spoke softly, but the Old Country lilt in his voice commanded attention. When he finished, spontaneous applause broke out.

Beside him, Granny Caldwell stood. She was a tall woman, nearly as tall as Sean.

"This city of ours, it has magic. To this day it bears traces of both the shame and the beauty of the past, and life here is a mix of the old ways with the new. But we love our city and hold it dear in our hearts. We come from different places, and different histories run in our veins. I have prayed at the altar of my beliefs, and I'm here to say that I believe in the man who stands before us. The readings say he is a good man, a man who will seek the truth. The father of lies is at work among us now, and we need to learn to see through the forest of his deceptions. In your hearts, don't be angry. Be strong, and look for the truth and goodness that surround you."

She fell silent and looked around at the crowd, as if to emphasize her point.

"Thank you, as always, Granny Caldwell, for your support," Jagger said. He wanted to run over and kiss the old woman. She was as strong as an oak.

She nodded and pointed a finger at him. "There are many paths that lead to God. but the important thing to know is that God exists. And in this, as in so many things, He will have his say. I have seen things while in a trance, and I know that the day will come when the murderer is caught."

The room was eerily silent.

The killer is here among us, in this room, Jagger thought.

He could feel it. Feel the truth as if it were a palpable thing. He wished that he could see *who* with the same certainty, but he knew the killer was there, smiling, nodding, speaking to his neighbors, watching....

Laughing.

And maybe feeling the slightest hint of trepidation after Granny Caldwell's words.

It was time to end the assembly, he decided, but before he could speak, that option was taken away from him.

"Where is the young lady who's the newest addition to vampire society?" Mateas Grenard asked.

Jagger was surprised when David Du Lac rose from his chair to reply. "Why, she is here, of course. I am grooming her for her new role in life."

"How can we be sure that she will understand and obey the laws of our community?" August Gaudin asked quietly.

"Would you like to ask her that yourself?"

"Of course," Mateas Grenard said smoothly.

David looked at Jagger, who shrugged.

Fiona was still standing. She smiled and walked over to David, who took her arm. They went out together.

"What about this witness at the strip club?" a shapeshifter who was also a reporter called out. "Is she reliable?"

"I'm going on instinct here, but I believe she is," Jagger said. "What concerns me is that no one has admitted seeing the man she described."

"I hate to say it, but in the interest of being open-minded and catching the killer, that suggests a shapeshifter to me," shapeshifting cop Michael Shrine said. "The problem is, a shapeshifter can be anything or anyone, then choose never to appear in that guise again."

Jennie looked as if she was about to object when a sudden hush fell over the room, for the first time that night making it feel like the consecrated church it had once been.

David and Fiona were back, escorting Abigail, and the three of them were walking down what had once been an aisle toward the podium. Jagger backed away, staring at Abigail.

She had undergone a complete transformation. Her long blond hair was now short and curly and red, her blue eyes were hazel and she was dressed in the kind of suit a new MBA graduate would wear to look for a job in a bank. With heels, she appeared taller. The overall look was both cute—and oddly sophisticated, half gamine and half urban sophisticate.

"Ladies and gentlemen, I'd like to introduce Annie Du Lac, my niece, who will now be living in New Orleans and working at the club," David said.

"Hello," Annie, nee Abigail, said to the crowd. Though she appeared to be a little bit overwhelmed, she had a beautiful smile, and despite the touch of sophistication, there was still something—naive and sweet about her.

Someone in the crowd suddenly stood.

Valentina.

"Annie, is it?" Valentina said. Jagger was surprised to realize that David Du Lac had been keeping his plan for Abigail a secret from everyone, even his hostess. "Annie, how do we know that we can trust you? You'll be working with me. How do I know that you won't look at my throat—and decide you're hungry?"

"Oh, there's absolutely no fear of that," Annie said. "David has been a wonderful teacher. I know how to find nourishment when I'm hungry."

"Right," Valentina snapped. "Because kids are always such models of self-control."

Fiona stepped up to the microphone. "David and I have complete faith in Annie. She will still need day-to-day help and guidance in negotiating our world, of course, and, Valentina, she'll be looking to you, especially, since you'll be working together. I have no fear whatsoever that Annie will be violent. On the contrary—I worry that her soft heart may be her undoing, if she sees her former friends mourning her death and feels tempted to reassure them."

"I have a question," Mateas Grenard said.

"Yes?" Fiona asked.

"Abigail—Annie, did Billy Harrington kill you?" he asked bluntly.

Annie stepped to the microphone. "No. He most certainly did not."

"How do you know that?" Valentina demanded. "Did you see your killer?"

"No, I didn't," Annie admitted.

"Then how do you *know?*" Jennie Mahoney demanded.

"Because I know Billy," Annie said. "I know in my heart." She put a hand on her chest. "And the heart is more than an organ. It's a part of the soul, and I have a soul, and I know Billy does, too."

"You can't know any such thing," Mateas said with a sniff.

Fiona took back the microphone. "I think we should leave the solution of these murders to the police and move on to the purpose of this meeting, which is that every one of us needs to work, and work hard, to keep the peace. My parents died for the peace we've enjoyed for so many years. Why do you think they did that? Because they believed. They knew in their hearts that peace could exist. And now it's up to all of you to keep the peace, and I know you'll do it. My sisters and I learned well from our parents. They taught us about strength, about wisdom and mercy and most of all, they taught us about acceptance. And no, I'm not talking about being blind or naive and just ignoring problems and differences. I'm talking about working together. About relying on instinct, the instinct that lets us distinguish between good and evil—even in one of our own—and believe love. Trust me. My sisters and I *will* keep the peace."

Caitlin and Shauna stood, walked to the podium, joined Fiona.

The three of them joined hands.

"There *will* be peace," Fiona announced. "Prejudice and intolerance killed our parents, and we're not going to let those attitudes win. We can promise you two things. The killer will be found. And the peace will not be broken. As Granny Caldwell said, our city is magic. And we intend to keep it that way."

Chapter 11

Jagger was exhausted. He'd joined David after the meeting, staying to speak with those who wanted a word, and he felt disheartened.

One of the werewolves was certain the killer was the vampire down the street.

A vampire was certain it was his shapeshifter hairdresser.

He stayed, he listened, he carefully noted every complaint and tried each time to remind the accuser not to cast suspicion unless they had evidence. Because of course none of the accusers had anything approaching proof.

Of course, he realized he had his own suspicions. While he believed in Billy Harrington, the nagging knowledge that Billy did have a motive in the second slaying kept him in the picture as a suspect.

Mateas Grenard was a newcomer and seemed to have a hidden agenda.

And then…any shapeshifter out there.

It was nearly light when he made his way to the Mac-Donald house, and he realized he was so tired he could barely make the shift into the mist that would allow him to enter unnoticed.

He slipped into Fiona's bedroom and discovered that he was not the only one who was exhausted.

She was sound asleep, lying on one side of the bed, as if she'd been waiting for him but been unable to stay awake until he arrived.

He watched her sleep. Not even Abigail, as young and innocent as she was, had ever looked so beautiful, he thought. Fiona's hair was splayed out in a glorious golden halo around her perfect face. Her lips were slightly parted, moist and so tempting that he was drawn to touch them with his own.

But he didn't.

He didn't want to disturb her.

She was lying on her side, her arms around a pillow, partially covered by the drape of the sheet, the beauty of one long leg bared to his view.

He sat carefully on the side of the bed and shed his shoes and socks, jacket, gun and holster, then stood to discard the rest of his clothing. He lay quietly down beside her but kept his distance, propped on his elbow to watch her.

Just to watch her.

He was hopelessly infatuated, he realized.

No, this was far more than infatuation.

He took pleasure in watching her sleep, in watching her breathe.

A sudden chill shook him.

She was blonde, with immense blue eyes. She was beyond beautiful.

She was the exact type the killer seemed to like.

He'd been so busy debating the possibility of vampire vs. shapeshifter that he'd somehow managed to miss making that basic connection until now.

He moved closer to her, taking her gently into his arms. She stirred, and a murmur escaped her, but she didn't waken, though she seemed to know, in the depths of sleep, that he was there.

And she was content to be in his arms.

He suddenly knew that if she was ever threatened, he would not be a cop. He wouldn't even be a vampire. He would be a man who would defend her in any way he could, with his very last ounce of strength and being. He would die a thousand times for her, or follow her into eternity, if that was where she chose to lead.

Holding her close, he felt the beat of her heart.

He was afraid, and he was renewed.

And he knew he would move heaven and hell to end the evil that had entered their world.

Fiona awoke slowly, aware that she wasn't alone, and basking in the comfort of being exactly where she was, in the comfort of her bed.

And in the sheer heaven of Jagger's arms.

She had thought that he would come. She had waited.

But the day had been too long, and sleep had won out over her determination to stay awake.

She felt his arms tighten around her, and she opened her eyes slowly to find that he was watching her. She smiled slowly.

"You certainly make me hope I don't snore," she said.

He laughed. "If you snored, I'm sure the sound would be pure music."

She felt a surge of vitality fill her, and she rolled, casting off the covers, to straddle him. "Tell me it's still early," she whispered.

Without answering, he slid his hands up her torso. He cradled her nape, drawing her down to him, and their lips met in a liquid kiss. Before she knew it, he had shifted just slightly, arched, lifted her and brought her slowly back down over his erection, drawing her closer, filling her completely and igniting a wild and abandoned desire in her.

His whisper touched her ear. "I'm not sure if it's early or late, so…"

Then he moved.

And she moved.

And the world moved with them.

In minutes, the earth itself seemed to explode, and she fell against him, awed and dazzled, and wondering how she had lived without this, without the sound of his voice, without him so solidly in her world.

Her sheets felt softer, the sun shone brighter, than ever before….

He kissed her quickly and rose.

"Another day, and another reason to work quickly," he said huskily, then started toward the bathroom.

"Oh, no! I get the shower first…or too," she said, racing after him.

It was a mistake—or would have been, if she'd had any interest in getting an early start on the day.

She loved to shower.

She loved it so much more when he was there.

They made love again, slick with soap, luxuriating in the suds and water and steam.

But as he held her, steam rising around them like a cocoon, the spell was broken by a pounding on the door to the bedroom.

Fiona swore softly.

"It's Caitlin, I'm sure of it, and she doesn't accept the fact that we're together," Fiona told him, angry. Then she left Jagger in the bathroom and, wrapped in her towel, hurried to open her bedroom door.

It wasn't Caitlin. It was Shauna.

Her face was white, her expression tense.

"It's on the news. There's been another murder."

Once again, the corpse had been found in a cemetery just outside the French Quarter, no ID anywhere to be found.

The dead woman was wearing a long white nightgown, blond hair streaming around her face. Her flesh was cold, her skin as white as snow.

She was lying on a tomb in the middle of a family vault—the Taussant vault, this time. Her hands were folded over her chest.

She looked like an angel.

Jagger managed to get his team out of the vault long enough to find the telltale pricks, so small that not even Craig Dewey would notice. This time the killer had gone for the throat.

The jugular vein.

The kill had probably been quick; that might have been the only mercy.

He was standing there, staring at the corpse, when

Dewey walked in. The M.E. was silent for a minute, staring at the corpse.

"Another angel," he said softly.

"Well, I'm not sure Tina Lawrence was an angel," Jagger said, shaking his head. "And we don't know anything about this woman yet," he added wearily. "She could be a nun or the biggest bitch in the city, for all we know."

"I haven't touched her yet, but I can tell you the cause of death is going to be the same as the other two," Dewey said. "I'll get this one straight into autopsy."

Jagger nodded, feeling ill. Another death. It was on his head. He should have caught the killer by now.

"Thanks, Dewey," he said. "The sooner we check her prints, compare dental records, the sooner we'll know who she is."

"I'll get right on it," Dewey said. "I won't leave her for a minute."

"Think you can give me a time of death?" Jagger asked.

"Sure."

The girl was dead, but even so, Jagger turned away while the medical examiner opened her eyes, checked her limbs, gave the body a cursory examination and checked the corpse's temperature.

"She hasn't been dead long. I'd say she was killed around five this morning. Just before light," Dewey told him. "I think someone is really trying to make this vampire thing look real."

"So it seems," Jagger said. "Thanks, Dewey."

"I'll be opening her up in about two hours, if you want to meet me at the morgue."

"Thanks."

Jagger walked outside.

He'd searched the tomb and the cordoned-off area around it. The killer hadn't left behind a single clue.

He looked across the cemetery. Celia Larson and her crew were coming to comb the cemetery for footprints, for any small piece of trace evidence the killer might have left behind.

He already knew they weren't going to find anything.

"DeFarge, I would have thought you'd have put a stop to this by now," she said. "You know, the city will rise up in a panic soon. Maybe they already are."

"Thank you, Celia. I'm glad to be aware of your thoughts," he said flatly. He started to walk by her, but then returned.

"It would be helpful if I were getting more from my technical support team," he said.

Her eyes narrowed. "We've gone over everything with a magnifying glass," she snapped.

"No, you haven't."

"The killer hasn't left any clues! Not so much as a drop of blood, nothing with DNA, nothing anywhere! Not a single victim scratched her assailant or—"

"Celia, there *is* a clue."

"What?"

"The nightgowns."

She looked at him blankly.

"Celia, they've all been wearing white nightgowns, different, but basically the same. Or did you think they all went to bed in white nightgowns? Where's my report on the gowns?"

She turned away, her face red. "They were killed at night. We didn't think—"

"I need to know where those nightgowns were purchased. Can you get on that?"

"You should have asked before," she pointed out.

She was right. He should have.

He didn't reply but headed over to the cemetery gates. The press was gathering outside. He saw Gina, and gave her a nod, assuring her that he was coming out to speak.

First, though, he walked over to where Tony was talking with the "City of the Dead" tour guide who'd found the body. The man was about fifty, dressed in an official uniform and obviously shaken.

"I...I suppose I shouldn't have been so shocked. Not after the other two murders," the man was saying to Tony.

Tony saw Jagger and interrupted the guide to say, "Jagger, this is Arnie Offenbach. He found the corpse. He had five people in his tour group, but when he saw the open doorway to the tomb, he made them wait while he went to check. The door is solid brass, so he knew it hadn't just blown open."

"Mr. Offenbach, thank you for calling us in so quickly. And thank you for keeping the tourists away," Jagger said, feeling unutterably weary.

Offenbach nodded.

"Did you see anyone in the cemetery?" Jagger asked.

Offenbach shook his head. "No, another group was coming in, but they were behind me."

"Where is your group now?" Jagger asked.

Offenbach turned and pointed. There were two men—retirees, from the look of them, one white-haired, the other balding. Two older women, probably their wives, were sticking close to them. The heavier of the two women had seated herself on the low stone wall around another family vault. She was fanning herself vigorously with a guidebook. The fifth member of the party looked to be around twenty-five, and was carrying a camera and a notepad.

"Thank you, Mr. Offenbach," Jagger said, and walked over to join the tour group. He introduced himself, and met the Winstons and the Smiths from Calgary, Canada, and Sophie Preston, from New York City.

"Did any of you notice anyone in the cemetery when you got here, or maybe somebody leaving?" he asked.

"The officers already asked us that," Mr. Winston said. "I'm sorry, I didn't see anyone."

His wife shook her head. The Smiths solemnly did the same.

"I didn't see anyone in the cemetery," Sophie Preston said. "But there was a man walking down the sidewalk, heading toward Canal, when we arrived."

"Can you describe him for me?" Jagger asked.

She was thoughtful. "He was wearing a short-sleeved, tailored blue shirt and blue jeans. Dark hair. He was walking fast, like he was hurrying, and he was good-looking, I'd say thirty-five or forty."

"Muscular?"

"Um, tall. Yes, broad-shoulders, and…yes, I'd say he was muscular," she said.

The description could fit half the men in the city.

It certainly fit Mateas Grenard.

"Could you possibly come to the station and work with a sketch artist for me?" he asked her. "I realize that we're asking for your time, and that it will be an inconvenience, but we need your help."

"Of course, I'm more than happy to help," she assured him.

"Come to think of it, I noticed him, too. And she's right. He did seem to be in a hurry," Mr. Winston said.

"Perhaps you could help with the sketch," Jagger said.

"I'm willing, yes, sir, I'm willing, but I didn't see his face. All I can say is that he was tall, and that he had dark hair. Honest to God, sir, I'd love to help you, but all I can say is tall and dark haired."

Fiona was with her sisters in the shop when more news started to flow in about the most recent murder.

Shauna was their internet expert, and she had been Web surfing all morning, looking for information.

"No ID yet," she told her sisters. "Another blonde. Like us." She grimaced. "I wonder if the brunettes in the city are feeling safe?"

Fiona felt sick.

Of course every paranormal who'd stopped by that morning suspected a vampire. And that made her, as the vampires' Keeper, at fault. She had to find out what was happening. She had to stop this. It wasn't that she didn't have faith in Jagger, it was just that…

She suddenly realized that both of her sisters were staring at her. She was the oldest and the vampires' Keeper. She was supposed to have the answers.

As her parents had always had all the answers.

"If anyone asks for me, I'm heading back to the frat house to talk to Billy," she said.

Just as she grabbed her purse and started for the door, the little bells above it began to ring.

They had a customer.

"Thank God, child," Granny Caldwell said as she spotted Fiona and hurried over. "Thank God you're here."

"What is it?" Fiona asked, tempted to help the old woman over to a chair at one of the tea tables by the counter.

But Granny Caldwell was strong and proud—and she didn't like being helped. She had told them all often enough that when she was ready for help, she would certainly ask for it.

"I just had to see you, Fiona. All of you, really," Granny Caldwell said.

"I just came from Papa Joe's House of Voodoo—you know, down toward the CBD?"

They all knew Papa Joe. He was as beloved as Granny Caldwell, and he was as old as she was, too. He catered to the people who lived on the other side of Canal Street, near the Central Business District.

"Papa Joe is a brilliant man," Fiona said.

"Yes, that he is," Granny said. "Well, he put together a mojo sack, and he went into a trance, and he saw many of his ancestors there."

"And what did his ancestors tell him, Granny?" Fiona asked, as her sisters came closer to listen.

"They told him that we all have to keep thinking beyond what we see. The day can be beautiful—and then a storm strikes by night. He wants to be sure that you know this, Fiona. We are not of the underworld, we are among this world, Papa Joe and I, and you three straddle the two. Papa Joe says that he prays you will pay him heed. His ancestors have told him that you must look beyond the gloss of the picture to the substance beneath. He prays that you will believe in faith—that all paths lead to God—and that you will listen to an old man who knows that the world is not black-and-white, but many shades of gray."

Fiona gave the old woman a warm hug. "I will always pay heed to you and Papa Joe, as will my sisters. You are goodness made flesh, and we listen to goodness, no matter how it comes to us."

"Of course," Caitlin echoed passionately.

"You bet," Shauna assured the old woman.

"Now you must go," Granny Caldwell told Fiona. "You must listen, and you must look beneath. You must also remember that God sees the soul in all living things, though it is invisible to us. And one more thing. Remember that you know what you must do."

Fiona nodded. Because suddenly she *did* know what she had to do.

"There is nothing that fills me with greater sadness than to have to tell you that yes, we have another victim," Jagger said, meeting with the press that had gathered at the cemetery gates. "I can only beg the public again for help, and assure everyone that we will not rest until the killer is caught."

"There isn't anything you can tell us? No profile of the type of guy we should be looking out for?" a reporter called from the back of the pack.

"We have been in contact with profilers at the FBI," Jagger assured him.

"So what does the Blood Sucker profile look like?" another reporter called out.

"He wants to be a vampire," Jagger said, groaning inwardly at the nickname the press had given the killer. "And, most importantly, he wants the world to think he really is a vampire—to believe that he actually feeds on blood."

He had heard that just minutes before the press briefing, in a call from Jarrett Gilfoy, a senior agent at Quantico.

"How exactly are the victims killed?" Gina asked, thrusting a microphone toward him.

She had her job, he thought.

He had his.

And there was no way to avoid her questions or the answers they required.

"First, Gina—and all of you—right now this is an active investigation, and we all know that it's imperative that we catch the killer as quickly as possible. It would only encourage copycats if we were to tell you everything we know about the killer's methods."

Someone else called out a question about rape.

"No, none of the victims has been sexually molested," Jagger said.

"Why would a killer want people to think he's a vampire?" a reporter from an overseas news station asked next.

"Perhaps he wants the power credited to vampires," Jagger suggested. "That's really all I can give you at this minute."

"Apparently not!" a woman from a local radio station called shrilly. "The police haven't done a thing—and this is the third murder."

"I can only repeat that the police force is working overtime, because all of us are committed to finding the killer. As I've said before, we need your help and that of the public. We will continue combing the area for witnesses, and we need any clue, any sighting, *any-*

thing, you can give us. What we don't need are crank calls, because every second of manpower is necessary if we're going to find this killer before he strikes again."

"What about the man at the strip club before the first murder?" a woman in the back called out.

Jagger craned his neck, but he couldn't see who had spoken. "I'm afraid we've had no reports from anyone who might have seen him," Jagger said. "We *are* still looking, however."

"Is it possible that there are two killers?" someone else asked.

"Possible—but I sincerely doubt it," Jagger said.

He noticed Tony watching him from the edge of the crowd, looking irritated by the tone of the continuing questions.

But one thing Jagger had learned over the years was to keep his temper firmly in check and answer every question as calmly as he possibly could.

Finally he excused himself, and saw Tony snap to attention and run to get the car. Sophie Preston had already been taken to the police station to start working with a sketch artist.

When Jagger arrived at the station he discovered that they had already come up with a picture of the man she had seen outside the cemetery.

Mateas Grenard.

Chapter 12

Fiona loved going to church. She loved ritual and ceremony, and deeply believed in one God, though she also believed that there were indeed many paths that led to Him.

Her beliefs had never been put to a test up to this point, but the time had come.

She didn't head toward the cathedral on Jackson Square. Although it was a beautiful church and a place of worship despite its location in one of the city's most popular tourist destinations, she didn't want to be seen on her mission, and there were always too many people there.

Instead, she headed across Frenchman Street, toward the small church she had attended with her parents—and last visited after her parents had died.

Their funeral services had been performed there.

As she walked in, she wondered if she was crazy.

No, this would be fine, she told herself. She would see Father Maybury. He'd been close to her parents, and he must have known…something.

And if he wasn't there, then she hoped to manage a few moments alone so she could fill up several vials of holy water without being stopped.

Oh, God, what she wanted to do probably *was* crazy. Admittedly, she wasn't sure it would work, so she might be risking harm to an innocent, but something in her somehow knew that holy water could be the key.

Jagger knew how to deal with vampires. A stiletto-style stake, straight to the heart.

But she didn't want to start indiscriminately killing vampires.

She simply wanted to know the truth.

When she arrived, she found that the church was quiet. The lowering sun was shining gently through the gorgeous stained-glass windows portraying various saints and key events in the history of the church.

She walked down the aisle, heading toward the center of the room, where a large stone vessel stood, holding the blessed water.

So far, so good. She was safe, and she was alone.

But as she neared the holy water, she noticed a young priest come in from the apse. He crossed himself and genuflected as he faced the altar, then walked up to her, his smile welcoming. He appeared to be about thirty-five, a handsome man with dark hair and dark eyes. His demeanor was friendly, easy—it seemed to say that he was comfortable in his beliefs and comfortable in himself—and calming.

Which was good—she had begun to feel a sense of panic stealing over her. She'd wanted to get quickly in and out of the church, and if not, at least a visit with a man who might have understood…something.

Where was Father Maybury?

"Hello, and welcome," the young priest said to her. "Can I help you? You appear to be at a loss."

"I'm sorry. Is Father Maybury here?"

"I'm afraid that I'm the one who is sorry. Father Maybury died last fall," he told her.

She must have appeared stricken, she realized.

"May I get you some water? Would you like to sit down?" he asked.

"No, I just needed to see him," she said quietly. "And—well, obviously, I can't."

"Perhaps I can help you," he told her.

"I'm afraid it's an unusual problem," she said.

"Try me," he suggested.

"Father Maybury was…he was a personal friend," she explained. "He was close with my parents before their deaths."

"I see. I am so sorry. I'm Father DiCarlo, by the way."

"It's a pleasure, Father," she said, shaking his hand. He was watching her with eyes that seemed at ease, knowing eyes. She wasn't sure if she felt comforted or wary.

"You're Fiona MacDonald," he said.

She started, almost yanking her hand from his.

"I haven't been here since my parents died," she said. "And I don't believe you were here then."

"No, I wasn't. But Father Maybury was my mentor," he said.

She nodded, not sure what to say.

"It seems that you have questions," he said very quietly.

Fiona noticed that an elderly woman had entered the church. She knelt down at one of the back pews and was quickly immersed in prayer.

"Well…" Fiona murmured uncomfortably, looking in the direction of the newcomer.

He smiled. "That's Mrs. Sienna. She's quite deaf. But we can talk elsewhere, if you prefer."

She flushed. "Father, you do believe in good and in evil, don't you?"

"I am a priest," he said, smiling, his expression friendly and open.

"Those of good heart, no matter what their circumstance, are always welcome in church, isn't that right, Father?"

"Absolutely. All are welcome in God's house," he said. "But you know that."

I need to take several vials of holy water. Is that all right with you?

She just couldn't manage to spit out such words.

"I'm getting the feeling that you might want to be alone in God's house," he said. "You don't know me, and you don't trust me."

"Oh, no, I don't mistrust you," she said.

Though of course she did, she realized. There was no guarantee that everyone who came into God's house was good. History had proven that evil men were perfectly capable of using religion as a cover for their misdeeds.

He laughed, and she had the uneasy feeling that he was reading her mind.

But he was definitely human. She would have known, would have sensed it, if he belonged in the underworld.

"I think I'll go and say a word to Mrs. Sienna," he

said "Please, say whatever prayers you intended, in your own way."

"Thank you."

She smiled awkwardly at him and started to turn away.

"Fiona MacDonald," he said softly.

"Yes, Father?"

"Sometimes," he said, "it seems that no goodness exists in the world at all. We question why terrible things happen. And none of us has the answers. Then again, sometimes, when we think we're alone, we realize that we're not, and we're filled with tremendous strength when we suddenly discover the help that can come from opening ourselves to a greater power. I believe that we are given only the tasks we can manage—and that, if we ask, we will receive the help of good to vanquish evil. I'll leave you now, so you may do what you must. The city needs you, and I know you'll rise to whatever task is asked of you. Goodness is in the heart, and in the soul, and those who are evil are afraid of all that is good. Belief, not just in God but in one's self, can be one of the most powerful weapons known to man. Even the angels learned the importance of faith and belief."

She stared at him, a tremor rippling through her.

He knew. He would never admit that he knew, but he did. He was a man of faith, and his faith led to the belief that things existed that the eyes couldn't always see.

"Thank you," she whispered.

"Bless you, my child," he said softly, and turned away.

He knew, she was sure, that she had come for holy water. Was he telling her that it would work for the project that she had in mind?

"Thank you," she told him again.

"I'm always here," he assured her.

Somehow those words managed to impart some of his confidence to her. She had been afraid, she realized. She had never really been challenged—until now, when she was being challenged in so many ways. But now she realized that she could indeed take her place in the world, just as he would take his and be there for her.

As he smiled and moved away to speak with the elderly woman at the back of the church, she hurried forward with her vials to collect holy water.

"I think I've seen this guy," Tony Miro said, tapping a copy of the picture of a man's face, which had been copied and passed around. "Maybe in the market…maybe the Square. Somewhere."

Jagger, with the support of his chief and other key members of the task force, had decided against handing the likeness out to the media just yet. Witnesses had seen Grenard in the area where the latest body had been found, possibly leaving the cemetery, but there was no proof that the man had actually been *in* the cemetery, or that, if he had, he was guilty of murder.

Of course, Jagger, along with a few other members of the force, knew there was the best reason in the world that Mateas Grenard might have been guilty of behaving like a vampire.

Jagger wanted to find Grenard himself. If he *was* guilty, Grenard would never be willing to go to trial. If someone else attempted to arrest Grenard, they might find himself with at least one dead police officer, along with the three dead women.

"Listen," Jagger told Tony, "I'd like to start walking

through the tourist sections, see if I spot him. I need you to go talk to Celia Lawson."

Tony frowned at him. "Hey, two of us walking the streets would be better."

Jagger shook his head. "I want you to hound Celia until we find out where those white nightgowns were bought. And then I want you to take a trip back over to the college and check on everything there, find out if anyone has remembered anything about the night Abigail was killed. When you're done there, we'll meet back at that strip club—Barely, Barely, Barely. What I'm worried about is panic in the streets, so be careful when you're questioning people. Make sure it's clear that all we're looking for are witnesses. Oh, and if you find anyone resembling the sketch, call me immediately. Don't go after the man alone. I told everyone that when we handed out the sketch, and I mean it."

"All right. But don't run around thinking you have to protect me, Jagger. I'm a good cop," Tony told him.

"I never thought you were anything but," Jagger said.

Tony studied him, nodded and offered a tight smile. "I'm on it, then."

Jagger nodded. "I'm going to check in on the autopsy of the newest victim, and then I'll hit the streets."

It was the truth.

Almost.

He meant to be at the autopsy.

And he would be out on the streets.

Because he intended to find Mateas Grenard.

"It's Fiona. I need to talk to you," Fiona said, as soon as Billy answered his phone.

"I'm in class. Out in an hour," he said in return, his voice low.

"All right. Where?"

"Wait a minute! Is this about Abigail? She's all right, isn't she?" he asked anxiously.

She was officially dead, and now she was a vampire. If "all right" could be defined in such a way, then Abigail was all right.

"There's nothing wrong with Abigail. I just need to speak with you. I'm hoping you can help me, that's all," she said.

"Where?"

"The cemetery where they found the first body," Fiona said.

"Fiona, if there were any clues there that Jagger De-Farge missed, we won't find them," Billy said solemnly.

So innocent. But they had to look past what they saw on the surface. Or did they? Maybe everything was all exactly what it seemed. A vampire was committing the murders. Perhaps that vampire appeared to be honest and aboveboard, and *that* was the surface she needed to see past. There was still good reason to believe Billy was guilty, and that good reason even had a name: Abigail.

"Please, this is getting worse by the day. I'm afraid we'll have riots in the streets soon. And we all know that no matter how good a detective Jagger may be, we're not looking for a normal murderer, so normal police procedures don't apply," Fiona stressed.

"You *are* the Keeper," he said softly. "If you tell me to be somewhere, I'll be there."

They'd taken the dead girl's prints but so far there was no match on record.

She had died in the same manner as the others: exsanguination, though the manner was eluding everyone—except Jagger.

Eventually, of course, the marks would be found. But Jagger wasn't really afraid that the city would instantly start believing in vampires. Instead, they would start looking even more closely at the cults and the self-proclaimed vampires.

That day, feeling dread and pain unlike anything he had experienced in a very long time, Jagger watched while the beautiful blonde victim was autopsied on the sterile table in the sterile room, the scent of chemicals rising around them, barely hiding the natural release of body gases.

But none of those scents meant anything to him. Nor did it particularly bother him to watch the M.E. make the Y cut on the body, or listen to him drone on into the overhead voice recorder as he listed facts and figures on the healthy young organs, pristine liver—she hadn't been a drinker—clean lungs—she hadn't been a smoker—and perfect heart. Life had stretched ahead of her. She shouldn't have been dead. She should have been joining friends for coffee after work, or attending classes, meeting a lover...*living*. Somehow, this girl seemed to epitomize the tragedy and the loss present whenever life was stolen from one so young. He knew that professionally he should be keeping his emotions in check. Still, this hurt, almost as much as if he had known her. Or maybe she reminded him of Fiona, and that was why he felt the pain of her death more deeply.

He waited until Craig Dewey had finished, leaving his assistant to sew up the beautiful young woman who would never have a husband or children, never laugh or love again.

Craig shook his head. He had nothing new to offer.

Jagger knew that she was still a mystery woman, and that somewhere, a mother, father, lover, brother or friend was missing her, praying for her safe return.

Not knowing yet that she would never come home.

By day, New Orleans' cities of the dead were unusual places. They were sites of strange and twisted beauty, filled with unique vaults and monuments, their walls often lined with "oven"-style graves. Over the years, many tombs had collapsed, and on occasion neglect had interrupted the normal process of natural cremation in "a year and a day," leaving bleached pieces of bone lying atop crumbling masonry.

Not these days, of course. This was the modern world. Care was taken so that the living would not be offended by the dead.

And still…when the day came to an end, when the heat of the sun died away and the great orb began to fall toward the western horizon, the cemeteries were transformed by shadows from something spiritual into— something frightening.

Certainly some of the danger came from the living—those who prowled behind closed gates in to deal drugs—and worse.

Some originated in the mind, because in the darkness and the mist that came when rain and heat collided, monsters rose from the depths of the subconscious to haunt the night.

And some monsters were real.

Fiona arrived just before the gates were closed, and she knew where to hide when the guides urged the last of the day's visitors to leave.

She stood near the Grigsby tomb, watching as twi-light came. At first the light was gentle and beautiful. Soft pink rays falling on the serene faces of angels, wrenching the heart as the light darkened to mauve over a monument for a child, an infant sleeping peacefully by a lamb. Then the shadows came in earnest, transforming the mausoleums stretched out in awkward rows, here a grand vault from the eighteenth century, there a more modern mausoleum with touches of bronze. Some had broken windows, as if the dead had sought a way out, and some were still whole, with stained or etched glass windows, opaque, so no one could look in, and—more importantly—no one could look out.

As she was watching the light and the colors fade, she heard someone nearby. It was just a touch against stone, a whisper of movement in the air.

"Billy?" she said quietly, but no one responded. She decided she must have imagined it, so on edge that she was hearing things.

She slipped around the Grigsby tomb and hurried si-lently along a path that led toward a monument to the Italian workers in the city. She skirted the rusty iron-work fence and paused behind the monument, listening.

Nothing.

She checked her watch, certain that Billy was due any minute. Perhaps the noise *had* been Billy.

Perhaps he hadn't heard her call his name.

But then she heard something again, and this time it was like the rush of giant wings.

She headed for a grand marble mausoleum owned by a family named Tricliere. She saw that the door—which should have been tightly closed—was open, and she held very still, listening.

The sound of wings slicing the air came again.
Nearer.

She slipped past the slightly open gate in the rusting fence surrounding the small stone building, then into the mausoleum itself, steeling herself to see a corpse lying on a stone coffin in the center of the room.

There was no corpse. No newly deceased victim lying bloodless and still. The vault was old, probably one of the earliest in the cemetery. The mortar used to seal the vaults in the walls had long since crumbled away, and there were gaping dark holes where the bodies of the deceased had lain, and might lie again.

But now, in the darkness, she felt surrounded by the scent of the damp earth. Not death, just the smell of the earth itself, and the dust of the ages. And it *was* dark. Not a silent or complete darkness, for she could distantly hear the street sounds, unintelligible messages from the world of the living, and a tiny trickle of gray light seeped in through the broken, barred window at the rear of the vault.

Gray dust motes fell in gray air.

She heard the wings again, flapping just outside the mausoleum.

She didn't speak.

She slid into a broken vault, lying on the ash and bone shards of the last Triclieres to be buried there.

And then, just as she pressed herself more tightly against the wall, her hand falling on a broken skull, she heard a sound, and she winced.

The gate.

Creaking farther open.

And then she knew.

It had been a trap.

* * *

The city had changed so much over the decades, and yet in so many ways it had stayed the same.

Street names and numbers, old houses, awkwardly slanted second-story balconies, filigree and decoration…these were the same as they had always been. Modern storefronts punctuated rows of houses that, by night, looked no different from when they had been built, nearly two hundred years before.

Jagger hardly even noticed all that history as he walked quiet streets where frightened residents had holed up for the night, afraid of a killer who'd already claimed three victims. It had been easy for most residents to feel safe when the first victim had turned out to be a prostitute, but Abigail's death had ruined that illusion of safety. Still, he was certain that plenty of people were feeling safe for different reasons—they weren't female, for one. Or they weren't young. Or blonde.

Some might even have been happy, perhaps for the first time, not to be considered beautiful.

Still, most of the residents of the city were frightened. The most common theory was that some psycho who thought he was a vampire was on a killing spree, so what if he decided that he just desperately needed some blood? He might strike anyone then.

Even Bourbon Street was quiet—though far from shut down.

Walking along, Jagger tried calling Fiona's cell phone for the third time that night.

Once again, it went straight to voice mail.

He headed down toward Esplanade and David Du Lac's club, Underworld.

Walking the streets had done nothing. He had not

seen Mateas Grenard, Billy—or any other vampires who might have fallen under suspicion simply by being out and about. The only vampires he saw at all were those on the force, who were searching as diligently for the truth as he was himself.

Calling the morgue—where there was still no word on an identity for their latest victim—also brought him nothing but frustration. Tests for toxins, for semen, for fibers on the body, threads in the hair—had all revealed nothing of any use.

He was glad, at least, that he hadn't needed to worry about *being* at the morgue.

Sinner or saint, the latest victim was really, truly dead, not *undead,* thanks to the fact that all her organs—particularly the heart—had been removed in the course of the autopsy.

He was about to head toward the shop to talk to Fiona's sisters when his phone rang.

It was Tony Miro.

"I'm having trouble with the nightgowns. Celia told me that they're a cotton polyester blend—available at major department stores all around the parish and beyond. Even some of the boutiques carry them. I realized I couldn't cover the city by myself, so I have some of the men questioning sales people, too. It's like finding a needle in a haystack. Just at the mall across from Harrah's, they've sold twenty similar gowns in the last week, eighteen through credit card sales, and two for cash. Lord, Jagger, we don't even know how long ago the murderer bought them. He could have been planning ahead for these killings for months."

"I know, Tony, but you and the guys need to stick

with it. It's all we've got, and those officers have to be on the streets no matter what."

After the call, Jagger turned and headed toward the sisters' shop, but it was closed. He wasn't thrilled about heading to the house to talk to Caitlin and Shauna, but he had no choice. He could still see the beautiful blonde woman on the autopsy table, and he was growing edgier by the minute, even as he tried to tell himself that Fiona was a Keeper—that she had the power to keep herself safe.

The power to change.

The house was just down the street from the shop, but even as he started in that direction, his phone rang.

He was expecting Tony again.

But his hello was greeted with a second's silence.

"Hello?" he said again impatiently, and checked the caller ID.

The number was listed as "Unknown."

"Who is this?" he demanded.

"Good evening. Such impatience, Detective." The voice was hoarse and raspy, making it impossible for him to tell whether his caller was male or female. Someone was playing him.

And doing it well.

"May I help you?" he demanded.

"I was just wondering if you had noticed…how blonde and beautiful they are. I read the papers, and they're all blonde and beautiful."

"We're aware of that fact," he said, turning back toward Bourbon Street, searching for another officer—or anyone—whose phone he could nab and call in to the station to get a trace put on his phone.

But the caller was smart and knew what he was doing.

"Don't bother trying to trace this call, by the way. We won't be talking long enough. Just remember…blond, beautiful—and dead. Just like Miss Fiona MacDonald may be at this very moment. Just as she soon *will* be, I promise."

Jagger fought desperately to keep from throwing the phone away in denial, to keep from screaming at the speaker.

He didn't know if he had a quack on the phone—or the killer. If it was the killer, then he was talking either to a vampire or a shapeshifter. But Fiona was a Keeper. She had power…if she got the chance to use it.

If she didn't…

She was as vulnerable as any other beautiful young woman.

And if she trusted the killer, she wouldn't think to use her power until it was too late.

"Do you know something about the killings?" he asked, keeping his voice as low as possible.

He'd reached Bourbon Street and searched the crowd, knowing that a mounted patrolman should be within quick reach. All he needed was time, a minute, seconds…

Sean O'Casey, uniformed and on foot, was standing on the corner across the street. Jagger waved him over, and Sean instantly sprinted across the street.

The caller was chuckling softly.

Jagger covered the mouthpiece of his cell and silently mouthed the words, "Get a trace on my phone."

O'Casey nodded.

"Look, we've asked the public for help on these killings," Jagger said conversationally. "If you're willing to help us, if you know something, we'll be grateful for anything you can give us."

From the corner of his eye, Jagger could see that Sean was already on his phone, calling the station, asking them for a satellite trace.

"Oh, Detective, please. I can almost hear her screaming now." Then the chuckling started again, and before Jagger could respond, the phone went dead.

Chapter 13

The old, rusty iron gates were impossible to open, no matter how slowly and stealthily, without squealing.

The noise was like nails—talons!—against a blackboard.

Fiona held her position, praying she was hidden in the darkness, planning her next move and praying it would work.

She was certain the killer had found her, had known exactly where she would be and then had driven her into this dead end.

Because the killer was Billy?

She swallowed hard, waiting.

She was startled to hear shouting from out near the street. Someone calling her name.

The voice was far away, but thunderous.

The squeaking of the gate stopped.

"Fiona?" A different voice, closer, the tone quizzical.

She must have made a noise, because she heard the gate open noisily, and then the door swung wide.

"Fiona?"

It was Billy.

He homed in on her position, hidden in the vault, and came closer.

She was ready. She tossed the holy water into his face....

"What the hell did you do that for?" Billy demanded, wiping his face and obviously completely puzzled. "It's me—Billy. Hey, I just heard Jagger out there. What's going on?"

She stared at him from her hiding place, still hidden in darkness, incredulous that he hadn't screamed in pain, hadn't blistered hideously or turned to ash.

"Billy, did you see anyone out there?" she asked.

"No—I didn't even know you were in here until I heard the gate creaking a minute ago. I was over by the Grigsby mausoleum, waiting for you."

"Fiona!"

Jagger's voice was closer, and he sounded frantic.

"We're in here, Jagger!" Billy called, stepping out of the tomb.

The next thing Fiona knew, Jagger, as impressive as any action hero in the movies, was suddenly slamming open the door to the tomb. "Fiona!"

"I'm here. I'm fine."

Jagger turned to Billy, who lifted his arms in confusion. "What the hell is going on?"

Jagger turned to Fiona, puzzled himself. "What are you doing here? In that vault?"

Before she could reply, Jagger reached for her. She was glad that her remaining vials of holy water were shoved deep into the pockets of her jacket. He took her arms, and she slid to the floor, a plume of ash and dust coming with her.

He stared at her, searching her eyes, then he drew her close against him, shaking for a moment.

Then, suddenly angry, he pushed her away. "What were you doing in there?" he demanded.

"I was meeting Billy here," she murmured.

"Why were you meeting him? And in a tomb?"

"Just in the cemetery."

"And what are *you* doing here?"

He was silent for a long moment.

"Jagger?"

"I asked you a question you've yet to answer," he said firmly.

"I was meeting Billy because…"

Billy suddenly gasped. "You asked me to come here because you didn't believe me! You thought—oh, my God! You really thought I killed those girls. That I wanted Abigail so badly that I would not only kill her and make her a vampire so she could be with me for all eternity, but I'd kill two other women just to make it look like some demented serial killer was on the loose! And then…then you threw holy water on me."

"You threw holy water on him?" Jagger asked.

"Yes," she admitted. "But it didn't do anything." She smoothed back her hair, trying for dignity. It was difficult when she was covered in the ash of a long-dead Grigsby. "Don't you see? If it didn't burn him, he's not evil. He's not the killer. I don't know how I knew it would work that way, but I did."

"Fiona, do you know what kind of danger you could have been getting into?" Jagger demanded.

"I know how to take care of myself," she said. "I'm a Keeper, remember?"

"You're also human," Jagger reminded her.

She inhaled. "It made sense. Billy was a suspect. Now he's cleared."

Billy stared at her incredulously. "I can't believe you really thought I could be a murderer."

"You *are* a vampire," Fiona reminded him.

"I'm a civilized vampire," Billy said. "I'm—I'm a student. I'm American as apple pie."

"Billy, I'm sorry, but I had to know. It's—it's my job. I'm the Keeper," Fiona said.

"You may be the Keeper," Jagger said softly, "but you're in danger.

"Someone—and I think it was the killer—called me to make sure I know he intends to kill you."

"What?" Fiona and Billy asked in unison.

"Billy, give me your cell phone," Jagger said.

"Hey! It wasn't me. I'm a good guy, remember? She just proved it," Billy said.

"Billy, your phone," Jagger said.

Billy shook his head, reached into his pocket and produced his phone. Jagger took it and checked the call history.

"That the only phone you're carrying?" he demanded.

"Search me," Billy said, lifting his arms, then looked indignant when Jagger took him up on the offer and patted him down.

"I didn't call you," Billy said.

"All right. And neither of you saw anyone else in the cemetery?" Jagger demanded.

"No," Billy said.

"Someone else was here," Fiona admitted.

"What? And when were you going to tell me this? Who was it?" Jagger demanded.

"I don't know—I heard…noises, so I ran in here. And then I heard the gate creaking, but then you and Billy showed up, and whoever it was ran away," she said.

"It was the killer," Jagger said.

"How can you know that?" Fiona asked him, feeling even more uneasy than she had before, because instinct told her he was right.

The killer had been close. But she hadn't been helpless; she had been ready to fight. Even if the holy water had only been enough to wound but not kill, it would have bought her the time to turn, and that would have given her the strength to fight.

She shuddered, spooked by the knowledge that she was a target. She was the vampires' Keeper, and yet a creature was out there, ready, willing—no, eager—to kill her.

"I found Sean O'Casey on Bourbon Street, and we put a satellite trace on my phone. The killer hung up before we could pinpoint his location, but we were able to target this part of town, and given this case, I was sure he had to be in the cemetery." He took her by the shoulders and stared into her eyes. "Look, you've got to get out of here. Now. I don't want to have to explain your presence to the police. I'll just say it was a lead that didn't pan out, that if he was here, he got away. Fiona, please, go home and stay there. Billy, stay with her."

Fiona steeled herself mentally and drew herself up with all the dignity she could muster. "I am the Keeper," she reminded him. "This is my business as much as it's yours."

"Fiona," Jagger said, "I'm begging you, for everyone's sake, to take care, now more than ever. Please. Go home, and let Billy stay with you and your sisters until I can get there. This killer is after you. Somehow he knew you were meeting Billy here. He intended to catch you unawares. Please. You are responsible not only for us but *to* us—and in turn, *we* are responsible for *you*. I balance dangerously between a police force that has no idea we exist and the reality of what we are. I have to be here when backup arrives—and I have to be here alone."

With the situation put in that perspective, she felt like a fool, but she had no intention of betraying that fact.

"All right. Billy, let's go," she said.

"Of course," he agreed, nodding earnestly.

Together, they hurried out the door, and she and Billy headed away from the main gate. They could already hear sirens, and with the police arriving soon, they would have to scale a wall to get out.

A minute later, after leaping gently to the pavement, they hurried back into the French Quarter.

Looking at her, Billy laughed.

"What?"

"You look like a corpse."

"Thank you."

"No, you're all gray and dirty from hiding in that vault."

"Oh, that makes it so much better."

"I'm just hoping we don't meet anyone on the way back."

"Me, too. When we get there, you explain to my sisters while I hop in the shower, okay?"

"They won't suspect me, will they?" Billy asked.

She shook her head. "Not when you're with me," she promised, even though she was all too aware that Caitlin certainly seemed to hate Jagger. Maybe she just felt threatened by his close relationship with Fiona.

"It'll be fine—you'll explain, and I'll shower and try not to look like a corpse."

"Okay, deal. And then, perhaps…" Billy murmured as they walked.

"Perhaps what?" Fiona asked.

"Perhaps I could see her tonight?" he asked wistfully. "Abigail, I mean."

"Billy, David is working with her on her new identity," she reminded him.

He swallowed. "But her memorial is tomorrow. It will be a tough day for her. She might need a friend tonight," he said.

"Perhaps," she said softly, feeling suddenly very fond of Billy.

Someone out there was planning to kill her.

It wasn't Billy, and there were very few others she could be so certain about.

Tony Miro arrived in the first of the screeching police cars.

Jagger met him at the front gate, which had been opened by a representative of the church, as a number of other officers spilled from their cars.

"We need to get some floodlights and search the entire cemetery," Jagger said. "Someone was in here tonight, and we need to find him or at least whatever traces he left behind."

Police with portable floodlights went marching grimly into the cemetery. With three bodies so far, no one complained that it was a tedious task that would probably lead to nothing, as the other cemetery searches had.

But it didn't lead to nothing. They hadn't been there long before Sean O'Casey, who'd been among the first arrivals, shouted, drawing Jagger and a half dozen others to where he stood.

He was over by the Grigsby vault, hunched down by a gargoyle that guarded the family gates.

"What?" Jagger demanded.

"I haven't touched it," Sean said, pointing. "There!"

Jagger knelt down and saw that something was stuffed behind the stone monster.

Celia Larson and several of the crime-scene techs ran up just then. She pushed her way through the cluster of officers, shouting, "Damn it, don't go touching anything without gloves on!"

Jagger didn't have gloves, so he waited for Celia, who immediately reached behind the gargoyle.

"Damn," she said, looking at him, her eyes wide.

"What the hell is it?" Sean demanded.

"A nightgown. A white nightgown. Just like the others," Jagger said and stood. He felt sick, thinking how close Fiona had come to being a victim tonight, but he had to remain stoic. It was his job to keep the balance.

He was suddenly nothing less than desperate to be with Fiona.

But he was the lead investigator; he had to supervise the search for clues that was going on with such grim determination.

While the officers and techs continued to comb the cemetery, he put through a call to Fiona. When she answered her phone, his relief was limitless.

She and Billy were both at her house, and he spoke to Billy for a few minutes before hanging up, glad to hear that both Caitlin and Shauna were being courteous. They were all watching a comedy Shauna had rented, Billy reported. Yes, Fiona seemed ready to crawl the walls, but they had gone through the house, closing and locking windows and doors, and they were armed and ready in case of attack.

There wasn't going to be an attack on the house, Jagger was certain. But it didn't hurt that they were on the alert.

He thanked Billy and hung up, then called David Du Lac. It took a while to get him. Valentina answered the phone, her voice low and sultry as she questioned him, then explained that she would have to find David, implying that it could take some time.

Jagger suggested that he really needed her to hurry up.

Finally David came to the phone.

"David, have you seen Mateas Grenard?" Jagger asked without preamble.

"Grenard? No," David said. "He hasn't been around at all today. Pretty much no one has. The place is more than half-empty. People are getting scared."

"Yes," Jagger agreed. "And things will get worse if we don't find this guy."

"Why are you looking for Grenard? Do you actually suspect him? Personally I think the guy is all mouth," David said. "Mouth, not teeth."

"A witness gave the police artist a description of someone seen in the vicinity of the cemetery after the last murder. And that someone looked pretty much identical to Mateas Grenard," Jagger said. "So keep an eye out for him. And if you see him, call me. Immediately. All right?"

"Of course," David agreed. "Of course."

Jagger closed his phone and began to pace in front of the Grigsby tomb. It seemed forever ago that they had found the first victim.

Forever…and yet the murders had taken place in almost no time. If the killer kept up this pace, they were in serious trouble.

The nightgowns…the nightgowns were his only real clue.

And they had found one here tonight.

One intended for Fiona.

He could barely restrain himself while the team went through the cemetery. Finally they determined that they weren't going to discover anything else that night, so he said his goodbyes and left.

Forgetting his car, heedless of those around him, he slipped out the gate, around the corner of wall, turned to shadow and flew—like a bat out of hell—to Fiona's.

The mood was, beyond a doubt, tense.

When they heard someone knocking on the front door, all three sisters and Billy Harrington leaped from their chairs. Fiona wanted to kick herself for overreacting, then wondered why she cared, when the whole evening hadn't gone well. Caitlin and Shauna had been horrified by her appearance when she and Billy had walked into the house, and it had only gotten worse when they'd heard the story.

She had told them about her trip to the church, and the holy water, and that Billy had passed the test. After that they had tried to relax, watching a movie, even laughing on occasion.

They were still as tense as taut wire.

"It's just the door," Caitlin said.

"It's Jagger," Fiona said and hurried to answer.

"Don't open it without checking!" Caitlin warned, running after her.

Fiona paused, looking back at her reproachfully. "No, of course not," she said.

"Jagger doesn't need to knock, does he? He's been invited in," Caitlin reminded her.

"He would knock anyway," Fiona said. "He's polite, okay?"

She looked through the peephole, and it was indeed Jagger. She quickly let him in.

He didn't care about Caitlin standing there staring at him with ill-concealed hostility, as he pulled Fiona into his arms. He didn't do anything, though; he just held her. She could feel him trembling again, and she realized she'd been angry earlier when she should have been gratified.

He was afraid for her. As afraid as she had been in the tomb, hiding in the vault, hearing the gate creaking as it opened.

As afraid as she was now, because her parents had seemed all-powerful to her, and they'd had to use all that power and give up their lives to stop the violence that had broken out before, and now it was all up to her.

She held Jagger in return, drawing strength from him. She wasn't alone. She had her sisters…and she had Jagger.

Caitlin cleared her throat. "So now the killer is

threatening my sister. What's taking so long? Why haven't you found this monster?"

Jagger was still holding Fiona close, but she could tell from the sudden tension in him that he was staring at Caitlin.

Just as Billy and Shauna came running up, Jagger said, "I will find the killer, Caitlin."

Fiona looked up at him. "*We* will find the killer." She turned to Caitlin. "We'll find him. I swear it."

"Before the next victim dies?" Caitlin asked. Without waiting for an answer, she turned and headed for her own apartment.

"She's just scared," Shauna said, when Caitlin was gone.

Not to mention that she hated vampires and always had, Fiona thought.

Billy ignored the tension and turned to Jagger. "I'm so glad you're here and I can go. Jagger, please, I need to see Abigail. I mean, come on. It's not like I haven't been to Underworld often enough before. And there's going to be a memorial service for her tomorrow. She needs me," Billy said.

"I think it would be fine," Fiona said.

Jagger looked at her, and a small smile just barely lifted his lips.

"Fiona is the Keeper," he said. "If it's all right with her, it's all right with me. I'll call David and arrange it. Just make sure you're back in your room by morning."

"Of course," Billy assured him. "Of course."

"Just make sure everything is locked up, okay?" Shauna said. "I'm going to try to get some sleep."

"Good night," Fiona said.

"Good night. And don't worry. I'll make sure the door is locked and the house is safe," Jagger promised.

Shauna nodded and headed up the stairs. Jagger pulled out his phone and called David Du Lac, and in moments Billy was on his way out, a happy man.

When the house was locked, Fiona said, "I was afraid you weren't going to let Billy see Abigail."

"I couldn't stop him tonight," Jagger said.

"Because—you were going to defer power to me?" she asked.

"I never even had to think about it," Jagger said. "I knew how desperate I was to see you tonight, Fiona. And I couldn't deny Billy."

She walked back into his arms.

She wasn't sure how they made it up to her bedroom.

She only knew that in minutes her flesh was against his, and his hands were on her, drawing her close. There were intense moments in which he just held her, drawing her closer and closer, as if he could pull her underneath his skin and into his very being.

Then there were moments when all that was separate and distinct between them was erotically enhanced, when his lips found the most erogenous zones of her body, when his tongue teased. And then he thrust into her, and they came together in a flood of passion and urgency, writhed and arched together with a wild and abandoned need, then climaxed ecstatically, shuddering, holding on, holding in, cradling one another as they drifted down to the coolness of the sheets and the air around them.

That night Jagger didn't sleep. He lay, staring up at the ceiling, cradling her against him in the darkness.

"I have to find the killer," he said.

"*We* have to find the killer," she told him. "I told you that."

He shook his head. "Not anymore. I have to find the killer—before he finds you."

Jagger was awakened by his cell phone.

It was Tony Miro.

"Jagger, I think we know the store," Tony said excitedly.

Jagger frowned, still trying to blink sleep from his eyes. He seldom needed much sleep, but when he did sleep, it was deeply.

"The store?" he murmured now.

"Where the killer bought the nightgowns. Hey, where are you?"

"On my way in. What time is it?" Jagger asked.

"Ten-fifteen," Tony told him.

Jagger tried not to groan aloud. He'd overslept.

"Where are you—that's the question. I'll be right there."

"Ooh La La," Tony told him.

"What?"

"It's the name of a shop over on Royal Street. I'm not a hundred percent certain, but…just come on down here. You'll see what I mean."

"On my way."

Jagger leaped out of bed. Fiona was still sound asleep. Apparently her sisters had decided not to interrupt the two of them.

Maybe Shauna had said a good word, because Caitlin certainly wouldn't cut him any slack. She hated the fact that he was in the house.

After he showered and dressed quickly, he looked down at Fiona.

She made him tremble inwardly, constantly. He watched her sleeping, the gentle rise and fall of her breasts, the pulse at her throat. Her lips were slightly open as she hugged a pillow.

Her back was sleek and long, and every inch of her arresting and arousing. The golden spill of her hair would have stopped his heart if it still beat. He was ridiculously in love.

He pressed his lips against the gold of her hair, but she didn't waken.

He slipped out.

Afraid that if he waited longer, he would remember the killer's threat and be afraid to leave her side.

The sound of the phone was shattering, but Fiona tried to ignore it. She wanted to sleep and dream. She wanted to think of the future—of a vacation.

Time away.

Long days on a beach…

Mexico, the Caribbean. Texas or Florida. Anywhere…away.

Finally she gave in and answered. David Du Lac was on the other end of the line.

"Hey," he said tensely.

"Hey what?" she asked.

"He's here," David said.

"Um—who?" Fiona asked.

"Mateas. Mateas Grenard. Jagger thinks he may be involved in all this somehow, and he wanted to know if he showed up here. Well, he's here."

"Jagger isn't with me. Did you try his phone?" she asked.

"Yes, I don't know why he isn't answering," David said, sounding worried. "I'm not sure what to do."

"David, I'm on my way over," Fiona told him.

"Wait! If he's the killer…"

"It's daytime, I'm forewarned and you'll be there. And I'll try to get ahold of Jagger myself, so he can join us."

"All right," David said, sounding uncertain. "No, I'll try calling him again. You just get over here as quickly as you can. I don't like this."

Fiona said firmly, "Call Jagger's partner, and call the leprechaun—Sean O'Casey. One of them will find Jagger soon enough if he's not answering his own phone. And have some faith in me, okay? I am your Keeper, after all."

"I just don't want to lose you, kid," he said.

She smiled, though of course he couldn't see it. "Thanks. I'm going to call August Gaudin, too. It will look like friends meeting by chance for lunch. Oh, you should call Jennie Mahoney, too. All right?"

David agreed and hung up.

Fiona bounded out of bed and into the shower. As soon as she was dressed, she hurried downstairs. She found a note on the door from her sisters.

We're at the store. You stay home.

They had each signed it individually.

She left a note in return.

Love you two so much. Gone to David's.

After taping it on the door, she headed out.

Tony Miro was an excellent cop, even when given a tedious task. Jagger started off at a quick pace to meet him at Ooh La La.

The owner and shopkeeper, a woman of about thirty-five with the improbable name of Misty Mystique, was charming and determined to be helpful.

She was slim, blond, pretty—and worriedly talking to Tony when Jagger arrived, leaving her assistant to help the customers.

Tony introduced Misty and Jagger, explained that she carried all four nightgown styles they'd found so far and let Jagger take it from there.

"Did you sell the nightgowns yourself?" he asked. When she nodded, he said, "All to one person, or were they sold to several people?"

"Each one was sold to a different person," Misty told him, her dark brown eyes huge. "They were all men, though. Do you really think I sold one of those nightgowns to the killer?"

Jagger showed her the artist's renderings of Mateas Grenard and the unknown man from the strip club.

Her eyes widened farther.

"Yes! I sold one of the nightgowns to each of these men."

"What about the others? Please, this is very important. Can you remember what they looked like? Did they pay cash, or do you have the credit card receipts?" Jagger asked.

"How odd. Every one was sold for cash," Misty told him.

"Is it possible for you to leave the store?" he asked her. "I know I'm asking a lot, but perhaps you could help our artist create sketches of the other two customers."

"Yes, of course. Except that I'm afraid to leave Lilly alone these days," she said quietly, nodding toward her assistant.

The girl was perhaps twenty-five, pretty.

And blond.

"We'll call in an officer to keep an eye on her," Jagger promised.

"But if a cop just hangs around in here, I'm not sure I'll get any customers," she said, then sighed. "This is so terrible. Everyone is afraid and tourism is down—and I want to be smart, but I don't want to go out of business."

"Don't worry—he'll just be out on the street, in plain clothes, watching the store but not getting in the way or drawing any attention himself," Jagger assured her.

Misty agreed, so Jagger put through a call and arranged for Michael Shrine, one of the best cops and most trustworthy shapeshifters of Jagger's acquaintance, to take the assignment—and use a few of his "talents" while he was at it.

Michael could stand guard all day—and no one would ever know he was out there the whole time, much less that he was a cop.

As soon as Michael got there, Jagger, Tony and Misty headed down to the station.

It took about a couple of hours, but at the end he had a very curious bunch of sketches.

First there were the two they already had: Mateas Grenard and the unknown man from the strip club.

The third drawing was of Billy Harrington.

The fourth was of David Du Lac.

Chapter 14

Valentina was standing at the hostess desk. The luncheon courtyard had only just opened when Fiona arrived, but already Valentina was guarding her stand with buxom majesty.

"Good morning," Fiona told her. "David is expecting me."

Valentina arched a brow with royal disdain. "I don't believe so."

"I spoke to him earlier. I assurc you, he's expecting me," Fiona said and stared hard at the other woman.

Valentina's eyes fell. "Look, maybe he *was* expecting you, but if so, he didn't tell me. And he left around half an hour ago, muttering something under his breath."

Had something happened? If so, Fiona wondered, why hadn't he called her? She checked her cell phone for missed calls. Damn! His number was listed.

"What about Mateas Grenard?" she asked.

Valentina waved a hand in the air. "I don't know. He comes here…sometimes."

"What about now?" Fiona asked. "Is he here now?"

Valentina wrinkled her nose. "So good-looking," she murmured. "But…a vampire. The vampires come and go as they please."

"All right, I'll try again. Have you seen him since you got here today?" Fiona asked.

Valentina gave it some thought. "No, I do not believe I have. But the vampires often go straight into the main room." Suddenly Valentina smiled sunnily.

"August Gaudin is here—with Jennie Mahoney," she offered.

Fiona decided that maybe Valentina was more than a shapeshifter.

She had to be a schizophrenic, as well. She was nice one minute, haughty the next.

Fiona looked out toward the courtyard and saw Jennie Mahoney and August Gaudin chatting away.

"Thanks. I'll join them," Fiona said, deciding that would be safer than checking the main room of the club, the massive core of the old church, on her own. "Did you catch anything David was saying? Do you have any idea where he went?"

Valentina shrugged. "No, but I'm sure he'll be back. I think August and Jennie were expecting him, too."

Fiona walked past Valentina and headed for the small table where the werewolf and the shapeshifter were sitting, deep in conversation.

"Morning," she said.

They both looked up.

"Ah, Fiona!" August said, and, ever the gentleman, he rose.

Jennie offered her a smile that wasn't much warmer than Valentina's usual attitude.

Fiona accepted the chair August drew out for her. "Lovely to see you both."

"We're a bit perplexed, but now that you're here, maybe you can clear things up. You and David called us, asking us to lunch, but he isn't here," August told her.

"Something needs to be done," Jennie said firmly. "Three murders now. One corpse missing. And the police still don't have an ID on the last victim."

"They're doing everything possible," Fiona said, knowing she sounded defensive. Too bad. She *was* defensive. Jagger DeFarge was working nonstop—as a vampire *and* as a policeman. She found herself leaning forward. "Jennie, you know that the police don't have a prayer of solving this case, but Jagger is doing everything he can. As to not putting a name to the latest victim, that's…that's not that unusual. Her prints aren't in any system. She doesn't match the description of any missing women. And you know damned well where that 'missing' corpse is."

"Yes," Jennie said primly, wrinkling her nose. "She is another vampire—despite all our unspoken agreements."

"Abigail will be an asset to our community and… you know it," Fiona said.

Jennie shook her head and sighed. "I'm sorry, Fiona. It's a terrible situation, and even I can't help but be afraid. And please forgive me for saying this, but it does seem as if vampire society is having trouble managing its own."

"We're managing just fine," Fiona said, deciding not

to argue the point that no one had yet ruled out the possibility of the killer being a shapeshifter. She rose.

"Aren't you going to wait for David?" August asked her.

"I'm going to find David," she said.

And Mateas Grenard, she added silently. There was no reason to tell Jennie and August her suspicions. The lynch-mob mentality could take root as easily among the inhabitants of the underworld as among the humans.

"All right," August told her. He pulled out his old pocket watch and checked the time. "I'll wait awhile longer—might as well have lunch while I'm here—so call me if you find him. I have a meeting with the tourism board this afternoon," he said, grimacing. "Anything positive to tell them will be most welcome."

"I'll stay for lunch, as well, and then my poetry group is meeting," Jennie said. "So please call me, too, if you find out anything—if you find David."

"Yes, of course," Fiona said and smiled.

She left the courtyard and the club and started down the street, then found a dark alley and…changed.

She was mist, had substance but not. She could move with the air, with the breeze. She was a cloud, she was a shadow and, like both, she could become an illusion that teased at the senses but passed otherwise unnoticed.

She reentered the club and slipped unseen into the body of the church.

By day it was an oddly haunted place, even more Gothic than it seemed by night. In the evening and into the wee hours, music throbbed in the air, and the beat itself could be felt in the walls. Patrons danced, drank and laughed. Men and women flirted—and more—with each other, or with their own sex. Everyone was welcome, everyone was accepted. Colors, religions, sexes, sexual orientations, old and young. Everybody came to play. Laughter was a melody that complemented the melody of the music.

Now the huge room was empty.

The massive stained-glass windows let in a whisper of light broken into a myriad of colors.

Medieval and Victorian art lined the walls.

St. George regally sat his horse and stared down at the dragon in its death throes.

The old stone of the deconsecrated church kept the heat of the city at bay and created an aura of time gone by. The place had an atmosphere all its own.

Bodies had once been buried beneath the floor, and some of the headstones that were set between the marble pavers were still legible. All the bodies should have been removed and taken to one of the local cemeteries, but politics and money were always a factor, and some had been left behind. Now the place was silent and steeped in a potent brew made up of the combined energies of the living and the dead.

Fiona stood still, *feeling* the space. She looked around and saw no one, but there were side altars, and nooks and crannies, a choir loft behind what had once been the high altar.

She sensed that she was not alone. But she was ready, waiting and wary.

"Fiona?"

It was Billy Harrington's voice, calling to her softly from the shadows surrounding the choir loft.

She didn't answer, and he stepped out, holding hands with Abigail.

He looked even more afraid than she had felt, and she let out a silent sigh of relief.

"Billy, are you alone here—you and Abigail?"

"Yes."

"Do you know where David is?" she asked.

"No," Billy said, puzzled. "He isn't here?"

"No, and he was supposed to meet me," Fiona told him.

Billy looked at Abigail. "We saw him at breakfast," she said.

"Do you think he might have gone to my memorial service?"

"Abigail wanted to go. I convinced her that she couldn't," Billy said.

"You definitely shouldn't be there," Fiona said. "I'm sorry."

"I—I suppose it's better this way," Abigail said. She wore a look of indelible sadness. "I'd want to comfort the nuns. I'd want to tell them that I was really all right, that things would be okay."

"Precisely," Fiona said softly. "Won't people be surprised that you're not there?" she asked Billy.

"They'll understand that I couldn't bear it," he said, looking at Abigail with such adoration that Fiona wondered how she had ever doubted the boy. He would have died a thousand times over rather than do the slightest harm to her.

"I think I'll go over to your memorial, though," Fiona said. "Where is it being held?"

When Billy told her, she realized that it was the same church where the service for her parents had been held, and where she had just gotten the holy water.

She imagined that she knew just which priest was reading the service.

David might have gone—but if so, why hadn't he left her a message about his change of plans?

"All right, you two stay low—and I mean low," Fiona said.

"We're staying right here—we're not budging," Billy assured her.

Fiona changed, drawing a little gasp from Abigail, who whispered to Billy, "She's so good. She's a human being, but she has such power...."

"Well, of course," Billy replied. "She's the Keeper."

Fiona wished she felt as powerful as Abigail thought she was.

Still, it was good that others saw her that way. In fact, it was crucial that they did.

She slipped away from the deconsecrated church.

In an alley, she found her substance again.

She decided to hail a cab and get to the memorial as quickly as she could. On the way, she tried calling David again, but he didn't answer.

The driver let her off right in front of the church. Mourners were walking in slowly, some chatting softly, others quiet and thoughtful.

She saw a number of the students she had interviewed, along with what could have passed for a flock of very tall penguins. Every nun in the city must be attending, she thought.

She started to head in herself, but as she did so, her cell phone rang. Quickly, without even looking at caller ID, she answered, "David?"

There was silence, then a husky laugh.

"Is it true that blondes have more fun?" a raspy voice asked.

She froze, certain that the murderer was on the phone.

"I *will* find you. And I *will* destroy you," she said.

"This city was founded by the French, ruled by the Spanish, and peopled by those of all colors and faiths—along with all kinds of creatures, of course. Like vampires. Drinkers of blood. Killers."

"Men kill, too, but they don't have to, and neither do vampires."

"Ah, that's where you're terribly wrong! Man loves to kill. And vampires long not only to kill but to possess, to capture a beauty and watch her eyes as they consume her blood and her life drifts away."

"You're sick," she said, realizing with a nauseous feeling that the killer was a vampire. One of hers gone over to the side of darkness and death.

That husky laughter that seemed to slip right beneath her skin sounded in her ear again.

"Then there were three. Three little Keepers, and all of them blond. I'm watching you right now. And you should know—I have a little blonde beauty. She's not you, but she's so like you. She isn't dead yet, but she will be soon. When we hang up, you will close your phone. You will start walking back toward the French Quarter, and you will keep walking. If anyone calls, you will not answer your phone, because I will be watching you all the way. Will it be a long walk, you ask? Yes, it will. But if I see you reach for your phone, if I see you so much as say hello to a stranger, I will kill your sister before you can reach your destination. Do you understand?"

Fiona felt as if she had been stabbed through the heart with an icicle.

Caitlin.

Shauna.

Oh, God.

Who did he have?

How could he possibly have gotten to either one of them?

Maybe he didn't have one of her sisters. Maybe it was a bluff.

How could she take that chance?

She looked at the church. David might well be there. Jagger, too. So close, and yet…

"Do you understand?"

"Where am I going?"

"I'll call you when you're closer."

"I thought I wasn't supposed to answer my phone."

"I can see you. I will see you all the way there. It will ring once, stop and then start to ring again. Then, only then, do you answer your phone."

"If you're following me, you can't be holding one of my sisters hostage," she said.

The laughter sounded again.

"Whatever made you think I was working alone?"

Fiona wasn't answering her phone again, but today Jagger had no intention of wasting any time. A storm was rolling in, bringing early winter darkness and rain. He wanted to be back with her before the darkness came.

He called the shop. "This is Jagger. Where is Fiona?" he asked without even trying to figure out which sister he was talking to.

"We left her sleeping at home."

"She's not answering her phone," Jagger said.

"Oh, Lord, I'll have to close up shop."

"I'm sorry," he said flatly, "but is this Shauna or Caitlin?"

"Shauna. Caitlin went out. August Gaudin called, something about a meeting with the tourism board. Said he was looking for Fiona, too, and Caitlin said she'd go talk to him. Personally I think it was my place to go. I'm the Keeper for the werewolves, after all."

"You're alone at the shop, and Caitlin is out?" he asked.

He wasn't sure why that worried him so much. He trusted August Gaudin. Or did he? Did he trust anyone anymore?

"You stay where you are—and while you're at it, stay up front, where people can see you. I'm not far, just at the station, and I'm on my way. I'll go to the house with you," Jagger said.

"All right. But…Fiona's probably just sleeping and didn't hear the phone. What do you think is the matter?"

"I don't know. Maybe nothing. Just wait for me."

"I'll be here, Jagger," Shauna said. "For whatever it's worth, I believe in you. I know you're doing your best."

"Thanks," he said and hung up.

He hit the street and started walking, but by the time he hit Royal Street, he was running.

It was a long walk. Visitors to New Orleans had a tendency to stay in the French Quarter, where they could walk to anything. If they were headed to the Garden District or Uptown, they were usually bright enough to drive, grab a streetcar or take a taxi, options that were forbidden to her.

Her phone rang half a dozen times.

She didn't touch it.

He had said, *Whatever made you think I was working alone?*

He could have a partner. And his partner could have one of her sisters while he was watching her.

Or he could be lying.

She didn't know which.

She looked up at the sky. Clouds were roiling above her, and it was growing darker by the minute. A breeze had picked up, and as she walked, the trees were being stripped of leaves. In the wind, they seemed to reach down for her as if they had bony, skeletal arms and fingers. The sound of the rustling leaves was like the laughter of the man who had called her.

Darkness was coming.

The killer wanted darkness. The false darkness of a storm, fading to the ebony blackness of a moonless night.

Her fingers twitched on her phone.

He might be bluffing.

But he might not be.

Caitlin…Shauna…

She couldn't take a chance.

As she got closer and closer to the French Quarter, she felt the shadows darkening around her and began to imagine she heard the whoosh of wings.

Giant wings.

Shadow wings.

Following her.

She had to come up with a plan.

And she had to save her sister.

Those two thoughts kept her moving.

And all the while, the shadows were darkening.

Shauna was standing right inside the doorway of the shop, waiting for him. She was ready with a sign for the door: *Must close early—our deepest apologies. Please come back.*

He nodded to her as she locked up and they started down the street.

"Thanks for coming with me," he said.

She glanced at him sidewise. "Are you kidding? I'm losing my mind. Neither one of them is answering her cell phone!"

"Caitlin isn't answering, either?"

"No," Shauna said. Her face was white with worry.

He pulled out his cell phone and called August Gaudin. A secretary answered.

"May I speak with August, please? This is Jagger DeFarge."

"Oh, Detective. I'm so sorry. He left—he said something about lunch, and then he had a meeting to attend."

"This is his cell phone, isn't it?" Jagger asked, perplexed.

"Yes, yes—he's a brilliant man, but forgetful. He left it on his desk. I just heard it ringing because I was dropping off some papers that needed to be signed," the secretary said.

"I see. Well, if he comes in, please ask him to call me," Jagger said.

Shauna looked worried. "He's not there?"

"It's all right. We'll get to the house, see if we can

find out where Fiona went and then I'll get my men looking for both of them," he promised her.

She stared at him with huge eyes. "But they won't know what they're looking for."

"Shauna, there are...*others*—on the force. We'll find them."

They reached the house. As soon as they went in and closed the door, they found the note Fiona had left.

Jagger swore softly.

As he did, his phone rang.

He answered it crisply, praying it was Fiona.

It was Sean O'Casey, and his voice was excited.

"I've been going through the FBI database, and I got a hit, Jagger. I just got a hit."

"On what? The last victim?"

"No, the sketch of the man at the strip club. The guy no one has been able to find. And you're never going to believe who he is."

The rain was just waiting to fall.

The clouds were growing oppressive, and Fiona knew it would be sweltering if not for the strange breeze blowing through the trees.

Streetlamps, whose sensors told them to turn on when darkness fell, began to light up, but their illumination seemed oddly weak, creating only small pools of brightness against the shadows.

She could change, she reminded herself.

And she was still armed. She felt surreptitiously for the holy water in her pocket.

It didn't matter if a creature was Jewish, Hindu, Christian or worshipped aliens—any touch of the one true goodness that ruled all religions would work against any personification of evil.

Or so she believed...

She had to trust in that belief. Power lay in belief, and most of all, she knew, she had to believe in herself.

Leaves rustled.

And the growing darkness seemed to become one massive shadow, hovering over her.

Her phone rang once. Stopped. And rang again.

She answered.

"Know where you're going yet?"

"No."

"Then I'll tell you. There's a cemetery near the Quarter where they haven't yet found a beautiful blonde. I'm sure you know which one. There is a mausoleum there, one I know you know—well."

Her heart seemed to stop.

She knew exactly what he was referring to.

"It's quite a glorious memorial, large and magnificent, with rows of crypts, and a massive sarcophagus right in the middle holding two Keepers not long gone. Have you figured out what I'm talking about yet?"

"Of course I have," she said, praying that she could keep her tone flat and dry. "Obviously."

That wretched laughter sounded again.

"Where else to find a beautiful blonde MacDonald than atop a MacDonald tomb? Move quickly," the voice added harshly. "Time is everything now."

"Thomas Anderson," Sean O'Casey said.

Jagger blinked and waited. When Sean didn't explain, Jagger asked, "Am I supposed to recognize the name?"

"Yes. Well, maybe. He was a serial killer who preyed on women here—in the 1940s."

"The 1940s? He'd be way too old," Jagger said. "Can't be the same man."

"Get this—he was killed in 1949, hanged by the neck until dead," Sean said.

So a ghost had been haunting the strip club.

Or the man had been hanged by the neck until dead—but bitten by a vampire while no one was looking?

Or…the man in the strip club had been a shapeshifter. But was he also their killer?

"Okay, Sean, thank you. I need you to get over here to the MacDonald house and stay with Shauna Mac-Donald."

"I'm on it."

"What?" Shauna protested. "Wherever you're going, I'm going with you."

"No," he told her.

"Hey, I'm not a damsel in distress—I'm a Keeper. I can turn into a wolf with massive teeth and long, long claws whenever I desire."

"Shauna, if anything happens, you have to survive. Do you understand? One of us has to be here to—to be the one to pick up the pieces if I don't manage to…"

"Don't you dare say it! My sisters have to be all right."

"Shauna, I'm begging you—it's imperative that we all think logically right now, and I need you here. What if I need help? I need to know there's someone I can reach."

"You better not be patronizing me," Shauna told him.

"I'm not. Sean O'Casey is coming over and—"

"I don't need police protection."

"He's a leprechaun—" Jagger began.

"A leprechaun?" Shauna asked, frowning fiercely. "You have a *leprechaun* coming to watch over me?"

"He's one of my best, trust me," Jagger said.

"A *leprechaun?*" she said again.

Just then there was a pounding on the door. He checked the peephole, then threw the door open and let Sean in.

Shauna stared at Sean O'Casey, then at Jagger.

"He's a *leprechaun?*" she demanded.

"It's the hormones in the milk," Sean said wearily. "Shauna, I know who you are—I saw you at the assembly. Please, I know your capabilities. Have some faith in mine."

She turned back to Jagger, shaking her head. "At least he's a very good-looking leprechaun."

"We're all good-looking. We just don't tend to be tall," Sean assured her.

They would be fine together, Jagger decided, as he paused in the doorway. "Hang on to your cell phones, and be ready to go wherever I send you whenever you get a call."

"Whatever you say, sir," Sean promised.

Shauna nodded, and Jagger was on his way.

The gates to the cemetery were still open.

Fiona walked in, aware of the chill tendrils of the growing breeze at her nape, aware of the shadows taking shapes between the monuments and mausoleums.

The family vault was toward the far end, where once things had been pristine and beautiful, but where time and the elements had led to corrosion and decay. She and her sisters kept up the MacDonald tomb, but many of the surrounding families were long gone, and the three of them couldn't maintain everything that should have been maintained.

She walked over weeds and stones, and wove through broken bits of funerary art, past a row of fine vaults and toward a towering angel.

Past the angel, she reached an expanse of grass that led toward the family tomb.

And someone was standing there, waiting.

David Du Lac.

Jagger headed straight to Underworld.

Valentina was at the hostess stand, but he didn't bother to stop and speak with her. He strode straight into the courtyard, looking around. When he didn't see David, he turned and headed for the main room, bursting through the double doors.

Valentina came running up behind him. "What are you doing, Jagger?"

"Where's Fiona?"

Valentina shook her head. "She was here around lunchtime, but she left hours ago."

"I want to see David. Or Mateas Grenard. Is either of them here?"

"Mateas Grenard is here right now," a voice boomed.

The man rose from a shadowed table against the wall and strode toward Jagger. "What is it? Why are you looking for me?"

Jagger drew a copy of the sketch artist's rendering from his pocket.

"You were seen leaving the cemetery immediately before the third murder was discovered. And now I can't find Fiona MacDonald—or her sister. So you will talk to me, and talk quickly, or—"

"I was never anywhere near that cemetery!" Grenard interrupted in protest.

"You also purchased a nightgown like the ones worn by the victims in all three murders," Jagger said.

"I've *never* bought a nightgown," Mateas protested.

Jagger reached into the lining of his jacket for the stake he carried at all times.

"You've spoken against our ways," Jagger said softly.

"So what? I'm innocent!" Mateas cried. He started to bare his teeth, his fangs growing, saliva dripping from them. "Where is your law?" he asked. "I'm innocent."

Jagger felt his own fangs growing, felt the fury begin to ripple through him.

Fury born of fear. Fear for Fiona.

"Stop, please!" a voice interrupted.

It was Abigail. Or Anne, as she was now called. She rushed forward, holding Billy's hand and dragging him with her. "Please, stop!" she said. "I don't know what's been going on today, but Mateas has been here with us for hours. He's been teaching me all kinds of history, and how to behave and things I need to know."

"She's telling the truth," Billy said.

Jagger's phone rang. This time it was Tony Miro.

Apparently Tony had taken over the database search when Sean left to stay with Shauna.

"Hey, boss. I went further on that dead-guy thing— you know, the murderer who died in the forties. He wasn't just hanged. Folks in the city were crazy. They dug him up right after he was buried and chopped him into pieces. He wasn't walking around this city in any way, shape or form—not unless he had a doppelgänger of some kind. Sorry, boss, wish I could be more helpful. Says he died without children, so this has to be some kind of a fluke. I'm sorry."

"Don't be sorry, Tony. You might just have given me exactly what I need."

Jagger snapped the phone shut and headed straight to the hostess station. He didn't see Valentina, but he did see her friend Sue.

He walked up to Sue and took her by the arm. "That was you before, wasn't it?" he said.

She flushed. "So what? Valentina just wanted some time off, so she asked me to cover for her. But there's this really cute guy over there, so…I wanted to see if he would like *me*."

He didn't reply. He was already halfway back to the church.

"Billy, you stay put with Abigail. Mateas, you come with me."

"Where are we going?"

"Where are the bodies found?" Jagger asked.

"In cemeteries," Mateas said. "But…which cemetery?"

"I think he's taken at least one MacDonald, so we're heading to the MacDonald vault."

"David," Fiona said. "It was you? I don't believe it."

"You don't believe what?" he asked. "That one of your precious vampires was a murderer? That you weren't in control? Well, believe it. Now it's up to you. Pick. I can kill you—or I can kill your sister."

"Or I can kill you," she said.

David shrugged. "Caitlin is not alone. She has supposedly been out all afternoon—with August Gaudin.

But August is really in a meeting, and Caitlin —well, one bump on the head and…let's just say she's a bit tied up right now. So here, you see, is the problem. Either Caitlin goes free or you do. Either way, it's such a beautiful ending. Your precious sainted parents expended the last of their strength to stop the fighting. Now one of you will die on their tomb, and the races will go to war again over the evil of the vampires."

"Take me to Caitlin," Fiona said.

"Lift your arms," David said.

"I have no stakes on me," she said, lifting her arms as directed. She had to pray he wouldn't notice the little vials in her pocket.

"Jagger will be here to save me," she said.

David Du Lac laughed. "Jagger will be too busy chasing Mateas and hunting for someone he'll never find."

"What are you talking about?"

"A long-dead serial killer," David said with pleasure. "A will-o'-the-wisp he'll never find."

"Take me to my sister."

"Do you really think you can save your miserable lives?" David asked.

"Of course."

He laughed. "Fine. Follow me."

He turned, knowing full well that she wouldn't do anything with Caitlin at risk. But as she followed him, a shadow suddenly loomed up before her.

"Stop!"

The voice…

The shadow resolved itself into a man, stumbling as he tried to walk forward.

David Du Lac swore, striding toward him. "You're harder to kill than I thought."

"Wait!" Fiona cried out.

For a moment she felt a shiver of uncertainty wash over her, but then she knew.

David Du Lac was the man struggling to reach her. And David Du Lac was the one going over to finish off a murder. The murder of a man who had wanted peace, who had opened his heart and his club to all of them.

"You're not David," she said to her captor. "And if you kill the real David, I swear, you'll never get a chance to murder me or my sister. Touch him and you die."

"Fiona, watch out!" the real David Du Lac cried.

Too late. The blow caught her on the head. Her last thought was that she'd never even sensed the shape-shifter's accomplice coming up behind her.

And when she awoke, she was lying on her parents' sarcophagus, next to her unconscious sister.

"I don't understand," Mateas said.

"The killer wants a war. He wants all vampires destroyed. First he tried to turn us against each other, and then he wants to turn everyone else against us," Jagger explained. It was difficult to speak. They were traveling as night and shadow, flying through the tempest the breeze had become.

"So the serial killer from the past—how does he fit in?" Mateas said.

"When I learned he had been dismembered, I knew then. The killer's a shapeshifter. He allowed a witness to see him in the guise of a long-dead killer just to confuse us, so if we ever identified the man in the sketch, we wouldn't know what to think. And he appeared outside the cemetery as you," Jagger explained. "Now he believes the deaths of the Keepers will give him the opportunity he wants to control the entire New Orleans underworld."

"God help us," Mateas said.

They had reached the cemetery. Jagger motioned to Mateas to stay dead quiet as they tried to see what was happening.

Silently they made their way to the MacDonald mausoleum.

It was large, adorned with cherubs and angels. It sat past a shrine to little children who had died of yellow fever, and a monument to fallen Confederate soldiers.

Jagger noted the stained-glass window in the back, which had been broken in a recent storm and not yet replaced.

He motioned to Mateas to follow him, then moved in that direction.

They must not have expected that she would regain consciousness so quickly, because she could hear her attackers whispering as they struggled to tie her ankles, making so many things clear. She looked at Caitlin, who still seemed to be unconscious. Then she saw Caitlin open one eye and mouthed two words.

"Holy water."

Caitlin tried to nod, but she was clearly very weak.

Fiona looked at her captors and wasn't surprised to see Valentina.

Bitchy shapeshifter? Oh, yeah. She was a bitch, all right. And a murderess.

It made sense that the victims hadn't been sexually

molested. The killers weren't sexual predators; they simply loathed vampires, wanted power and were willing to do anything to create chaos and blame it on the race they despised.

"I should have expected you," Fiona said. "Really. I mean, you are a jealous bitch, so this is really no big shock."

Valentina laughed. "I'm a bitch—but so are you. And tonight you'll be a dead bitch."

She wasn't beautiful anymore; she looked furious and mottled. She was going to change into something, Fiona thought, something ferocious, to slap her, claw at her...kill her.

But she was stopped by the person behind her.

The *woman* behind her.

"Stop it. Let's get this done. Don't touch her! If you wanted to hurt her, you should have hit her harder."

Fiona knew the voice. And as the woman stepped out of the shadows, she also knew the face.

It was Jennie. Jennie Mahoney. The brilliant, uncrowned queen of the shapeshifting community.

"I'll get it done," Jennie said, staring at Fiona.

And then she started to change—into a vampire. She took on Jagger DeFarge's face and form, laughing all the while.

Behind her, Valentina began to laugh, and she started to change, too, shifting into Billy Harrington.

There was no time. Fiona fought against the pain in her head as she began to change herself, at the same time reaching for one of the vials of holy water.

Valentina reached for her, and she threw the vial.

Valentina shrieked and fell, twitching, screaming, to the ground.

As she fell, the real Jagger DeFarge burst into the room, brandishing his stake. In a rage, Jennie Mahoney flew at him, already changing form.

But a shapeshifter's weakness was that she could never be as strong as the real thing. Even as Jennie ripped and tore at him, becoming a wolf, a tiger and finally herself, Jagger fought her, slowly but surely bearing her down.

Valentina was on the ground, twisting and turning, becoming an octopus and snaking out a suction-cupped arm to wrest Caitlin from the table. Caitlin was weak, but she became a mouse, escaping the attack.

Someone else was there.

Mateas Grenard.

Fiona didn't know who was who anymore, and she tossed holy water at Mateas, who stared at her blankly.

"Sorry!" she cried swiftly.

She dug in her pockets for another vial. Valentina was a tiger now, and she lunged at Fiona, who ducked behind her parents' tomb.

Jagger flew at the shapeshifter, tearing at her with his fangs.

"I need holy water!" Caitlin, back in her own form, cried.

Fiona freed the vial from her pocket and tossed the water over Jennie Mahoney, who screamed as she writhed. Fiona splashed the rest of the vial's contents over Valentina.

Then the smell of charred flesh filled the air, and thick smoke rose from the shifters' still forms.

Suddenly everything was silent.

Exhausted, the four of them looked at each other.

Fiona and Caitlin started hugging, both of them gasping for breath.

They all jumped as someone lunged through the doorway.

"Thank God," David Du Lac—the real David Du Lac—gasped out. "I've been out there waiting, hoping… Well, we were all fooled, weren't we?"

Epilogue

It wasn't quite Mexico or the Riviera, and Fiona wasn't on a beach yet.

But still…

Just being alive was quite enough for the moment.

The condition of the women's bodies meant things had to look as if they had died in a fire, and luckily they had brought a gas lantern into the mausoleum with them, so it had been easy to spill the gas and light it.

Easy to physically carry out the action, anyway, but a lot harder mentally. But the stone-and-brick tomb would survive, and the MacDonalds had given up their lives for peace—they would understand a little charring in the family vault.

The five of them had stayed to greet the police and firemen. Fiona had explained how she had been tricked into the mausoleum in search of her sister, and then she and Caitlin recounted how the two dead women had conspired to put the city in a panic and throw suspicion on the vampire cult. The murders themselves had been so bizarre that no one questioned such a bizarre explanation. Then there had been all the annoying paperwork, the even more annoying problem of dealing with the press, and then...

Then it was over.

No one could believe that Jennie had been behind the killings, and everyone wondered what demon had lived inside her. Sometimes hatred and anger could fester unseen, and the general theory was that that was what had happened with Jennie.

As far as Valentina went...

Fiona kept her own counsel on that.

Valentina was simply a bitch, as far as she was concerned, and that was that. She was a woman who'd wanted everything, and killing had seemed like nothing to her.

Some of the men mourned her. Even Fiona had to admit she'd been a beautiful bitch.

But the important thing was that they had brought an end to the situation. Jagger was upset that it had taken him so long to figure out the truth, but then again, no one in the human world or the paranormal community had suspected Jennie. And, of the two, she had been the leader. She had hated the vampires—and the Keepers—since the war. She had bided her time.

And now...

Now they were celebrating, and naturally the party was at Underworld. People from all over the city came, and not just the paranormal races but regular people were welcome, too.

The band was fantastic. The food was delicious. Alcohol flowed

Fiona and Jagger danced and danced. With each other, with shapeshifters, werewolves and even a leprechaun or two.

It was a party to end all parties.

Finally she and Jagger slipped out and stood alone under the stars.

"What do you think made Jennie so hateful?" Fiona asked, as he held her and she leaned back against him, gazing up at the night sky.

"Sue told me that she'd been in love with a vampire once. He rejected her," Jagger said.

"Do you think that's true?"

"I don't know," he said.

"Do you think that a werewolf and a shapeshifter, or, say, a shapeshifter and a leprechaun, could ever find true happiness? Or," she asked, turning into his arms, "a vampire and a Keeper?"

"Ah," he said thoughtfully. "Well, I know that I'm very much in love," he said. "In fact, I was thinking of slipping away and exploring just what love can be. I'd like to forget all about hate and evil and cruelty…and there's no better way than looking deeply into the possibilities that love holds."

She laughed and rose on her toes, and they kissed.

And then she whispered against his lips, "I'm quite ready to explore."

So they held hands and slipped away.

And looked deeply into love and all its endless possibilities.

* * * * *

YOU HAVE
JUST READ A
HARLEQUIN®
NOCTURNE™
BOOK

If you were **captivated** by this **dark** and **sensual paranormal romance story,** be sure to look for two new Harlequin Nocturne books every month!

⬧ HARLEQUIN®

NOCTURNE

Ⓝ

THE KEEPERS: L.A. miniseries continues in

KEEPER OF THE MOON

by Harley Jane Kozak.

When a mysterious outbreak threatens the Elven population, it's up to Sailor Gryffald, Elven Keeper, to put a stop to it.

Magic hour.

It was the last hour of sunlight, when the day was closing up shop, the light rendering even a plain landscape enchanted.

Sailor Ann Gryffald loved magic hour, loved to run as the sky turned red and the canyon faded to black. The name itself was a kind of incantation to her. But unlike most people, she knew that "magic hour" had other meanings, lying just under the surface the way L.A. herself could hide under a veil of smog. The moments separating the worlds of day and night were when portals opened, shapes shifted with little effort and even the most unimaginative human might stumble upon signs of the Otherworld.

Sailor was part of the Otherworld. She was a Keeper, a human born with the mandate to guard and protect a particular race—in her case, the Elven. These were not the tiny elves of popular culture but tall, intensely physical creatures whose element was earth, whose beauty was legendary, whose powers included healing, telepathy and teleportation. Of course, most people had no knowledge of the Others, and it was Sailor's job to preserve that ignorance.

She was new to the actual job, had taken it over from her father only months earlier, but with it came a fraction of the Elven powers and their beauty, so all in all, not a bad gig. She also had a strong sixth sense that told her things, such as—

There was something in the air right now.

She slowed her pace. She was a mile into her run, heading west on Mulholland at a good clip. It wasn't literal darkness she felt; the sun wouldn't set for another hour or more, and the moon was out already. It was a heaviness, making her want to look behind her, making the hair on the back of her neck stand up.

A rush of cold wind hit her, followed by a flutelike sound blowing in her ear, the flapping of a wing next to her cheek, striking her face. She swatted at it wildly, but something sharp sliced right down the middle of her chest, ripping through her shirt. *Man, that's going to hurt in a minute,* she thought as her legs faltered, refusing to hold her up.

And then, as the fading sunlight hit her full in the face, she found herself falling onto the gravel and pavement of Mulholland Drive.

Damn, she thought. *I'm checking out.*

Darkness.

**Find out what happens when Sailor wakes up in
KEEPER OF THE MOON by Harley Jane Kozak.
Available March 5, 2013**

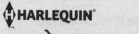

NOCTURNE

Dark and sensual paranormal romance reads.

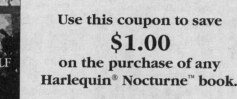

Use this coupon to save

$1.00

on the purchase of any
Harlequin® Nocturne™ book.

Available wherever books are sold, including most bookstores, supermarkets, drugstores and discount stores.